Town of Ellsworth

Town of Ellsworth

Meghan Apriceno

Apriceno, Meghan.
Town of Ellsworth / by Meghan Apriceno

ISBN-13: 978-1499175479
ISBN-10: 1499175477

For my Father –

Chapter One
Friday, September 4ᵗʰ

'Again,' I thought as the scene unfolded in front of my eyes. Not that I minded. The same entrancing dream played almost every night and had become somewhat of a playground for me. A classically decorated staircase wrapped in dozens of roses and yards of ribbon competed with one another down into a brilliant Beaux styled ballroom. Candlelight illuminated the hundreds of pristinely dressed guests who were talking and laughing amongst one another as I passed by. A violin played softly somewhere in the distance. The notes were mesmerizing, sounding like two separate strands intertwining.

The dream felt so real that if I hadn't known any better I would have believed it to be. This repetitive subconscious illusion had become my nightly reel, and always ended abruptly – never revealing a purpose.

As I woke up in my queen-sized, four posted bed I replayed the vivid scene that was ingrained in my mind for as far back as I could remember. Once my eyes adjusted, I looked around my bedroom and tried to remember what it looked like before my mother hired an interior designer. The room's redecoration was to my surprise, of course.

If walls could talk – scratch that, if walls could make sarcastic comments… well, things would be interesting. Over the past seventeen years my walls had witnessed many phases, paint colors, and restless nights. The one thing that hadn't changed much at all, besides the whole growing up thing, was me.

I could still picture the light shade of pink and scrapbook collages that had hung, scattered on these walls only two years ago. Now they were a rich plum with Victorian styled décor and lavish accents. It was very high-end, not my taste but it was a surprise from my mother and I had come to terms with it.

Across from where I was laying there was a fireplace set in a substantial white mantle with a large, oval mirror above it. Knickknacks were strategically placed for show purposes only; no memory or funny story was attached to them. In the corner to my left was a fancy armchair where some dresses had been tossed over. To the right of the chair was a window with an old fashioned table underneath it that probably cost more than any table should. To the right of that, in the far corner was a walk-in closet with a chandelier in the entryway. Inside were designer clothes, upscale shoes and accessories that I had accumulated. To my other side, my right, there was a nightstand and another window. In the corner was my father's old desk that I had kept meticulously structured, much like my life but mostly as an ode to him. Artwork hung on the wall in the space that separated the old desk and a fancy, opaque tri-fold vanity mirror with a matching stool. My eyes focused on the artwork; I still hadn't taken the time to try and understand the painting but, supposedly, it was tranquil and soothing.

Next to the vanity was the door to my bedroom which led to the rest of the penthouse – the empty penthouse. My mother, Dana Reid, was a self-professed 'workaholic', a title which only she believed. This past week she had been on yet another 'business trip'... to the Hamptons out on Long Island. My mother had been the mastermind behind the revamping of my room which was now perfectly fitted for royalty and adequately suitable for any uptown princess. I, however, missed my old pink walls and mismatched hand-me-down furniture.

I rolled over in bed to see the large vintage clock on the nightstand showing that it was five o'clock. Judging by the dark sky behind the satin curtains, it was 5:00 AM. I had another thirty minutes of mindless sleep before I would put my running shoes on and go for a jog in the park; the first part of my morning routine.

—

"Bethany, wake up. Beths..." I heard and opened my eyes seeing a figure standing next to my bed.

All I could mumble in my incoherent state was, "What?" as the familiar all-American profile became clearer. "Ryan! What are you doing here?" I asked sitting up to hug him. He looked the same as he did the last time I saw him about two months ago. With his unmanaged dark brown hair and brown eyes, he was undeniably a very handsome man to any girl, except to me. To me he would always be my dorky, older brother.

"I thought it was time to pay you a visit," he said humored by my reaction. As I leaned back out of the hug the skepticism that was now running through my mind must have translated onto my face because he quickly added, "You *are* my favorite person," in a tone higher than normal. I smirked and threw the remaining covers to the side, put my feet on the cool hardwood floor and looked for my robe which was somewhere in the redecorated jungle.

"How ya doing, kid?" Ryan asked taking notice of various dresses and crowns that were spread around the room. They added to the high-end décor. As I tied my robe around my waist I couldn't help but notice how Ryan stuck out. He was wearing a fitted, red t-shirt, blue jeans and construction boots. "It looks like you've been busy," my brother said as he gestured to the mountain of magazines sporting my face on the cover. My mother thought they were something I should showcase. They registered on her scale of 'life accomplishments' but not on mine. We had very different definitions. I wasn't exactly proud of my career and I definitely didn't gauge success on the level of her satisfaction. How could I when I didn't even use my real name, Bethany Taylor?

When my mother pushed me into the industry, shortly after Ryan decided to move down south with our grandparents, she thought 'Reid' sounded more professional. So, 'Bethany Reid' was born. I believed it had everything to do with 'Reid' being her maiden name and nothing to do with the way it sounded.

"Did you drive up?" I asked. It was a sad excuse for a conversation changer but, thankfully, Ryan went along with it.

"Yup, it only took me about twelve hours," he said looking around my room. With his hands in his pockets, he walked over to the nightstand which was the only territory in the room that reflected my taste. I had reclaimed it after the interior designer was long gone. The array of old frames held pictures that catalogued him and I through the years; the most recent photo was from his last visit at the beginning of the summer. Ryan picked it up and smiled before putting it back. Moving the curtain to the side, he glanced out the window and then down at the noise from the city streets humming below.

"So, what's the occasion?" I asked regretting my selection of words the second they left my lips. I was thrilled by his unscheduled appearance and didn't want him to think otherwise. The truth was I missed my brother. He had been my confidant and hero since... well, always. When he moved out two years ago, the place I called home became nothing more than a place where my mother and I resided. But I couldn't blame him for leaving. I knew it had everything to do with getting away from our relentless mother, and to be closer to Kate.

Kate was a girl Ryan had met in town while helping our grandfather at a summer football camp. She had stolen his heart and our mother was certainly wasn't enough reason to stay in New York. Knowing that I was the only thing keeping him here, after seeing how miserable he was one night, I told him to go and that I'd be fine. I made him promise to visit me, helped him pack and then he was gone. But the fact remained that my brother was my home and when he left, I wasn't home again until his next trip.

I took a few steps forward trying to think of how I could clarify what I meant by, 'What's the occasion?' but Ryan was staring out the window concentrating very hard on something. It was beginning to make me nervous. "Is everything alright, Ry?" I asked apprehensively.

"Yeah," he answered and looked sideways at our father's old desk before looking over his shoulder at me. "It's time for you to come home."

—

Ryan had thrown most of my belongings into boxes and was lugging them to the elevator, bringing them down to the lobby. He was eager, giddy almost, at the "sister napping" or, as he called it, 'Operation Bethany'.

While he made several trips, I scribbled a note for my mother telling her that I was okay, that I had gone with Ryan and would not be back to the penthouse. I left it on the table where she would see it the next time she decided to stop in.

The last thing I needed to do was to call my agent, Michael. Michael wasn't your typical agent. He had my back. He looked out for me, took care of me and always had my best interest in mind. He also had a clear understanding of what kind of person my mother was and offered support whenever I needed it. Michael had become my protector from the ugliness of the modeling industry and my mother on many occasions. He was sort of like a guardian angel. Over the past twenty-four months he had guided me away from the negative parts of the fashion world while fueling my career in the decisions he made on my behalf. He was a blessing in my life and had become a good friend. The phone rang twice before he picked up.

He was relieved when I told him that my brother was taking me out of the city and told me not to worry about contracts. Michael wanted me to take this opportunity with my brother to have a real family and to be away from all of the 'noise'. As for canceling photo shoots, designer appointments and scheduled runway appearances – he would handle it. Not knowing quite how to say goodbye, we both said, "Talk to you later," and hung up the phone. I felt a twinge of sadness at the sudden end but smiled when I looked up to see Ryan standing in the doorway with an 'are you ready to get out of here' look on his face.

–

Twelve hours later I found myself trying to recall when the city streets had turned into acres of farmland. The sun was burning its way to the horizon in shades of crimson. The clouds overhead stretched for miles over the southern terrain to the Appalachian range and a cool, crisp breeze blew through the opened windows keeping us company. We crossed state line after state line in my brother's 1975 blue Ford truck that he had bought from our grandfather. It had a super cab so there was additional seating behind the driver and passenger seat which was currently occupied by brown boxes and suitcases. The old but pristine truck was definitely not the quietest thing on the road or fuel efficient but Ryan didn't care. He was use to the racquet it made and had a fondness for it.

We had talked straight through the drive, laughing and joking about life, blasting music and stopping at several gas stations to fill up the truck which I referred to as 'the tank'. Our relationship had not changed if that's possible. We had this bond with one another... we had grown up but didn't grow apart.

—

Ryan lowered the volume on the radio even though 'the tank' still rattled loudly and asked, "How are you feeling?"

"Okay, I guess," I answered honestly. Half a day had gone by since I was lying in my bed in Manhattan. Now I was somewhere between the Mason-Dixon Line and the Gulf of Mexico.

"Last chance, Beths," my brother nodded towards a fast approaching mile marker on the side of the road. "Only ten more miles." Reality started to set in and I broke out in a cold sweat. By no means had Ryan dragged me out of the city. I didn't argue with him, didn't kick or scream, however, I was not jumping for joy at the idea of going from a population of eight million to a population of about a handful in comparison.

As I took a deep breath, I managed an optimistic smile and concentrated on the scenery passing outside my window. A historic sign drew closer... 'Welcome to Ellsworth'.

—

Ellsworth was not old, Ellsworth was *really* old. Not even the fading light from the fleeting sun could hide that. The houses had been handed down from generation to generation, cherished and beautiful. Property was not scarce and each home had an extensive yard where children and their imaginations could run freely. Oak trees at least a century old lined the wide, cobblestone streets. There were people walking down the sidewalks waving to one another, American flags flew proudly from front porches and Main Street was made up of mom-and-pop storefronts. Seeing my reaction to this strange world Ryan laughed, "You'll get use to it." I looked over at him and grinned skeptically. "You will!" he insisted with a grin of his own. Slowing down, he stopped to allow people to cross in front of 'the tank'; a gesture that is alien to city folk.

Ryan turned off Main Street and drove down another wholesome road and pulled onto a pebble driveway with a wildflower garden. Like the other homes, this house was also picturesque. It had a wraparound porch, was three stories high with white siding and navy blue shutters. Ryan got out and closed the heavy driver's side door. I tried to unlock my seatbelt blindly because my attention was focused on the life-size dollhouse in front of me with its simplistic lines, eaves and welcoming porch. My brother opened the passenger door and I stepped out of 'the tank'. The front door opened and a familiar face lit up when we saw one another. Instantly, Midtown Manhattan was a lifetime away.

"Oh my!" the recognizable older woman with white hair and loving smile said as she walked down the porch steps. She grabbed my arms at my sides and had a huge smile on her face.

"Hi Grams," I said and she pulled me in for a hug – a real hug; the type that leaves you trying to remember the last time you were held that way.

Over her shoulder, I watched as Ryan's face gave away his happiness before he threw a luggage strap over his shoulder, picked up some of the boxes and headed up the front porch steps in true pack mule style.

Grams and I walked into the house arm-in-arm a few moments later and I looked around not knowing what to expect. I had never visited; I only had ideas of what my grandparents' house may look like. What I saw before me was different than what I had envisioned but it was, nevertheless, enchanting. There was an old antique table underneath a rustic lighting fixture in the center of the open first floor. To the left was a living room with a large, comfortable looking, brown couch and matching end tables that faced a television hung up on the wall. It was perfect for watching football games which was something Ryan and our grandfather did whenever a game was on. Two armchairs sat side-by-side under the front window separated by Grams' knitting basket where an unfinished blanket was folded.

In the far corner of the living room there was an open door leading to a bathroom. From what I could see the tub had authentic ceramic lion's feet, something that isn't common nowadays. The staircase straight ahead had wooden, handcrafted banisters and went up eight steps before coming to a landing followed by two continuing sets of stairs that split to go up to the next floor. A large stained glass window above the landing was illuminated by light from the retreating sun. To the right of the staircase there was a swinging door to the kitchen. However, the space to my immediate right, the dining room, is what caught my eye. Here was the table where my grandparents and brother sat and ate around together every night. Family dinners were something I longed for, and now, I would have that. A smile washed over my face at the realization.

Behind the table and against the wall there was a hutch older than my grandparents that held Grams' good china, heirloom candlesticks and porcelain figurines. I was sure they each had meaning and story behind them. There was a history here.

My grandmother and I continued to follow Ryan up the stairs to the second floor. "I am so happy you are here, dear. Your grandfather called and wanted me to tell you that he is glad that you have decided to join us. He'll be back from his conference early Sunday morning."

"Thanks Grams," I smiled and as we reached the second floor. I took notice of the three doors off to the sides. It was sad that I had never visited them before but the relationship between my grandparents and my mother had turned hostile after my father's passing. Walking through this place was long overdue and I was taking it all in.

The door straight across from us led to a bathroom. The doorway to the left was my Gramp's and Gram's bedroom and from what I could tell it had beige walls with white crown moulding and dated mahogany furniture. I was sure my grandmother had sewn the quilted comforter spread over the bed. The room to the right belonged to Ryan and was chaotically clean. He knew where everything was, of course, and it warmed my heart when I saw a picture of us on his dresser.

Ryan, Grams and I turned the corner and there was another staircase to the third floor. However, instead of revealing a landing with rooms off to its sides, this set of stairs led to a standup, wooden attic.

I followed behind and when we reached the top, my brother put down the first trip worth of my belongings. "Sorry about the mess, Bethany. If Ryan had told me what he was up to, I would have seen to it that you wouldn't have to sort through this disaster," Grams explained as I took in the attic. Ryan put his arm around my shoulder and we smiled at each other, both knowing that the word 'disaster' was an understatement for this catastrophe. The third floor expanded the length and width of the house but unlike the rest of it, the attic was untidy; there were trunks, boxes and pieces of furniture scattered in a united disorder. Wooden beams that supported the roof along with its many awnings gave the attic a barn-like feel.

There were two large windows, one at the front and the other at the back of the house. The view from the back window was very different than the view I had grown use to in the penthouse. I could see trees for miles and there were sounds of birds chirping instead of taxis beeping.

"Have Ryan help you move the bigger things. He loves an excuse to pick up heavy objects," Grams laughed as she patted him lovingly on his back. Looking around the attic, an old mirror partially covered with newspaper, a mountainous armoire, a bed frame and a few lamps all stuck out as being useful. "I'm going to go finish cooking dinner. If you need anything, anything at all, just call down."

"Thanks Grams," I swallowed. She turned to start her trek to the kitchen but paused, looking back at Ryan and I, then smiled before continuing on her way.

"I'll go get the rest of your stuff out of the truck," Ryan said not too far behind. When I turned back to the mess it hit me that this, this attic, would be my new room. It was going to take some getting use to but I would be closer to my brother. I would also be a flight of stairs away from my grandparents who I hadn't seen since their annual visit during Christmas and whom I missed terribly. Even though my mother did not get along with her in-laws, they didn't allow for that to keep them from their grandchildren. Since I could talk, Grams and I spoke on the phone every Sunday morning. She knew all about my friends, including Michael, and most things about my life. We rarely discussed pageants, runways, and never talked about my mother. It wasn't that my grandmother was disinterested in that part of my life. I think she wanted to give me some sort of normalcy and she did every Sunday morning after I got home from Church. She listened intently and I grew fond of our phone conversations. Now, she and I were under the same roof.

There I was, hundreds of miles away from where I woke up, standing in the middle of an attic with a mishmash of objects that were older than me and covered in dust that had gone untouched for years. Walking to the far window, I pushed it open with a little effort and a cool, end-of-summer breeze blew through the space. I had always taken the path less traveled and this was just another bend in that road.

Looking back at the clutter and not knowing where to start, I reached into the outside compartment of my luggage, found my most recent playlist, put in my earphones and pressed 'Play'.

Saturday, September 5th

Early the next morning, after returning the cleaning supplies to the second floor linen closet, I walked back up the stairs to the attic and looked around at the progress I had made. In the past ten hours, the room had undergone a huge transformation. I had worked through the night, only stopping for dinner. Thankfully, it was looking more and more like one of those vintage lofts and less like an attic. There was something special about it; it had a charm that the penthouse I left behind could not compete with. It felt like a home.

Soot, clutter and disarray had been replaced by cleanliness and order. In the open area opposite the stairs stood the large armoire. After clearing it out, it made for the perfect closet. Next to it, I leaned the old, full length mirror – a find in the 'Great Clean'. I had also pushed a large trunk underneath the front window with the intention of using it as a desk or vanity; another much more normal accommodation for a seventeen year old girl compared to the plum prison.

On the other side of the attic, under the back window was the bed Ryan and I had assembled. Beside it was a nightstand, another pleasant surprise find. Slowly I had started unpacking my belongings and began to place things around the room. It was all coming together. Taking in the newly refurbished room, I smiled to myself – this was definitely more 'me'.

There were footsteps coming up the stairs and when I turned I saw Ryan carrying one more box. It must have been packed deep in the bed of his truck. The sun wasn't up yet so the windows on either side hadn't come to know their purpose. The current source of light in the room came from an old chandelier which now hung in the middle of the attic. "So," Ryan started. By the sound of his voice I knew something entertaining was about to be said. He leaned against one of the four wooden support posts and grinned, "That's the last box, princess. Is there anything else your humble servant can get you?" He then half-bowed.

"Hilarious," I smirked and stretched my arms over my head. "But I do actually need to get some toiletries."

"Okay, we'll stop by the drugstore. I have to go by the Lumberyard to check on an order anyway," my brother said grabbing the back of his neck with his hands which was followed by a growling yawn.

An aroma of coffee made its way up the stairs and I breathed it in. Smiling I said, "I smell coffee."

"Yes, but I also smell you," Ryan kiddingly pushed me. "You need to hit the showers, kid," he teased as he ran for the stairs before I could retaliate. He truly was a boy in a grown man's body.

—

"Well it could have been worse." Ryan said as we drove down Main Street in 'the tank'.

"Thanks Ry," I said shaking my head, recalling the massive spider episode that had occurred minutes ago. I was finishing getting ready and Ryan was playing with my phone on my bed. A spider crawled its way out into the middle of the room having been disturbed by the 'Great Clean'. Unfortunately, Ryan had witnessed my freak-out when I spotted it and was still laughing as we drove to the drugstore. I tried defending myself by imitating his response. "Mister, 'It's just a spider.'" I couldn't help but do the finger quotations, and, of course, he called me out on it.

"Real mature Beths," he smirked as he stopped at one of the few red lights on Main Street. There was hardly anyone around this early. Cool air drifted through the open windows and its purity was refreshing. It was so different from what I was use to that I kept taking in deep breaths, drinking it in, enjoying it. The morning sun was starting to shine through the tree branches stenciling dancing shadows onto the pavement below. Park benches and gazebos were common along the sidewalks and grassy street dividers. It was amazing to see that a town like this still existed. I guess I was more naïve about the world than I thought; close-minded even. It was ironic considering I had grown up and lived in 'the city that never sleeps'.

"You should have seen your face," Ryan said breaking out into hysterics again, hitting the steering wheel with the palm of his hand.

"That was the BIGGEST spider I have EVER seen, Ryan," I argued as I slumped back into the passenger seat trying to rationalize my reaction which had included pointing, jumping onto the bed and screaming for him to kill it in an octave unbeknownst to man.

"Oh, come on! It was funny," he argued and I smiled agreeing. "Really funny," he erupted again. I nudged his side but he didn't care.

When he turned his head towards me something caught his attention out of the window. There were two young women walking to a parked car, both blonde and pretty. The older of the two looked familiar and the younger girl looked to be around my age. Ryan honked the horn and they looked up and waved at the distinct truck and its owner. Ryan turned right as the light turned green, threw 'the tank' into 'Park' and jumped out as I tried to unbuckle my ancient seatbelt. After freeing myself, I managed to get out of the truck and watched as Ryan picked up the older, familiar looking blonde and kissed her lightly before placing her back down. "Good morning, beautiful," he said and I struggled to not feel awkward about his display of affection by focusing on a small squirrel that was prancing along a nearby white picket fence.

Hoping the greeting was finished I looked back at him and saw the two girls blatantly staring at me. "Kate, this is my sister," Ryan began.

But before he could finish the younger girl found her voice, "Bethany Reid?"

Kate, ignoring the younger blonde's comment, looked at my brother perplexed and then at me. She put her hand out and said, "It's nice to finally meet you, Bethany." I could tell she was just as taken aback as the other girl but her sincerity was genuine. Kate was plain but an irrefutably attractive woman. Leave it to my brother to find the perfect girl... But, in my opinion, he deserved nothing less.

Kate was a little taller than me and her hair was neatly pulled back out of her face. She had hazel, almond-shaped eyes and natural pink lips that complemented her complexion. She was wearing dark pink scrubs which usually hide a woman's figure but were flattering on her.

The younger girl, still in shock, looked from her older sister to Ryan and then back at me. Her hair was long, thick and naturally highlighted. She had brown eyes, was shorter than me and was dressed in distressed jeans and a white sweatshirt. She was cute and looked like she would fit in on one of those high school television shows.

"RYAN, your sister is Bethany Reid!" her voice reflected her utter disbelief.

"Ugh... yeah," he nodded and put his hands in his pockets, "Bethany *Taylor* actually," he amended. "Beths, this is Kate Connolly, the soon-to-be Mrs. Taylor," he beamed as he introduced his bride-to-be and she blushed. "And this is Olivia Connolly, Kate's younger sister and my soon-to-be, official-pain-in-the-butt sister-in-law," Ryan introduced, giving Olivia a playful wink to which she teasingly stuck out her tongue.

"I'm sorry for the initial shock, Bethany," Kate apologized. "Ryan told me that he had a younger sister but what he failed to mention was that you are..."

"Bethany Reid," the younger one said flatly.

"That was nice of him," I smirked with a humored expression. Guiltily, Ryan averted my eye contact by suddenly becoming fascinated with the sidewalk.

"How are you two related?" Olivia questioned pointing from Ryan to me, partly sarcastic but mostly serious.

"Hey!" Ryan shot back at her.

"Don't 'Hey!' me," Olivia said wide-eyed. It was clear their relationship was well-formed and accustomed to bantering.

"It's not my fault... it's not exactly easy to bring up in a casual conversation," Ryan tried to defend himself.

Not fazed by her fiancé or sister, Kate shook her head and said to me, "It's nice to finally meet you, Bethany. Aside from not mentioning you were a celebrity, believe it or not, Ryan has told me a lot about you."

"Thank you, Kate," I smiled and as she placed her free hand on my brother's bicep, I noticed her beautiful, oval cut engagement ring.

I had known Ryan was head over heels for Kate since they met. He had come home from helping our grandfather with a football camp two summers ago and told me that while he was in town he had met 'the one'. I had seen pictures of her and Ryan had talked about her. But, actually seeing him holding and kissing a woman, even if it was his fiancé, was something I was going to have to get use too – and get use too fast.

Kate looked at her watch and said, "I have to run. I'm going to be late getting to the hospital. Liv, do you want me to drop you off at the drugstore?"

"I can do it." Ryan offered. "I was just driving Bethany there to pick up a few things."

"Is that okay with you, Liv? Liv…" Kate said trying to break her sister's trance on me.

"Yeah, ugh huh," was her response.

—

"Kate," my brother said, "will definitely take my side. Don't make me bring up the Scrabble incident. She knows to stick by her man." Ryan nodded his head as he turned back onto Main

Street. Liv, short for Olivia, was sitting in the back seat. "Hey Liv, you breathing yet?" he asked sarcastically looking in his rearview mirror to check on her.

"Very funny, Ryan," Olivia said as she hit his shoulder. "It's nice of you to never mention that your sister is not only the SAME age as me but, oh, I don't know... famous!"

"Hey, I mentioned her a lot," my brother tried to defend himself while I enjoyed the free entertainment.

"Ryan Taylor! You never mentioned that your sister is a supermodel!"

"Super?" I asked oblivious to the status I had achieved. It only made Ryan laugh harder. I'm pretty sure his side hurt by the time we pulled up in front of an old, whitewashed, brick building with a weathered sign that read 'Druggist'.

"Thanks for the ride, Ry, but I'm still angry at you," Olivia said as she jumped out of the truck and slammed the door. Ryan rolled his eyes and then looked over at me. "I'll be back from the Lumberyard in fifteen minutes. I'm just helping Chris with an order." I looked at him pleadingly.

"Get out!" he said jokingly shooing me. As I closed the passenger door and walked around the front of 'the tank', Ryan called out to Olivia, "Watch her for me, Liv?" Her head snapped around and he continued to laugh as he pulled away.

When Olivia and I made eye contact we shrugged at the morning's chain of events. "Sorry about him," I apologized.

"I still can't believe that you two are related," she shrugged as she opened the paint chipped door. On cue, a little bell rang above us indicating that the door had opened. She walked behind the counter, clipped on a nametag then turned the sign in the window around for it to read 'Open'. "How can I help you?" she politely asked.

"You don't have to," I offered so that she didn't feel obligated.

"I'm sorry about before. I was just in shock, I guess. I think I still am," Olivia admitted somewhat embarrassed.

"It's okay. I'm sorry that my brother never..." I began and then lightheartedly joked, "Well, I'm just sorry that you've had to deal with him for the past two years." We both smiled finding middle ground in the uncharted territory of awkwardness. I pulled out the napkin I had scribbled the things I needed on and handed it to her.

—

Ryan's fifteen minute trip turned into a three hour excursion but it had given Olivia and I time to realize that we had a lot in common, including an almost identical sense of humor. We talked all morning, even after I had gotten everything on my list. She continued to work and I helped her. We talked about clothes and real celebrities while we restocked shelves. When the occasional customer moseyed on in she let me hide down one of the few aisles, unnoticed. I appreciated it more than she knew. One new introduction was enough for me to handle this morning.

When it came time for her to replenish the newspaper and magazine stand I picked up an issue that I was on the cover of and flipped it over so that the back advertisement was displayed. "What'd you do that for?" she asked turning it back around. "Oh," she said when she realized that the person on the front was standing to her left. "Weird," Liv said putting it back down.

"Yeah," I replied. "Weird."

She opened a different box but I also happened to grace the cover of that magazine too. "Does it ever end?" she asked kiddingly.

"Yes," I said answering more profoundly than the intention of the question. "Yes, it does."

Ryan had talked about Kate every time he visited me in New York – how she was this 'amazing' girl. It was now clear to me that it must be a family trait. The Connelly's – both Kate and Olivia, were good people.

—

I spent the rest of the afternoon focused on unpacking and settling in. I was blasting my music, wearing my favorite hangout outfit of high socks, boxer shorts and an old tank top, when I heard bells. I looked up at the ceiling and pulled out one of the earphones. 'God?' Nope. It wasn't that easy. 'Ding Dong' rang out again. I got to my feet and made my way downstairs. 'Ding Dong.' Was I the only one home?

When I got to the first floor I peeked into the living room only to see the back of Ryan's head. He was completely engulfed by the announcers and the pregame hype, lost to all reality. "Are you serious?" I asked laughing at him as I reached for the front door. At the exact moment my hand touched the door knob, Ryan heard me and he launched himself over the back of the couch, towards the front door and pushed me behind it as it opened.

"Hey," my brother said to whoever rang the bell and put his arm up casually leaning against the door, blocking me behind it.

"Took you long enough," a voice said carrying a six pack and walked passed my brother into the living room. A second stranger punched my brother playfully in the stomach and followed his friend over to the couch. Ryan peaked behind the door and a smile crossed my face amused by the breaking development. He uncomfortably looked back at his friends who were arguing over which team was going to win; the reason for the get together. "Ryan," one called out when my brother didn't respond right away, "which team?"

"Ah," Ryan processed the question and answered, "Titans."

I crossed my arms when my brother turned back to me. He rarely did anything that made him feel uncomfortable and right now he looked full-fledged panicked. Curious as to how this was going to play out, I jokingly whispered, "They don't know that we're Giants fans, do they?"

Ryan's forehead creased. He leaned in closer to whisper behind the cover of the door. "I might have not told them about," he said actively moving his hand between the two of us, "you know... the 'Bethany Reid' thing."

"And the brother-sister thing," I added.

"Yeah, that too," he said coming clean.

"Okay," I shrugged, "They don't have to know. I'll just sneak back upstairs and..."

Ryan touched my arm and apologetically, spoke softly, "Beths, I'm sorry, it's just that..."

"Ryan, really it's okay. I understand." I whispered.

"Dude," one of the guys asked concerned, "What are you doing over there?"

"You don't have to do this right now," I started to say but Ryan had made up his mind and before I knew it, he had closed the front door and pulled me into the view of the living room. The two guys stared with their mouths open. "Bethany Reid?" one of them uttered in awe.

"Bethany *Taylor*," Ryan corrected as he led me around the couch coming to a stop in between it and the television. "Chris, Gregg, this is my sister, Bethany." If I thought the two men were shocked before, they now looked stunned by my brother's revelation.

Slowly, very slowly, the taller of the two stepped forward and put out his hand. He was good-looking and was a little older than my brother. "Gregg," he introduced himself as I met his handshake.

"Nice to meet you, Gregg," I said lightly and smiled. He was the rugged type and had dark hair, warm eyes and an athletic build.

"Ah, I'm, ah, Chris," the other one said as he followed his friend's lead but was looking at Ryan searching for an explanation. Chris was lean, more of the soldier-type, and although the smallest of the three, he was still taller than me.

"It is nice to meet you, Chris," I said feeling more awkward than I did in seventh grade gym class.

"Bethany just moved down from New York," my brother explained looking from me to his bewildered buddies.

"Bethany Reid is *your* sister?" Chris said aloud trying to grasp the concept.

"Bethany *Taylor,* and yes," Ryan corrected defensively. Ryan didn't welcome the use of our mother's maiden name and hearing it multiple times today wasn't sitting well with him.

"And, she," Gregg started to say, but then looked at me directly and asked, "You're staying *here*?" to which I nodded.

"And Bethany is YOUR sister?" Chris asked Ryan again.

"YES."

"Bethany Reid," Chris repeated suffering from full-fledged 'Bethany Reid Syndrome'.

"*Taylor*. Bethany *Taylor*." Ryan corrected again, now annoyed.

"Whatever," Chris dismissed, not caring what last name was used.

"If it makes you feel any better, I didn't know Ryan had friends," I interjected sarcastically trying to break the Taylor/Reid cycle.

Chris and Gregg both started to laugh and Ryan, not knowing whether to or not, mumbled, "I'm going to get some dip," as he headed to the kitchen.

"So," Chris started a few seconds later.

"So," I said clasping my hands in front of me.

"You're Bethany Reid," Chris reiterated as he shook his head.

"Let's just go with, Bethany," I tried.

"I don't believe this," Gregg ran his hands over his forehead as he sat down on the couch.

"Me neither," Chris said plopping down on the other end.

"Me too," I agreed but under different circumstances. It was now clear that Ryan had not told anyone here who I was, not his fiancé or his best friends. I guess the baggage of being Bethany Reid's brother was too much.

"Want to join us?" Ryan asked as he walked back into the living room with two bowls of dip. He sat in between his two friends, placed the two bowls down, picked up the remote, made the television louder and leaned forward, closer to the snack covered coffee table, ready for the game to start.

"Um, sure," I accepted the invitation and chose the comfy, over-sized chair off to the side.

The pregame show had ended and the commercials were winding down to kickoff. I turned my head leisurely, feeling two sets of eyes on me.

Chris then looked at Ryan who was dipping a chip and said, "I just don't see it."

"See what?" Ryan asked thinking his friend was referring to the commercials on the television.

Chris glanced from me to Ryan and said seriously, "You're a good looking guy and all, Ry, but your sister is Bethany freaking Reid!"

Ryan dropped his chip and before I knew it, my brother was on top of Chris holding him down on the couch. Gregg reacted quickly; clearly this was not uncommon. I could hear Ryan saying bits of sentences like, "My sister," and, keeping with the cadence of punches, "I. WILL. KILL. YOU!"

"Get off of me!" Chris attempted to protect himself with one of Grams' throw pillows as Gregg, the strongest of the three, pried Ryan off. "Dude, seriously?" Chris asked as he stood up and readjusted his t-shirt.

"She's my sister!" Ryan said pointing at me while I sat frozen but highly entertained.

"I was just saying," Chris said as he sat back down on the couch. Reaching into a bag of chips, Chris continued, "You could have at least given us some kind of warning, not that I think *that* would have helped." Ryan then wailed the side of Chris' head with the very same pillow that had offered Chris little protection.

"You'll have to excuse them," Gregg said as he sat back down on the couch confident that Ryan wouldn't lunge again.

"Do they do this a lot?" I asked watching as my brother took the bowl of dip out from under Chris' chip before he could get some.

"It's a weekly occurrence," Gregg laughed. "Sometimes it's over things like who the best Ninja Turtle is but today might take the cake."

"Who won? The turtles..." I clarified when he looked confused.

Gregg leaned over and said lowly, "Raphael, but it's still a touchy subject." I shook my head and held back my amusement as the Titans kicked off.

Sunday, September 6th

I slept soundly due to the exhaustion caused by not sleeping the night before. It was strange though that my frequent dream missed its nightly visit.

Ryan was sitting at the dining room table in his Sunday best playing a game of Solitaire when I made my way downstairs. He cleaned up nicely and, coincidentally, today my sundress complemented his attire. I smiled at the sibling sixth sense.

"Ready for Church?" he asked hearing my wedge heels coming down the last few steps.

"Yes sir," I answered as I walked towards the table where he flipped over another card. When he looked up, he smiled to himself.

"What?" I asked suddenly feeling self-conscious.

"You look very nice, Beths," my brother said as he turned over the Jack of Clubs.

"Thank you?" I responded insecurely.

"No, you do. I just don't think you could fit in with any crowd if you tried," he let out a breath of air, collected the piles he had played and reshuffled the deck. "And that was in New York. Ellsworth is just a teeny, tiny bit smaller," he said sarcastically.

I took the seat across from him and folded my hands on the table, watching as he set up the next game. When he felt my gaze, he fiddled with the cards and then asked, "What?" when he couldn't take it any longer. I tilted my head and waited for him to explain yesterday – why he hadn't told his fiancé, his future sister-in-law or best friends about me. "Alright," he said not needing me to verbalize the looming question; it was something he had anticipated. "I am sorry," he started, "I didn't know how to bring it up. I've told Kate about you. She knows you as Bethany, my baby sister. And Liv, Liv gets all crazy when she talks about celebrities. I didn't want her obsessing. As for the guys… I didn't want them checking you out," he finished protectively.

"Okay," I said leaning back in my chair.

"Okay?"

"Yes, I understand," I tried to grin. Ryan placed the stack of cards down and reached for my hands, covering them with his.

"Beths, you will always be my kid sister. The girl who is too smart for her own good, who has the patience of a saint, is stunningly beautiful and someone I would *willingly* take a bullet for." There was a flicker in his eye; something funny was coming. "But you need to remember, as perfect as you are, you will always be number two on the favorite grandchild list." I grinned and looked down at the table then back up at him. Ryan's smile slowly melted away and he took a deep breath. "You make it hard to be an older brother, Beths. I hope you know that. I almost killed Chris yesterday," he said starting to crack up at the memory and so did I. Squeezing my hand, he said seriously, "I love you. You know that, right?"

"Yes. I love you too, Ry," I responded looking back at him.

"Good," my brother said sitting back in his chair, swept up the deck and directed, "Now pull a card out from under that pile."

"That's cheating," I smirked but did as I was told.

"Yeah, yeah," Ryan said flipping over the next card.

I heard the bathroom door open and my grandmother came out brushing a comb through her hair. She was smiling, happy that we were together and ready for Church. "You look lovely, Bethany," she complimented.

"Grams!" Ryan, for a laugh, stood up exuberantly gesturing to his outfit and posed.

"You look dashing, Ryan, as always," she smiled and kissed his cheek.

"Thank you," he said pleased and sat back down.

"Favorite grandchild award goes to…?" I taunted and Ryan's eyes narrowed playfully.

The front porch door opened and an older man, also dressed in his Sunday best, walked into the house with the morning newspaper under his arm. He was a kind, gentle looking man and was handsome. He and Ryan looked more like father and son than grandfather and grandson. My brother's frame was fuller with youth and his hair had not grayed yet but otherwise there was not much difference between the two. Walking over to my grandmother's side, my grandfather looked down at me. "Mornin' Bethany."

"Good morning, Gramps," I nearly giggled as I stood, hugging him and felt him kiss the top of my head.

—

The Church was what would be expected for a small town setting. Even though it had been taken care of by its parishioners over the years, it was dated. The cornerstone was marked '1885' and as we walked inside I was able to get a better look, it was not hard to believe.

I followed behind my grandparents as they made their way down the left aisle to the pew where they sat with Ryan every Sunday. Whispers and pointing started to break out as we filed into the row. You might have thought that I was the Second Coming or something by the way their eyes bulged. That's when I knew I had just walked into Ellsworth's spotlight. Ryan leaned over as he put down the kneeler. "And so it begins," he whispered.

"Great," I said kneeling next to him. Closing my eyes and making the Sign of the Cross, I took a deep, controlled breath. 'Ellsworth... really,' I laughed in my mind. This was my style of praying. It was an open conversation. 'You have a sick sense of humor,' I let my thoughts flow and a smile crossed over my lips. I had received what I had been pleading, praying and hoping for the past two years – to be closer to Ryan. 'I know, be careful what you wish for and even more careful what you pray for,' I rambled soundlessly. I opened my eyes and saw a little girl sitting in front of us staring at me. I smiled and waved. She looked away but was more at ease seeing that I was human. 'Help me ride this out until I'm old news,' I shot up before sitting back in the pew.

I felt Ryan's arm resting behind me along the top of the back of the pew. His actions spoke louder than words. It was a simple sign of his protective nature, the start of revealing our family tie, and the support that I needed. I tilted my head and he nodded knowingly. 'Thank you,' I added to my prayer as the music began to fill the space, bringing with it a sense of life.

—

After Mass, the congregation made their way out into the parking lot where they could talk freely with one another. My grandmother and I walked arm-in-arm while Ryan and Gramps followed behind us. We smiled at everyone we passed but they weren't receptive. Their surprise was two-fold: a new member to the Church as well as the revelation that the beloved Taylor's had another grandchild. This was big news in the small town arena.

'Good morning Ben, Leah, James, Lily," my grandfather said as we walked by a young family but received no response. My grandfather was now witnessing 'Bethany Reid Syndrome' firsthand.

Finally in the safety of 'the tank', Ryan started the truck and people parted like the Red Sea to let us through. "I would have thought it would have gone better than that," Grams said of the women of the town whom she had been friends with since birth.

"Give them some time, Claire," my grandfather encouraged her looking over his shoulder at his wife and then at me. I must have looked somewhat troubled at the effect the people's reactions had on my grandmother. I felt guilty that their lifelong friends were surprised by my existence. "Bethany," he said directly. "Just to be clear, we do not think of you as some family secret." I let out a smile at my grandfather's grin before he turned back around in the passenger seat. It was clear that my brother wasn't the only one who felt strange about the 'Reid' thing.

Ryan caught my eyes in the rearview mirror and was trying to gauge how I was doing. I brought my hands up to either side of my head acting as fake antlers and stuck out my tongue at his reflection. He immaturely made a funny face back at me and we both broke away silently laughing at one another.

—

I changed out of my sundress and was helping Grams in the kitchen with breakfast elated that we were having our weekly 'phone call' face-to-face. Moving here would not affect our Sunday talks that I had grown to love and look forward too. The topic of discussion this week was my new room and the potential rumors that would come about after today's appearance. Grams was not a gossiper, rather, she was truly looking forward to introducing me to her friends once the shock wore off and the dust settled. She had a sparkle in her eye for her granddaughter... Bethany *Taylor*.

—

As I put down a mound of pancakes and a platter of sausage on the dining room table, I took a seat across from Ryan. Grams handed me a plate from the antique hutch and instructed, "Help yourself, dear, before your brother eats it all."

"Hey!" Ryan said as he put a few pancakes on his plate and began to cut them into large pieces. I smiled and poured myself a tall glass of orange juice. Gramps had been reading the newspaper at the head of the table and folded it now that we were all sitting together. He noticed me watching him and winked my way.

"Hi Gramps," I said sounding like a little girl.

"Tell me, how was your trip?" he asked picking up his fork and pulled a few pancakes and sausages onto his plate. We hadn't had much time to talk before Church so now the flood gates were open.

"It was great," Ryan interjected between bites, "I only had to stop for gas like five times."

Gramps looked at Ryan and shook his head, smiling and then asked me, "Bethany, can you please pass me the syrup?"

The phone rang and he got up to answer it before I could hand him the candy-like topping. "Hello? Brad. Yes, thank you for calling me back," my grandfather said switching the phone to his other hand and brought it to his other ear. The name caught Ryan's attention and my brother's chewing slowed as he tried to listen. Not able to make out what the mumbled voice was saying on the other end, he turned in his chair. "Yes. I appreciate it, Brad. I really do," Gramps said and nodded towards Ryan who turned back in his seat. I saw a smile on his face before he took another bite. "Thank you and pass along my thanks to your father. Bye now," Gramps said before hanging up the phone and rejoined us back at the table. I watched as my grandfather and Ryan pretended like the last two minutes hadn't happened.

"Is everything alright," my grandmother asked also noticing the strange exchange and now the even stranger silence.

"Yes dear," Gramps assured her, drizzling syrup over his pancakes. As he picked up his knife and fork he added nonchalantly, "Bethany, you won't have to worry about any of those paparazzi folk. The Sheriff will be making it… difficult for outsiders."

At this news my eyes widened and excitement washed over my face. "No paparazzi?" The idea was heavenly.

"Yeah," Ryan said wiping his mouth with his napkin. "Let's just say that anyone who tries to 'wander' into Ellsworth over the next few weeks will not experience southern hospitality." With a smirk my brother continued, "I would imagine Brad and the boys will have fun giving those parasite photographers a hard time. And I know they'll be more than happy to introduce them to their state issued shotguns."

"Shotguns? Jonathan!" my grandmother said looking from Ryan to her husband.

"Claire, the fear of God never killed anyone," he said cutting his pancakes into small slivers. Ryan laughed so hard that he pushed himself away from the table. Grams picked up her tea and leaned forward worriedly.

She and Gramps had a complete conversation without a single word. An innocent smile broke over my grandfather's face calming her, assuring her, while her smile was one that showed her trust and respect for him. It was proof that a love like theirs still existed and, better yet, that it still worked.

The phone rang again and Gramps didn't hesitate; he walked back over and picked it up. "Hello? Yes, hello Tom. I'm glad you got my message," my grandfather paused, listening. Relatively uninterested, Ryan unfolded the newspaper and started to read the sports section of the *Ellsworth Edition*.

"Aha. I see," I heard Gramps say as I served myself a pancake.

"Would you like a sausage, Beths?" Grams offered pointing to the platter.

"No, thank you. But I will have some eggs."

"You and your brother... He eats all the time. You eat like a bird," she said lovingly, passing me the serving spoon.

"Thanks, Tom. She'll be there. So long," Gramps said as he hung up the phone and walked back to the table and sat down. "That was Tom Donovan. He is looking forward to meeting you, Bethany."

Confused by who Tom Donovan was, I waited for my grandfather to elaborate. While doing so, I noticed that Ryan was again entertained by what was transpiring. "What?" I asked my brother sitting across from me.

"Tom Donovan is the principal of Ellsworth High School," Gramps explained as he picked up his utensils for the second time. Before taking his first bite, he casually added, "And he's expecting you to be in his office first thing tomorrow morning."

—

With the anticipation and anxiety of starting at a new school it didn't surprise me that I had a restless night, but the dream itself was something I could not have expected.

It came with the same likeness that the familiar nightly reel brought, but the dream itself was different. There was no party; no violins playing in the background... Instead there was a wave of emotion unrivaled in intensity even before the images came into focus.

"ANDREW," I yelled frantically as I burst into the large Estate. I ran up the curved, master staircase and down the long hallway into the study holding the sides of my gown so that my feet wouldn't get caught in the heavy black lace. Finding no one in the room, I ran back into the hallway screaming, "Andrew! DREW!" at the top of my lungs as if the house was on fire and we needed to escape. Racing down the back servant stairwell into the kitchen, I opened the back doors and hurriedly strode out onto the extensive grounds. "Drew!" I shouted, hysteria consuming me.

His voice came from close behind me and I turned to see him following a few feet away. I spewed out the lie, "I hate you." The archangel wasn't wearing a mask when the words hit him. His expression showed the hurt and anger; his jaw clenched. I closed the space between us. It pained him to be this close to me but his deep, ocean blue eyes locked with mine.

Acting calmer I continued the lie venomously. "It should have been you." My words stabbed him like I knew they would. He took in a sharp breath; his eyes grew red, burning with welling tears that he would not let fall. It was working – I was pushing him away from this sick, twisted mess instead of us being torn apart.

After everything we had been through and with all that he had thought I should feel towards him finally coming from my lips, I yelled, "Are you happy now?" It was then that he realized my words had held no truth. "Andrew, he would forgive you. He would *have forgiven you. Take it," I pleaded. But Drew continued to fight against what I was trying to say to him. Frustrated, I repeated, "Take it," and pushed against his chest. "Take it!" I cried. He grabbed my wrists and held them from him. He knew I was right; that he had driven us to this but he still couldn't forgive himself. The tragedy was still so raw.*

"Forgiveness?" he mustered out. "I don't deserve it. You don't know what it's like... Every time I see you," he tried but sentences wouldn't form for him. He was beyond comprehensible. Finally to the point of meeting his pain head on, a grin washed over my face. Not understanding, his anger showed itself. "You get pleasure out of this? How could you get pleasure out of this?"

"No," I shook my head. "Drew, you don't earn forgiveness. It's a gift."

Without warning I was overwhelmed with a heavy, heavy weariness. My breathing became strange in my lungs and my heart was beating to a rhythm of its own. "Take it," I said again, placing my hands gently on his chest, hoping that he would release himself from the guilt that had paralyzed him; that had paralyzed us. "Take it," I whispered.

Something was wrong – something not expected. This weariness was not going to pass; its hold on me was too strong. When Andrew's eyes found mine I saw how he stood frozen, helplessly watching my strength leave me. He moved closer and had a look on his face as though I was betraying him. Perhaps, I was.

"Bethany," I heard him say in fear. My eyes blinked slowly. Struggling to keep my hands on his chest, he covered my hands with his and held them to him. "Beths," Andrew said again in desperation watching as I continued to falter. But then I felt nothing. No beat. No breath.

With one last look into his piercingly blue eyes, my lips parted in a soft smile. "Drew," I whispered, "Take it."

Suddenly, everything went black.

Monday, September 7th

Unfortunately, even in this time capsule of a town, Monday came after Sunday.

"This is impressive, Miss Taylor, really impressive." Mr. Donovan, a forty-something year old man with salt and pepper hair said as he looked over a copy of my transcript from my prep school back in Manhattan.

Mr. Donovan's office was that of a typical principal's. There were some framed articles showcasing the school's achievements on the walls and stacks of papers of new curriculum outlines on his desk. It sufficed for the very involved, hands-on principal; at least that's how Gramps described him.

"Saint Hale's Academy for Girls sounds like a fine institution. I only hope you are not bored in your classes here at Ellsworth High," he said placing my transcript down on the desk.

In the half hour I had spent in Mr. Donovan's office, the secretaries scurried to put a schedule together for me while he asked numerous questions about New York and my high school education. He had fallen prey to the 'Bethany Reid Syndrome' of shock and staring on occasion; however, he would circle back to the topic of Ellsworth High School, his true passion in the small town. "You seem to excel in the sciences and math," he acknowledged. "History and English on the other hand," he said taking notice of the significant difference in grades.

"I have a hard time with history and English," I confessed. History was always a challenge for me and when it came to English I was told that my writing style was of a different standard which was not considered 'current' and, therefore, was not acceptable. That's why I tried to steer clear from both subjects and immersed myself in classes that made sense to me... ones with numbers and formulas.

"Even though you have taken higher course levels than we offer here, your grandfather was clear that he wanted you to have a standard senior schedule," Mr. Donovan said looking across his desk at me. The pit in the bottom of my stomach grew as I realized this would include taking history and English. "You will not be taking any classes for actual grades. I think it's safe to say that you would kill the curve in the science and math departments. I will inform your teachers of this arrangement at our next faculty meeting but, for the time being, please keep this between you, your grandfather and me."

"That won't be a problem, sir," I assured him.

"I'm sure it won't," Mr. Donovan nodded. "Your grandfather is a good man. I am happy I can do him a favor, even one as easy as this." There was a knock on the door before it opened. One of the secretaries came in and smiled at me as she handed Mr. Donovan a blue piece of paper. "Thanks Laurel," he said standing up and his frame blocked out the light that came in from the window behind him. "Alright Miss Taylor, are you ready?" he asked and I nodded, picking up my bag.

I followed him out of the office and down a hallway lined with navy blue lockers. Bulletin boards were covered in flyers for an upcoming charity car wash, 'Welcome Back' posters hung over doorways, and there were sign-up sheets for various clubs taped to the wall outside the cafeteria. Other than for a few murmurs coming from behind closed classroom doors it was very quiet. My heels clicked with every step I took and I realized then that I was probably not dressed like the other students. I had gone to a private high school and was use to wearing a uniform. In fact, I was actually missing it as I walked down the hallway in designer denim and an emerald green Dolce&Gabbana top. Ryan was right, fitting in was not something I was particularly good at. Being my older brother, Ryan had also gone as far as suggesting on more than one occasion that I wear turtlenecks and sweatpants in public.

As Mr. Donovan and I got closer to my destination I thought more and more about the students behind the classroom doors. Most had no clue who or what they were going to be after graduation, whereas I felt like I was going in reverse. I had the 'career' and had seen life outside the safety of this small town. To me, being here was like retracing important steps that I had skipped over. Maybe Gramps knew that too and that's why he asked Mr. Donovan to give me a standard senior schedule.

First period had already ended according to the timely bells that echoed throughout the school while I was still in Mr. Donovan's office. So, it was safe to assume that everyone was currently in second period. "This is your stop," Mr. Donovan said as he handed me the blue paper that my schedule was printed on. I looked down and read 'Second Period: Calculus, Room 9'. He knocked on the door, proceeded to open it and then stepped into the room. "Excuse the interruption, Mr. Kingsley."

"Of course, Mr. Donovan, what can I do for you?" a much older voice said. Mr. Donovan stepped to the side and said, "New student. Bethany, you may take a seat." I walked through the doorway hating myself for wearing heels. Why did they have to be so loud?

"No way," I heard a girl gasp. I looked up at the class full of my peers and tried to find an empty seat. There was one in the back. Perfect.

As I walked to the unclaimed desk, whispers broke out and grew louder and louder. "That's enough everyone," Mr. Kingsley said calling the class to order as Mr. Donovan closed the door behind him. I tried to be as discrete as possible as I slid into the chair but I could feel everyone's eyes on me. 'This is what a fish in an aquarium must feel like,' I thought to myself. I chanced one look up to the left and a guy wearing his letterman jacket which had a 'C' on the sleeve gave me a kind, welcoming smile. That's when I realized looking around was a bad idea. Not only did I feel ridiculously out of place but, in that moment, I also redefined my definition of 'shy'.

Thankfully, Mr. Kingsley continued his lesson from the podium, "Where was I? Oh, right. We were going to justify the equations." I opened the notebook Ryan had given me earlier which had a Lumberyard logo on the front. Inside, on the first page, he had scribbled, 'Good luck' and attempted to draw a sparrow – the school's mascot. Smiling, I shook my head and looked up at the board gladly loosing myself in a topic with unknowns and infinities.

—

In a normal high school hierarchy, one could walk down the halls as a normal teenager and see who's talking to whom, overhear party plans for the weekend, watch people pass notes, etc. HA! As I walked out of calculus it seemed like everyone stopped what they were doing. Maybe even time stood still too. I tried to be friendly, smiling at the people I passed but nothing seemed to register – a side effect of 'Bethany Reid Syndrome'. I really couldn't wait for it to wear off.

As I opened my locker the PA system sounded, "Bethany Reid, excuse me, Bethany *Taylor*, Coach Taylor would like to see you in his office." Both relief and anxiety washed over me. Gramps would be a haven from the gawking and whispers but, there was one small problem... I didn't know where his office was.

"Hey," Liv said coming up next to me like a guardian angel. "Cute blouse."

"Thanks," I said happy she had found me and took notice of what she was wearing: jeans and a t-shirt. I felt that much more out of place but made a mental note for my future outfit selections.

"I heard you were spotted in the Main Office."

"Spotted?" I laughed.

"Yes, like an endangered species," she said in a funny accent to add to the safari-like comment. Then she handed me a folded piece of paper. "It's just a note. My locker is twenty-seven whenever you want to write back."

"Cool," I smiled and realized that by standing with Olivia, my nerves had settled. Not only was she my friend, but thanks to our siblings, we would soon be sisters-in-law; I was grateful on both counts.

"Didn't you get called to your grandfather's office?"

"Yes," I said closing my locker, "but I have no idea where it is."

"Come on," Liv rolled her eyes dramatically and we walked down the hall together as she gave me fun, impromptu tour.

—

"It's open," I heard Gramp's voice say from the other side of the office door.

"You wanted to see me?" I asked while Olivia continued on to her next class.

"Yes," my grandfather said as he picked up a remote from his desk, pointed it at the television across the room and pressed 'Pause'. Gramps was dressed in khaki slacks and a navy blue polo that had 'Coach' embroidered on it. "I was just looking over some passing routes for the scrimmage on Friday. You wouldn't be interested in playing?" he teased.

I grinned and sat down in an old chair on the opposite side of his desk. His office had school colored streamers of navy and gold, school memorabilia, tons of article clippings and trophies from previous teams' accomplishments. He had a reputation for turning out great players and for winning championships.

"So, how's your first day going?" he asked sitting down and leaning back in his chair.

"Well, I've only had one class so far," I smirked at him.

"I know, but I figured you could use a break. You are quite the talk of the school," my grandfather said while trying to read my face.

"Gramps..." I started.

"This will be a good experience for you, Bethany." With a growing seriousness he continued, "I've seen your transcript and know that classes won't be hard for you." Looking me square in the eyes, he continued, "However, I want you to do me this favor."

"Favor?" I asked with a raised eyebrow.

"I want you to do as many high school things as you can," he said leaning forward and folded his hands on his desk.

"High school things?"

"Yes."

"Okay," I replied skeptically.

"Just try to enjoy your experience. That's it," was his explanation. I shrugged, agreeing to what he was asking. Gramps then passed me the morning paper saying, "You look like you could use a free period."

"I thought you wanted me to get the 'high school experience'?" I asked confused.

"Skipping, my dear, if I remember correctly, is part of it," he smiled as he brought his coffee mug to his lips.

—

I spent the next ninety minutes, when I was supposed to be in physics, with my grandfather discussing Ellsworth football as we ate homemade cookies Grams had packed for us. Unlike his players, Gramps was not nervous for the upcoming season and thought of Friday's game as nothing more than a motivation booster. With a record like his – having more undefeated seasons and state championships than any other high school football program in the state – many could not understand why he had not accepted college coaching offers over the years. Even though my grandfather told people that he didn't take the positions because he felt like he had no experience with college football, only having played high school football himself, the real reason was that he didn't want to leave his hometown; a town which he loved and which loved him back. He also measured his success in the fact that his players were accepted into good colleges based not only on athletic ability but academics as well. He believed that his legacy was what his players could not only do on the field, but also in the opportunities that waited for them once they stepped off.

There was a knock on the office door. Gramps called out, "Come in," and a man in his early thirties entered the room. He was an old kind of handsome, striking. He had brownish blonde hair, brown eyes and carried himself well. I read over his classic profile as he greeted my grandfather.

"Good morning, Jonathan," he said rather articulately. He was holding a leather bound book in his left hand which I recognized as being the team's playbook. I couldn't help but feel like there was something remarkable about this stranger. What it was exactly, I couldn't pinpoint but I instantly felt like smiling.

'Charles,' I thought to myself and, like an echo, my grandfather spoke, "Charles," as he stood and the two shook hands. My eyes widened realizing I had known this person's name before hearing it. I stared again at his facial features trying to place where I knew him from while my grandfather searched for his copy of the playbook on his desk. "Charles, this is my granddaughter, Bethany," Gramps said without looking up. I stood as Charles' head turned and his eyes narrowed in disbelief at the sight of me. It wasn't the 'Bethany Reid Syndrome' reaction; this was stunned amazement matched by an exceptional distrust, anchored by a sense of longing to believe what he was seeing. Recovering from his lapse in composure, he nodded towards me, never putting out his hand. I didn't take offense because it was an old gesture leaving me to feel as though I should... curtsy? Taken aback by my impulse, I looked over at my grandfather who had found his leather bound book and picked it up. "Charles is the assistant coach for the varsity football team and is also your biochemistry teacher, Dr. Landon, Coach Landon, whatever the kids call you," my grandfather laughed. There was another knock on the door. This time it was a nervous looking freshman.

"Fischer, I left the permission slips in the locker room." My grandfather instructed as he walked towards the door and led the boy out of the office. Dr. Landon and I were alone.

"Bethany," he swallowed and took a step closer to me.

"Yes," I answered and added, "It's nice to meet you," even though a part of me believed that I already knew him. I was hoping he would correct me and tell me that we had met before and where, but he didn't. Instead, he looked sideways in disappointment. "We have met before, haven't we," I smirked tilting my head. His eyes came back to mine and he nodded with a promising smile.

"Beths," he began but stopped himself. Other than my family, no one called me 'Beths'. However, when he did, it sounded natural.

"Charles," came from my lips and my eyes flickered. Images flashed in front of them, of him, but placed in a setting identical to the ones in my dreams. Feeling a little off balance, my right fingertips felt for the top of my grandfather's desk. Dr. Landon put out his arms, prepared to steady me if needed. The concern he showed and the way his eyes were fixed on me was more than any stranger or acquaintance would demonstrate. Our eyes crossed each another's – mine searching for something that his looked like they'd found.

"Make sure you have one of your parents sign it and bring it to me first thing tomorrow," Gramps called after Fischer in the hallway. My grandfather walked back around the corner and into the office, snapping Dr. Landon and I out of the gaze we had fallen into.

"I should go," I decided, reaching for my bag.

"Of course," Gramps said as he sat down in his chair. "Have fun in class."

"Thanks," I answered. Like a gentleman, Dr. Landon stepped to the side, allowing me to pass.

I crossed the room and when I got to the door, I looked over my shoulder at my new acquaintance who was watching me carefully. When our eyes met, I had the urge to smile and did so, involuntarily. His eyes narrowed again but he smiled to, and then shook his head in continued disbelief. My left hand traced my collarbone, a nervous habit of mine. Seeing this, Dr. Landon let out another breath as though the wind had been knocked out of him. Oddly enough, my smile didn't leave my face and as the bell rang, I closed the door separating the time, space and moment between us.

It had been a long first day at Ellsworth High. Now in the safety of the attic, I distracted myself by focusing my energy on mindless time killers like putting the finishing touches on some homemade wall art. My playlists were on shuffle and I enjoyed the randomness which consisted of country ballads, some Christian rock, obscure preteen British pop and even a few classical compositions. The notes filled the attic, changing the feeling with every song.

"Hey!" Olivia yelled over the music, scaring me half-to-death. She was still dressed in her cheerleading practice clothes.

"Hi," I said holding my chest and lowering the volume.

"Sorry. I thought you heard me coming up the stairs," she apologetically shrugged and handed me a small, white pharmacy bag. "Here's the prescription you needed filled from Saturday."

"Thanks Liv," I said checking the bottle and putting it in my nightstand drawer. "Make yourself at home."

She walked over to the huge armoire and when she saw the selection of clothes and accessories, her face looked like a kid's in a candy store. "This is insane," she gawked.

"Help yourself," I offered as I picked up the finished embellishment, jumped up onto my bed and felt around for the nail to hang it from. Loud footsteps marching up the stairs told me that Ryan was home.

"Hey Beths, how was school?" he asked as he got to the top, dirty from working at the Lumberyard. Kate was right behind him in her scrubs and looked around the room like her sister had seconds ago.

"It was okay." I answered.

"This place looks great," Kate admired, resting her hands on the top of the banister.

"Grams said dinner will be ready soon," my brother mentioned as he walked over to Olivia and moved his hand in front of her face. She was spellbound, staring at a pair of European branded sunglasses.

"They're yours," I insisted.

"What? Are you serious?" she squealed holding them in the palms of her hands like they were a glass slipper.

"Yes, a gift for not acting like I have the plague." Liv's eyes whimsically floated from me back to the glasses.

"Was it that bad?" Kate grimaced.

"Oh, come on!" Ryan challenged. "You're telling me no one talked to you today?" he asked plopping his two hundred and twenty-five pound body on my bed.

Before I could answer, Kate came to my defense, "Not everyone can have the same high school experience as you did, Ry."

"Ha! Those were the days," my brother said putting his hands behind his head, looking up at the ceiling and amusingly added, "What can I say... People love me."

Olivia, sporting her new eyewear, was enjoying her reflection in the old mirror when she interjected, "Bethany is like the biggest thing to happen to Ellsworth. Maybe even bigger than Ryan's ego, if that's possible." She and Ryan shot each other fake scowls and then she abridged, "Everyone's curious; gossiping... you know."

"What are they saying?" Kate asked sitting next to Ryan on the edge of the bed. Olivia gave the same report she had given to me in the notes we passed back and forth between classes.

"Bethany is going to go into rehab, Ellsworth is a publicity stunt, she's taking a break... launching her singing career."

"They have *clearly* never heard you sing," Ryan commented in only a way an older brother can. I threw a pillow at him which he caught and put behind his head.

"Would you two want to go see that new movie after dinner?" Kate asked. She didn't need to dwell on people's speculations and kindly offered a distraction from the rumor mill.

"I thought we were going on a date?" Ryan asked leaning up on his elbows.

"We can double," Kate smiled and looked at Olivia and me.

"Sure. Sounds like fun," Liv bounced in place and I nodded, happy to spend more time with the people who were quickly becoming my every day.

—

"WOAH OHH," my brother belted out the last lines of the song blaring on the radio. The truck windows were rolled down and the sun was long gone. There were no streetlights – only headlights; something I was neither use to nor fond of. How could anyone drive like this? Don't tell me those little yellow plastic reflectors every few feet sufficed. I guess my city eyes were still use to the well-illuminated glow of Times Square and bustling avenues.

"Where's the movie theater?" I asked when I realized we weren't in Ellsworth anymore.

"Coverly. It's a town over," Kate explained from the passenger seat.

"The theater is new, super clean and ginormous!" Olivia said trying to reapply her makeup. "A lot of kids from school hang out there."

"That's because Ellsworth doesn't have..." Ryan started to taunt.

"Hey!" Kate softly elbowed him. "Not everyone can be from the city."

"I love you babe, but sometimes I wonder," he said humorously before kissing the back of her hand which was intertwined with his.

As we entered Coverly, it was easy to see that they had sold out their Main Street to high-end chain establishments in exchange for making them categorically more affluent. In contrast, Ellsworth had chosen to keep its mom-and-pop shops which preserved and protected the small town feel but limited its commercialism. Personally, I enjoyed Ellsworth's loyalty and the atmosphere that came with it.

Ryan turned into the movie theater parking lot and as we got out of 'the tank' Liv giggled, "Isn't this place huge?" I smiled to myself knowing that her definition would change with one glance at a skyscraper but, in comparison to the buildings I had seen since moving to Ellsworth, this was 'huge'.

Arm-in-arm, she and I followed behind Ryan and Kate as we walked towards the box office. "Hi, four tickets for…" Ryan began to say but stopped and looked up from his wallet feeling the tension coming from the other side. "Hello?"

"Ah, sorry," the surprised teenage ticket vendor said looking away from me and at Ryan.

"Four tickets for the eight o'clock showing of that new movie. The one with the guy," my brother mumbled as he pushed money through the opening in the glass.

"Right," the vendor said sliding the tickets and change back underneath. "Aren't you…" he added, pointing my way.

"Brad Pitt. I get that all the time," Ryan answered intercepting the question. I smiled and Liv, who was now laughing, pulled me along with the group.

"That wasn't nice," Kate whispered to my brother who held the door for us.

"Neither was his drooling over my sister," he countered while giving other people who started to stare a childish growl.

"I want Snowcaps," Olivia announced as we walked through the pristine lobby that had a glass dome overhead and every possible amenity you would need at the movies. "What are you going to get?" she asked looking back at me as we approached one of the concession stands.

"Umm, popcorn is good." I decided after reading the lit up menu.

"Welcome to the…" the attendee started. "Bethany Reid!"

"Hi," I half-waved. This 'famous in a small town' thing was getting old, fast. After today, with school and everything, even Olivia had met her quota.

"Can we have Snowcaps and a small popcorn?" she asked ignoring what was taking place.

"Can I have your autograph?" the attendee asked grabbing a napkin and pen and handed them to me, disregarding Olivia's order.

"Sure," I said scribbling, 'Bethany Reid' in a bubbly script for the full effect.

"The guys are never going to believe this," the concession employee said more to himself than to anyone else.

"Dude! Snowcaps and popcorn!" Liv repeated agitated. She was cute and blonde at a glance but I was quickly learning that her sarcasm had the potential of being lethal – and hilarious.

"Ugh, right. Yeah," he said scrambling for a popcorn bag. After handing us our snacks he nodded and said, "It's on me. You ladies have a good night."

"Thhhhanks," Liv said slowly as we turned and looked at one another before finding our way over to Ryan and Kate who were in another line.

"What did you get?" Kate asked her sister who showed her the Snowcaps box.

"What can I get you folks?" their concession attendee asked.

"I would like…" Kate started but Ryan, who was eyeing the candy options, didn't realize that his bride-to-be was about to order and cut in.

"I'd like a soft pretzel, a box of Peanut Chews and Milk Duds." Kate looked at him and he shrugged, "What? I'm hungry!"

"I'll have the Sour Patch, please," she said shaking her head.

Trying to maintain straight faces, Olivia and I headed towards the theater. "We'll save seats!" Liv yelled over her shoulder to them as we started laughing.

—

"Liv, can I ask you a question?" I asked bravely now that we were alone.

"Yeah, of course," she said opening up her candy.

"The biochemistry teacher," I started but Olivia ran with it.

"Dr. Landon. I don't have him for class but he's super nice. He's the assistant coach of the varsity football team, so he and your grandfather talk a lot. He's married… and totally cute."

"Umm, yes," I said not having seen him in quite that way but, she was right, he was a good looking man.

"His wife is Mrs. Landon. I think your schedule said you have her as a teacher too. She's nice, strict though, teaches physics... She's pretty, like that classic kind."

I was hoping that Liv would continue to give me the rundown on the Landon's but Ryan and Kate were filing into the row and the lights started to dim as trailers began to play.

—

The movie was almost as good as the fun that surrounded the 'double date'. With Kate and Liv dropped off at home, Ryan and I pulled into our grandparents' driveway. The porch light was on.

"How was the movie?" Grams asked when we came in the front door. She had stayed up, waiting for us and was knitting in her chair.

"Good, but I'm beat," my brother said reaching down and untying his work boots. "Gramps is already in bed?" he assumed, looking around the empty first floor. "I'm going to turn in too. Night," he said as he walked over and kissed our grandmother on the cheek then kissed my cheek, "Night, Beths."

"Night, Ry," I said as my brother headed for the stairs.

"Bethany, would you mind sitting with me for a minute?" Grams asked.

"Sure," I said curling up in the armchair opposite hers. My grandmother's fingers moved seamlessly, wrapping the strand of yarn around the needles which gracefully crisscrossed forming stitch-after-stitch. With years of experience she could easily hold a conversation and work without losing her count.

"Is anything bothering you, dear?" she questioned with a hint of concern in her tone.

"No," I answered too quickly.

"No?" she repeated, not fooled. I began to trace my collarbone nervously. The feelings that I had been suppressing for the past two years were on their way to my eyes. It was only a matter of time. "Honey," she said putting aside what she was working on and touched my knee. With this, the tears began to stream down my face. "It's okay," she said but I shook my head. The sound from Ryan's bedroom door closing on the floor above us made her and I look up at the ceiling. "He's so happy you're here. We all are," she smiled as our eyes came back to one another's. "And, you and Olivia seemed to have hit it off."

"She's really funny," I laughed as I dried the tears away.

"She is definitely a firecracker, that one," Grams grinned.

"Thank you for letting me…" I started but she chimed in.

"We love you. Do you hear me young lady?" she asked and waited for my acknowledgement. When I nodded my grandmother said, "Good." We both stood up and she gave me one of her all-encompassing hugs.

"Night, Grams," I whispered as I let go.

"Good night, sweetie."

Tuesday, September 8th

Just like my clothes, my car had a hard time fitting in. It had magically appeared in the driveway this morning and had Ryan's doing written all over it. I don't know how he managed to get my pride and joy to Ellsworth but I appreciated it. My brother knew how much I loved my car. It was the only indulgence I had purchased for myself and something I took very good care of. After all, it was a top-of-the-line, fully loaded, crystal red Corvette. Just looking at it brightened my day. The rest of my money was in bank accounts no one could touch; they were something my father had set up before his unexpected passing while I was still a baby. The accounts were set in stone way before the whole 'Bethany Reid' thing and every one of my paychecks had been directly deposited into them. Not even my mother could interfere or 'redistribute' the money I had earned or funds I inherited. I didn't know what I was going to do with it, but it was quietly and safely accruing thanks to his financial knowhow.

Driving the Corvette to school today was only the second time I had actually driven it. Before buying it, I hadn't considered that I lived in Manhattan. Right after signing on the dotted line, I ended up parking it in the private garage underneath the penthouse to keep it safe, assured that no crazy city drivers could scratch, hit or damage my prized possession. I would go down to the garage and sit in it on occasion, enjoying the sound system and escaping from the plum prison. On Ryan's last visit before 'Operation

Bethany' I had told him about the car and even let him sit in the driver's seat. He clearly hadn't forgotten and had made arrangements for it to be delivered to Ellsworth. After all, it was the only thing that wouldn't fit in the back of his truck. Leave it to my brother...

I parked the beautifully engineered masterpiece in the school parking lot far away from everyone else, not wanting to risk it getting dinged or scratched. As I got out, I heard the warning bell for homeroom. I looked back over my shoulder and smiled when I chirped the doors locked. I loved that car.

—

I managed to get myself through first and second period by focusing on writing a long note to Liv which included the news about the Corvette. I found a seat towards the middle of the room in third period, physics, and looked down at my blue schedule. Liv was right, I did have Mrs. Landon.

A woman in her late twenties strolled into the classroom. She had reddish brown hair that was pulled back in a neat bun and she wore a pencil skirt with a conservative, ruffled blouse. Mrs. Landon was plain but a very pretty woman, and, like her husband, she too carried herself differently than most people. There was an air of elegance about her, a subtle poise. Mrs. Landon's eyes were focused on the floor in front of her and at her arrival, the class turned in their seats without being told. I watched the students around me, prepped for the exam they were about to take. She moved up and down the rows placing the packets on each of their desks. I turned over my packet, wrote my name on the top and read through the questions. They seemed easy enough; basic high school physics questions – things I had studied before. Feeling pretty confident I penciled in the first answer and then showed my work in the space provided. It took me about ten minutes to finish the entire exam and that was with checking it twice. I tried not to draw attention to myself as I put down my pencil. However, when I looked to the front of the classroom, Mrs. Landon had been watching my every move.

Our eyes met and everything other than her blurred in my sight. It was like my mind was short circuiting again. I saw her, her profile and flashes from an older time. A slight smile crossed my lips for no reason at all. Feeling as uncomfortable and unsure as I had while meeting her husband, my hand began to anxiously trace my collarbone. She walked over to my desk and asked, "May I," before picking up my packet. I noticed her engagement ring – it was unlike any I was use to seeing and somehow I had seen it before. The center stone was a large, radiant cut ruby bordered by small diamonds in an intricate gold setting. It was stunning and somehow I knew her husband's initials were engraved on the inside of the gold band. I shook my head at the moment of insanity.

Mrs. Landon walked back to the podium where she scanned over my test. She then wrote something on the top of the packet, returned it to me, and continued to walk down the row, proctoring the rest of the class. I turned over the corner of the paper to find written in a cursive script, 'See me after class.'

'Great,' I thought to myself. I should have held my head longer or at least put in a wrong answer or something…

—

The rest of the period was long, almost painful. I watched other students struggle and moan over the questions. But to their relief, the bell rang and their torture came to an end. After everyone had left the room, I stood with my belongings and walked to the front. Mrs. Landon was stacking the tests in a neat pile. Feeling my presence, she turned, leaned her hip against the desk and crossed her right foot in front of her left. Looking at me she held my packet and said in a sweet voice, "Remarkable."

"Thank you," I answered cautiously; her voice eerily familiar.

"I heard you met my husband, Charles, yesterday."

"Yes," I confirmed.

It was then that she took a deep breath and made eye contact. Her eyes softened and her lips widened into a smile. If she didn't look so refined I might have thought her reaction was unhinged. Looking away from her and around at the empty classroom I felt quite awkward and only looked back at her when the silence became deafening. She was in a state of disbelief but not in the typical 'Bethany Reid' way. Her chin rose when she asked, "May I ask you a personal question?" to which I nodded, agreeing.

"Did you inherit your green eyes from your mother or your father?" she questioned in a low but smug voice as if she already knew the answer.

"My dad," I smiled to myself. My emerald green eyes were identical in color to those of my late father. It was something I was proud to have; a constant reminder of a man I barely knew but deeply loved. Even Ryan said he wished he had my father's eyes instead of my mother's brown shade. "I don't mean to be rude, Mrs. Landon, but I really don't know what this has to do with the exam," I said with the discomfort from the situation inspiring me to speak.

Mrs. Landon focused on her reason for asking me to stay behind. "My apologies. Mr. Donovan pulled me aside to talk about your previous education in the sciences and bearing witness to it today, I was wondering if *you* would like to explain it to me?"

"Explain what exactly?" I asked. I could feel heat start to rise to my face.

"Well, you can only learn so much about a person from a piece of paper and, I daresay, while your transcript is impressive, I believe there is more to the story." I didn't answer; I couldn't answer. I was taken aback by the terminology she used and was failing to understand why she was probing more than even the principal had. "Bethany," Mrs. Landon said and caught herself. I looked up at her unknown unease in saying my name as she continued, "The exam you just took was a twelfth grade physics exam. I am hoping you could explain to me why you used physics equations from a higher level of the subject, and better yet, how you managed to get the answers without using a calculator?"

I hadn't anticipated the 'not using a calculator' thing at all even though I should have… and I definitely didn't think twice about what equations I had used. I mean, I answered the questions correctly! That usually means the teacher leaves you alone. I was a bad liar and when it came to incriminating evidence, well, I had left plenty. I knew I couldn't answer her without giving myself up. Her eyes narrowed as she waited for my response. For a second, I looked back at her forgetting about the informal interrogation and found myself caught trying to recall where I was. She, like her husband, somehow resonated in my mind. 'Abigail,' I thought to myself. I knew her name but no one had told me it.

"Abigail," slipped out of my mind and onto my lips. Mrs. Landon clasped her hand over her mouth and her eyes welled with tears.

Immediately breaking the gaze and composing herself, Mrs. Landon focused her attention on restating her question, "Do you… Do you have an explanation for your exam?"

"I, ah…" I stuttered and admitted, "I've taken a few college courses."

She nodded. "Mr. Donovan missed this bit of information?" she asked, sounding more like a fact than a question. I nodded. "How many classes have you taken?"

"A few," I replied.

"And how old are you?" she asked waiting for me to answer.

"Seventeen," I said glad that it was nonnegotiable.

"Seventeen," she repeated.

"Yes."

Forcing herself out of the thought she was in, she lightly folded her arms in front of her. "And your equations?"

"A mistake," I admitted sarcastically and took a deep breath. "Abby…" escaped. Her eyes went wide again and I froze in place. "I'm sorry, Mrs. Landon," I said recalibrating my seriously confused brain. "I'm only in class because my grandfather wants me to be. No one knows that I have already graduated from high school… not Mr. Donovan and not even my grandfather. The only reason I've taken higher classes," I said readjusting the bag on my shoulder, "is the result of boredom mixed with too much free time and an interest in Architectural Engineering."

"Which university?" she asked wearing 'a grin on her face, not surprised by my advanced level of education. It was strange to me that the revelation about my education didn't faze her nearly as much as me calling her by her first name… twice.

"Columbia," I answered. She nodded and smiled at her confirmed assumption.

"And no one knows?" she asked.

"No and I would prefer if no one…" I started.

"Found out? Fair enough," Mrs. Landon cut in, grinning. "How far along are you in your study?"

"Credit wise? My second year."

"Good for you, Beths," Mrs. Landon said truly happy for me – proud even. She looked down at the floor and then back up at me. She, like her husband, had called me by my nickname. "Your father would've been very proud," she began to say as her composure became less and less professional and more and more unguarded.

My eyes narrowed at her mention of my father which Mrs. Landon noticed and quickly redirected, "What are your plans to finish your education?"

"Um, I'll go through this year here at Ellsworth High, and then when it comes time to pick colleges, I'll find a school somewhere close by that will accept my credits and I'll finish there."

"There are a few southern Ivies that you could look into. Duke, for instance..." she started with a growing enthusiasm. She sat down at her desk and I pulled a chair under me. It was innate, too innate. We sat across from one another so comfortably; the moment was surreal. Mrs. Landon and I both stopped and neither spoke. We just stared at one another and smiled. There was an expected relationship between her and I, and it was strong – like there was some sort of history. I looked down at her engagement ring again and the wedding band next to it, and then back up at her.

"I... I," I said shaking my head slowly blinking. Unnerved and feeling embarrassed, I stood and gestured to the door, "I should get to my next class."

I began to walk away but heard her say, "May I ask you just one more question?" I was not annoyed, but rather felt more like a caged bird. I turned and waited. "What made you come back to Ellsworth?"

"My brother, my family is here," I answered. She nodded without saying a word and I opened the door and found myself in the crowded hallway. Closing the door behind me, I stopped mid-step. 'Did she just say, 'Come back to Ellsworth'?' I thought but quickly disregarded it as the next bell rang out overhead.

—

Luckily, the rest of the school day went by smoothly with no further impromptu interrogations taking place. No other teacher noticed symptoms of my exposure to higher education like Mrs. Landon had, especially my history and English teachers; those subjects were a completely different story.

As I was walking up the front porch steps after school I noticed my grandfather sitting next to someone whose little feet were swinging back and forth. "Hi," I said when I reached the top step.

"Bethany, this is Cole. Cole, this is my granddaughter, Bethany," Gramps introduced me to the smiling nine year old boy with platinum blonde hair. "Your grandmother usually babysits for the Landon's at their house but there was some sort of family emergency and they had to fly out of town."

"Hi," Cole said jumping off the chair and put his hand out, "I'm Cole. It is a pleasure to meet you."

"The pleasure is mine," I grinned and shook his little hand. I looked incredulously over at my grandfather who was smiling.

"Cole, why don't we go see what Mrs. Taylor is up too?" Gramps suggested as he stood up.

"Okay," Cole beamed and used both hands to open the screen door. Before it slammed shut, my grandfather caught it and held it open for me.

"After you, my dear," he said motioning for me to go before him.

"Thanks Gramps." I stepped inside saying, "Cole's adorable. Where did he get that blonde hair from?" Neither Dr. nor Mrs. Landon had traces of light hair.

"Charles and Abigail are foster parents," my grandfather explained.

"Coach," Cole said sticking his head out from behind the kitchen door with excitement that could not be hidden. "Mrs. Taylor said we can have a cookie break now." I looked back at my grandfather whose expression matched the little boy's.

"Cookie break," Gramps winked at me and headed to the kitchen behind Cole. I smiled as I climbed the steps.

I decided to take a long, hot shower during which I heard 'the tank' pull into the driveway, then Ryan's voice coming from the porch. A few minutes later, I could hear him and Cole playing downstairs where a lot of 'fee-fi-fo-fuming' and laughter was coming from. I wrapped myself in my towel and headed up to the attic but stopped halfway. The light was on and I knew I hadn't flipped the switch. Walking slower, I heard a small voice and as I reached the top, I saw a little girl dressed in a light pink dress with platinum blonde curled pigtails sitting in the middle of my bed. She was humming happily to herself and was playing with some of my ribbons. One of my tiaras was sparkling between the pink bows on either side of her head and she was wearing a pair of my heels which were much too big for her small feet. Holding on tighter to my towel, I couldn't help but think that this was the perfect scenario for a horror movie – a beautiful little girl humming, an old attic...

"Hi," she said in an adorable voice.

"Hi," I smiled as I walked towards her. "I'm Bethany," I said before sitting on the edge of the bed.

"I'm Gracie," she answered in her innocence.

Ryan came roaring up the stairs with Cole on his back. "Where'd she go?" my brother growled. Cole was laughing hysterically at Ryan's attempt of sounding scary. Gracie jumped up and hid behind me, giggling into her hands. "Hey Beths, have you seen a little troublemaker around?"

"Nope," I smirked but her giggling got louder and gave her away.

"Get her!" Cole pointed.

—

The rest of the day was packed full of games like hide-and-go-seek and a new game Ryan called 'suck-the-energy-out-of-the-kids' which consisted of him throwing a football as far as he could in the backyard while Cole and Gracie chased after it. They had passed out on the living room floor shortly after dinner from pure exhaustion. Ryan was sleeping in one of the armchairs and I was close behind them. I had found my way to the couch but with a caffeine kind of rush, I felt like a fifty pound weight had been laid on my chest. I assumed that this is what a panic attack felt like and, strangely enough, even though my mind was racing, my eyes closed from the day's fatigue.

Then I was in that kind of dream again, except this time I wasn't in a ballroom or on the grounds. I was sitting on a sofa in the study of the same Beaux turn-of-the-century styled house. It was dark out and there was a large fire burning in the fireplace across from me. The lamp lit on the end table next to me shed light on the pages I was reading. "What part are you up too?" a paternal voice asked from the doorway. As I looked up, I smiled. He was tall, handsome... the gentleman type and, my father. I closed the book and watched as he entered the room. "There are other books in this world," he said with a grin on his face as he sat down in his evening chair to my left.

"The lack of binding..." I began to joke.

"Is evidence that you take part in that adventure quite often," his smile widened. "Beths, I have to leave for Coverly for business in the morning," he explained knowing that I would not be happy with the news. I looked at him upset but he grinned and *added, "It will be a quick trip, I promise." It was my father's piercing green eyes that stayed with me as the dream melted from my sight.*

I woke not having moved on the couch but Ryan was now sitting on the other end. He was watching television and eating a midnight snack to try and satisfy his forever-hungry appetite, however, with his metabolism, it was nearly impossible. Cole and Gracie were still asleep on the floor and Ryan had thrown a blanket over them and put down a few pillows. Pretending as though I was still sleeping, I rolled over and tried to get my bearings.

I had never *really* met my father; I was too young to remember him before he passed. I didn't know what my imagination was doing but I was somewhat grateful for the sweet vision – for the chance to see what it would have been like if he was still alive, even if it was only a dream. But it didn't feel like a dream; it felt real. Closing my eyes again, I hoped that I would fall right back into it.

Wednesday, September 9th

I love mornings. I guess I was just one of those people; a polar opposite of my brother. Over the years I had developed different morning routines which I followed religiously until something caused them to change. When things did change, a new ritual was born. After Ryan moved out, my routine changed. After

I finished high school early, my routine changed. When I decided on Columbia, well, it changed again. Nevertheless, morning runs were always a priority. I loved it and at the same time, it had become a necessity.

I had been diagnosed with a heart defect when I went for a mandatory physical as a result of my early admission to Columbia. With a combination of prescription medication, regular cardio and routine checkups, the doctors said I should be fine. Their orders were even more incentive to make sure running stayed in my regimen.

Moving to Ellsworth was another one of those 'changes' and it was time to adapt. I woke up early and put my blanket over Ryan. I snuck around Cole and Gracie, pranced quietly up the stairs to change into my running clothes, threw on my sneakers and grabbed my earphones. After softly shutting the front door behind me, I was ready.

It was still pretty dark out by the time I reached the edge of Ellsworth but I felt good. I decided to cross over the town lines and increase the volume of the playlist. The way I played music, I was going to be hard of hearing by the time I turned thirty but I didn't care. I figured with the racket Ryan's truck made… well, we were going to make an interesting pair.

The pavement passed faster under my feet, the scenery didn't change much – trees, picket fences, the occasional squirrel, maybe even a bunny. There was no one around. The sun, finding me, hit my face as it came over the horizon. It was an endless game of hide-and-seek for this morning person. Don't get me wrong – there was pain in my legs, the start of a stitch in my side from the pace I was keeping, and the idea of slowing down was a faint thought in the back of my mind but I didn't. I pushed because running was time that I had to myself – to pray, to let go, to hand everything over. My body was on autopilot. The dream that was still so fresh in my mind replayed hauntingly, hanging in front of my eyes.

Not knowing exactly how long or how far I had run, the road vibrations from morning traffic under my feet were the signal to me that it was time to make my way back to my grandparents' house and get ready for school. Watching as the town came to life, I smiled at the nine-to-five pace. And before I knew it, I was making my way back up the driveway, pulling out my earphones.

Grams was eating breakfast with Cole and Gracie when I left and, at school, it came as no surprise to me that the Landon's were absent. After all, I was helping babysit their foster children while they were out of town. However, it did become clear that the rest of the student body was not use to their teachers being out; the substitutes didn't stand a chance.

—

It was about dinner time when the phone rang. Grams wasn't home because she had taken Cole and Gracie to their house after school and was waiting for Dr. and Mrs. Landon to get in from the airport. On the third ring Ryan picked up the phone. "Hello? Sure Grams... love you too," he said before ending the call.

"Grams needs a ride home from watching the monsters," Ryan stretched and handed me the remote before getting to his feet.

"They're not monsters," I said also standing, "and I'll pick her up."

"You don't even know where they live," he argued.

"I have GPS. I think I can figure it out," I shrugged as I slid on a pair of shoes that I had left by the front door. "Plus, I miss them."

"You are sick and twisted if you miss those…" Ryan began to say but Gramps walked in from the porch. Ryan quickly finished with, "children," through gritted teeth and with much effort. My grandfather grinned, not missing a beat, as he continued to the kitchen. "Fifty-six Emerson," Ryan called over his shoulder sitting back down on the couch and changing the channel. I reached for my keys from the table and closed the front door behind me.

With music blaring, the windows down and the sun getting ready to set over the tops of the trees, I felt alive driving along the streets of Ellsworth. According to my GPS, the Landon's lived three miles west.

The road was long, the double yellow lines curved slightly. There were woods on either side and there was no sign of life. "The destination is on the left in point two miles," the automated voice chimed in over the music but there was no road to turn onto.

I was about to curse the navigation system and call Ryan, admitting defeat when I saw cobblestone barely visible under broken pavement. Looking closer, I noticed two old widely spaced trees separated by a dirt path. Coming to a crawl, I decided to make the turn and, sure enough, the dirt path led to a fully exposed cobblestone drive.

The forest thinned into a clearing and the drive was lined with two rows of massive oak trees that created a high arching ceiling of branches, both protective and beautiful. As I reached the top of the small incline, a breathtaking Estate came into view sitting at the end of the pathway. My tires felt the vibration of the cobblestone underneath them and I slowed even more as I took in the extensive, manicured grounds surrounding the gorgeous, white, turn-of-the-century Estate. It was untouched. I would have never thought a house of this grandeur would be so close to the modest town of Ellsworth.

The wind blew through my car windows and the tree limbs swayed overhead. The calm, peaceful sound of thousands of leaves rustling together made me smile as the shadows danced below.

I came to a stop in front of the Estate and stepped out of the Corvette completely awestruck. Even for its age, the Estate was in perfect order and very well taken care. There were no traces of Mother Nature's forces on her and the vast amount of scenic land stretch farther than my eyes could see.

I took my time walking up the front steps, enjoying this hidden treasure. The inimitable front door was at least ten feet in height and was rounded at the top. The substantial frame complimented the earthy stone foundation and white exterior. I reached for the steel iron knocker and, eerily aware of its familiarity but unable to place it, knocked twice.

There was no answer. I knocked again but still, nothing. I turned the door knob and felt amazement wash over my face as I took in the entranceway.

An ample antique table was positioned in the center of the high ceilinged space. To the left there was a majestic, master staircase that bent slightly as it climbed to the second floor. The wall that should have been directly across from the front door was over a hundred yards away and there were cathedral-like windows that cascaded down to the level below, allowing the massive archway framing to showcase the extent of the grounds. Walking passed the table I realized I was at the top of an ostentatious staircase that descended into a marble floored ballroom. The floors below glistened and reflected the dramatic, ornamental ceiling and lighting above it.

I turned back to the front door. To the right and left there were doorways leading to what I imagined were more amazing rooms. Above the table that was now in between me and the front door, hung a chandelier that was a beautiful statement of an early American influence.

"Hello?" I said hoping Gracie would come running around the corner but it was silent other than the echo of my own voice. "Hello?" I said again and looked back down into the ballroom and out the far windows onto the grounds. Then I heard faint notes being played on a piano, a sign of life. I began to climb the master staircase leading to the second floor and when my hand glided along the banister, I stopped. I knew these stairs. I had seen them, climbed them... I knew the entranceway and the ballroom... and the grounds. The dreams came rushing at me. I put my hands out on the stairs in front of me, steadying myself until my eyes refocused. Desperately wanting to not be alone in that moment, I called out, "Hello?" again but this time a little louder. The music stopped abruptly. I found my balance and took the last few steps up the staircase. A door to the right had opened and I saw Dr. Landon walking towards me, down the long hallway.

"Bethany," he said surprised.

"Hi, Dr. Landon, how was your trip?" I asked moving to the side not wanting him to think I expected to go any farther than the stairs. He tilted his head almost as if he hadn't heard me. I took the cue and elaborated, "My grandfather told me there was a family emergency... is everything okay?" But before he could answer the question which had caused him some sort of mental delay, Grams and Gracie came strolling down the hallway from the other side of the house.

"Bef-fany," Gracie yelled as she ran into my leg, clinging tightly.

"Hi Gracie," I said wrapping one of her blonde, curly pigtails around my finger.

"Did you come over to play too?" she asked adorably.

"No Gracie," Dr. Landon said swinging her up into his arms. "Bethany is here for her grandmother."

"Maybe she can play next time?" she asked.

"Maybe next time," Grams winked as she touched Gracie's shoe that swung energetically.

"You have a lovely home, Dr. Landon." I admired the architectural luxury as we walked down the stairs to the front door.

He smiled as though I had said something funny. "Thank you," he said placing Gracie down and she took off, ready for her next adventure.

"Have a good night, Charles," Grams kindly bid as she stepped out onto the front steps.

"Claire, thank you again," he nodded. As my grandmother walked to my car, I turned back to say goodbye. Dr. Landon was leaning with his one hand against the doorframe and his other ran tensely over his mouth. He looked tired, worn even, and he hadn't anticipated that I would catch him.

"Are you alright, Charles?" I asked instinctively and then closed my eyes. I had used his first name and not the appropriate 'Dr. Landon'. What was wrong with me?

"Beths," Dr. Landon responded but stopped himself. I heard my grandmother try to open the locked passenger door, so I turned my head and clicked it open for her. "Nice car," he remarked in a changing demeanor.

"Thank you," I said as I looked back at him. Sure enough, he had regained his bearings which had flickered seconds ago.

"You are always welcome here, Bethany," he added kindly.

"Thank you," I nodded writing off his invitation as southern hospitality. "Have a good night, *Dr. Landon*," I distinctively said, focusing on using the right name.

He smiled saying, "You do the same," then waved to my grandmother who was patiently sitting in the car.

I couldn't help but look in the rearview mirror when I pulled away. Dr. Landon watched from the front door as I drove down the cobblestone oak alley until we lost sight and I turned back onto the main road.

—

Later that evening I had the dream that played almost nightly while I lived in New York, but this time I saw it differently. I saw it with an unparalleled awareness.

I was standing in the ballroom surrounded by women in beautiful gowns and men dressed in formal attire. There were candles lit everywhere and I could hear violins playing. I took my first steps up the ostentatious staircase wrapped in roses and ribbons leading to the now recognizable entranceway. The table under the chandelier was the exact same antique table I had seen earlier today except it was new. My heart raced as the setting of my dreams now had an address. The Estate which I had not known existed until this afternoon had been the setting of the nightly dream for as long as I could remember. I did not wake up because of the implausible understanding of my surroundings. Rather, I awoke when I reached the inimitable rounded front door only to see that the guests, the people in the Estate, were arriving in carriages, not cars.

Thursday, September 10th

It was only the second day of my new routine but I was already in love. Running in this small town meant there were no taxis to dodge, no bikers to jump out of the way of, and no other runners who didn't acknowledge your existence as you passed. And, above all else, the air was clean.

I quickly found out that the best way to measure how much time had gone by during my jogs was by the amount of movement coming from houses as people left for work. On my way back to my grandparents' house, neighbors would say, "Good morning," to me as they reached their cars. I would return the gesture with a smile or a wave; it was a sweet exchange.

After my shower, I went downstairs to the kitchen where Grams had left breakfast for me with a handwritten note.

Bethany,
I had an early meeting with the Ladies Guild for the County Fair. Hope breakfast is still warm. See you later.
Love, Grams
P.S. Ryan, DO NOT TOUCH.

As I picked up my fork I noticed that half my eggs were gone, there was no sausage – only a space where they had been, and there was leftover syrup on my pancakes... make that pancake. "RYAN," I yelled and then heard him sneak out the front door and start his truck, chuckling as he pulled out of the driveway. I couldn't help but laugh too, eating what was left.

—

Liv was waiting for me when I pulled into the school parking lot. She had been dying to see my car and had made it known in every note since I told her about it. However, she had cheerleading practice and work after school so her time was limited. Today we spent lunch and a free period sitting in the Corvette, talking and giggling... girl moments. The day had not been all smiles though. I found out that I had an English reading assignment and a quiz in history tomorrow. Let the torture begin...

—

Later that night, after I read and re-read the English assignment and finished studying for history, I crawled into bed. That's when I had another dream, the strange kind.

"Bethany?" Dr. Landon said. I didn't answer him. I was standing over a fireplace with both of my hands on the mantle. He came in from the doorway and touched my arm. I looked at my knuckles, white with tension, grasping around the carved wood.

"Bethany..." he started.

"Charles, please," I said through clenched teeth; I was incensed. My eyes were filled with tears that had not fallen yet. My stomach was in knots. My heart, aching.

"Bethany," Dr. Landon said again. I looked up at him with one of the traitor tears slipping down my face.

"They," he paused also distraught as he tried to say what he had too. "One of them... They didn't say who."

"No... No, no," I said as the fear turned into hurt. My knees weakened as I broke down crying. Dr. Landon held me up and led me out of the study and down the long corridor to a bedroom at the other end of the house. Mrs. Landon was there silently looking out the large window into the night. She was dressed in a light green Victorian styled dress which was cinched at the waist. Light from an oil lamp was the only brightness in the room and she watched worriedly as my head found the pillow. I knew she had heard the commotion I had made and was also clearly upset over the news. After Dr. Landon had placed me on the bed he walked over to his wife and whispered in her ear, then left the room quietly returning down to the first floor. Mrs. Landon walked towards me and I rolled over on the bed, away from her. "Abby, don't," I let out defeated. Tears continued to run down my face and I felt like I was dying inside or at least a piece of me was. I closed my eyes and hoped only for the white light.

Instead, there was noise that came from downstairs – the front door. I heard a man's voice... two voices... and they were getting closer. One belonged to Dr. Landon. "Drew," I said *recognizing the other. Relief washed over Abby's face when she saw her brother and ran to him meeting him in the hallway right outside the room. I saw his arms hug around her and then he stepped passed her. He stood frozen in the doorway at the sight of me, a mess. I pushed myself up, my hair falling over my shoulders and my feet found the floor underneath the hem of my dress. Then our eyes met.*

He was handsome, a striking man who was only a few years older than me. He had brown hair and piercingly blue eyes. His jaw line was strong and he was very attractive even with the cuts and bruises – mere traces of humanity. He wore a white button up shirt and black pants which only slightly revealed his masculine physique. A bandage was wrapped around his left forearm, red with blood. He was injured but very much alive.

In disbelief I made it less than halfway across the room before he walked towards me, closing the gap between us, and taking me in his arms. Seeing that he was alright – the relief was instant. His presence and his health meant that the other person had not made it. This sent my mind into denial; a safe place but only temporarily.

"Bethany," Andrew said placing his hands on either side of my face as new tears began to fall. "I am so sorry," he said with a splintered voice as though he could feel the mourning that would come. Mrs. Landon began to weep and Dr. Landon held her, hiding his own face.

Looking back at Drew, I said, "I know." He was tortured by what had transpired; burdened with a guilt that he shouldn't have to carry. His eyes closed but not before I saw the shame in them. "I know," I repeated and began to cry harder; his arms pulled me into his chest. I felt the archangel's right hand run into my hair and he kissed the top of my head before his own tears fell onto the cold, hardwood floor.

I woke in a sweat in the dark room with tears still in my eyes. My breathing was erratic and the pain I had experienced in the dream was very much still with me. The anxiety, fear, and hurt were fierce and bottomless. The striking man had become a reoccurring character in my dreams and I had a pull towards him that was intense and alarming, but I was not alarmed by this. 'Relax,' I told myself as I laid back down. Oddly enough, I fell asleep instantly as though my time awake was a breath of air after being submerged.

Chapter Two
Friday, September 11th

It was the last day of my first week in Ellsworth and until now I hadn't fully comprehended the meaning of high school football in a small town. That is until this morning.

There were cheerleaders, Liv included, and football players completely decked out in their uniforms for the pre-season pep rally. All of the football players proudly wore their lettermen jackets – a hierarchical symbol. They were the royalty of the school; the highest in the social chain of command. I smiled to myself at the safety of this falsity but was still taken by its charm.

The student population was giving off an electric charge that could be felt in the hallways. The excitement was contagious as the countdown to the start of the football season began. The scrimmage, a tease, was going to be played at the opponent's field in a neighboring town but it didn't put a damper on school spirit. I had never witnessed anything quite like it.

I got my books for the morning, closed my locker and turned, walking into someone. "I'm sorry," the voice said immediately. Rebounding, I looked up and saw one of the football players unmoved by my insignificant momentum. "I wasn't trying to scare you. I just…" he started. He was cute with his dirty blonde hair and hazel eyes. He was definitely the athletic type and there was a big 'C' on the sleeve of his letterman jacket confirming that status. I had run into the 'king' of the school and smiled to myself again at the mental, hierarchal reference *and* its charm.

"My fault," I nodded. "I'm Bethany," I said putting out my hand.

"Jackson," he said meeting my hand with his. "We're in the same homeroom together... I sit behind you in biochemistry," he half-smiled shyly when it was clear that I was oblivious. He was a good looking guy, had a great smile and didn't come off over-confident or smug like I had stereotyped. He seemed nice and sincere. Maybe I had this football hierarchy all wrong.

"Oh," I said embarrassed for being in the same vicinity as him for a week without acknowledging his existence.

"And we're in about every other class together too," he laughed realizing I had paid little attention to my surroundings. But his last comment made me recall my very first day at Ellsworth High and my very first class.

"I remember. Mr. Kingsley's class," I said sounding pathetic as I linked the memory with the 'C' on his jacket to the guy who had smiled at me.

"Yes," he said as his face turned the slightest shade of pink to whose embarrassment I am not sure.

Trying to redeem myself I changed the subject and asked a safe and obvious go-to question, "Are you excited for the game?"

"Yeah, but I'm a little nervous," Jackson admitted as we started to walk down the hallway together and rounded the corner headed to physics. He had a relatively deep voice but it still had the boyish flare to it.

"I think you guys will be fine. At least my grandfather thinks so."

"I think we'll be okay. It's just the 'beginning of a new season' nerves," he smirked. "Are you coming to the game?"

"No," I answered shaking my head, "but I'll be at the home opener next week. I'm kind of excited about it. I've never been to a game before."

"Really? Wow," he laughed.

"What?"

"It's just never occurred to me that someone would never have been to a football game," he explained. "Especially since your brother and grandfather are who they are."

"Yeah, well... I'm not normal," I joked.

"Oh, I know," he grinned as he held the classroom door for me.

I looked curiously at him and he quickly added, "I didn't mean that in a bad way, it's just you're... different?"

"Different," I repeated as we found our seats which were embarrassingly close for me to have not noticed him before.

Leaning across the row that separated us he gestured for me to move closer to him so I could hear when he whispered, "No offense Bethany, but if you were a *normal* girl, I'm pretty sure you would have noticed that half the football team sits by you when they can." Jackson smiled as I looked around. Sure enough, I was surrounded by letterman jackets. "For the record," he said pointing to his seat, "this has been my seat since freshman year." His smile widened as I began to laugh. I didn't know what to say; he was right. Any *normal* girl would have noticed the football players around her.

"I'm shy?" I shrugged to which he laughed. Then I offered, "I'll try to be more observant."

"That's a good start," Jackson grinned as the announcements came over the PA system.

—

It was difficult sitting through physics and biochemistry and it wasn't because of the material. Seeing Dr. and Mrs. Landon was perplexing and uncomfortable. After all, they had leading roles in my haunting dreams. I could feel my face wince whenever we locked eyes during their lectures. I would then awkwardly look away and was finding it harder and harder to keep my composure without coming off as being rude. It only took a quick smile from Dr. Landon to push my adrenaline to new levels. 'This is insane,' I thought to myself when I got to my locker after his class and slammed it shut before heading to my car.

Having no plans for the rest of the day, I got to observe it peacefully as it unfolded. The weather was gorgeous: clear, bright, crisp and brilliant, mountainous clouds billowed across the sky. With Gramps and Liv at the away game, Ryan working late at the Lumberyard and Kate working a double shift at the hospital, Grams and I spent the evening baking cookies, playing cards and watching a movie. A life of normalcy was finally finding a rhythm and I couldn't be happier.

Saturday, September 12th

On the front page of the Saturday *Ellsworth Edition* the headline read, 'Ellsworth Sparrows Take Flight'. The in-depth article on yesterday's scrimmage gave a detailed description of the victory and hope for another winning season. It came to no one's surprise that the Sparrows won; it was more an article of pride for their small town heroes. Gramps didn't bother to read it in its entirety because he had witnessed it firsthand. Also, nothing they wrote would surprise him – he was a town legend himself.

Around noon Ryan came up the attic stairs in his Lumberyard clothes. "Hey Beths," he said when he reached the top step.

"Hey," I answered as I picked up two boxes full of magazines that had made it from New York.

"Need help?" he asked taking them from me.

"Ugh, sure," I said with no other option as they were already out of my hands and in his.

"Where do you want them?"

"In the garbage," I shrugged lightheartedly.

Ryan rolled his eyes and started, "You should keep these. Show your kids someday…"

"You sound like Michael," I whined but then directed him, "Could you put them BEHIND the armoire until you're an uncle?"

"Fine," Ryan said half-defeated as he put the boxes out of sight.

"How was the Lumberyard?" I asked folding some clothes that were over the back of a chair. Judging by the amount of dirt my brother was covered in, it had been a busy morning.

"It was okay. We got a couple of orders out. Chris stopped home to shower and Gregg said he'd be by after he helped his brother-in-law with something. Are you going to watch the game with us?" Ryan asked. Almost on cue, two sets of heavy footsteps made their way up the attic stairs.

"Wow, nice place," Chris said making it to the top first.

"Thanks," I smiled closing the doors to the armoire.

"How'd you guys get here so fast," Ryan asked faking a punch at Gregg's shoulder.

"What are you talking about? We left the Lumberyard over two hours ago," Chris said grabbing Ryan's wrist and looked at his watch.

"Stop at the hospital to see Kate?" Gregg guessed and Ryan nodded. That's where the time went.

"Well you better hit the showers so we don't have to put up with the smell," Chris said with a disgusted face.

"Yeah, yeah," Ryan said jogging down the stairs headed towards the bathroom. Chris and Gregg were wearing the unofficial guy hang out outfit: drawstring shorts and t-shirts.

"So…" Chris cleared his throat. "How are you, Miss Reid?"

"Chris, there's no 'Reid' and it's just 'Bethany'," I deadpanned.

"How's school going," Gregg asked shaking his head at his friend's comment.

"Alright I guess."

"What teachers do you have," Chris curiously questioned as he sat on the edge of one of the trunks behind him.

"I have Dr. Landon for biochemistry, Mrs. Landon for physics," I listed first. Neither Chris nor Gregg had them as teachers because they came after the two had graduated. "Wiman for homeroom…"

"He's still alive?" Chris asked surprised to which Gregg sniggered.

"I have Prather for history, Ogno for English," I said feeling the pit in my stomach for my weakest subjects. I had been putting off the homework for both classes and even though Mr. Donovan said my grades wouldn't count I still felt anxiety over the material. "Oh, and I have Kingsley for calculus."

"Kingsley's," Gregg and Chris spoke at the same time each finishing with a different opinion. Gregg's was, "awesome," while Chris' selection was "sucks". Gregg crossed his arms and said, "Just because Kingsley failed you, does not mean he was a bad teacher."

"Hey, I actually studied for that class!"

"First off, you should have never been in that class to begin with," Gregg argued.

"Hailey Buchanan was hot! It was worth the 'D'," Chris tried to justify.

"Kinglsey is a good teacher," Gregg said looking back at me. "Einstein over here charmed our eighty year old guidance counselor into signing him into calculus when he was barely passing algebra."

"What are you trying to say, Gregg?" Chris challenged.

"I'm saying you can't expect to learn how to run if you can barely walk," Gregg answered with his hands out in front of him.

"I, I... I got nothing," Chris surrendered and looked down at the floor laughing. "I am horrible when it comes to disciplined math."

"Disciplined math?" Gregg couldn't resist asking what he meant by that.

"I'm great at Lumberyard math but anything that has limits and crazy differentials... and I'm lost," Chris said with blank eyes. Gregg continued to shake his head at his buddy's remarks. "Is anybody giving you a hard time at school, Beths?" Chris said turning the attention back on me.

"No," I answered freely, "not at all. Besides Liv and Jackson, everyone else seems to stay away."

"Jackson Turner?"

"I don't know his last name," I said embarrassed. "He's the captain of the football team..."

"Yeah, that's Turner. He's the safety, nice kid... I graduated with his older brother," Chris added. "He and I played for your grandfather. I miss playing for Coach. He was great."

"Yeah, that doesn't surprise me," I smiled and noticed Gregg looking at me. Caught, he looked at the floor and then back up at me. My smile grew wider as I tried to hide it. The water shut off from the shower on the floor below then the bathroom door opened.

"Let's go," Ryan yelled up to his friends as he threw a clean shirt on over his head at the bottom of the stairs. Ready to watch the game, Chris and Gregg turned.

Chris asked over his shoulder, "Beths, you coming?"

Flattered that they expected me to join them I said, "Sure, I'll be right down."

About ten minutes later the living room was filled with football analysts... the ones on the television who got paid to be analysts and the ones sitting on the couch: Ryan, Chris and Gregg. The three of them all had their opinions about today's match up, so much so that I could barely hear what the announcers were saying. I chose to sit in the armchair with a bowl of popcorn. There were bags of chips and homemade dips on the coffee table for the festivities that had become a weekly tradition for the trio. Grams had gone to the Landon's to watch Cole and Gracie again. Mrs. Landon had called earlier asking if she could come by for a few hours.

The score was close and after a few beers the guys were full out yelling at the television. It was highly entertaining.

"OH COME ON," Ryan shouted as the final seconds counted down to halftime. His team of choice was losing by fourteen points. "Refills?" my brother asked standing up with his empty beer. Chris handed him a bowl with a few tortillas crumbs at the bottom, Gregg pointed at his beer and I handed Ryan my empty glass of water.

As soon as the kitchen door swung closed Chris looked over at me and said, "Do you know that you are Bethany freaking Reid!" I laughed; unlike most people, Chris' drunken words were the same as his sober ones.

"Seriously," Gregg repeated. His usual standoffish behavior was more forthcoming now that he had a few beers in him.

"Guys," I started knowing it wasn't worth the attempt of trying to explain to them that I was an exceedingly boring person who could not possibly live up to the hype.

Chris nudged Gregg's arm and said, "Slap bet." Gregg nodded in agreement to the proposal without knowing what the terms or conditions were. Chris turned his attention back to me and asked, "Who would you date?"

"Chris," Gregg said, uncomfortable by his friend's selection of words. Ignoring Gregg, Chris posed the question again.

I let out a laugh but two sets of eyes were on me. "I'm not answering that," I said feeling awkward even though Gregg's name basically screamed itself in my mind. "What exactly is a 'slap bet'?" I tried to change the subject hoping that the alcohol in their systems would make them forget the question they'd asked. Deep down, I knew there wasn't enough alcohol in either of their systems for that to be a possibility; there wasn't enough alcohol in the house for that matter.

"A slap bet?" Ryan asked returning to the living room with bottles of beer under one arm, a refilled bowl in one hand and my glass of water in the other.

"Yes," I said taking the glass from him. 'Thank God,' I thought. Chris and Gregg leaned back against the couch with a look of unease as Ryan took his seat in between them. I couldn't help but bite down on my lip.

"A slap bet is when the person who loses the bet gets slapped by the person who wins," Ryan finished as he opened up his beer and flipped the top into the community beer cap pile on the coffee table. "Why? What was the slap bet for?" he asked. I looked at Chris and Gregg who were now staring desperately at the television.

"Nothing," I said taking a sip of water before looking at the television too.

Ryan looked at Gregg and then slowly at Chris. When neither of them moved, Ryan guessed that whatever he had missed while in the kitchen had caused the now palpable tension in the room. He stood up and pointed at Chris who immediately pointed at Gregg.

"What?" Gregg said throwing his hands in the air. "Ask your boy, Christopher, he's the one that proposed the slap bet."

"Oh, and you weren't thinking it," Chris sneered at Gregg but he retracted further into the couch when Ryan caught a glimpse of him.

"What bet?" Ryan asked. "What was the bet," Ryan repeated looking over his shoulder at me.

"Ugh…" I said not wanting anything to do with what was about to transpire. Ryan looked at Gregg who looked at Chris.

"Somebody better start talking," Ryan said with his voice elevating.

"It was just a stupid bet," Chris tried sounding nonchalant.

"About? About Bethany," Ryan guessed and then narrowed in on Chris.

"Maybe," Chris looked up at Ryan and grimaced.

"Oh really," Ryan said with broadening shoulders.

Chris stood up, backing away from Ryan with his hands in front of him. "Dude, really…" but Ryan took a step forward with every step Chris took backward. "It was a stupid bet. We were just fooling around," Chris began to plead.

"Gregg," Ryan said still walking towards a retreating Chris.

Picking up the refilled bowl of chips, relaxed and ready to enjoy the impending beat down, Gregg explained, "He asked Bethany which one of us she'd date."

"What?" Ryan said turning his head sharply towards Gregg then looked over at me. I shrugged not offended. This little exchange gave Chris a two second head start to the front door. However, as he went down the porch steps Ryan quickly gained ground and with a football-like tackle, the two landed on the front lawn. Gregg and I stood at the window watching the two grown men beat each other on the grass.

"Chip?" Gregg offered me as I offered him popcorn.

"Shouldn't you, like separate them?" I asked after Ryan tried to pin Chris who somehow rolled out of the hold.

"Eh," Gregg said taking some popcorn from my bowl. Just then Gramps pulled up, parked the car, stepped over the two twenty-something's and continued up the walk and into the house.

"How long have they been going at it?" Gramps asked joining us at the window, taking a chip.

"A minute or two," I said as Ryan got a strong hold on Chris.

"And that's my cue," Gregg handed off his bowl to my grandfather and headed outside to separate his buddies. Gramps reached into my popcorn bowl and I stole a chip as we watched the three best friends on the other side of the glass.

—

After dinner the house was quiet. Grams had gone to her Ladies Guild meeting shortly after she got back from the Landon's, Ryan was picking up Kate from the hospital after her shift and Gramps was on the phone talking to some college scout about one of his players that they were interested in. I had just finished washing the dishes and was getting ready to sit at the dining room table to do my history and English homework. I could study history for hours but some things never stuck no matter how hard I tried. It was like I had a slightly different account of how certain historical events were presented and as much as I tried to memorize the pages in front of me, my brain wouldn't allow me to 'override' my gut. They were cemented in my mind. As for English, I was told that my reading comprehension was not the problem but that my writing style was of a different standard. My argument was, if a teacher could read what I wrote and understand what I meant, then where was the problem? 'Ugh,' I complained as I opened my history textbook with a backlog of homework assignments.

"Hey," I heard Liv say from the other side of the screen door.

"Hi," I said surprised when I looked up. I walked over and let her in. It was dark out and the bugs were congregating around the porch light.

"I thought we could use a girls' night," she said stepping inside and handing me a few movies. I smiled and was moved by the simple gesture. Other than in between classes, Liv was busy with cheerleading and she also had her job at the drugstore. This was spontaneous, unplanned; something that real friends do. "I hope you have ice cream," she bounced.

"Ryan lives here," I said hiding my emotional response and smiled, "of course we have ice cream."

—

It was late when Olivia and I had finished watching the last of the movies in my room but we were still wide-awake, talking and laughing about school. "Oh, I forgot to tell you. I think I made a new friend," I said remembering Jackson's introduction yesterday.

"Oh really, who?" she asked as she finished the pint of chocolate chip.

"Jackson Tur..." I began to say but her eyes widened before I finished.

"Turner," she gulped.

"Yeah, he introduced himself. We're actually in the same classes."

"He *talked* to you? Wow," Liv said with eyes wide in excitement.

"What?"

"Jackson doesn't talk to anyone other than the guys on the team. He's usually super quiet."

"Really?"

"What did he say," she asked eager to know more.

"He just introduced himself, we walked to class..."

"HE WALKED YOU TO CLASS!" she gasped.

"Well, no, I mean technically... I guess. We were both headed the same way."

"How did I not hear about this from anyone?" Liv asked aloud, upset that she hadn't heard the gossip.

"Because it was nothing," I shrugged.

"Bethany, you do know what this means, right?"

"No. What?" I asked finishing the other carton of melted deliciousness.

"Jackson and Bobby," she began.

"Who's Bobby?" I cut her off.

"Umm, Bobby Thompson, aka: possible love of my life," she said in a 'you should have known this' voice, "who happens to be on the football team with Jackson."

"Oh," I said never having heard about this 'possible love of her life' before. "What's Bobby look like?"

"He's tall, has red hair, always has a baseball cap on..." Liv said trying to describe him.

Not knowing who she was talking about I said, "Not ringing any bells but I'll keep an eye out. How long have you had a crush on him?"

"Well, we sat next to each other in the second grade," she started. I smirked as I put down the carton. Then something caught my attention out of the corner of my eye. I turned and spotted IT. There was a bug; a HUGE bug. It was scampering its way across the wood floor. I don't know if Liv or I screamed first, but Liv was yelling, "Get a boy!"

"A boy?" I shouted back as we both jumped onto my bed.

"To kill it!" she said in a very high pitched voice. When the mother of all bugs was halfway across the floor she yelled out the second best option, "Get a shoe!" I reached down and picked up the closest one and handed it to her.

"This is Versace!" she said outraged. Not getting off the bed, I reached for a flip-flop with the tips of my fingers and handed it to her and BAM! – the bug was gone. Well, not exactly... I was the cleanup crew. Two tissues and a flush later, our little friend was off to sea.

Sunday, September 13th

When I got back from my run, Cole and Gracie were waiting for me at the front door dressed in their Sunday best. Dr. and Mrs. Landon had dropped them off after going to an earlier Mass. Grams said they had some sort of family emergency again but this time they wouldn't be catching a flight; we would only be watching the kids for a little while. Grams didn't mind. She enjoyed babysitting for the Landon's because she treasured having a full house.

After Church, my grandmother and I had our weekly conversation over tea and coffee as Gracie colored next to us at the table. Grams asked how the night before had gone with Liv. She also asked about my classes and teachers and was thrilled to hear that I loved Ellsworth. I had gone from buildings to barns in a week's time and had no problem with the trade off. Although the pace was substantially, and sometimes, painfully slower, it was calming when I realized there was no need to constantly rush. What I liked most was the house I called home and the people who made my transition worthwhile. I knew this was the start of the life

I had always wanted. Laughing daily and smiling because I could –
I wouldn't dare turn back. There was something about this place,
this town. It was as if the sands of time had little consequence on
the simplicity of it, yet, I couldn't help but feel like something
more was coming.

The rest of the day went by with little children playfully
yelling and Ryan's energy quickly dissipating. "Please, it's your
turn," he said handing me Gracie from his back when *SportsCenter*
came on the television.

"Lunch!" I heard Grams call from the kitchen. Cole and
Gracie loved Grams' cooking almost as much as Ryan and I did.
However, for the first time in a long time Ryan was not the first
one to the table. In utter defeat I plopped down next to him on the
couch.

"I'm exhausted," I admitted melting into the cushion.

"What happened to you two?" Gramps kiddingly asked as
he came in from the front porch.

"I want to sit next to Bef-fany!" I heard Gracie yelling.

"Bef-fany, you're wanted in the kitchen." Ryan laughed
making the volume on the television a little louder as the segment
came on.

"I want to sit next to the Ryan-a-tor!" Cole shouted.

"Ryan-a-tor? Ha. Ha," I yawned as I stood up and stretched.
Ryan picked me up from behind.

"Yeah, like allig-a-tor," he said attempting to sound scary as he carried me over his shoulder. I was kicking my feet as he swung the kitchen door open, and Cole and Gracie shrilled with excitement.

—

Lunch had been delicious. I was rinsing the last of the dirty dishes at the sink and handing them to Gracie who was standing on a chair next to me, drying them off with the dishtowel. She was such a pleasant little girl, always watching and always pretending. "How old are you," she asked looking up at me as I carefully handed her towel-ready hands a Mason jar.

"Seventeen," I answered and her eyes shot open at the 'large' number. "How old are you?"

"Five," she said matter-of-factly.

"Wow, you're old!"

"No I'm not," she giggled. "I'm only one hand," she said placing down the glass and showed me five fingers.

"What's your favorite color?"

"Cole's favorite color is orange," she started. "My friend Lindsey's favorite color is purple. Ryan's is red," she listed. "Uncle Drew's favorite color is green. And I love pink." My heart was in my throat as I looked over at her. She was clueless to the sudden loss of air in my lungs.

"Uncle Drew?" I asked slowly as my mind began to race, having matched the names with my dreams. Dr. Landon… Charles, Mrs. Landon… Abby, Uncle Drew… Drew… Andrew.

"Uncle Drew likes green," she said again taking the next plate from my hands; I stood still, dazed almost. Then I heard Dr. Landon's voice coming from the porch where my grandparents were sitting. Gracie heard him too, put down the towel and plate then jumped off the chair. I followed behind her as she and Cole met at the front door and rushed out onto the porch together. Ryan had gotten up from the floor where he had been playing blocks with Cole and returned to the couch. He turned and mouthed, 'Thank God,' at me.

"Stop it," I said walking farther into the living room, eyeing Dr. and Mrs. Landon through the front windows. The rush of anxiety still in my veins from what had just taken place in the kitchen sent my nervous hand to my collarbone. Just then Mrs. Landon looked away from the conversation she was in with my grandparents and looked through the window feeling my stare. Our eyes locked but it was the sound of my brother's voice that made me turn my head.

"Next time I think we should try to direct their energy towards… I don't know… cutting the lawn or, or washing cars!" The porch door opened and in walked Cole and Gracie who hopped, skipped and jumped towards Ryan giving him 'thank you' hugs. Then it was my turn and Gracie tugged my hand so that I would come down to her level.

"I had lots of fun playing with you," she said in her adorable little voice.

"I'm glad to hear that. I did too," I smiled. As I stood, Grams and Abby were walking into the house followed by their husbands. Ryan had gotten up and walked over, kissing Mrs. Landon's cheek and shook Dr. Landon's hand.

"Good to see you, Ryan," Dr. Landon nodded.

"Likewise," my brother answered standing next to me. "Did you like what the guys did with the refurbished woodwork?" he asked and unconsciously put his arm around my shoulder.

"Yes. Again, quality work," Dr. Landon said taking notice of Grams looking down at Cole who had also put his arm around his little sister's shoulder. Gramps brought his hand up to his chin and smiled at the sibling moment, as did Dr. and Mrs. Landon. Ryan and I looked at one another and then at Cole and Gracie.

"Cole, a little sister might be a pain in the butt sometimes," Ryan joked and I poked his side, but my brother pulled me closer. "But you take care of her. It's your job."

"Right," Cole said like a solider taking orders. A grin crossed over Mrs. Landon's face as she looked from Cole and Gracie to Ryan and me. Her head tilted in thought but a comforting smile crossed her lips.

"Did you say thank you to Ryan and Bethany," Dr. Landon asked the children after exchanging a look with his wife. Cole and Gracie nodded vigorously. "Okay," he said holding the screen door open with his left hand for them while shaking my grandfather's hand with the other. "Thank you again."

"Thank you," Mrs. Landon echoed and walked out the door in front of her husband. Dr. Landon closed it behind him and the small family made their way to the car – a perfect black Bentley.

Grams retreated to her knitting and Gramps made his way into the kitchen for a glass of sweet tea. I watched out the window as the car pulled out and made a left onto the street, headed back to the Estate. "What's wrong with you," Ryan asked looking at me funny.

"Nothing," I played off. But truthfully, I was experiencing the strange effect that Dr. and Mrs. Landon's presence had on me. "I'm going to go finish doing the dishes," I announced and turned back towards the kitchen.

"Whatever," Ryan said jumping over the back of the couch, making himself comfortable.

'I'm losing my mind,' I thought as I scrubbed an already clean plate in the sink for the third time, staring out the window into the backyard. A few trees shaded the country scene and the tall grass beyond the property danced in the wind. Dropping the sponge, I rinsed my hands and turned off the faucet with force. Placing both hands on either side of the sink, I looked down into the suds and continued to pray, 'I don't know why I am so fixated on the Landon's but for the sake of my grandparents and the relationship they have with them, please help me to be less awkward. They're going to think I am out of my mind… which is something I haven't actually ruled out yet, myself.' I let out a laugh at my own sarcastic remark and my grandfather looked over at me from the other side of the room.

"Care to share with the class?" he asked bringing a glass of Gram's sweet tea to his mouth.

"Have you ever felt... have you ever had a dream and then..." I paused, turned around and gave up. "Gramps, I think I'm going to go lie down for a little while."

"Naps are a good thing." I heard him say as I left the kitchen, perplexed by my teenage girl behavior but amused.

Monday, September 14th

I stirred the next morning in my bed as the dawn crept in through the windows. Since hearing Gracie speak of her 'Uncle Drew' I found myself caught replaying the dreams I had collected over the past week. They stayed with me even as I ran through the morning mist that lay over the town in its early hours. The images of the subconscious illusions were still vivid and the emotions linked to them were just as strong.

Nevertheless, it would be another typical day in Ellsworth, nothing complex; I had learned that much. I took my time getting ready for school, successfully curling my hair in large barrel-like curls. My makeup looked clean and natural as I picked out my outfit; a white dress that stopped above the knee with a brown braided belt at the waist and matching brown cowboy boots. It was a much more sensible look and I felt pretty.

As I walked down the first flight of stairs I could hear Ryan singing in the shower which was awfully amusing. Gramps was on the porch reading the morning paper and Grams was eating her toast with homemade jam in the kitchen. "Hi Grams," I said as I poured myself a glass of orange juice.

"Good morning, dear," she said handing me my lunch in a brown paper bag. "I love that dress. It's very… Bethany."

"Thanks," I smiled as I gave her a kiss on the cheek.

"Have a good day at school."

—

Stepping out of my Corvette and onto the grounds of Ellsworth High, I took notice of the new flyers and banners that were already hung up for Friday – the first official game of the season. Even though it was four days away there was a buzz of anticipation throughout the hallways.

Olivia found me before homeroom. She was cramming for a math exam she had second period. "When will I ever need to know this?" she moaned as she leaned up against the lockers. I took her book and started quizzing her. We made up a few acronyms to help her remember some of the fundamental rules. By the time the bell rang she had phrases like 'Ellsworth's Football Team Has Cute Cheerleaders'.

I sat in first period English, vaguely acknowledging Mr. Ogno's attempt at finding what material the majority of the class had read and stared out the window. The dreams weren't losing their luster and I couldn't seem to find a way to detach myself emotionally from them. Able to recall everything about the images: the rooms, the feelings, the faces… they were all becoming… clearer? I focused on the attractive man that had stood in front of me and held me in his arms. That only caused more confusion.

In physics, Mrs. Landon came in the classroom and the class turned at her arrival. She, like always, looked prim and proper, walked straight to the podium to start the day's lesson with no delay. She was extremely focused, more than usual. I opened my book ready to distract myself.

Classes other than history and English were hard to get through because I was bored. So, I had started reading the math and science textbooks in an effort to entertain myself. In the first five chapters of the physics textbook there were two grammatical errors, five formatting mistakes and twelve problems that were explained in a way that was more complicated than necessary. No wonder why most high school students dreaded the subject. I rewrote a few of them in the margins; a true testament to my level of OCD and proof that I had way too much time on my hands.

There was a loud bang and I looked up to see that Mrs. Landon had accidentally dropped her book. She looked my way, flustered. She then gracefully picked up the textbook and flipped through the pages finding her place again. She was nervous, anxious even. 'Odd,' I thought. She was so refined, so put together. It had been a week since my impromptu interrogation and since then she had paid little to no attention to me in class. Today, however, I had her attention.

There was a knock on the door and Mrs. Landon turned. "Yes," she called out. The door opened and Mr. Donovan appeared. "The paperwork came through for your brother, Mrs. Landon. Take a seat," he added looking over his shoulder to the person behind him.

That's when *he* walked through the door.

Ghostly familiar, it was like a wave washed over me. It was *him*, the one from the nightmare on the grounds, the one from the dreams that had been intensifying. The tall, very attractive man walked passed Mr. Donovan holding a book with a blue schedule tucked inside of it. He was wearing a pure white button up shirt with cuffed sleeves and black pants. He had playfully brown hair and he was a specific kind of handsome – my kind of handsome. He was amazing.

It was his face I'd been seeing in my dreams; a face I already knew. I blinked uncontrollably at first, my mind running a mile a minute. He hadn't looked in my direction but I was certain that his eyes were a deep, ocean blue… What was wrong with me? And where did I get the confidence to know that I was right?

Mrs. Landon's brother walked down the row without acknowledging me but my body was aware of his presence. He carried himself with an unrivaled poise, another thing that made him stand out from others. It was neither arrogance nor pride that emulated from him; rather it was a subtle, underestimated chivalry.

He took a seat a few desks behind mine and to the left, closer to the window. My eyes continued to blink and my hands were wrapped tightly around my pencil. I could hear the students whispering about the archangel-like addition. I shut my eyes and mouthed his name trying to make my mind work but couldn't get farther than that. Slowly opening my eyes, I looked up to find Mrs. Landon staring back at me; I was definitely not invisible to her. I knew my expression was pained by the racing machine behind it. My mind was short circuiting again. Mrs. Landon broke the trance and called for the class' attention. Maybe I wasn't imaging things. Or maybe I was and she knew I was borderline crazy.

—

Ninety minutes later the bell rang but I stayed in my seat, barely comprehending that people around me were collecting their belongings. Mrs. Landon had walked to the back of the classroom after she had announced the homework assignment. The clicking of her heels as she elegantly strode down the aisle awoke my muscles, triggering them to move. I stood up and placed my bag over my shoulder. I turned my head slightly to see her speaking very quietly to the new student, her younger brother.

In the few seconds that I stood there I was certain that I had no brainwaves. He was possibly the winner of the DNA lottery. I watched as he said something back to her and then his eyes looked straight into me. It was as if all the feelings from the strange dreams joined forces and imploded in my chest. He looked at me with such an intensity that I looked away feeling embarrassed by my own insanity. Mrs. Landon, witnessing the exchange, whispered something to him again but this time with a desperate fervor... pleading. I was very self-aware and took my first steps towards the hallway.

"Pardon me," I heard Dr. Landon say after colliding with him as he walked into the classroom at the same moment I tried to escape. I was encompassed by his frame that protectively caught me after being pushed off balance. He steadied me with both of his hands on either side of my arms. Dr. Landon looked more surprised than me when he saw who he had bumped into. "My apologies, Bethany," he said as we settled in the doorway.

"It's alright," I blushed, collecting myself. The hallways were a mess with bustling students in between periods. A loud noise came from where Mrs. Landon and her brother were standing in the far corner, diagonally across the classroom. Andrew had started to move desks out of the way which stood in between him and where Dr. Landon and I were. Without pause, Dr. Landon acted, meeting Andrew halfway and grabbed his arm.

"Andrew," Dr. Landon said firmly causing him to look from me to his brother-in-law. Andrew regained his composure and Dr. Landon let go of his hold. Meanwhile, my anxious right hand habitually found its way to my collarbone and traced it nervously.

"Charles," the archangel's voice said lowly as he watched me. His face softened and he looked at me as though I was a mirage.

"I know," Dr. Landon whispered looking from his brother-in-law to his wife who stood motionless in the back corner where Andrew had been moments ago.

"Beth... Bethany, you should get to your next class," she said in a weak voice. For the first time looking away from Andrew, I nodded at her, turned to go but stopped and looked over my shoulder one more time at the scene that had unfolded. Mrs. Landon's perfect posture, Dr. Landon's ideal disposition, and Andrew, who nodded at me without breaking eye contact, were hauntingly reminiscent. When I smiled at Andrew's old gesture he allowed himself to smile back. It was such a sweet exchange that even Dr. Landon's breath escaped him.

Someone in the hall slammed a locker close by which made my head turn snapping me out of my trance. I stepped into the hallway and was engulfed by the jet stream of backpacks and 'get to class' mentality.

I had made my way to my locker but in the state that I was in, I couldn't remember my combination. I heard people already talking about the new student as they hurried by. The addition had caused gossip pandemonium. "Bethany Taylor, Bethany Taylor, please report to Coach Taylor's office. Bethany Taylor, Coach Taylor's office," the loud speaker rang. Grateful for the distraction, I decided to take the long way around the building to my grandfather's office. When I reached the exit doors, I felt the much needed fall breeze.

"I think the secretaries are getting annoyed with my announcement requests," Gramps laughed as I walked in. "Bethany. Are you okay?" he asked concerned as I took a seat. "Do you feel sick? You look pale," he added handing me a bottle of Gatorade from his team's back up supply.

"Thanks," I said twisting the cap. "Gramps, do you know anything about the new student?"

"You mean Andrew Wicks? He's Abigail's younger brother," my grandfather said uncertain why I was asking. My anxiousness only grew as I processed Andrew's full name – 'Andrew Wicks'. It was becoming almost unbearable to be in my own body.

"Her brother… Andrew Wicks," I swallowed as the dream echoed through my consciousness.

"Yes, Mrs. Landon's brother. It's my understanding that he just moved into the Estate with them. Have you met him yet?" he asked distracted by whatever it was on his desk.

"No, not formally," I answered. My mind and heart just couldn't catch each other. My erratic reaction was brought on by something other than my heart condition; I had been taking my medication and doing cardio workouts faithfully. This was strictly emotional; it was as if I had been hijacked.

"Well, I am sure you will. Charles mentioned that they were glad that he was coming to stay with them," Gramps said as he looked up and I quickly stared down at the bottle in my hands not wanting him to think I was losing my mind even if I was. "Anyway, I called you out of class because I have a favor to ask."

"Sure," I said taking in a deep, calm and counted breath, "What's up?"

"It turns out that the hospital is falling on hard times. Folks around here can't provide the means necessary to keep it running the way it should and we can't keep relying on the Landon's to carry the weight."

"Dr. and Mrs. Landon?" I questioned lost by the last part of his statement.

"Yes, Charles and Abby are quite dedicated to the hospital's sustainability," he said leaning back in his chair.

"Dr. and Mrs. Landon?" I asked again knowing that there was no way that two teacher salaries could support a hospital.

"The Landon's come from very wealthy families, old money. Their efforts have single handedly kept the hospital running from the moment they moved to town."

This new revelation surprised me not because of their generosity – I knew they were good people. I was surprised that no one had said anything. There was no talk about the two teachers being from old money; Liv had even failed to mention it. It was as though it was old news and unimportant. I sat waiting for Gramps to continue. When he didn't, I asked, "So, what is this favor?"

"There is a fundraising event that was planned by the hospital's Board of Directors. I was hoping that you could… help."

"Okay," I said as I unwillingly recalled the charity banquets and award dinners my mother made me attend when girls my age were going to slumber parties.

"It is a little over two months away, December 11th, which is two weeks after Ryan and Kate's wedding. I was hoping that you would help endorse it," he said simply.

"Sure," I agreed.

"Unlike most high school students, your 'platform' could help the cause by leaps and bounds, publicity wise," my grandfather explained unnecessarily. "There are going to be many well-to-do people there. Dr. and Mrs. Landon are networked among the who's who in…"

Catching on, I cut in, "Money."

"Yes," he nodded happy that I understood, "money."

"So you want me to 'make an appearance'?" I clarified and he shook his head. "Sure Gramps," I shrugged my shoulders knowing that he was torn in asking me. It was a loop hole in his request that I try and be a 'normal' high school student. But for one night I would put back on the 'Bethany Reid' act because it was for a good cause. There was no harm in that.

"I know this is an exception to our agreement. But I wouldn't have asked if I didn't think it would truly help the hospital."

"Of course and who knows, it could be fun! You get to see me in action. You know the whole standing, smiling, and walking thing. I'm pretty good at it," I teased of my model behavior.

"I'm sure you are my, dear. I'm sure you are," my grandfather grinned and relaxed his shoulders.

I stayed in Gramps' office for the rest of the day. I was too confounded by what had happened in physics to be able to focus on classes or anything else for that matter. His office was a safe haven where we watched football films in preparation for the game on Friday.

—

'Andrew Wicks, Andrew Wicks, Andrew...' my mind repeated over and over as I cleaned my room, cleaned Ryan's room and was now sitting cross-legged in the small laundry room off the kitchen, folding another clean load.

"Everything okay, Bethany?" my grandmother asked as she walked into the kitchen and saw me on the floor.

"Yeah Grams," I said snapping out of the mental conundrum. "I think I'm going to go for a walk."

"Okay sweetie. Don't be late for dinner."

Main Street seemed to be a good place to start my impulsive adventure. There were people walking down the sidewalks, cars stopping at stoplights and a few birds flying overhead. I took extra notice of the gazebos on the grassy dividers and park benches set under rustic lampposts. The sky was crystal clear and a slight breeze blew through town. I was window shopping when I heard my name being called and turned to see Jackson on the other side of the street.

"Hey," I said as he crossed over.

"Out for a stroll?" he asked with his hands in his letterman jacket pockets.

"Yes," I said looking around as people passed by. With my sarcasm restored I added, "I did say that I was going to try and be more observant…"

"Well then, Main Street is a good place to start," he grinned. "Mind if I join you?" I shook my head and we continued down the sidewalk together. "So is playing hooky something you do often?" he asked watching me out of the corner of his eye.

"Hooky?" I questioned, then realizing what he was referring to I replied, "No, I was in my grandfather's office. Did I miss anything in class?"

"Nah," Jackson stopped as we came to an intersection. "In calculus we reviewed for the exam. Biochemistry, well, you can have my notes and for history… our papers are due tomorrow."

"Wow, we really are in *every* class together," I laughed and silently dreaded the reminder about history.

"Yes, yes we are." Jackson said and made a funny 'I told you so' face which made me laugh harder than I had in a while.

"Excuse me," a small voice said and I felt my shirt being tugged. I turned and looked down to see a little girl with dark brown hair holding a crayon and coloring book.

"Hi," I smiled at her and saw her mother standing a few feet away carrying an infant. She had an apologetic look on her face and reached for the little girl's hand.

"Can I have your autograph," the little one asked sweetly and I knelt down so that we were eye-to-eye.

"Sure, but only if I can have yours too."

"Okay!" she said and dropped to her knees. Opening her coloring book, she scribbled on top of an already colored picture of a princess. "Here," she said ripping it out and handing it to me.

"Emma is a pretty name," I admired the purity of how she colored with shades and scribbles that disregarded sense and boundaries. In clear print I wrote out my first name on the next page and she announced each letter.

Handing her the coloring book and crayon back, I stood up. "It was nice to meet you, Emma, and thanks for the autograph."

"Any time!" the little girl giggled as she took her mother's hand. The woman mouthed, 'Thank you,' before turning and walking away.

"Looks like you have a fan club," Jackson joked as we resumed our stroll.

"Yes sir," I smiled at the priceless moment.

"Have you had a tour of town yet?" he asked and when I didn't answer he put forward, "Would you like one?"

"Sure," I smiled.

"Okay," Jackson gestured for us to cross the street. When we reached the well-kept grassy divider he began to point out different places along Main Street turning in a circle. After one full rotation he looked back down at me and grinned, "And that's Ellsworth."

"Thanks," I let out a laugh.

"You're welcome," he joined in with me as we crossed over to the other side of the street. "So is Main Street everything you expected it to be?"

"Yes," I said taking in a deep, refreshing breath as another breeze blew by.

"You *really* like it here don't you," he asked with a confused expression.

"Yes," I answered honestly to which he rubbed the back of his head and squinted his eyes.

"What?"

"Nothing, I just didn't expect..."

"Me to like it here?" I finished.

"Yes," Jackson nodded. "I guess I thought you would be…" he hesitated.

"Stuck up? Mean? Vindictive," I listed, "Perhaps have a drug problem, suffer from an eating disorder or walk with my nose in the air?" I threw my chin up mimicking what most people probably thought I would be like.

"Yeah, something along those lines," he chuckled.

"Well," I said returning to my normal stride, "I'm sorry for being a relatively uninteresting individual."

"Not uninteresting," Jackson said holding a door as he passed a grocer carrying crates. I could not nor did I ignore his innately kind ways. It was refreshing.

"If I believed everything I heard you wouldn't be talking to me right now," I grinned and when my statement reached his ears, his expression changed.

"Why's that?" he asked curiously.

"Jackson Turner: eighteen, captain of the varsity football team, straight 'A' honor student… You have one older brother who is in the army and three younger brothers. You drive a Tahoe. Your mom works for the newspaper. Your dad's a former marine who owns a landscaping company which you help him out with on the weekends and during the summer. Not to mention, other than your teammates, you pretty much keep to yourself," I repeated everything I had learned about him from Olivia and my grandfather.

"You did your homework on me?" he said with a smirk.

"It is a small town, Jackson," I joked lightheartedly. "But," I clapped my hands in front of me, "the question is, if you keep to yourself why then are you talking to me?" He shrugged and smiled with his eyes. "I have two theories," I said holding up my index finger in front of me. "One: You are shy but a nice guy and you noticed that I really don't talk much and felt sorry for me, or," I said putting up a second finger, "Two: There was some kind of bet where the loser had to talk to me and you lost."

"The first one," he laughed.

"Then, thank you," I said sincerely.

"From one shy person to another, you're welcome," he smiled. "I'm really glad you like it here, Bethany. I love Ellsworth and anyone who can appreciate it, is alright in my book."

"I'm glad too," I smiled and looked around at the picturesque town. Not knowing where to take the conversation, I asked, "Do you know my friend Olivia Connelly?"

"Yes," he said somewhat surprised by my question.

"Have you ever actually spoken to her?" I inquired even though I knew he hadn't. "Jackson, there are only like a hundred people in the graduating class and you two have been in the same school since…"

"Kindergarten," he finished with a smirk. "We shared a cubby." I shook my head disbelievingly. "I'm shy too, remember?" he laughed as we continued to walk down Main Street.

Jackson was a sweet guy, funny, smart, kind… he was simply beautiful. We had spent the next hour together and he even walked me back to my grandparents' house. Not once did I feel anything more than friendship, and I was pretty sure he felt the same way. I was glad that I made a friend like him. He was the perfect small town hero – a rarity – an untouched, hidden, still naïve, secretive, but everyone thinks that they know him, life-watcher sort that just takes it all in. Jackson is the guy who has gone unscathed by an undeserving girl. He was the real deal – one in a million. He was the boy that a girl prays will find her… and yet there was nothing but the beginning of an awesome friendship between him and I. Logically and hormonally, I should be swooning. I was really starting to think that there was something wrong with me and I knew Liv would agree.

—

Liv agreed. She had stopped by after dinner as promised to finally take a ride in my car before it got too dark outside. News traveled FAST around Ellsworth – really fast. After she threw my car keys at me from the table, she clung to my side as we walked to the car and squealed, "I heard you went for a walk with TURNER!"

"How did you…" I began to ask.

"Oh, please! I know everything," she said before opening the passenger door.

The windows were down, my brunette and her blonde hair blew freely around our faces and the radio was at an unreasonable level. Olivia held her hand out of the window and let her fingers ride the invisible wave of air that wiped next to the accelerating vehicle. Once we were on the highway, she lowered the music and I put the windows up. It was time for girl talk.

"Okay, I want to know EVERYTHING," Liv said shifting in her seat so that she could see my face.

"Liv, nothing happened. We just walked around," I said checking the speedometer making sure there would be no reason to get pulled over in the easy-to-speed-in, not-so inconspicuous, red bullet.

"I don't think you understand," she shook her head but I cut her off.

"By the way, how did you find out?"

"Well the guys didn't have practice because your grandfather gave them the day off to relax from their morning lift session but Zach and Duke stayed to watch our practice and so did Bobby," Liv said and her eyes widened in excitement at the sound of his name. "And Zach found out from Joe whose brother is Mike Fenmore who works at the gas station who saw Jackson and you walking down South Broad Street. Then Zach told Duke who told Amanda who is friends with Christina and, well, she loves Jackson – always has. So," Olivia inhaled a good amount of air, "when Jessica saw that Christina was upset she asked her why and Christina said it was because Jackson and you were going out. When I heard your name I was like, 'They are not going out.' But then Christina was like, 'How do you know?' and I said, 'Because I *would* know.' So then Kerry asked Duke if he knew if Jackson liked you and he said he didn't know but that you and Jackson were in like every class together and talked to one another. But I don't know how Kim knew because she wasn't even there in the beginning of practice. Do you?"

My eyes blinked as I tried to comprehend what Olivia had just said but all that came out of my mouth was, "My head hurts."

Olivia huffed and started all over again. "Never mind Liv," I tried to interject and laughed while we crossed over county lines.

We drove around for a while just being us.

"I think it's safe to say that we've reached a new level in our relationship," Olivia said as she got out of my car outside of her house. She lived in a colonial styled home with grayish siding, black shutters and a large tree in the front yard. A rickety mailbox and a dark stone driveway added to the whole 'southern living' thing. "I know it's only been like ten days since you moved to town but I feel like we are those two girls in grade school who went home on the first day and told our parents that we are going to be best friends forever."

"I couldn't agree with you more," I smiled.

"Night, Beths. And by the way, your car is awesome."

"Thanks," I agreed as she closed the passenger door. It was nice to share moments like this with her – my irrefutable best friend. As I drove the nine blocks back to my grandparents' house I recognized the blessing that she was.

—

Unfortunately, my history paper was still due tomorrow and it was not going to write itself. After three hours, I fact checked it against my textbook one more time to make sure I wouldn't be accused of fabricating anything. Glad it was finished I climbed into bed but couldn't fall asleep. As I unwound the day I found myself stuck in a reel. 'Andrew Wicks, Abigail Landon, Charles

Landon… Andrew Wicks, Abigail Landon, Charles Landon… Charles, Abby… Drew,' I repeated over and over again until my eyes closed.

I could see them, all three of them. Images moved so fast that I could feel the mental strain. I knew I was dreaming because it brought with it the same feelings the other dreams brought with them. My mind was racing, running somewhere, in circles it felt like. In short glimpses I saw Dr. Landon adjusting his tie in a mirror. In another, I watched Mrs. Landon brushing my hair in our reflection as we laughed. I felt it. Then I saw Andrew talking to a group of men. He was midsentence when he saw me looking at him and he grinned. I felt a blush on my face and looked down at the patterned rug that met the hem of my dress and then I looked back up at him. He had excused himself from their company and was happily making his way over to me.

An instant later my father was holding a door for me which led to a dining room where Dr. Landon and Andrew were busy discussing a matter over structural drawings and other documents on the polished dining room table. Both men, fully involved with the topic of discussion, turned their heads at my father's voice, 'Charles, Drew,' I heard him say. They beamed at the sight of me joining their company. I was surprised when someone's arm wrapped with mine and looking over I saw Mrs. Landon cheerfully by my side.

I tried with all my might to slow this image, this scene, to put on the brakes in order to make some sense out of it. But I couldn't. These flashes weren't figments of my imagination, not a daydream that you can pause and rewind or even rework. They were more like... memories or at least fragments of memories. I couldn't control them or change them; they were simply for me to watch.

My alarm clock went off waking me up from my restlessness. Being so abruptly interrupted, I felt like my head might explode.

Tuesday, September 15th

I completed my morning routine despite my massive migraine. I was putting my books in my bag when I heard Grams call up the attic stairs, "Bethany, telephone."

"Hello," I half-whispered into the receiver of a rotary phone – another find in the 'Great Clean'.

"Bethany, it's your mother," the voice declared on the other end. 'Well, if I didn't have a headache before…' I thought to myself. This call was overdue; I had left the note for her in the penthouse a week and a half ago saying that I was going to Ellsworth with Ryan. "What do you think you are doing?" her voice rose.

"Hi mom, how are you?" I asked sitting on my freshly made bed.

"I had to come home from MY trip because I was getting phone calls and emails from people who heard rumors that you left. When, I called Michael, he had the *audacity* to tell me that he didn't have time to talk to me but if I cared to reach you that I should try *my son's* phone number!" she now yelled angrily. I let out a huff of air partly in annoyance but partly humored by Michael's instructions to her because he knew the history between the two of them. But then I became upset because she realized *today* that I had left the penthouse... *today*. Whether it was the distance from Manhattan to the Hamptons or from the penthouse to my grandparents' house, it made no difference; she hadn't even noticed I was gone.

My mother continued rambling out her anger. Feelings that I had been suppressing since I left New York started to seep their way in. Even though I was finally happy here, I never wanted to disappoint anyone, not even my mother. But now I was seeing things differently. I had chosen this path because it was a life that I wanted. I put my happiness first and mentally reminded myself that the reason for this phone call was not for her to see how I was doing, it was motivated by dollar signs and the reputation that came with it. "We've worked so hard," I heard her say and then there was a third voice on the line, one that I was not expecting to hear so soon.

"Bethany, could you help me with breakfast?"

"Sure Grams. I'll be right down," my voice cracked as my emotions reached my vocal chords. I hung up the phone and dried my cheek where a tear had fallen. I heard my grandmother hang up the phone in her bedroom as I made my way down to the first floor.

Ryan was standing in the laundry room alcove off of the kitchen. He was dressed in his usual Lumberyard getup of jeans, a Lumberyard emblem polo and construction boots as he folded his clean clothes from the dryer. "What's up?" he asked as I leaned against the wall.

"Mom called," I said taking a shirt from him, folded it, and then placed it onto the pile he had started. "She says hi," I added sarcastically.

"What? What did she want?" Ryan questioned protectively. I answered by shrugging my shoulders. I wasn't expecting a bear hug but I found myself in one.

"Hey," he said with his chin on the top of my head and his arms still wrapped around me. "Want to go to the football game Friday with me and Kate?"

"I have to go," I mumbled. He loosened his hold and looked down at me. "Gramps' orders," I grinned.

"I'm glad you're here kid," Ryan said stepping back to the dryer and threw a pair of shorts at me to fold, "I missed this."

"I missed you too, Ry," I said neatly adding them to the pile.

"No, really, I hate folding. I'm glad you're here," he teased and we both laughed.

I handed in my history paper. I could hear my teacher back at Saint Hale's saying, 'There is no room for the imagination when it comes to cold, hard, indisputable facts, Ms. Taylor.' Ugh, Mr. Klendeski had truly scarred me. I was hoping Mr. Prather would be a little gentler.

After lunch I had biochemistry and when I walked into the classroom I saw Dr. Landon at his desk talking with the archangel. I was so panicky I could hear my heartbeat in my ears; I focused on getting to my seat. There was no way to know what classes I shared with Andrew because I had taken refuge in my grandfather's office yesterday. So far it was just physics and biochemistry – coincidentally, the same classes his sister and brother-in-law taught.

I opened my textbook and found today's topic: Cloning. 'Well I'd know who I'd like to clone,' I humored myself and let my eyes fix on the young, dashing blue eyed man in the front of the room. 'You are crushing hard, Bethany Taylor,' I mumbled as I looked down and opened my notebook. Then two perfectly cultured, shiny black leather shoes met by well tailored pants slid into the desk in the row next to mine. I turned my head, already knowing who they belonged to. His attention was at the clock over the board in the front of the classroom. His distraction allowed me time to read over his perfect profile defined with a strong jaw line. Unhurriedly and unknowingly, he turned his head and met my unexpected gaze. His piercing eyes had gone from stern and determined to captivated and absorbed when he saw a smile wash over my face. It was innocent and natural. Seeing my happiness, his happiness sparked.

A student arriving late to class walked down the row that separated Andrew and I, breaking the exchange. Feeling out of sorts and trying to prevent myself from breathing erratically, I looked down at my books. I may look like I had it together from the outside but I felt like my mind was malfunctioning again as my heart picked up its pace.

"Today, we are going to do group work," Dr. Landon announced. I found my left hand rubbing my collarbone and put both of my hands in my sweater pockets to try and inhibit the nervous habit. My fingers felt my phone, something I hadn't had use for in the past two weeks. I took it out and slid it under the cover of my opened textbook to make more room for my hand. I felt Andrew's eyes on me again and just like the first time I saw him, butterflies took flight. 'Should I look over at him? Or could I actually control myself and not look for the entire period? If I looked over would he think I was crazy? Crazy... he definitely would think that I'm crazy.' I argued with myself.

"Let's see," Dr. Landon said as he picked up a piece of paper from his desk. "Matt Wiley and Jennifer Palmer, Jackson Turner and Christina O'Neill, Peter McCarrie and Marissa Kent..." he read off the pairs, "Andrew Wicks and Bethany Taylor." My eyes shifted, reacting to the sound of the two names together. It triggered a deep, hallow ache inside of me to be ripped open. I leaned forward in my desk and steadied myself. Then looking over at Dr. Landon I noticed him give a slight nod in my partner's direction. Andrew kept his eyes locked on his brother-in-law. Great, the new kid did notice my fixation, and, unfortunately for him, he now had to spend the next ninety minutes with me.

I swallowed hard, still overcome by the effect of hearing our names together. All of the deeply harvested emotions that the dreams had left me with were mounting, and there was nothing about it.

At first, neither Andrew nor I moved as the other students paired with their partners as Dr. Landon walked around handing out the assignment. When I finally looked over at Andrew, he had stood up and was moving his chair with little effort so that it was across from mine. As he sat back down, he fixed one of the cuffs of his white shirt that had unfolded, exposing his strong forearms. Andrew dressed very plain but classic; simple, timeless. Again, my eyelashes fluttered and I felt a blush rise in my cheeks.

Dr. Landon placed a worksheet in front of Andrew for the both of us and continued down the row without a word. At the top of the page Andrew wrote, 'Andrew/Bethany' in a flourish of his pen. The tip rested on the end of my name for a few seconds and he silently exhaled as though he was somewhere else.

We didn't speak as we filled in the blanks. I could feel him watch me whenever I wrote in an answer and I watched him when he wrote in answers. It was like a game of cat and mouse. I wanted so desperately to make conversation with him but just the thought of it took my breath away. The more time passed, the harder it was to break the silence. Before long, we had finished the assignment and still had a few minutes before the period ended.

Trying to look everywhere but at each other, our eyes finally overlapped. That's all it took for the quiescent feelings to ignite again. Andrew looked like he was about to say something but changed his mind. When the bell rang, I put my books in my bag and left the classroom with the rest of the students.

As I walked down the hallway annoyed that I hadn't even introduced myself, I reached in my pocket for my phone. I then frantically looked through my bag, scrambling until I realized where I had left it – back in the classroom. 'Fantastic,' I thought and momentarily debated whether it was worth going back for but knew I was being ridiculous. Everyone would have cleared out by now, including Andrew Wicks.

My hand was on the classroom door knob when I heard the archangel's voice sternly ask, "What was that, Charles?"

"My apologies but I thought..." Dr. Landon responded coolly.

"Merely that I needed a push? Come on, Charles," Andrew added irritably.

Dr. Landon didn't answer at first but then said, "Drew, might I ask *when* exactly were you planning on speaking with her?"

"That's not the point and you know it," he retorted.

I knocked on the door as if I had just approached it and Dr. Landon's voice called out, "Come in." I opened the door.

"I'm sorry... I forgot something," I said in the most controlled tone I could manage. Both Andrew and Dr. Landon were stunned seeing me in the doorway but, regaining his composure, Dr. Landon picked up my phone, walked over and handed it to me. "Thank you, Char..." I started to say and quickly corrected myself, "Dr. Landon." Dr. Landon restrained a smile.

'I am such an idiot,' I screamed in my head when I was back in the crowded hallway. 'Get control of yourself woman!'

This was so much worse than I thought and I needed to talk to Olivia and tell her everything – even if it was lunacy. I couldn't hold it in anymore and there was no way I could write it all down in one note. I had to do this in person. So, I bee-lined it to the football field knowing she would be at cheerleading practice.

—

"Come on girls!" the cheerleading captain yelled as they attempted a three tier pyramid. Liv was on the second tier; now was probably not the best time to distract her. I walked over to the bleachers and sat down. At the other end of the football field my grandfather walked among his varsity players who were stretching in the end zone. I released the tight grip I had around my phone and looked down at the metal bleachers. 'What. The heck. Was that?' I continued to think as I replayed the conversation I unintentionally eavesdropped on minutes ago. Looking around, I saw Dr. Landon walking along the stands on the other side of the field headed over to football practice. Hoping he wouldn't spot me, I looked over in the direction of the parking lot acting as though I was preoccupied with people-watching. Students were walking to their cars and waving to their friends as they left for the day. My eyes, of course, found Andrew in the sea of people. He had reached his car, a beautiful, black Camaro. He got in, closed the door, started the engine, backed out of his spot and pulled away.

Why had Dr. Landon asked Andrew when he was planning on speaking with me? And why was Andrew so angry that Dr. Landon paired us together? My eyes closed. I had been doing nothing but making excuses over the past few days for my mind's 'short-circuiting' and writing off dreams that seemed to keep building. 'Drew,' I thought, 'Drew Wicks'. Involuntarily, a smile washed over my lips.

At that precise moment, Olivia came jogging up the bleachers, glistening from her difficult stunts. "Hey! Come to join the team?" she laughed as she saddled the bleacher in front of me so she could watch the boys practice and talk to me at the same time. But, when she saw the distress on my face she took the seat next to me. "What's wrong?"

"Have you ever thought you were going crazy?" I asked in all seriousness.

"Um, pretty much every other day," she said tilting her head and laughed.

"Then I have a story for you…"

—

"You're not crazy," Liv said from my passenger seat looking out the windshield. I had told her everything starting with the dream in New York and she rarely asked questions. We were parked outside of her house and it was starting to get dark.

"I'm not crazy?" I asked. I thought I sounded like a lunatic for sure, especially after hearing it out loud for the first time. The things I had been dreaming, thinking and saying…

"No," she said shaking her head. "I think you have gone through a lot in the past month and your mind is, like, overwhelmed. I have weird dreams when I'm going through stressful stuff," she said reassuringly and added, "And your life is much more exciting than mine."

I put my hands on the steering wheel. "Maybe it is stress. My mother did call this morning."

"SEE. I mean, I don't blame you for thinking the new guy is gorgeous, because he is," my best friend said flatly and I smiled at her frankness. "But it is weird how you dreamt of him before you actually met him… but you know how dreams are. Maybe it was some faceless guy and when you saw Andrew in school you thought it was him. It's got something to do with your Freud I think."

I started to laugh and corrected what she had said. "You mean it has something to do with my subconscious which is part of Freudian theory."

"Yeah, that's what I meant," Olivia approved.

"Thanks Liv. I really needed that," I grinned.

"Any time," she bounced in the passenger seat then stroked the dashboard. "Plus, I got to drive home in the red bullet!"

—

Maybe she was right. Maybe I wasn't crazy but I couldn't disregard how detailed the dreams had been and how aware my senses were in the false reality. And what I would not talk myself out of was my certainty that it had been Andrew's face in my dreams. There was not a doubt in my mind. But the fact that my dreams preceded his starting at Ellsworth High was a timeline issue and that couldn't be ignored either.

—

Gramps, Grams and Ryan were sitting around the dining room table when I walked in the front door. "I was starting to get worried, Bethany," my grandmother said standing and clearing away some dishes.

"I gave Olivia a ride home."

"Oh that's nice," she smiled. "I saved you a plate. It's on the stove."

Ryan was still eating; he was probably on his third helping of dinner and he and Gramps were in the middle of a conversation. "Do you think he'll be any good?" Ryan asked.

"Supposedly he has a better arm than Trent. If that's true, it's saying something," our grandfather said taking a drink of water.

"What about Peterson?" Ryan asked before eating another forkful. Grams came back through the kitchen doorway with the plate of food for me. I sat down in the seat across from my brother as the tennis match conversation between him and Gramps continued.

"He went to see the specialist today."

"Wow, what'd they say?"

"He's out for the season. That kid had a lot of potential too," Gramps said shaking his head.

"Do you think this Wicks kid can step in and be ready for Friday's game?" Ryan questioned. I looked up trying to comprehend what I had just heard.

"We'll see. I'm meeting with him first thing tomorrow and if it goes well he'll run a few plays with the team after school to see if it's a good fit." Could I not escape thinking about Andrew Wicks for more than one freaking minute? Maybe this was what was fueling my insanity; the small town gossip mill just kept throwing it in my face.

Ryan agreed with our grandfather's take on the situation and looked down at his plate not expecting it to be empty. Moving it to the side, he turned his attention towards me. "How was school?"

"What?" I asked even though I had heard him.

"School," he repeated, "How was it?"

"Good," I answered pulling my fork through a mound of mashed potatoes.

"Did you make any new friends?" Grams inquired.

"Umm… I talked to Olivia and saw Jackson," I said taking my first bite of pork chops with homemade applesauce.

"He's such a nice boy," Grams smiled.

"Turner had the nerve to talk to you?" Ryan interjected surprised.

"What?" I asked confused. What did Ryan mean by 'the nerve to talk to me'?

"Jackson walked Bethany home the other evening," our grandmother added and Ryan's head pulled back slightly.

"Interesting," he grinned as he turned towards Gramps.

"I'm sorry, how is that interesting," I questioned looking across the table at Ryan.

"Well, word is that the football players think they'll be benched if they talk to the coach's granddaughter," Ryan explained as he leaned back in his chair and the grin on his face grew.

"Oh Ryan, leave your sister alone," Grams chimed in thinking he was pulling my leg.

"Benched?" I asked not having missed the look he had just given in my grandfather's direction. "I wonder where they would get that idea from," I said curiously looking over at our grandfather who looked guilty but not ashamed of the rumor.

"I haven't the slightest clue," the old man said trying to hide his smile behind the napkin he wiped his mouth with.

"Jonathan Taylor," my grandmother said placing her hand on the table.

"I can neither confirm nor deny anything like that has been said," my grandfather responded and put his hands up in front of him which only caused Ryan to erupt into hysterics.

Wednesday, September 16th

Olivia was enthusiastically flipping through magazine after magazine as we walked through the front doors of school. "I want one like that but I don't like the back of it," she critiqued pointing to a gown that some actress had worn to a red carpet event. "What are you going to wear to the Gala?"

"I don't know," I answered honestly as I twirled my locker combination and opened it.

"What do you mean, 'You don't know'?" she asked confused. "Beths, the Gala is on December 11th which is like two months away. You have to start planning now," Olivia insisted and handed me one of the magazines.

Smiling, I put it in my locker. "Maybe later," I said not wanting to do anything that could constitute as being 'Reid-like' for as long as I could postpone it for.

"Do you think I should wear my hair up or would it look weird with this neckline?" Liv asked showing me another picture as we walked through the crowded hallway. "Beths," she asked holding her hair up with one hand to try and give me a visual.

"Sorry, umm, up would look good," I said giving her my opinion. But I was distracted – I knew Andrew was meeting with my grandfather during first period. Trying to focus on Olivia and her battle of the ball gowns I suggested, "I have a lot of dresses. You should come over and try them on. If you like any of them, you can borrow it for the Gala."

Her face lit up and her mouth dropped open, "Are you serious?"

"Of course, I've only worn them once or twice. They just hang in my closet."

"That would be awesome!" she said squeezing in between students who were headed in the opposite direction. "When someone asks me what I'm wearing I could be like, 'I'm wearing Dior!'" I laughed at the pose she struck imagining the moment. "I'll see you later?" she asked stopping at her locker.

"Sure," I nodded.

"I'm going to figure out how I can lose ten pounds before this little shindig," Liv called out to me over the noise. I continued to laugh as I walked towards homeroom.

Jackson was staring blankly into his locker when I came up next to him. "Hey Jackson…"

"Hi," he said snapping out of the fog he was in.

"Everything alright?" I asked watching his unusual behavior.

"Ugh, yeah," he said closing his locker.

"Are you sure?" I challenged knowing that something was clearly on his mind.

"Just football stuff," he shrugged. I assumed he had learned of his quarterback, Peterson's visit to the specialist yesterday. As the captain, I could tell Jackson felt sorry for his friend but also worried about what it meant for the rest of the team and the season that hadn't started yet. The bell rang overhead as we turned the corner and walked into homeroom.

Taking our seats a row apart I whispered, "Hey Jackson," as the morning announcements rolled over the archaic PA system. He looked at me and I smiled saying, "Breathe." He exhaled and a grin crossed his face.

—

Unfortunately, in first period Mr. Prather had handed back our graded history papers. I was disappointed when I saw a 'C' in red ink at the top of mine. 'Wonderful,' I thought allowing myself to wallow momentarily. I had worked hard on this one. I had fact checked and everything! If that wasn't bad enough, there was a deadline for an English paper due soon. Stupid APA and MLA formatting… My rant ended when the PA system summoned me to my grandfather's office.

"Come in," he called out after I knocked on his door. There was no sign of Andrew Wicks; part of me was relieved but the other part was disappointed. Folding a paper he had just scribbled on, Gramps stood up and handed it to me. "Would you mind giving this to Dr. Landon? I know you have him for biochemistry soon."

"Next period," I nodded.

"Good. Well, I wouldn't want to keep you from a class you've already taken," he laughed. "Have fun, Bethany."

"Thanks," I said walking back to the hallway.

On the way to my seat I placed the note on Dr. Landon's desk. He nodded in acknowledgement and didn't miss a beat in his lecture. I could feel the archangel's eyes on me as I sat down. Trying to pretend it had no effect, I turned to the page in the textbook where class had ended yesterday. Sure enough, Dr. Landon was now discussing the next bolded subtopic. 'Let's see how long I can pretend to be distracted by this,' I thought in an attempt to waiver my attention from Andrew.

I had only gotten to the second paragraph when the fire alarm sounded. "Everyone please remain quiet and file out," Dr. Landon instructed as the class got up from their seats. Like cattle, the student body filed into the hallways, exiting out the emergency doors and poured into the parking lot.

"Bethany this way," I heard someone say in a low voice. That someone grazed my elbow and when I looked sideways I saw that it was Jackson.

"Thanks," I whispered back. Not familiar with Ellsworth High fire drills, I had no idea which way to go. Jackson and I got separated again but at least I knew I was headed in the right direction. In the organized disorder, I turned around only to find Andrew behind me. He was close enough to touch and it was apparent that he had been following me. This was a routine fire drill with no real emergency but it was almost like he was making sure that I was… okay? I looked up and with him as my focal point the encircling swarm of students around us became nothing more than a blur. Being caught off guard at my discovery of him tailgating me, he blushed with a gentleman's charm. Smiling back I felt as though a piece of me fell into place; a piece that I didn't know was missing. As quickly as the moment had come, it passed. A teacher close by was taking a roll call of her class and the sudden noise made my head turn. I saw Jackson standing by Dr. Landon a few feet away. Engulfed again by the last traveling students, I made my way over to the biochemistry group on the lawn near the first row of cars. A few other biochemistry students followed before Andrew Wicks joined the line. His brother-in-law and he nodded at one another when things had settled.

I could not ignore Andrew's behavior even in its subtleness. It was not a figment of my imagination and I knew in that instant that this, whatever 'this' was, was something more.

Liv's Freudian theory went out the window.

—

The rest of my classes went by quickly after that – chalk it up to adrenaline.

I was walking to my car after school, fumbling with my keys when I heard Olivia call my name. I looked over my shoulder and saw her jogging passed a few students, including Andrew Wicks who had looked up from the trunk of his Camaro at the sound of my name. Wordlessly, he and I locked eyes and I felt another round of unexplained emotions pulsate through my body. "Hey," Liv said slowing to a walk a few feet away from me observing what had stolen my interest. "I, ugh, I'm glad I caught you. Ryan called. He's running late at the Lumberyard and asked if I could pick Kate up from the hospital but I have practice... Would you mind getting her?"

"No, I don't mind at all."

"Thank you! You're the best," Olivia said gratefully and then winked like best friends do signaling that she saw Andrew looking over at us.

"See you later," I grinned as I got into my car.

"Later Beths," she laughed as she ran towards the football field for practice.

I started my car and watched as Andrew pulled out a duffle bag from his trunk and slung it over his shoulder with ease. With his other hand he took out football pads. I purposefully didn't look in the rearview mirror for fear of being caught staring. But, when he closed the trunk and turned to walk towards the field, it occurred to me that he had the tryout with the team that Gramps talked about last night. As I drove in the opposite direction, the distance between Andrew and I grew larger and soon enough we were out of each other's sight, but he was anything but far from my mind.

—

"Good afternoon. Can I help you?" a helpful nurse sitting behind the ER desk asked.

"Hi. I was wondering where I could find Kate Connelly?" I requested looking around the emergency room. It was unlike any hospital I had ever seen. It felt more like a fancy hotel lobby with its decor and warm lighting.

"Hey Beths!" I heard Kate say surprised as she came out of an exam room and placed a chart on the counter.

"Hey, Ryan's working late and Liv has practice so I'm your ride."

"Oh, okay, great," she smiled. "I have to finish up a few things. If you want you can get something to drink in the cafeteria; it's passed the elevators and through those doors," she directed.

"Thanks. Do you want anything," I asked to both Kate and the other nurse.

"No thanks. I've had at least a pot of coffee today."

"I'm fine too, but thank you," Kate said appreciatively.

I walked by the elevators and noticed the shine off the marble-like floor. I didn't know what to expect on the other side of the doors leading to the cafeteria. Usually people have horror stories about hospital food but this hospital was already an exception to that rule.

The cafeteria had a high, glass greenhouse-like ceiling with the sun shining through it. There were different food and drink stations, all of which had more than decent options. On the far end of the cafeteria there was a plethora of seating with the alternative of sitting on the outside patio.

I decided on an iced coffee even though I knew that a nap was in my future. I felt exhausted. As I opened the paper covered straw, I looked around deciding where I would sit in the few minutes before Kate finished her rounds. She knew I was in here and I would easily spot her thanks to the aquamarine scrubs she was wearing today. Looking around I noticed Mrs. Landon at a small table by herself off to the side. She was sipping on tea and had a stack of papers in front of her. Knowing that it would be rude not to say hello and that I should at least acknowledge her existence, I walked over to her. "Hi Mrs. Landon," I said politely and she looked up surprised to see me.

"Hello," she answered with an excited smile. "Please," she said motioning to the empty chair across from her and closed her pen.

"Oh, no I just wanted," I began to say.

"Please, sit," she gestured to the wrought iron chair. Now, I couldn't refuse.

Getting a closer look at what she was working on I saw that it was not high school tests, rather it was one large document at least two hundred pages thick and it resembled a contract. Noticing that I had glanced at what she was working on, Mrs. Landon explained, "The hospital's Board of Directors are revamping a few things and I have the 'privilege' of grammar checking," she said in jest. I grinned and took a sip of my iced coffee. "So, how are you?" she asked and I looked up to meet her waiting eyes.

"I'm fine, thank you." My sheer exhaustion must have been playing with my head because once again I felt as though I was sitting across the table from a friend, not a teacher.

"How are your classes?"

"They're okay," I shrugged. "Unlike physics, I have a hard time in history and English," I disclosed and her eyebrow rose and I swore she was holding back a laugh. As an educator, how could she find my struggle in any subject amusing?

"Beths, I..." she began and the ease in her voice at my name made her stop herself. My eyes dropped as I thought to say, 'Abby,' instinctively. My left hand was at my collarbone, nervously tracing it back and forth before I looked back up at her again.

"Mrs. Landon," I said forcing myself not to use her first name. "I think," I stuttered, "I think that I," I paused. How do you tell someone that you feel like you know them... that you have been having dreams about them, their husband and their brother.... and that you have no idea why.

"What is it?" Mrs. Landon pushed encouragingly as she leaned forward. I knew I couldn't say the things I had been thinking but, I was about too.

"Found you," Kate's cheery voice said as she came up to the table. "Hi Mrs. Landon," she added.

"Kate, how are you?" Mrs. Landon smiled kindly even though there was disappointment in her eyes.

"I'm doing well," Kate said pleasantly. "How are the kids?"

"Great," she answered sitting perfectly poised in her chair.

"That's good to hear. Bethany, are you ready to go?"

"Yes," I said not looking away from Mrs. Landon and as I stood up she said, "Oh, Bethany I wanted to thank you for agreeing to help the Board with the Gala. *Charles* and I appreciate it."

"Of course," I said not missing her purposeful use of her husband's first name or the spike of adrenaline that came with it.

"Well, you girls have a nice evening," Mrs. Landon smiled politely and Kate and I walked towards the doors to the lobby. I couldn't help but look back a few yards away and when I did I saw that Mrs. Landon had placed her elbows on the table and her head was in her hands. As she took in a deep breath, she saw that I was watching her. It was the sound of the automatic doors opening for Kate and I that broke my stare with Mrs. Landon whose glassy eyes were filled with rising tears.

—

My future sister-in-law and I were listening to the radio as I drove her home. "Thanks for picking me up, Beths. I really appreciate it."

"Any time," I said honestly. My mind was preoccupied with what had just played out in the hospital cafeteria.

"I've been meaning to ask you... Liv and I were thinking about going wedding dress shopping tomorrow. If you're not busy, I would love it if you'd join us."

"I'd love too," I smiled thrilled that she invited me.

"Good," the bride-to-be beamed.

"I like that one on you," I said to Olivia who was wearing a yellow satin gown with a deep v back that I had worn to an exclusive movie premier about a year ago. I was sitting on my bed looking through the magazines she had been reading this morning while she tried on gowns for the Gala.

Walking to the mirror to see her reflection, Liv smiled and twirled. I shook my head and grinned as I looked down at the magazine in my hands. There was a picture of me at some event with a smile only I knew was fake and forced. Those days felt like an eternity ago. I tossed the magazine to the side and watched Liv continue to spin. "I really like this one," Olivia said with a growing enthusiasm.

"Good," I said. *"Take it,"* caught in my throat while the haunting flashes from my nightmare on the Estate grounds crossed in front of my eyes, triggered by the words I had spoken.

"Are you okay, Beths?" Olivia asked watching me in the reflection as I silently freaked myself out. I closed my eyes and nodded as anxiety laced with unexplained emotions swooshed through my body. I could see him standing in front of me with panic stricken eyes and recalled how I had felt nothing. No beat. No breath. '*Take it*,' echoed in the distance.

"Are you sure, you look like you're going to be sick," I heard Olivia say and when I opened my eyes she had started to walk over to me in my moment of silence.

"I'm fine," I assured her. In my effort to refocus on her I asked, "What about shoes?" Her eyes lit up when I opened one of the trunks filled with heels.

"It's like a treasure chest," she said carefully kneeling in front of it. We both laughed and then played the girl game of 'Which Shoe'. Liv stood on one foot at a time, switching and balancing to see which option went best with the gown. The sparkle encrusted ones won.

—

"Where are you going?" I asked Ryan as he turned in the opposite direction of the restaurant.

"Need to pick up Grams before we pick up dinner," he said pulling onto the long, winding road.

"I still can't believe you ordered three meals for yourself," Olivia chimed in from the back seat cranking down the windows, allowing the fresh air to blow through 'the tank'.

"I'm a growing man," Ryan said cranking down his window too. My stomach started to turn but it was not from hunger pains. I realized where we were headed. I stared out the windshield as we made the left onto the dirt path that then turned into the cobblestone drive lined with century old oak trees showcasing the beautifully manicured grounds and exquisite Estate.

"Wow," I heard Olivia say as she saw it for the first time. "*This* is where the Landon's live?"

"Not bad, right?" Ryan let out. My brother had been here many times to pick up our grandmother but the view had a wonder about it which clearly never got old. He parked 'the tank' as I looked at the front door and then back at him. "Well, are you going to get out or what?" he asked not sure why I was being reluctant.

"You can do it," I said almost pleadingly. He leaned over, grabbed the handle and opened my door. I unclipped my seatbelt and got out slowly.

I knocked twice, admiring the familiar crest as I did. My heart pounded in my chest when I heard movement on the other side of the door. "Bethany," Mrs. Landon said taken aback when she opened it. "It's nice to see you again so soon. Come in," she offered. I took a step inside and we stood in silence in the entranceway as I took in the old beauty that the home possessed. She was waiting with a warm smile when I looked back at her.

There was a sound of one car door, then another. Before I could say anything, a figure came up the front steps stopping in the rounded doorway. Andrew was wearing a football uniform that was dirty from practice which only added to his attractiveness. He was surprised by the scene in front of him and looked at his sister for an explanation, who nervously grinned back.

Outside, I heard my brother's voice and Dr. Landon's. Not a second later, Dr. Landon came up behind Andrew and saw why his brother-in-law had stopped short – because of me. "How did tryouts go?" Mrs. Landon asked as the tension in the entranceway thickened. Dr. Landon hesitated, looking at his wife, then at me and, finally, at Andrew.

"It went well," Dr. Landon spoke breaking the silence that had called for someone to speak.

"Bethany is here for Claire," Abby made clear.

"Of course," Charles smiled and nodded in my direction. Thankfully, I heard my grandmother off in a hallway close by.

"Hello dear, let me just get my things," she said with Cole and Gracie following behind her.

"UNCLE DREW," Cole called out as the two little ones ran to him. Gracie clung to his right leg immediately.

"Hey pretty girl," Andrew unguardedly smiled as he scooped her up into his strong arms.

"How was work," Cole asked as they gave each other a high-five.

"School, Cole, Uncle Drew was at school," Mrs. Landon corrected timidly as she took Gracie from Andrew. "Come on, let's go check on dinner. Claire, thank you again," Mrs. Landon smiled at my grandmother as she lead the children down the other hallway towards the kitchen.

"Oh, I forgot my glasses," my grandmother said after she looked in her purse. "I'll be right back," Grams added before disappearing from the entryway, leaving Dr. Landon, Andrew and I alone. I knew that this was my opportunity to introduce myself to Andrew, to try and prevent any future awkward moments. However, he spoke before I had formed my words.

"Bethany Taylor," he nodded. Hearing my name from his lips awoke every sense and caused a smile to cross my face.

"Andrew Wicks," I said meeting his waiting eyes. His smile matched mine, and the boyish grin that lingered at the corners of his mouth sent a blush to my cheeks. "It's nice to formally meet you."

"The pleasure is mine," he said not breaking eye contact. The intensity of his piercingly, ocean blue eyes ignited feelings that I could not define nor compute, and for the first time the rush didn't bother me. "My brother-in-law has told me that you are new to town as well," Andrew said glancing over his shoulder at Dr. Landon who stood silently but attentively listening and watching the two of us.

"Yes."

"Your grandfather mentioned that you're originally from New York," Drew said looking back at me. The sunlight coming through the open door caught the side of his face and stance casting a handsome shadow next to my feminine one.

"New York, yes," I answered. "Where are you from?"

"Most recently, I've been in Fort Collins, Colorado, but I am originally from Coverly."

"Coverly? As in a couple of towns over?" I asked recalling the place where the movie theater Ryan, Kate, Olivia and I had gone to one of the first nights I was in Ellsworth.

"Yes," he replied. I smiled again simply because he had. Then I took a quick glance at Dr. Landon who was wearing a look of amazement at the two of us. Andrew noticed my observation which unintentionally then made Dr. Landon the focal point.

"Don't mind me," he somewhat laughed and placed his car keys on the table as he headed passed us to the curved staircase. "Bethany," Dr. Landon said when he was halfway to the second floor. "If you don't mind me asking," he turned unhurriedly. "You live with your grandparents and brother, but your parents…?"

"My mother still lives in New York, and my father passed away when I was a baby."

"If I may, what did he pass from?"

"There was a car accident, and he didn't make it," I stated.

"I'm sorry for your loss; your family's loss... Truly," Dr. Landon said and I saw a twinge of sadness on his face before he turned and continued to climb the remaining stairs. When I looked back at Andrew, he also wore the same troubled expression.

"Found them," Grams announced as she returned to the entranceway with her glasses in hand. "Good to see you again, Andrew," she said kindly.

"Likewise, Mrs. Taylor," Drew nodded and politely moved to the side, holding the door open.

"I'll put in a good word for you with that football coach," Grams teased patting his arm as she walked out.

"Thank you, ma'am," he laughed at her spunk while she made her way to 'the tank'.

"It was nice to finally meet you, formally," I half-smiled, following my grandmother's exit but came to a stop next to him. My brother and Olivia were arguing over the radio, Grams was busy climbing into the passenger seat, I could hear Cole and Gracie giggling with Mrs. Landon in the kitchen and Dr. Landon had retreated upstairs. It was just Andrew and I. The sun in its later hour glowed golden on us standing in the strong, framed doorway.

"Until next time," Andrew said in what was almost a whisper and bowed ever so slightly. It was an old gesture that left me enchanted.

"Until next time," I echoed.

—

"Are we ready? I'm starving," Ryan said as I climbed into the back seat next to Olivia. She was looking at me out of the corner of her eye wordlessly confirming that she had witnessed the moment that had just transpired between Andrew and I. Ryan, unaware, drove down the long cobblestone driveway fiddling with the radio and made the right onto the main road. With the Estate out of sight, I started to my breath again.

"Okay, maybe it's not in your head." Olivia whispered as my brother and Grams got out of 'the tank' and headed into the restaurant to pick up our order. "I could feel 'that' – whatever 'that' was from the car," my best friend said after seeing firsthand the mysterious dynamic I had been trying to explain to her.

"Tell me about it," I said sarcastically resting my forehead on the back of the seat in front of me and closed my eyes.

"Not to get off topic here or anything, but, Andrew looked *really* good in that uniform."

Happy and willing to recall his appearance I grinned, "Yeah, yeah he did."

—

"Everyone out!" Ryan ordered as we pulled into our grandparents' driveway. "Ladies and children first," he continued as he opened the passenger door for Grams and then jokingly closed it on Olivia and me.

"Real mature Ryan," Liv yelled as I opened the door for the both of us. We were all laughing as we walked up the front porch steps where Gramps was reading his newspaper.

"Well, it's about time," he said with a smile, folding the paper under his arm. "Where's Kate?"

"Sleeping, she worked a double," Ryan explained switching the bags of food from his one hand to the other. "Saw Wicks at the Landon's place... how'd his tryout go?"

Liv threw me a quick look as my grandfather answered, "Wicks lived up to his reputation. He'll make a fine replacement quarterback."

Thursday, September 17th

I slept through the night and felt refreshed after my run. Ready for school, I stopped outside Ryan's bedroom door which was open a few inches. He was sleeping, sprawled out across his bed, wearing a pair of gym shorts. I picked up his dirty work clothes from the floor and placed them in the hamper before lightly sitting at the foot of the bed.

He stirred but didn't wake up. "Ryan," I said softly and he readjusted the pillow underneath his head. "Ryan," I said again and he sniffed but was still out cold. In my best impersonation of our mother's voice I ordered, "Ryan Jonathan Taylor, you are going to be late for school! Get up right now!" Ryan's eyes shot open as if he was having a nightmare and I burst out laughing at his reaction. He looked at me and realizing what I had done, threw a spare pillow in my direction.

"I think I just lost ten years off my life," Ryan grumbled as he rubbed his hands over his face and then stretched.

"*That* was hilarious," I giggled and hit my knees. He looked at me and I looked back at him. I knew I only had a few seconds to try and make an escape before he would reach me. I pushed myself off the bed and ran out of his room. He was right on my tail as I trampled down the steps using the walls for support.

"You are SO dead," I heard him say close behind me. Once on the landing, I spotted Gramps on the porch through the living room window and knew that like freeze tag he would be base – a safe zone. I bolted across the floor and threw open the front door stumbling onto the porch. That's when Ryan got one hand around my waist.

"No!" I laughed as my brother picked me up, "RYAN!"

"Good morning," I heard Gramps say calmly. Ryan slowly placed me down and I turned fixing my disheveled hair only to find that our grandfather was not alone. Dr. Landon was sitting across from him and stood with a smile on his face.

"Hello Ryan. Good to see you again," Dr. Landon said putting out his hand. Ryan, still only wearing his shorts, returned the handshake.

"Good morning," my brother said a little embarrassed and looked sideways at me with flared nostrils. I shrugged; I didn't know that there was company. "Well, if you'll excuse me," Ryan said reaching for the screen door.

"Ryan, before you go inside would you mind checking the mailbox for me? I'm waiting for an important letter," Gramps said gesturing towards the mailbox at the end of the driveway.

"Sure, let me just throw a shirt and shoes on," Ryan said opening the door.

"Could you look now," my grandfather asked with a straight face. With a guest present Gramps knew Ryan wouldn't protest or postpone his request. Nodding with a forced smile Ryan tiptoed his way across the dirt and pebble driveway barefoot and shirtless.

Amused, Gramps, Charles and I watched from the porch as Ryan got looks from neighbors and passing drivers. As he made his way back over the stone landmines Grams came out the front door. "What on Earth," she said seeing Ryan and then looked at her husband. "Jonathan, what is Ryan doing out here like that?"

"Here you go Gramps," Ryan said handing him two pieces of mail knowing that they were both useless advertisements.

"I've been waiting for this," our grandfather said choosing one and pretending to look it over.

"No you haven't," Ryan snapped comically as he reached down between his toes and pulled out a small rock. Then my brother stormed back into the house. I could barely contain myself.

"You are turning into a mean, old man, Mr. Taylor," my grandmother said adjusting the dishtowel over her shoulder. I would have continued to enjoy the humor of the situation but the sound of Dr. Landon's laughter brought images in front of my eyes so quickly that I had to steady myself, placing my hand on the porch railing.

The Estate, the backdrop for all of my strange dreams, flashed vibrantly in front of my eyes. There were doorways, corridors, a grand clock, oil paintings, ornamental fireplaces, Beaux-style archways, the beautifully manicured grounds and Charles Landon – clear as day.

When the visions subsided I looked at Gramps and Grams who hadn't noticed my momentary glitch, but Dr. Landon had and was looking at me intently. I half-smirked nervously and finding my right hand anxiously tracing my collarbone, turned and walked back into the house.

Inside and out of sight, I leaned up against the wall next to the door and slid down to the floor with my arms wrapping around my knees. Closing my eyes, I listened as Dr. Landon spoke to my grandparents. His voice was so distinct to me – familiar, composed and resounding. A car door closed and as I got to my feet, I saw his black Bentley pulling out onto the street. I leaned back against the wall and looked up at the ceiling unable to gauge the new level of frustration I was feeling.

—

"Hey Coach," I heard two letterman jacket wearing students call out close by which made me look around for my grandfather. He was standing outside the biochemistry classroom talking with Jackson. I knew that it was crunch time for the football team especially with the switch in quarterbacks.

"Bethany," my grandfather said as I unsuccessfully tried to slip by not wanting to disturb his impromptu meeting with his captain.

"Hi Gramps."

"Hey Bethany," Jackson said and by the way he said it I could tell he was stressed over the football situation.

"Guys," my grandfather called to the players who said hello to him seconds ago. The two varsity players stopped dead in their tracks and about-faced, obedient to his authority. "Zach, Duke," he said over the hum of hallway voices.

"Mornin' Coach," the bigger of the two guys said before looking at me.

Gramps didn't miss the glance and politely asked, "Have you been introduced to my granddaughter, Bethany?" while crossing his arms in front of him.

"No sir," the other one replied after he too made eye contact with me. They were both victims of 'Bethany Reid Syndrome'.

"Well then, Bethany this is," Gramps began.

"Zach Till and Duke Pierce," I finished.

"You know who we are?" Zach, the bigger of the two, questioned taken aback.

"Yes," I grinned at Jackson. "A friend told me I should be more observant." Both Zach and Duke hit each other on the arm, fueled that I knew who they were. Still smiling wide the two looked back at my grandfather who was not pleased by their behavior. Like whimpering puppies the guys continued down the hallway with their tails between their legs.

Walking into biochemistry together, Jackson and I were laughing at his fellow teammates' uncensored reactions. Nevertheless, I was very aware that Andrew Wicks was already at his desk having stolen a look the moment I walked into the classroom. "That was priceless," Jackson said holding his side as he slid into his seat behind mine. "I needed that. Thank you," Jackson sighed relaxed as I turned in my desk so we could continue our conversation.

"Any time," I shrugged. Sitting in the row next to us, Andrew moved forward in his seat, resting his forearms on the desktop but his back remained straight and strong. He was matchless in every way.

"Hey, it's Wicks, right?" Jackson asked at Andrew's slight shift. The archangel turned at his surname a bit taken aback and nodded at Jackson.

"I'm Jackson Turner. I didn't get a chance to introduce myself yesterday. You had a great tryout. Welcome to the team," the Captain said putting out his hand. Jackson was such a nice person – a rare breed; like a breath of fresh air.

"Thank you," Andrew said shaking Jackson's hand appreciative of the stranger's reception. I stole another look at Andrew whose jaw line was masculine, his eyes were the bluest I'd ever cared to notice, and he had the most alluring lips. He turned back in his seat as I traced his profile with my eyes. I felt the rush of adrenaline and a blush heat my cheeks.

"Bethany," Jackson said.

"Ya, yeah," I said looking back at Jackson.

In a chuckle he whispered, "Are you okay?"

"Fine," I swallowed.

"Ha," Jackson smirked as he looked at Andrew and then at me.

My eyes widened in hopes that he wouldn't let the cat out of the bag. "Fair," Jackson understood as I turned back around to the front of the classroom. A few seconds later and in a different tone Jackson asked, "Beths, can I ask you a question?"

"Sure," I said looking over my shoulder and placed my elbow on Jackson's desk so I had a better angle of my friend. I, of course, made sure to steal another glance of Andrew whose hand was now tightly grasping a pencil. Jackson's expression was serious and he restlessly tapped his textbook with his fingers.

"What's up?" I asked now concerned.

"I was just wondering if you knew anything about Bobby and Olivia?" At this, Andrew's hand let go of his tense hold, making it clear to me that he was listening to our conversation.

"Umm, no but I do have a note from her that I haven't read yet," I said taking a folded paper out of my pocket.

"Oh," Jackson said leaning back in his seat.

"Is everything okay?" I asked him before unfolding the paper with Liv's small but bubbly penmanship written all over it.

"Yeah, everything's fine. Just locker room stuff," he said trying to shrug off whatever it was that was bothering him.

"Okay," I nodded not wanting to push further. I turned back around in my seat and began to read what she had written. 'HE ASKED ME OUT,' was the first line. In an 'Olivia styled rant' which consisted of hearts, bolding, underlining and capitalizations emphasizing her excitement, I stopped a paragraph in and turned back towards Jackson. "About Bobby and Liv..." I started and Jackson waited. "He asked her out and she said 'yes'." Jackson wasn't surprised, rather, it confirmed what he had overheard. He forced a small smile and then looked out the windows next to us. I turned slowly back around in my seat feeling horrible. "Jackson," I said turning sharply.

"It's alright," he said readjusting in his chair and opened his notebook. I placed my hand softly on the open pages so that he had to look up at me.

"It's really not alright," I said tilting my head and continued, "I could tell you that you're a good guy, Jackson…" he smirked and shook his head. "But the truth is you're a *great* guy."

"Thanks," he smiled through his heartache.

"Whoever is lucky enough to be with you is one very blessed girl. She's probably bending God's ear about you right now."

"You think so?" he said with a laugh.

"Yes. I bend God's ear all the time about my future husband," I admitted sheepishly.

"Thanks Beths," Jackson grinned. I left him alone as his eyes traveled back towards the window. Turning back, I continued to read Liv's note only sliding it back into my pocket when Dr. Landon called the class to order.

—

The classroom had almost emptied when Jackson passed by my desk on his way out saying, "See you tomorrow."

"See you, Jackson," I responded closing my pen. I stood and felt for my bag on the back of my chair but Andrew was already holding it out towards me. Surprised, I hesitated before saying, "Thank you," as my eyes trailed up his hand to his arm until they met his eyes.

"You're welcome," he said with a small grin. We stared at each other but it wasn't uncomfortable. He was brilliant, tall and broad. His crisp, light blue shirt, brown, playable hair and defined features complimented his piercing ocean blue eyes. All of this and how I hadn't expected this moment, encouraged what I felt coming.

Images from an older time and place crossed in front of my mind with a speed and force that made my breathing catch in a low gasp.

In the wake of it I found myself looking straight ahead – at my eye level – which was Andrew's chest. I slowly looked up but before I could process anything, I spoke in a splintered voice, "Drew?" He blinked rapidly and his shielded expression crumbled. His hands brushed the sides of my face as he stared captivated by me. Swallowing hard, he tilted his head slightly, truly locking in on me.

"Bethany," he whispered. My body reacted naturally – I was unafraid and welcomed him. A smile washed over his face and there was something he wanted to say but before he could the classroom door opened and both our heads turned at the sudden noise that poured into the room. Dr. Landon stood in the doorway not expecting what he saw. His hand stayed on the doorknob, he didn't move. I looked back at the archangel and with my mind catching up with the outrageousness I broke away from Andrew, walked passed Dr. Landon and out of the classroom.

The hallway, deafening as it was, barely gave off the volume at which I wanted to scream. My emotions were running high, extremely high, and I could feel my eyes burning when I saw Liv standing by my locker. I shook off as much confusion as I could and smiled when I reached her

"What's wrong?" she asked, seeing right through my charade.

"Nothing," I lied looking aimlessly around the hallway.

"I'm not buying it," she said flatly.

"Do me a favor and tell me about your day first."

"Didn't you get my note?"

"Yes," I remembered the news about her and Bobby. Liv's eyes widened and we walked arm-in-arm to the parking lot. She basically skipped to the car as I chirped it open and got inside. Once the car doors were shut she shrieked and had a complete teenage girl fit.

"Liv, I'm happy for you," I smiled, being a part of her 'cloud nine' moment.

"I just can't believe this. We haven't even gone on an official date yet but like this is AMAZING," she said emphatically.

"So how did it happen?" I inquired even though I had read the very detailed note. As her friend I was elated to see her so excited but a part of me felt a sting of pain recalling Jackson's somber look. 'Jackson likes Olivia,' I thought and then things started to make sense. His quiet nature – Jackson wasn't shy around people he wasn't attracted too. Then I had another revelation – it must be hard for him considering Bobby and him were both on the football team. They were teammates and Jackson would be succumbed to hearing about Bobby and Olivia's dates, relationship... that had to hurt. My train of thought was derailed when Liv's phone rang.

"Hey Kate, we're on our way," she said to her sister. "Okay... yup... no idea," she answered questions Kate asked on the other end. "Oh and he asked me out! Yes! I definitely will. We'll see you in a few," Liv squealed as she ended the call. "Just a warning, Kate was freaking out last night about this wedding dress shopping thing."

"Why?" I asked as I put on my directional, pulling out of the school parking lot headed towards the bridal boutique.

"She wants it to be perfect. And even though she could wear anything and pull it off, she wants *the* dress," Liv explained as she turned on the radio.

"I think we can help her with that."

"Absolutely," Liv said confidently. "How was your day?" she asked as she skimmed through the stations. All I could do was look at her in response to the question. She said, "What?" knowing from my nonverbal response that something had happened.

—

"This is a new sample gown we just got in," the hostess of the bridal shop said as Kate came around the corner from the fitting room. Liv and I both looked up from our conversation about my biochemistry run-in with Andrew pausing sporadically with the appearance of every wedding dress Kate tried on.

"Eh," Liv advised in her role of candid sister and Maid of Honor.

Turning on a platform in front of the large tri-fold mirror Kate said defeated, "It's not the one."

"What do you think, Bethany?" she asked directly.

"It's a pretty dress, I just don't think it's for you," I critiqued gently.

"What do you think I should try on?" she asked turning around to look at Olivia and me instead of asking us through the reflection.

Much too naturally I spewed, "I think you look good in almost any style but if I were you I would stick with the sweetheart neckline, a natural waistline, Venetian lace and a cathedral veil." Liv perked up and she scanned the room while Kate turned and looked at the hostess who was not familiar with a dress that would meet the request.

"I would have to check to see if we have any of those styles," the small, bright redheaded woman said trying to buy some time. But Liv stood up and walked over to one of the many organized display closets on a mission.

The gown she pulled matched my description and Liv handed it off saying, "Try this one." The bridal assistant led the soon-to-be-bride back to the fitting room and Kate mouthed, 'Thank you,' to the both of us as she stepped off the platform.

"You found that gown way too fast," I laughed at Liv.

"I've been eyeing that one since we walked in," she smiled. It was clear that we both had the same vision of Kate for her big day.

"So, am I crazy?" I asked continuing our on-and-off again conversation about Andrew Wicks.

Liv took a deep breath and answered honestly, "Yes." I knew she was right.

"What do I do?" I moaned holding my head in my hands.

"Avoid him and see a psychiatrist?" she advised sarcastically.

"Fantastic," I played back at her. But how could I blame my friend for the advice she offered even if it wasn't completely serious? What else could she possibly say to me?

Kate came around the corner, looking absolutely stunning. "Wow," Olivia said as she gaped at her older sister. Kate, thrilled with the initial reaction, walked over to the mirror to judge for herself. She glowed with excitement adding to the beauty of the gown.

"I love it," my future sister-in-law said with her hands touching over the exquisite lacework.

"Me too," Olivia said as she got up from the couch to stand next to Kate and take a closer look. Kate looked at me in the reflection as I joined them.

"Do you think Ry will like it?" she asked.

"Kate, you look beautiful. Ryan's going to love it," I answered with a sweet smile.

"I'll tell you one thing," Liv chimed in. "Mr. Tough Guy might even get choked up when he sees you at the end of the aisle in this."

"You think?" Kate looked back at her reflection.

"Slap bet?" I joked and the two started to laugh. Thinking about my brother and seeing how happy his future wife was, I touched her hand. She turned and looked down at me. "I'm pretty sure he will," I grinned at the thought of them on their big day. With that Kate's eyes filled and Olivia jumped up on the platform hugging her older sister.

—

Ryan pulled up in front of our grandparents' house right behind us. "How'd it go?" he asked shutting his truck door.

Before Kate could respond Olivia interrupted, "It is bad luck for the groom to know *anything* about the dress." Ryan rolled his eyes at Liv before kissing Kate on the side of her head. Ryan knew the trip had been successful – Kate was still beaming ear-to-ear.

"How was work," she asked her fiancé who shrugged before turning towards the house and put his arm around her.

"Expecting anyone?" Liv asked looking at a blue rental car parked next to the house. The four of us made our way up the front steps. I almost ran into Ryan and Kate who stopped abruptly after opening the front door. Looking beyond them I could see her – my mother, sitting at the dining room table across from Grams. She was a pretty woman but neither Ryan nor I resembled her. Luckily for us, our father's genes seemed to have dominated during natural selection. Ryan resembled Gramps more and more the older he got and I was the feminine version of our father, the striking man I never knew – emerald eyes included. People might not believe that we were actually our mother's children; something Ryan and I wouldn't mind given that she was as wicked as they come.

Her appearance was always sharp, making it a priority that she be presentable at all times. Her high expectation for the type of company she desperately wanted to keep was evident in her material possessions and the designer clothes she always wore. Our mother had tried to rub that desire off on me, her doll, but was unsuccessful.

The silence in the room was deafening until she snapped, "Bethany, outside... now," pushing passed Ryan and ignoring both Kate and Olivia, she charged out the front door onto the porch. I could feel my heart in my throat.

She turned when she heard the screen door close behind me. "You have ten minutes to get your stuff. We will send for the rest." I stood there frozen. "Bethany Ann, I am not joking. This little hiatus is over," she blasted furiously.

"I'm not leaving," I said calmer than I felt.

"I talked to Michael and he said he would take you back after this 'vacation'. Although, if I was him, I wouldn't after the way you just abandoned him," she said as her hands found her hips. She had no idea how I had left things off with Michael, she had no clue that he understood exactly why I left, or that he was actually happy for me. She took a step forward and said through her gritted teeth, "You have responsibilities young lady. Go and get your things."

"I'm not leaving," I repeated. My mother's shrill laugh echoed on the porch.

"What? Are you saying that you *want* to stay here?"

"Yes," I answered.

"Stop acting like a two year old and go get your stuff," she said running her hands over her outfit as though she were wiping off any 'country' that might have attached itself to her. When I didn't move she looked up at me. "Go." And with those words, she hit a nerve. I was not leaving Ryan, and not for anything, but he was not only 'my brother' but he was also 'her son'.

With a newfound confidence I asked annoyed, "I'm sorry did I stutter when I said I wasn't leaving?"

"Excuse me," my mother said taken aback.

"I. Am. Not. Leaving," I responded simply.

Stepping even closer so now we were an inch apart she said sternly, "Bethany Ann Taylor, go and get your things. We are leaving... NOW."

"Well at least you got my name right," I sneered. I was detached from this woman. I had cut the cord – she had no control over me. And it felt amazing.

"What? 'Bethany Reid' isn't good enough for you?" she said ready for a battle.

"No."

"Haven't I given you everything you've wanted?" she had the audacity to ask.

"The only thing you have *given* me is Ryan – and I will always choose him over you."

"You spoiled little," she began.

"I am seventeen, mom. I am not an adult but I am sure as hell not some business pawn. I'm done with New York. You're going to have to get used to that." She impulsively slapped me in the face. I don't know if she or I was in more shock that she had actually hit me. I touched my cheek and looked in utter disbelief at her.

"How dare you talk to me like that!" she barked with ferocity.

The screen door swung open and Ryan stepped in front of me. "You are leaving," he said firmly to our mother obviously having heard and watched our conversation. Her hitting me was more than Ryan would allow. I felt Kate take my hand and pull me into the house where Grams was standing shaken at what just transpired. Olivia had stepped onto the porch blocking my mother's view of me inside. I could hear Ryan and my mother exchanging muffled shouting, then a car door opened and closed, and an engine came to life.

Ryan flew back into the house slamming the front door behind him. "IF SHE THINKS THAT I WILL PUT UP WITH THIS SH..." He trailed off and coughed on purpose, his eyes apologizing to Grams for his almost cursing spree. I had never seen him this frenzied before; not even during their heated discussions while he still lived under the same roof as her. Ryan turned and we locked eyes with one another. "Beths..." he said shaking his head.

"It's fine," I said trying to harness the resentment I felt towards the woman who just smacked me; my own mother.

—

Grams placed a tray of homemade cookies on the dining room table about a half hour later; twenty minutes of which I spent in the bathroom rinsing my face with cold water, sitting on the edge of the lion footed tub, trying to calm myself down. I let a few tears fall – sad and angry ones mixed together. My emotions had been so out of whack lately that even though I was furious at my mother, I was happy I could at least identify where the feelings were coming from.

The result of my mother's unexpected visit was a large consumption of delicious cookies and an unplanned Scrabble marathon with Ryan, Kate, Liv and I at the dining room table.

"BOAT," Ryan said proud of his move.

"If you keep putting words like that down, Ry, you might beat your record," Olivia said jokingly.

While making a face at Liv, he asked, "What's the score?"

"Kate has one hundred thirty-seven. Bethany has one hundred twenty. I have ninety-three and you have fifty-four," Liv said reading off the scorecard.

"Bethany, it's your turn," Kate said handing the bag of tiles to Ryan. "By the way, I was going to ask you..."

"What's up?" I asked trying to find the right place for my word.

"Well, I know the timing might not be appropriate with tonight's events and all, but I've been waiting for the right time to ask you if you would be one of my bridesmaids?"

I looked up at her, then at Ryan and finally at Liv who was smiling. "Umm..." I said surprised.

"I know it's sort of short notice, with the wedding being a little more than a month away. It's just that I wanted you to get comfortable before I sprung something like this on you," she explained.

"I would love to be a bridesmaid," I answered. Kate touched my hand and her smile grew.

"Okay, I'm going to have to put my foot down for the sanctity of our Scrabble games," Ryan said looking around the table.

"Sorry," I said picking up my tiles, "Umm...TAVERNS, on a triple word score and a fifty point bonus for using all seven tiles."

"I quit," Ryan said pushing his seat away from the table. Liv and Kate laughed as they counted the points.

—

Falling asleep that night wasn't hard. I took a long, hot shower, used my favorite mint shampoo and tried to unwind as I brushed my wet hair in the reflection of the bathroom mirror. 'Why have her come here,' I asked looking up at the ceiling. 'Wasn't I already losing my mind with the whole 'Andrew Wicks/Landon' thing?' I laughed and placed the brush on the skirt of the sink. Throwing my hair over my left shoulder I began to braid the dripping locks. Distracted by my multitude of requests for the Man upstairs, I messed up the simple braid. I took out what I had already started and then messed it up again. Putting my hands on each side of the porcelain sink I looked down at the drain stopper then at the girl in the mirror. Taking a deep breath and closing my eyes, I quieted my mind. Tears began to build and I shook my head before sitting on the closed toilet lid next to the sink. My face found my hands.

I had gotten what I had prayed for – a home, a life with my brother, great friends… a quiet, full, daily life. He had heard my two year plea even when I couldn't see this possibility on the horizon. He had given me more than I deserved and yet I still had the nerve to ask for more. 'I'm sorry,' I thought. 'I'm sorry for being this way. I'm sorry for always having requests, lists. I'm… I'm… just…'

"Beths, are you done in there?" Ryan asked knocking on the bathroom door.

"Ugh, yeah," I said drying my eyes quickly and flipped the lock. He opened the door and threw his towel over the towel bar, took off his shirt and reached across me for his toothbrush. I ducked underneath his arm and stepped out of the bathroom. With his toothbrush in his mouth he began to say, "You forgot your hairbrush," and tossed it to me when I turned.

"Thanks," I half-smirked.

"Hey," he said spitting his first round of toothpaste into the sink and ran the facet. "Are you alright?" he asked taking a closer look at me.

"Yeah, fine," I shrugged. "I'm just…" I said continuing my prayer out loud. "I'm just afraid… tired…"

"Of what? Of mom?" he supposed in a tone higher than normal.

"No," I said looking passed him. "I always pray for things to get easier. I think I need to change the way I've been praying," I said dumbfounded by my own observation. Ryan crossed his arms and rested his shoulder against the open door listening as I went on. "Instead of asking for things to be easier, I should be asking for strength to overcome whatever it is. Sort of like running I guess," I said lost in my own thought as I drew a parallel. "If I'm in shape, it doesn't matter if the hill in front of me is steep… I'm in shape and I have the endurance to run up it. I've been praying for the 'hills' in my life to get smaller or even to disappear. But I should be asking for the grace to have the strength to run them. Then it wouldn't matter how steep the hills were after a while because I'd be in good shape and could run them no matter what." Ryan was staring at me when I looked back at him. A smile crossed his lips before he looked down at the old floor, then back at me before giving me a bear hug and refusing to let me go.

"Ry," I finally said patting him on the back. He released me and stepped away, biting down on his lip very hard. "Hey," I said pushing his arm like little sisters do.

"Do you mind if I steal your prayer?" he asked.

"Nope," I smiled realizing not only had he listened to me but he had *heard* me. "You can totally steal it," I tried to tease to lighten the mood. I knew it had worked when he let out a breath of air.

"I love you, kid," he said sincerely and kissed the top of my head.

"I love you more, Ry," I said as I walked up the attic stairs. 'Thank you,' I thought as I turned off the light, crawled into bed and let go.

Chapter Three
Friday, September 18th

Unfortunately, the night's rest didn't extinguish the fire that was burning in my chest as a result of my mother's visit. I woke angrier because while I slept I guess the shock had worn off. Now I couldn't get over the nerve she had coming to Ellsworth – the thought was like adding gasoline to a fire. I was nothing short of irate even though she was back in New York by now. My detestation read clearly on my face; even Liv hadn't attempted to make conversation. "Can you believe her?" I said out of nowhere as we walked from the parking lot to the school.

"Let it out," Liv said relieved that my pent-up frustration was showing itself.

"Seriously, though! What was she thinking? You know what she was thinking..." I started to answer my own question. "She thought she was going to throw her little temper tantrum, I would whimper and do what she said, then we would fly back to the city, she would hang out for a day or two and be back in the Hamptons by Sunday while I was walking a runway somewhere." Intelligently, Olivia shrugged and said nothing as she leaned up against the lockers while I switched my books. Liv was thankful that I didn't ask for her opinion on the matter but obviously she was also angry at my mother's behavior. "Sorry," I apologized.

"Please, I'm sorry you have to deal with her." My best friend said wide-eyed, "Stressful much?"

"Ha," I smirked after slamming the metal door shut. "She hit me. She actually hit me," I said and the pain in my voice hurt more than the slap.

"You're coming to the game tonight, right?" Liv asked putting her arm in mine as we walked under a banner that read 'Go Sparrows'. When I didn't respond to her question, she said with an evil grin, "Yes, you are – Coach's orders."

I mumbled as I now leaned up against the lockers so she could switch her books, "Cruel, you're cruel."

Olivia rolled her eyes. "Can I borrow the white top with the sparkles for after the game?"

"Of course," I assured her while acknowledging people as they passed by. Some were more receptive than others.

"Thanks. Oh, and I picked out your outfit for tonight and left it on your chair," she grinned as I looked over at her. "What? It's fun! It's like dressing Barbie!" she expressed, bouncing in excitement.

—

The PA system sounded after morning announcements, "Miss Taylor, Miss Taylor. Please report to Coach's office." My grandfather hadn't even given me a chance to pretend to learn today. I smiled to myself and headed towards his office.

—

"Bethany, the reason why I called you out of class," he began in a serious tone, "is because I just got off the phone with your mother... and she is rather resolute on getting you back to

New York. So resolute that she has threatened to get the authorities involved being that you're a minor." I looked up from my lap at the news. Gramps had been at football practice yesterday when my mother decided to pay us a visit and give us a show. When he had gotten home, Grams and Ryan had filled him in on what had happened. He spoke nothing negative about his daughter-in-law even though he had every right too. But he did make it clear that behavior like hers was not acceptable in his home or towards his grandchildren.

Gramps continued, "After speaking with your mother, my dear, I am afraid there is no talking her out of it." I was speechless. I didn't think she would go to this extreme. She was desperate. "So," my grandfather said, "you have two options. You can move back to New York... or you can stay here and the authorities will take you back." I closed my eyes in defeat. Either way, she was going to win. "Are you giving up that easily?" he asked with a smirk on his face.

Intrigued, I asked, "What are you up to old man?"

"My dear, there is always another option. Always," he said opening a folder on his desk. "After Ryan brought you to Ellsworth, I took the liberty of contacting your personal trustee. I hope that is okay with you," my grandfather said looking up over his reading glasses. I shrugged, indifferent because I had nothing to hide. He continued, "It appears that your father's old college friends from the city, a Mister Joseph Davis and a Mister Louis

Sturman, looked out for their friend's daughter even after his passing."

"They did?" I asked only recalling meeting the men once or twice.

"Your lawyer, Mr. Sturman, and your accountant Mr. Davis, were kind enough to send me a copy of your legal options and financial accounts in case a situation such as this, were to occur." As the executor to my father's Will, Gramps had unfortunately witnessed firsthand my mother in the arena of legality. Money brought out the worst in her and when my father passed, my grandfather tried to settle the financial minutia of his son's accounts while also trying to heal the wounds death left on our young, mourning family. My mother did not make any of it easy for him.

Gramps continued, "According to them, your accounts are impenetrable to anyone other than yourself. I must say that they contain quite notable amounts, Bethany." I knew that there was a good amount of money tucked away in the accounts but it was comforting to know that they were truly foolproof. "Also, Joe and Lou recommended that it would be of your best interest to either petition for a change in your legal guardianship or file for emancipation."

"It was never about the money, Gramps." I said wanting to make myself clear.

"Oh, I know dear. Trust me, I know," he said sympathetically.

"So," I said taking a deep breath, "What needs to be done?" My grandfather turned the folder around and handed me a pen.

I read over the paragraphs slowly and carefully, flipping page after page. When I was about to sign the document, my grandfather touched my hand causing me to pause, "Are you sure? You can take time to think about this," he said checking that this is what I really wanted.

"I'm positive," I said and signed on the line. Satisfied, I handed the folder back to him.

"Okay. Well I'm sorry I had to pull you out of class for this but the paperwork needs to be sent as soon as possible," he said standing up with the documents. He was surprised when I walked around the desk and hugged him. "I'm sorry," he apologized. "Your father would never have wanted this for you."

"I have you, Grams and Ryan and I'm pretty sure he'd want that for me," I smiled through whelming tears. My grandfather kissed the top of my head and hugged me tighter.

After a moment he asked, "What class are you headed too?"

"Biochemistry," I answered after looking over at the clock on the wall. I dried under my eyes with my fingertips and getting my bearings, picked up my bag.

"Oh, well that sounds important," he laughed. Jokingly shooing me he said, "Well, off with you! Have fun in class, my dear."

"Oh but Gramps... there is always another option," I grinned. "And if I remember correctly, 'Skipping is all part of it',"

I quoted him kiddingly. I could hear him laughing as I shut the door behind me.

—

Despite the previous day's odd encounter with Andrew, he gave no indication of it. That didn't stop me from stealing every look I could of him during the rest of the period. He was dressed up like the rest of the football team was on a game day; wearing a suit and a new letterman jacket. He looked amazing – like the 'not-fair' amazing. I really had to try to not stare but I slipped once and he caught me; in that moment his guarded expression faltered and a smile appeared. It replayed in my mind for the rest of class and every time sent an electric pulse through my veins.

Jackson and Andrew were glued to one another discussing their football plays and strategies for tonight's game. With only a twenty-four hour window to learn all the routes, it was crunch time for Drew.

Jackson was doing his best to teach the new quarterback everything the team had trained for all summer. I couldn't help but eavesdrop as I collected my books before leaving the class even if it was football lingo. The sound of Andrew's voice alone gave me goose bumps.

—

After school I called Ryan as I walked to my car. It rang once before he picked up.

"Beths?" he answered. It was very noisy in the background; there were loud machines and louder voices that were shouting over them.

"Hey Ry," I said.

"Are you okay?" he asked over the racket.

"I'm great actually," I smiled.

"You signed the papers?" he questioned enthusiastically.

"You knew about them?"

"Yup," he said and a sawing noise erupted on his end. "Of course I knew. You honestly thought Gramps and I wouldn't anticipate mom being mom? What are you up to now?" he yelled into the phone as the background noise escalated again.

"I'm about to get in my car and head home."

"I'll be there with Kate in a bit. I'm finishing up at the yard," my brother borderline screamed.

"Cool. I'll see you soon."

"Later, kid," he shouted before hanging up. I turned my key in the ignition, upped the volume of the music playing and rolled down the windows.

I relaxed after school, celebrating the fact that as soon as the paperwork was filed, I would no longer need to deal with Dana Reid. Following an almost celebratory dinner, I retreated to the attic. About a half hour later I heard Ry call up from the first floor, "BETHS, I'M LEAVING NOW."

"OKAY," I answered. Liv had to be at the games early for cheerleading and Ryan and Kate enjoyed getting their seats before everyone showed up. The plan was I would meet them there closer to kickoff.

Fortunately, Liv had laid out an outfit for me for the game. I put on the cropped pants with a high-end top and slid my feet into simple, matching wedges, then looked into the old mirror. I added my long, key necklace, undid the bun on the top of my head so that my hair fell down with a loose curl to it, sprayed myself with perfume and put on a pair of earrings I would didn't normally wear. I felt good. I felt pretty. I felt like I was on the verge of something, something bigger than me. Perhaps it was the legally breaking ties with my mother circumstance. Whatever it was, I felt like I was on fire.

As I pulled into the packed parking lot an hour later, I could hear the roar of the crowd. This game was the highlight of the week for the small town population of three thousand. I quickly realized that by not being early to one of these things meant that finding a parking spot was like trying to find a needle in a haystack. Thankfully, I found one but it did entail an extensive trek across the blacktop. During my walk to the stands I realized that finding my brother and Kate in the crowd was going to be more difficult than I anticipated. Once on the bleachers I looked up nervously into the mob for Ryan. That's when I heard his voice bellowing not too far away, "WHAT! ARE YOU KIDDING ME?"

I laughed to myself, all too familiar with the vocal fan. I could see Kate tugging at Ryan who sat back down, but he was still yelling at the referees who he obviously disagreed with. A loud horn rang out signifying that a timeout had been called and the players on the field ran off to their respective sidelines. I walked up a few rows and then slid passed people to where my brother and Kate sat at about the fifty-yard line. I said 'Excuse me,' and 'Hello,' as I made my way. Finally reaching where Ryan and Kate were, I was relieved to see that they had saved me a seat.

"It's about time," Ryan commented and I stuck out my tongue. He then proceeded to do the same.

"Hey Beths," Kate said kissing my cheek after elbowing Ryan's side. The cheerleaders were taking the field during the brief break in the game and Olivia looked up into the stands trying to find Kate, then saw Ryan and waved when she saw me sitting next to them in the outfit she had picked out.

The cheerleaders impressively pulled off the stunts that they had not yet mastered in practice. As they jogged to the sidelines when the routine was over, the crowd applauded, hooted and hollered. The horn rang out again and the announcer's voice echoed through the stadium. I caught sight of my grandfather standing next to Dr. Landon, both men were dressed in their coach shirts and beige slacks. Like Olivia, my grandfather searched the crowd for Ryan and smiled when he saw me sitting next to my brother making sure I was keeping good on the 'high school promise'.

Gramps' attention returned to the game when one of his players who held his helmet at his side walked up next to him and Dr. Landon. I could only see his profile but I knew what the back of his jersey would read. After reviewing a play on Gramps' clipboard, the player put his helmet on and secured the strap under his chin. My grandfather patted him on the arm pads and the new quarterback took the field joining a waiting huddle. The back of his jersey read, 'WICKS' with the number '7' underneath it.

"Are you cold?" Ryan asked taking his Lumberyard jacket off.

"No," I said not taking my eyes off the back of 7's jersey. Not listening, Ryan hung his jacket over my shoulders. "Thanks Ry," I said tucking my arms inside. The truth was, I was cold. Liv had underestimated the weather when she 'dressed' me. The autumn nights brought with them less degrees.

For the rest of the game I watched Andrew's every move. I watched him call for plays, complete passes and run on and off the field at the change of the offensive and defensive lines. I even watched the back of his head when he was on the bench going over formations with Gramps in between possessions. Jackson, who was the safety, was not on the field at the same time as Andrew but was relentlessly encouraging the team to trust the last minute replacement quarterback who was doing remarkably well. Based on Andrew's performance, the crowd and his fellow teammates didn't mind his late edition. As for me, I was grateful that I could finally look at Andrew Wicks and no one would know I was blatantly staring.

When the final whistle blew the Sparrows' victory was secured and the crowd roared as both teams shook hands and retreated to the locker rooms. Ryan and Kate left after I told them where I had parked and how I was going to wait for the bulk of the mass exodus to pull out before attempting to leave. "Alright, we'll see you back at the house," Ryan said as I handed him back his jacket. I smiled and watched as he led Kate down the bleacher steps, holding hands and having their own conversation as they disappeared into the mob, heading towards the parking lot. They were adorable.

There is something about an empty football stadium at night. I don't know if it's the lights, the crisp air, the heart and sweat that was left on the field or the quiet that exists after the cheering ends, but it's extraordinarily peaceful. I sat there staring up into the night sky.

A strong, cold wind picked up and it caused me to come back to reality. I looked around to find that the parking lot had emptied – completely. I had lost track of time. Slightly embarrassed at my spacing out, I stood and walked down the bleachers and decided it would be easier to cut across the field. As I walked onto the grass I saw someone walking from the end zone to my left from where the locker rooms were. I had only taken a few steps from the sideline onto the actual field when he called out my name. It sounded amazing coming from him.

I stopped and watched as Andrew walked towards me. I was in awe yet again by him, by everything about him; his handsomeness, his masculine build and an undeniable attraction that I was aware of. He had redressed in his pregame day attire consisting of black dress pants, shined shoes, classic white shirt button up with a black tie that was loosened around his neck and his letterman jacket. Andrew carried his black suit jacket over one arm and had his game pads and bag over his shoulder. I knew that all the football players had the same dress code but I felt sorry for any of them that had to stand next to him. They couldn't compare.

Andrew stopped a few feet away from me. "Hello," he said breaking the silence in a way that made it clear he hadn't anticipated running into me.

"Hi," I said, finding my voice. Not daring to make direct eye contact, I congratulated him, "Good game."

"Oh… ugh, thank you," he said not focusing on the game, but graciously accepted the small accolade. Andrew's stance shifted as he contemplated whether or not to say something to me; I could tell that much. A slight breeze blew the night air between the two of us and, reactively, I folded my arms. Lowering his bag and equipment onto the field, he took his black jacket and wrapped it over my shoulders. With his hands still on the collar, I tilted my head up, surprised at how close he was and how he had done it so naturally. It was a basic gentleman character and a gesture he felt comfortable doing *for* me. Realizing our close proximity he looked down and met my eyes. I could see how his were tortured once again. He let go of his hold on the collar and hovered for a second, but then stepped back. I looked down and to the left, focusing on the grass as I slowed my breathing.

But my mind was racing and so were the flashes that broke through. Unable to anticipate the strength and duration of the emotions that came with them, I was helpless. Random images of a marble floor, dim candle lighting, beautiful cathedral archways, and Andrew standing in front of me in a black suit much like the one he was wearing now, showed themselves.

When it stopped, I raised my head back up and saw him looking intently at me. I felt lightheaded and he took a step closer ready to hold me up. I put both my hands out to stop him from coming any closer so I could solidify my consciousness. My hands were shaking and my eyes were still refocusing. As my balance steadied, I saw Andrew's expression mixed with fear and anxiety. The anxiety was a gaffe on his part, giving me the little assurance I needed. "Why didn't you tell me?" I asked not exactly sure what I was asking but positive he had the answers. He squinted, knowing he was caught holding the secret he carried. "Why?" I said again sounding wounded.

He didn't answer and turned his head, looking at the empty bleachers. I took a step, closing the distance between us and he looked down at me stunned that I had done so. I could feel the warmth coming off of him; our eyes were locked again. "Drew," I said pleadingly. His breath escaped him in a sigh at the sound of his name from my lips. He surrendered and in one quick motion his hands brushed my hair back and his lips met mine. He pulled away but only to lean in again, and again, slowly and fully...

His hands ran through my hair and his fingers grazed my neck as I opened my eyes hoping he was still there. Relief had washed over the tortured archangel and for a moment all the world was still. I reached out and touched his lips with my fingertips and he closed his eyes and kissed them softly. I dropped my head in amazement of this moment. My hand slid to his chest and he pressed his lips to my forehead while his arms protectively wrapped around me, bringing me even closer to him. My eyes flickered as my memory recognized his cologne – I breathed it in knowing I could never get enough. My mind was finding new awakenings as the scent rekindled once nameless emotions.

Then something caught his attention behind me. I turned my head to see the distraction. Truck headlights were turning into the far end of the parking lot. "You have to go now," he told me as our eyes met, "But I will see you tomorrow." I slowly shook my head back and forth, not wanting to leave. A smile crossed over his face. "Beths, I *promise* you. Tomorrow," he whispered. Believing him, I nodded. He picked up his equipment effortlessly and walked toward the far end zone, leaving me under the Friday night lights.

–

"Bethany!" I heard someone shouting from the parking lot. I turned to see Olivia sitting in the driver's seat of Ryan's truck. I somehow made my way across the field and got into the passenger seat. I looked straight ahead at the dashboard while she said, "Everyone was getting worried about you..." but then she stopped, noticing what was over my shoulders. I slowly turned my head in her direction as she eyed the black suit jacket. "Whose is that?" she asked, her curiosity almost exploding from her petite frame. "Jackson's?" I shook my head. Her face went blank as she thought of other possibilities. Liv's eyes widened as she said the next name, "Wicks!"

"Yes," I said trying to understand it myself.

"What!" she shrieked as she hit her hands on the steering wheel several times. "Are you kidding me?"

"Liv, I don't think I'm crazy," I said looking blankly out of the windshield.

"Now, that is debatable," Olivia laughed, "but maybe he's into that," she added in the way best friends can.

"No, Liv. Really," I said looking at her seriously.

She rolled her eyes and put 'the tank' in 'Drive'. On the short ride home, I told her what had happened and when we pulled up in front of my grandparents' house I could see Ryan and Kate in the porch light already heading towards us. Liv, breaking her short silence advised, "I think that you need to see what Wicks says tomorrow."

"See what he says tomorrow," I repeated.

"Hopefully, he'll have an explanation," she shrugged her shoulders. "I wouldn't say anything to him about, you know… just let him do the talking. This way you don't sound crazy and scare him away or embarrass yourself."

"Right," I said as I got out of the truck. It was a rational suggestion. Somewhat snapping me out of my daze, I looked back at my friend who was climbing over into the back seat. "By the way Liv, that shirt looks really cute on you." She beamed at my compliment. I hadn't forgotten that tonight was her and Bobby's first 'official/unofficial' date.

"Thanks," she said with a contagious enthusiasm. I held the door for Kate who got into the passenger seat while Ryan jumped in on the driver's side. "Wish me luck!" I heard her say over the noise 'the tank' made.

"What happened? Where's your car?" Ryan asked leaning across Kate.

"Umm… at school," I said trying to remember where I had parked it last.

"What kept you so long," he asked nonchalantly.

"I, ah, lost track of time," I answered honestly.

Saturday, September 19th

Today the road was mine. The quiet and peaceful town could not hear the music blaring in my earphones, they could not feel the pounding of the street under my feet and they did not understand the internal conflict that was and had been wreaking havoc on me for the last seven hours let alone these past two weeks. I didn't know what today would bring but I wanted it to come. I needed answers to questions I could not form.

After my shower I had curled my hair with a massive curling iron and was now applying minimal makeup without really seeing my reflection through my anxious eyes. He had kissed me last night and every time I thought about it, I caught myself smiling. It wasn't just some kiss. It was... an incredible, 'can't-feel-my-knees', 'want-another-one-please' kind of kiss.

Opening the armoire, I looked for another outfit that Liv had thrown together which I really liked. Dressed in a high-waist sundress I looked in the old mirror knowing that I was reaping the benefits of her styling. I heard a car door close in the driveway; Ryan must be off to the Lumberyard early again. I was making my bed when there were footsteps on the stairs. "Good morning," Grams said as she reached the top step with her hand resting on the banister.

"Morning," I said as I flattened the sheets.

"I made breakfast... if you want to come down before it gets cold," she said tucking one of the corners under while I got the other side.

"Thanks, I'll be down in a minute," I answered pulling back the curtains to let the morning light into the room. She paused but changed her mind and walked down the stairs. I pushed my desk chair in and ran my fingers over the black suit jacket from last night. Picking it up, I walked over to the mirror and put it on over my outfit. It was big on me but it felt good to wear. I turned my head, closed my eyes and took in a deep breath, enthralled by the smell that so strongly reminded me of him. It was wonderful. Opening my eyes I saw my reflection and laughed at myself for the level of 'girl' I had achieved.

Sliding out of the jacket, his words resounded in my mind, 'You have to go now but I will see you tomorrow.' When would we see each other, where… and how? Would today really happen? Was he going to call me? I reached for my phone wondering if he even had my number. Realizing that I was acting like an idiot, I put the phone down and decided to go have breakfast, taking his jacket with me downstairs.

I had reached the top of the first floor when I heard Grandpa's voice in the dining room. "St. Anthony's has a strong defensive line but the key is the kid, Matthews. If Duke and Kiel can contain him, St. Anthony's line will definitely be weakened. They also have Cunningham. He's quick but Turner is the best safety I've ever coached so I'm not concerned." It wasn't unusual for Gramps to be talking football at the table, in fact it was a given; it was like saying Grace before each meal. "But after your performance last night, I can guarantee St. Anthony's is scrambling to put together a new strategy for Friday's game," my grandfather finished. My eyes shot up as I started down the last set of stairs. Did he just say 'your' as in Andrew's? He couldn't have. Could he? My hand tightened around the banister. Nearing the bottom steps where I would be able to see for myself, I silently laid the suit jacket over the railing.

"Thank you, sir," a familiar masculine voice said.

I stood frozen at the foot of the steps. Gramps looked up from the dining room table. "Good morning, Bethany," he said before taking a sip of his coffee.

"Good morning," I said forcing my feet to move. Andrew who was sitting with his back to the stairs turned and stood at my arrival. I smiled nervously at Drew then looked back at my grandfather who had taken notice of Andrew's manners.

"Andrew came to talk about last night's game," Gramps said not fooled for a second, eyeing the two teenagers that stood in front of him. "I believe your grandmother put a plate aside for you in the kitchen," my grandfather smirked. Without saying a word I looked from Andrew to Gramps and excused myself, softly pushing the swinging door. Once on the other side, I stood breathless at the highly anticipated yet somehow unexpected archangel run-in. Grams turned at the sound of my entrance and grinned, "Nice boy, that Wicks is." Continuing to cook over the stove she added, "Handsome too."

I walked over to the counter next to her and leaned my hands on it for support. "Grams, I'm not hungry…" I said feeling the butterflies in their delay finally taking flight. She looked out of the corner of her eye and smiled. Just then I heard Ryan trekking down the stairs. All together it made sense to me that the car door I had heard from my room was not Ryan leaving, it was Andrew arriving. Then panic hit; Ryan was coming downstairs. I looked at Grams, "Oh, no," I said helpless as I heard mumbled voices on the other side of the kitchen door. I put my ear up to it and tried to decipher what they were saying from the safety of the kitchen but it was impossible. As the door swung open, almost knocking into me, Ryan walked in wearing gym shorts and was looking at me through sleepy eyes confused by the near accident. "Sorry," I shrugged. Without saying a word, still half asleep, he stopped next to Grams and took a plate.

"Good morning, dear," Grams said as she served him breakfast.

"Morning Grams," he answered in a yawning slur. "It smells delicious." I opened the refrigerator and poured myself a glass of orange juice trying to hide my face. "Where are you going all dressed up?" he asked curiously. I shook my head back and forth and took a sip.

"Nice boy that Wicks is," Grams repeated throwing a look at me from behind Ryan's shoulders.

"Good player," Ryan added between bites as my grandmother's hint went right over his head. I put my glass in the sink and leaned up against the counter looking everywhere in the room except at Ryan. He was walking towards the door when he stopped and turned slowly. All hope of him overlooking my awkwardness dissipated as he placed his plate on the counter next to him and walked back towards me. He looked behind him at the kitchen door where the mumbled conversation was coming from, pointed at it and then pointed at me wordlessly putting two and two together.

We were at a standstill and I couldn't take it any longer. "What?" I finally asked. As my brother opened his mouth the kitchen door swung open and Gramps walked in with his empty dish. I took the opportunity to use my grandfather as a pick and slide out of the kitchen before Ryan could ask my grandfather his thoughts on the situation. I smiled as the door swung shut behind me, glad to have avoided the inquisition. However, now I found myself in the same room as Andrew who was looking at pictures hung on the wall. He turned at my sudden entrance and the butterflies got their second wind.

"Hello," he said with his hands behind his back.

"Hi," I said timidly noticing how different he looked wearing jeans and a plain white v-neck t-shirt under his letterman jacket. The casual clothes he wore were almost like a costume that went along with the small town setting.

I was startled when the kitchen door opened behind me. Grams grinned at the two of us as she walked over to the dining table to clear it off. Nonchalantly she asked, "Bethany, where's your car?"

"Umm," I muttered trying to think with the nearly perfect man standing in front of me, "It's at school."

"Do you want Ryan to drive you over there so you can pick it up?" she asked with an underlying cunningness in her voice.

"I would be happy to drive you to your car," Andrew offered with a smile having heard my grandmother's not-so-hidden intention.

"Well, that would be sweet of you, Andrew," Grams said pushing in one of the dining room chairs. "Bethany," she said looking at me.

"Ya, yes Grams," I said focusing on her.

"You should get going then," she said nodding towards the front door.

"Right," I said reaching for my keys from the bowl on the center table and picked up the suit jacket from the banister.

"It was nice to see you again, Mrs. Taylor," Drew said as he held opened the screen door for me.

"Likewise," Grams responded.

When I reached the bottom of the porch steps I was still breathing; that is until I realized Andrew was a step or two behind me. Expecting to see his black Camaro next to Ryan's truck, I was surprised when I saw a flawless, white Mustang. Andrew opened the passenger door for me and seeing my where-is-your-Camaro confusion, he explained, "This is my other car."

'Other car,' I thought to myself and tried not to appear too impressed as I got in gracefully. When he had closed the door I looked around the new, fully loaded, top-of-the-line work of art. Getting in on the driver's side, Drew put the key in the ignition. "Thanks for… this," I said holding out his suit jacket.

"You're welcome," he grinned while placing it in the backseat. I nervously looked out the front windshield as he put on his seatbelt with one hand and glanced over at me before putting the car in gear. I held my keys in my lap to keep my hands busy so they would not trace my collarbone.

I quickly glanced over at Andrew and then back out the window. I couldn't believe that I was sitting in his passenger seat. As the houses passed by my window in a blur, my mind kept saying, 'Oh my gosh. Oh my gosh. This is happening.' But in an attempt to take control I thought, 'Calm down or he'll think you are crazy.' Liv would be proud. However, what stopped the girly overture in my mind was the red light in front of us. Wanting to steal another look at him, I turned. He had one hand on the steering wheel, the other on the gear shift and was already looking at me. A blush warmed my face and my heart sped up. My right hand was at my collarbone… traitor.

"Weird weather," I commented looking out at the changing sky as ominous clouds started to roll over Ellsworth. My attempt at trying to break the ice or the 'ice-berg' that had formed in the car was pathetic. Andrew nodded politely. I couldn't believe I mentioned the weather. It was the official time-of-death stamp and I had killed a conversation that we hadn't even started yet. 'Typical Bethany' and 'Way to go' were thoughts that came to my mind. I sat on my right hand to prevent it from irritating the skin over my collarbone. Knowing I would be unable to recover mentally from my last statement I pushed forward fearlessly. "So, I was wondering… about last night… if you do that a lot… the whole kissing girls on the fifty yard line?"

"No," he responded with a laugh and shook his head. The light changed and he shifted gears causing the speedometer to go up a few notches. His eyes thinned in concentration before saying, "I apologize for being so untoward. I hadn't planned on seeing you and my behavior was inexcusable."

"Oh," is all I could muster as he pulled up next to my lonesome Corvette. Did I really just hear him say, 'I apologize for being so untoward,' and 'my behavior was inexcusable'? Although it caught my attention, I couldn't dwell on his selection of words because our time together was coming to an end. Despite the bombardment of butterflies I looked over at him wanting to steal every second. It was moments like this that stirred the emotions from the dreams, both the good and the bad. Those images were again, fresh on my mind.

To my surprise, Andrew put the car in 'Park', unhinged his seatbelt and walked around the front of the Mustang. Opening my door, he instinctively offered me his hand, helping me out of the car. Placing my hand in his for the first time, I carefully got out only finding myself standing very close to him. His eyes were blinking unfocused and erratically. When I released my hand he swallowed hard and looked down at me. His momentary flicker was the same reaction I had when the flashes raced in front of my eyes.

We were inches from one another and I was taken by the pull I had towards him. Although I never really thought about 'forever' and what it meant, I was certain I could look into his piercingly ocean blue eyes longer. He went to say something but stopped himself. I whispered encouragingly, "What?" Happiness washed over his face and he lingered close to my lips as though he were going to kiss me.

"Bethany," he said unguardedly, which sent chills over me. Andrew looked up at the sky at the changing weather and then back at me. "Follow me?" he asked pleadingly. Confused by his words I looked back at him. A wind from the impending storm rushed all around and through the little space between us, blowing strands of my hair that he sweetly tucked behind my ear. His fingers then tangled into my locks and he brought my face closer to his.

"Follow me, please," he begged and nodded towards my Corvette. There was no decision to be made. I was going to follow him.

With my windshield wipers slapping wildly against the torrential downpour, I watched as the left turning blinker and brake lights from the Mustang slowed at the secluded driveway; the only light in the daytime darkness of the storm. The black clouds rumbled thunder, shaking my car as the Estate came into view down the tree lined path. The garage doors opened, revealing his black Camaro and Charles' Bentley. Pulling into one of the open spots, I parked my car and turned it off. Andrew was there to open my driver's side door and he took off his lettermen jacket putting it over our heads. Motioning to the front door which was barely visible through the sheets of rain, he asked loudly over the cracks of lightening and rolls of thunder, "Shall we?" I smiled and moved closer to his side as we stepped out from under the safety of the garage awning and into the rain.

We ran laughing at the ferocity the storm was unleashing. Upon reaching the top steps, Andrew opened the front door with one hand still holding his jacket over us. Mrs. Landon had just walked into the entryway from the hallway off to the left and Dr. Landon entered the space from the right. They both stopped in the entranceway with expressions of uncertainty at our arrival. "Andrew," she said looking at her brother as he hung his drenched jacket on the carved wood coat rack next to the door.

"Abby," Andrew said as he suspiciously put out his hand for his brother-in-law to shake which he did without hesitation.

"Bethany, it's so nice to see you again," Mrs. Landon said distracting me from the unnecessary gesture between the two men.

"Bef-fany!" Gracie giggled as she came from the direction Mrs. Landon had.

"Come in, come in," Dr. Landon said softly picking up the little girl as he closed the front door against the howling wind. Gracie wrapped her arms around Dr. Landon's neck when the thunder growled.

"Hi Gracie," I smiled at her. "Don't be afraid of the storm."

"Are you afraid?" she asked loosening her grip.

"Nope," I shook my head.

"Oh," the little girl contemplated. Another grumble shook the Estate but she and I kept eye contact. When it was over a wide grin crossed her face. She had made it through her first thunder without being terrified. Excitedly, she kicked her feet and Dr. Landon placed her down. He was amused by my remedy for the little one's phobia.

"Abby and I were just talking about you," Dr. Landon said looking from me to his wife, who was exchanging a satisfied look with Andrew.

"Bethany! Hi Uncle Drew," Cole said as he entered the room from the direction Dr. Landon had. Cole was holding a deck of cards. "Want to play War, Gracie?"

"Sure," she said in her perfect, small voice. She skipped alongside her brother up the stairs. When they were out of earshot, Mrs. Landon looked around awkwardly and spoke uneasily, "Weird weather," which made Andrew and I smile – I had already used the conversation killer in the car.

"Why don't you two go sit in the dining room," Dr. Landon suggested to Andrew and I, pointing to the hallway behind his wife. "Abby and I will join you in a moment."

Andrew opened the wooden double doors to the beautifully restored dining room. I felt the warmth of a fire which was roaring underneath a large mantle. The light illuminated the rest of the room where a long table with matching chairs were meticulously placed. I walked alongside it admiring the craftsmanship. I turned back around and continued to marvel at the room's décor as I reached the source of the warmth again. Above the mantle there was a large oil painting. It was very old, maybe even as old as the house. I looked over at the sound of pounding rain hitting the windows across from the table. Beyond the glass panes and heavy curtains the storm outside impaled the extensive grounds. I looked back into the fireplace before I noticed that Andrew was leaning against the doorframe with his hands in his pockets, watching me.

"What?" I asked insecurely.

"Nothing," he said walking into the room closing the distance, his eyes still unmasked. He slowly placed his right hand on the small of my back. With my eyes, I followed his arm up to his shoulder, then to his face. I had no defense at his innocent touch. He slowly raised his left hand and brushed back my hair. I felt vulnerable and, yet, in control. Feeling both confused and overwhelmed my eyes shifted from side-to-side as my mind frantically raced. I knew I was reaching the brink. I knew that I would either snap at the insanity that was burdening me or I would surely embarrass myself in front of the very person that had become my secret fixation.

"Yes," he said as though it were okay to breakdown.

"No," I argued and took a step back and side stepped him walking to the halfway point of the long table. The door that connected this room to the kitchen, opposite to the fireplace, opened and I saw Dr. Landon. He too looked like a potential flash. I stood in the timeless room between both men. Looking down at the floor I felt my hand tracing my collarbone. I felt my other hand reaching for the back of a chair in front of me for support. I was lightheaded and then I felt my knees give way. Both Dr. Landon and Drew converged; holding me up before pulling out a seat for me to take. I sat dizzily, holding my head in my hands.

"Bethany," I could hear Dr. Landon say kneeling in front of me, "I need you to look at me." I didn't move. I felt his fingers looking for my pulse at my wrist. "Beths, look at me," he ordered and I unhurriedly moved my hands away from my face surprised at how natural my nickname sounded coming from him. Because Dr. Landon was kneeling we were eye-to-eye. A shot of adrenaline pushed through me as the flashes I had of him aligned with the sound of his voice. "Can you hear me," he asked now trying to examine the dilation of my pupils.

I nodded. "I think I'm losing my mind," I said touching my head again.

"No, you're not," he said moving my forearm gently away so I couldn't hide my face. Mrs. Landon walked through the door and upon seeing the scene in front of her, she rushed to my side. "Beths, are you alright?" she asked panicked.

Still fixed on Dr. Landon, I mechanically answered, "Abby I'm fine. Charles was just…" Stopping midsentence I slowly turned my head towards her, becoming conscious of how easily the words had flowed from my mouth. She wore a wide grin on her face as our eyes met and then she threw her arms around me, hugging me tightly. I patted her on the back watching Dr. Landon's smile unfold. Releasing me, Abby exchanged a euphoric look with her brother who had his hand on the back of my head, also on bended knee. "Someone… please tell me that I'm not as crazy as I think I am," I almost moaned.

"You are not crazy," Abby started laughing.

"I'm not?" I asked making sure.

"Absolutely not," she confirmed as she stood up. It was then I let my suppressed inclinations rise to the surface.

"Abby?" I asked after a few seconds.

"Yes," she nodded receptively.

I turned my head, so that I was looking directly at Dr. Landon. In the silence I studied his face and placed my right hand on his shoulder. He looked over at it and then back at me. "Charles," I said with a smile that could be heard in my tone. His eyes dropped to the floor and then looked back at me with nothing short of ecstasy in his eyes.

"Yes," he nodded.

Carefully standing, I turned to my next victim, Andrew, who also stood. I studied him with a new intensity, tilting my head, concentrating. "And you…" I said as my hand covered my mouth and I tried to hold back undefined tears. His lips opened slightly but he said nothing. He took a step back. With a sweetness I had never heard in my voice before I said, "You." He let out a breath of air at the wonderment in which I spoke; they all did. I took a step to close the space between us. My fingertips touched the crease of his arms which he had outstretched for me, ready to catch me if I became weak again. But I wasn't weak – in fact, I had never felt so strong or certain.

My fingers moved up his biceps and over his white, v-neck t-shirt as I hugged him tightly. I felt his arms wrap around my waist and he nestled his nose into my neck. I could hear Abby crying, Charles was caught with emotion too. Andrew's hands trailed up to the side of my face and I felt him kiss the top of my head. I closed my eyes, rested against his chest and whispered, "Drew." His arms protectively held me, pulling me closer.

"Yes, Beths," he said for only me to hear. "It's me."

—

The four of us sat around the polished dining room table with the reflection of the fire glazing off of it. Charles was at the head of the table and his wife sat to his left. I was to his right, across from Abby, and looked at them absorbedly, tracing their faces with my overworked mind. Turning to my right I looked at the last of the three, Andrew, who was watching me. The only noise came from the rain on the windowpanes and the crackling of the fire at the other end of the room.

"So," I heard Abby say but I did not break my stare with Andrew. "So," she repeated causing a grin to wash over Andrew's lips as he too did not want to look away.

"Bethany," Charles began, "Are you feeling alright?"

"Fine," I fibbed.

"Lie," Abby called me out. I looked at her and she crossed her arms with a playfully smug expression. Both Charles and Andrew grew concerned as the truth of how I was feeling was questioned. "What," Abby said looking at them. "She twirled her ring," Abby pointed to my hands that were on the table and, sure enough, I was twirling my ring around and around. I stopped immediately and could feel the blush of embarrassment.

"How did you know that I do that when…" I asked confused.

"You always did," she shrugged.

"Abigail, slow down," Charles asked of his wife but Abby continued from a different angle.

"Bethany, tell them how you struggle in history and English," she said celebratory over my shortcomings.

"Excuse me," I asked taken aback. Charles and Andrew looked at one another, then at Abby and finally at me. "What does that have to do with anything?"

"You have different impressions of historical accounts than those told in textbooks?" I nodded apprehensively at Charles. "And as for English, is it your writing style that is criticized?" I nodded again. With this, Charles began to laugh.

"I'm sorry but how are my weaknesses funny to you," I asked somewhat annoyed. "You are teachers."

"Beths, we all have that 'problem'," Andrew grinned putting his arm over the back of my chair and leaned close to me; closer than any new acquaintance would.

"Bethany," Charles said calmly, indirectly calling everyone to order. "Have you experienced anything out of the ordinary lately?"

"What do you mean," I said defensively, trying to follow Olivia's advice.

"Do you feel as though you may have been *here* before?"

"Yes," I replied withholding details.

"I told you she remembered," Abby said from across the table. "What have you seen? When did it start? What about Jonathan…" she rattled off before Charles placed his hand firmly on the table.

"Abigail, please," he said and Abby reluctantly sat back in her chair.

Andrew began listing the dreams and flashes I had experienced, "The banquet, the night before he left, the night of the accident," he paused and finished with, "and the day on the grounds amongst a slew of random images." Abby's mouth dropped at the revelation. I turned and looked at Andrew at a loss for words for what he knew.

"It's certainly remarkable," I heard Charles say as he leaned back in the chair and ran his hand over his mouth.

"How… How did you know that?" I asked looking at Andrew who exchanged a look with Charles. "No," I said to Drew, "Don't look at him, look at me. What is going on?" I demanded as I stood up.

"Bethany," Charles started and although I had all intention of not looking away from Andrew, Charles' voice, soothing and authoritative called for my attention. "Beths, please, you need to stay as calm as possible."

"I can't," I said shaking my head wanting to know what was happening. I turned straight to Abby and pointed, "Abigail, tell me." A girlish smirk washed over her face which opened into a smile.

"Some things never change," Andrew chuckled as his hands folded on the table.

"No, they don't," Charles half-laughed. I poked Andrew's side naturally and then covered my mouth shocked by my own behavior. I couldn't believe I had just done that. I felt as though I was slipping back into something I already knew.

"Beths," Charles grinned at my most recent reaction and at Andrew who was now rubbing his ribs. "You've been feeling confused lately… inundated with things you can't quite explain?" I nodded and he motioned for me to take my seat again which I did. "What has made you feel this way besides the instances that Drew mentioned," he evaluated.

Trying to walk the fine line of sounding like a sane person while actually knowing I was insane, I answered, "I'd rather not say."

"I highly doubt you can say anything that would surprise us," Abby sarcastically added from across the table as she gracefully adjusted in her seat, perfectly poised.

"Go on Bethany," Charles prompted while leaning forward in his chair ready to listen.

I was hesitant to comply but I needed answers. "The dreams feel very real... they're more... they are..." I tried to describe their complexity.

"Memories," Abby answered.

Andrew silently turned his hand over on the table, exposing his palm. I looked over at him. With trusting eyes, he nodded and without instruction I placed my hand in his.

I saw myself as though I was looking through someone else's sight: Andrew's eyes. I could see myself dressed in an ivory gown across the ball room smiling to a group of people that I was being introduced to. This connection not only allowed me to see but to feel. Andrew was anxious, something he was not used to feeling and he kept his eye on where I was in the room throughout the evening. He was captivated.

Flashes of wordless encounters in the halls of the Estate flew in front of my eyes. Our rooms were close to one another's and he was laying in bed one night with his right hand behind his head, his left on his stomach thinking about the beautiful girl that had stolen his heart sleeping in the room next to his.

It hadn't gone unnoticed to him that his sister and I were inseparable, that his brother-in-law had an instant affinity for me like that of a second father, or how I had managed to win over the affection of everyone without trying. I fascinated him for being who I was. He struggled more and more with whether to make his feelings known or to keep them to himself. But the more he tried to deny those feelings, the more he felt as though he wouldn't be able to do it for much longer.

The images slowed as another memory showed the two of us at the bottom of the staircase coincidentally meeting, both coming from different directions but headed in the same. He put his hand out gesturing like the gentleman he was for me to go first. As we walked side-by-side up the stairs he could not deny that although he had been raised to have manners and knew only to act a certain way, he enjoyed extending those behaviors towards me. To him, I was different – special – and he wanted to protect me and have me at the same time. In the loudest silence he had ever heard we walked up to the second floor and down the North Corridor. We stopped when we reached the far end; my door was straight ahead and his was to the left, diagonal from mine. Neither of us wanted to say goodnight and cross our thresholds so we found ourselves sitting in the doorways, talking and laughing with one another at a volume that would not wake the rest of the Estate as night became day again. Because the memory reel was rushed, I could not make out what exactly it was that we talked about – all I knew is that he felt like he had found his other half, his better half – what he had been praying for.

Another flash and Andrew was staring over numbers trying to rework some sort of complex business projection of losses and gains. My father was sitting at his desk across from Andrew working on a drawing of a new building and Charles was reading over a contract in a chair close by. It was late in the afternoon and I heard my father's voice telling Drew to take a break, go for a walk and clear his head. However, Andrew was close to getting the result he had been working towards for hours and he didn't want to step away until it was finished.

The sound of the front door opening and women's laughter filled the office. The three men turn their heads towards the office door which led to the hallway and back to the entranceway where the giggling faded. Andrew recognized the laughter – it belonged to his sister and, to me. Realizing that my father had taken notice of his attentiveness, Andrew watched as my father leaned back against his leather chair clasping his hands together and brought them to his mouth. With narrowing eyes and a grin on his face my father joked, "Charles, I daresay we may have just witnessed a miracle."

"Perhaps," Charles let out a chuckle as he put his work aside, stood, joining his brother-in-law and patted his tense shoulder.

"Drew," my father said sitting forward and rested his forearms on the desk. "This is the first time anything has distracted you from your work. Are you feeling alright?" Andrew felt very

uncomfortable at the current direction the conversation was taking and his pulse began to race.

"Fine," Andrew nodded.

"Are you sure," my father asked with a raised eyebrow still wearing the same faint grin. "You've seemed to be on edge for the past week... That wouldn't happen to coincide with the timing of my daughter's arrival, would it?" At this, Andrew broke out in a nervous sweat and in his hesitation, my father continued fluidly. "If I should take your silence as an answer to my question – that it does in fact have to do with Bethany's arrival, I only see it fit to inform you that I have received numerous offers from potential suitors." Andrew's anger flared at the thought of another man inquiring about me. His grasp on the fountain pen tightened. "And I have told her about each and every one... seventy-two I believe is the running count." Andrew's grip constricted even more but, otherwise, he maintained his composure.

"And?" Charles inquired out of his own curiosity as well as on behalf of his brother-in-law's. Charles knew of Andrew's interest in me from the beginning. The brotherly bond they shared was extraordinary; there were no secrets between them and they always had each other's best interest in mind.

"And, Bethany is exploring her options," my father said, busying himself by unnecessarily organizing papers. More laughter reverberated off the ornate ceilings and into the office from a farther distance than before. Andrew's eyes shifted once more to the door before they sheepishly trailed back to my father's; he had been caught again. *"Are you sure you don't have anything you'd like to ask me? Because if you do Drew, now would be the time."*

Andrew placed his pen down knowing that what he was about to say would either be well-received or be grounds for betrayal of trust. The expertise Andrew had gained in risk assessments somehow hadn't prepared him for this situation; he felt unprepared. *"Jonathan,"* the archangel said looking directly at the man sitting across from him; his mentor, father-figure and friend. *"The opportunities which you have afforded me, the knowledge I have acquired from working for you... As well as your kindness... opening your door to myself, Charles, and Abigail,"* Andrew spoke with a deep sincerity, *"Jonathan, I owe you a debt of gratitude which I will not be able to repay, and I will not soon forget that."* My father listened as his beloved apprentice continued. *"You are right in saying that I have not been myself lately. I have barely been able to focus, let alone think,"* Drew admitted. Rubbing the back of his neck, Andrew then set his eyes on my father. *"Jonathan, I did not know a woman like Bethany existed outside of my dreams."* It was at this that my father's eyes gave way to a smile as he glanced from Charles then returned his attention back to Andrew.

Exploring this admission my father queried, *"Why not say something sooner, Andrew?"*

Without hesitation, Drew answered, *"If I thought that I was worthy of the privilege of courting your daughter, I would have asked for your consent – your blessing – at our introduction."*

"I see," my father nodded solemnly and looked down at his desk then unswervingly back at him. "Drew, you are the only man in the town of Ellsworth, or the surrounding counties for that matter, who I would consider suitable for my Bethany." These words brought relief to Andrew; a relief that was followed by the highest of spirits. "I know the quality of the man you are, the unmatched work ethic you possess and the kind of life you lead and have led. You, surprisingly enough, have not only stolen one heart but have robbed another." With this Andrew became confused and, like a true apprentice, waited for an explanation. "I had a conversation much like this one earlier today with Bethany. And I can assure you that in her eyes, there have been no other suitors... Her interest lies solely with you." Andrew's emotions spiked again. My father stood from his chair and walked around his desk and Andrew got to his feet. "While you have stolen her heart, you have robbed me of mine," my father grinned at the bittersweet paradox. "As her father, it's not easy to watch my little girl have eyes for another man." The silence that followed framed the significance of the moment that was coming. "But, if that man is you," my father said putting out his hand for Andrew to take, "then I wholeheartedly give my blessing."

"Thank you, Jonathan," Andrew said and my father nodded as they exchanged a strong handshake.

Charles patted my father on the back offering comfort at a rather difficult milestone for his friend. The two shared somewhat of a burdened look which melted into an expression of elation. The matching of the families was a beautiful, unplanned compliment to the lifelong friendships they had formed – the courtship was ideal.

"Well gentlemen," my father said reaching into his suit vest pocket checking his gold pocket watch. Noting the time, he breathed in refreshed. "Shall we join the women for an early supper?"

The next flash consisted of multiple images. Andrew was fast forwarding through memories of courting, of butterflies, anticipation and tomorrows full of promise – all things I wanted to see, wanted to remember but he was pulling me through them purposefully. There would be time for all of that but right now Drew was centered on something very specific. The images slowed.

There was a fireplace with a dying light barely filling the room. I had fallen asleep on the sofa across from the fireplace with my book next to me. Andrew walked into the study after getting home from a late meeting in town and smiled before carefully sweeping me up and carrying me to my bedroom at the other end of the Estate. He pulled down the covers and placed me as gently as he could onto my bed. I stirred slightly and through heavy eyes managed a smile at the sight of him and at his closeness. He pulled the covers over me and I ran my hand over his, wordlessly asking him to stay. He knew he shouldn't. He knew that his quarters where a stone's throw away but he didn't want to leave my side. He wanted to wrap me in his arms. He wanted to fall asleep holding me, smelling the mint of my hair, the softness of my skin, the beating of my heart and the warmth of my soul.

Sitting down on the side of the bed, he untied his shoes sliding them off then moved the straps from his suspenders from his shoulders so that they fell to his sides and moved the covers over him. It was natural how he reached for me, natural how I rolled into him, curling into his chest. He felt very protective of the woman he was falling for and as he watched me drift off to sleep, he kissed my neck softly. "Hmmm," I heard myself say to him sleepily. A smile crossed over his face upon hearing my response. His prayers now began for the one in his arms, the blessing she was in his life and the grateful plea of a righteous but humble man. He too found his eyes growing heavy and fell into a near perfect sleep.

I was upset when the memory left and more images flew fast in front of my eyes. I wanted to slow them down; I wanted to see more of the happiness that I would soon remember of the moments he had never forgotten. Before the flashes slowed enough for me to watch, I felt his labored breathing.

Andrew swung his foot around his horse dismounting before the stallion came to a complete stop. He handed the reins to one of the servants while his adrenaline streamed through him. He walked straight towards the carriage that had pulled up in front of the Estate ahead of him. The driver left his seat, jumped down and opened door. Andrew could see the hem of my gown as he walked around the carriage to meet me. He put out his hand for me to take but I ignored it and placed my hand in the driver's instead. "Thank you, Thomas," I said before heading towards the front door. Andrew exchanged a look with Thomas who made no opinion on the matter that had caused this dispute. Instead, Thomas shrugged his shoulders as Andrew's attention then turned towards following me.

"Bethany," he called out confused but partly angry and somewhat burdened. Drew picked up his pace and reached the door before me. When I looked up to see him there, I stopped in my tracks and turned left, walking along the front of the Estate and around the side. It was clear I was refusing any of his advances. "Bethany," he called out from behind me watching as I picked up my skirts and trekked over the grass alongside the exterior wall. It was midday but the sun was nowhere in sight. The heavens had opened and they looked like they would again at any moment. "Won't you at least let me explain," Andrew said when we were about half the length of the house. I watched through his eyes as I turned on a dime, anger clearly written on my face – something he was seeing for the first time. Although he was taken aback, the fleeting thought of how cute I looked when I was cross did divert his mind... momentarily.

"Explain then, please," I said with my arms at my sides holding my gown above the grass and mud. Andrew also came to an abrupt stop in his pursuit. We stood a foot apart. He was taller

than me and from his eyes I could see what he saw in me. He didn't just see my appearance but he 'saw' me – for who I was, who I wasn't and there was nothing he wanted more than to have me for all his days.

"I thought," he began to defend himself, "it right that you receive the credit for your work," he stated flatly.

"But I didn't want the credit or recognition," I rebutted. "I made the suggestion about the design to my father. He presented the idea and they liked it. The matter was handled. There was no need for you to mention that I had anything to do with it."

"You're embarrassed," he asked and I shook my head annoyed by his statement but he was right, I was, and he knew it. Turning on my heels he watched as I continued to the back of the Estate. "And you're angry," he called out as he followed behind me.

"Furious actually," I shot over my shoulder. "But with your omnipotence over the people of this town, I am sure my opinion of your performance will not tarnish your pristine reputation," I added at the corner before heading towards the doors to the kitchen.

"And what is that suppose to mean," he asked defensively but even still, he opened the door and, forfeiting to his relentless manners, I stormed inside.

"Exactly what it sounds like, Andrew," I said turning when he closed the doors behind us.

"You're indignant because, yes, in a moment of pride, I told them that you were the one responsible for the work they valued so highly?" he asked touching his chest as he spoke.

"No, I'm indignant because I do not need praise nor want praise! Perhaps next time you decide to speak in such boldness you will keep in mind my wishes," I said in a fit of rage, hitting the counter in between him and me with my hands. Without another word, Andrew heatedly walked out of the kitchen into the dining room and slammed the doors.

His fingers were clamped around the doorknobs and his shoulders were bent inward. Drew looked down at the floor and even with the frustration he felt, he knew the moment he left the kitchen, it had been a mistake. He was wrong in mentioning my association with the drawing; he had not done it intentionally but he knew I was right. Opening the doors, he saw me leaning with my back against the counter and my hands covering my face. I was crying about the argument but looked up when I heard the doors open.

"Are we done fighting now," he asked tilting his head with 'please forgive me' eyes. I sniffled, nodded and then cried harder as he walked to me putting his arms around me. "I'm sorry," he said and heard me say the same thing into his chest. A smile broke over his face before he kissed the top of my head. I looked up at him with tear stains on my cheeks. Instead of using his hands to dry them, he kissed where the tears had fallen and then down to my lips as my hands found the sides of his face. The intensity grew and with little effort he placed me on the counter and my legs wrapped around him. Then his hands on either side of my waist ran up my back and then back down.

Andrew heard a few of the servants coming down the servant stairwell so he picked me up in his arms, opened the back door and closed it with one hand behind him, while our lips met again and again. As he pushed me up against the wall, I grinned as we continued to say 'I'm sorry' without words. "Ah hmm," Andrew heard to his left and he and I both looked at the source of the noise. Charles had walked onto the elevated terrace next to us, cautioning Drew and I to slip away before my father joined him on the terrace.

Taking my hand, Drew started back around the house headed to the front of the Estate swooping me up on occasion over mud puddles so that the hem of my dress would not be sacrificed. We laughed like children and he smiled as I held onto his hand with both of mine, trusting as he lead.

Thomas greeted us as we walked up the steps. "It would appear that you two have straightened things out," he said happily greeting us at the entranceway.

"Yes," Drew heard me almost giggle and looked down at me with a grin only to find that I was already smiling up at him.

"Mr. Wicks, if I had a woman like Miss Taylor look at me the way she looks at you, well, I'd consider myself exceedingly fortunate."

"I do," Drew said staring into my faithful, emerald eyes and softly kissed my hand as the scene withered away.

More flashes flew by at top speed and the feelings that were tied to them were blissful, heavenly. I wanted so badly to slow him down, to see them, to relive them and remember. But then it changed. Memories came like shadows and the dark emotions connected to them pulled at me with a weight not measured in strength. Beginning with my father's accident and the days that followed, I realized Drew was trying to avoid them all together. Fighting against his own mind, he didn't want me to have to relive or experience the ache they brought. But it was too late.

I saw myself come into focus, yelling at him in hysterics on the Estate grounds. I had my own memory of how this ended but now watched from his point of view. His feelings of pain and devastation over the sudden loss of my father, his mentor was unbearable. Drew was broken inside. The agony was all too recognizable and no matter whose perspective you saw it from, it was excruciating. Knowing what was about to happen, I let go of Andrew's hand before I had to witness our untimely goodbye.

With my hand free, the connection was over. I stood up quickly – too quickly – and stepped away from the table, panicked. Uneasy and not reacquainted with the room or my balance, I felt my knees give and reached for the table for support.

"It's okay," Charles said catching me and lowered me to the floor. "This is why I told you two to take it slow," he directed at his brother-in-law and wife who were also at my side.

"I…" I started to say as their faces aligned in front of me. "I didn't mean it. I was trying to make you understand," I let out, explaining to Andrew why I had challenged him on the grounds. Still very aware of the raw emotions that were attached to the scene that I had just revisited, tears poured down my face.

"I know. I know what you were trying to do. How unreasonable I was…"

"This is too much, too soon," Charles whispered lowly finding my eyes to steady me. "We should give you more time so that your mind can catch up."

"But Charles," Abby started to argue but stopped as she watched him help me to my feet.

"Drew, Abby, please, give me a moment with Bethany, alone." Andrew nodded and led his sister to the kitchen, looking back before closing the doors behind them.

When the room was quiet, I turned towards the fireplace filled with the fury of flames. "How old is this house?" I asked composing myself and glanced up at the oil painting above the mantle.

Charles came up next to me with both hands behind his back, "Old."

"How old?"

"It was completed in 1888," he answered.

"How old are these dreams? Memories," I said for the first time.

"They are from the same year," he answered. I swallowed hard before asking the next question.

"How old are you?" I waited and watched him out of the corner of my eye.

Without hesitation he answered, "I was born in 1860."

"This house," I paused. "This is your house?" I spoke expecting his answer to be 'yes'.

"No, I was born in the same small town as Andrew and Abigail. Coverly," he stated.

"Coverly," I repeated and now as I let the name of the town set in, somewhere in my mind, hidden recollections showed themselves. They hit me quickly, blurring into recognition as they linked the timeline together. It was the town where my father had told me where his business trip was the night before his accident. It was the place where Andrew's self-torture began – the cause for the scene on the grounds.

"Bethany," Charles said disrupting my mental perplexity.

"How old is Abby?" I asked needing more answers.

"She was born in 1864," he spoke not at all bothered by my inquisition.

"Andrew?" I continued.

"1868." Then there was complete silence.

"You haven't... aged?" I asked looking up at him. He, like his wife and brother-in-law, had remained timeless into both the twentieth and twenty-first centuries. The only thing that changed were their wardrobes, acting like costumes for the generations that passed by them.

"We realized shortly after your passing that we somehow had the ability to exchange memories with one another. We didn't understand how or why until it became evident that we were also not aging like we should. The memory connection and inability of growing older was some sort of a package deal," Charles explained. I tried to grasp what he was telling me but he asked a question which distracted me from any attempt at quantifying the phenomena. "Do you remember what year you were born?"

"Before today I would have said seventeen years ago," I laughed attempting to ease the lunacy. Charles smiled and adjusted his stance. I looked over at him and noticed his dashing profile like I had during our first encounter in my grandfather's office. He was an old kind of handsome.

"When was I born back then?" I asked staring back into the fire.

"1871," Charles answered with great certainty.

Seconds ticked by before I spoke again, "These things that I am seeing, these flashes, are from 1888?"

"Yes. We met in 1888," he answered watching me out of the corner of his eye making sure I wasn't on the threshold of lightheadedness again.

Thinking about the dreams, the nightmare and the undeniable connection I felt towards them, I formed the next question. "On the grounds when Andrew and I were fighting…" I started. Even with just the onset of remembering, the heartache flooded me once more.

"That," Charles nodded, "was the day you passed."

"I died…" I repeated before looking up at him.

"Yes," he answered looking ill as he too thought of the memory.

"But you, Abby and Andrew haven't died?"

"Correct."

"So, am I like a ghost or something?"

"No," he laughed. "Although when I first saw you in your grandfather's office, I admit that did cross my mind."

"And you…" I turned to face him, "You didn't take a drink from the Fountain of Youth or anything like that?"

"No," he grinned and shook his head.

When we both settled I asked, "Why and how is this happening?"

Calmly, Charles answered, "The three of us have our theories."

"What's yours?" I questioned.

"Does it matter?" he issued with caring eyes.

"I suppose not," I said understanding. It didn't matter what the reason was. What mattered was that it *was* happening. Letting whatever was left of my guard down I met Charles' eyes and smiled sheepishly. "We," I said pointing in between him and myself. "We were close weren't we?" I asked recalling fragmented memories which were unhurriedly revealing themselves.

"Yes," he nodded, "very much so."

"Abby?" I said looking at the closed doors knowing she was somewhere on the other side.

"You were best friends... like sisters," he verified something I instinctively knew.

"And Andrew and I?"

Charles didn't waver; he just smiled and said, "I believe you already know the answer to that." I looked down at the wooden floor and blushed at the thought of the archangel. "Beths," Charles said checking to see if I was alright.

I smiled up at him with eyes filled with tears, none of which had fallen. Charles understanding, joked, "He's most likely pacing by now."

"Probably," I laughed through my web of emotions. I felt strange knowing and not knowing so many things. But knew every part of it held truth. "How did this happen?" I asked again in a tone of disbelief.

Charles grinned and put his hands in his pockets. "We don't know, Bethany, but we're glad it has."

Charles accompanied me out of the dining room, through the entranceway and led me down the hallway to my father's office. Andrew was pacing the length of the room and was rubbing the back of his neck, looking anxiously out the large windows which showcased the side of the grounds. He was nothing short of perfect to me and when he turned at the sound of Charles and I entering the room, my heart fluttered. Without a word, Charles left us alone.

We walked towards one another and Andrew motioned for me to take a seat on a sofa identical to the one across from him. A gentleman by nature, he waited for me to sit before he sat down. We said nothing at first, gracelessly dancing around the silence. I looked down into my lap, not knowing where to start. That's when he asked, "Are you alright?" When I looked up at him, he leaned forward with his forearms on his knees and was waiting on my response. He was trying to get a read on me. I nodded but he wasn't convinced.

"I'm fine, really," I smiled back at him. The old clock in the corner ticked rhythmically back and forth and when my eyes traveled to it, the room we were sitting in caught my awareness. It was exactly the same. I knew the details… I knew how the light came through the windows... I knew.

He was watching me when my eyes came back to him. He was taking me in just like I had been taking in the room almost like he knew *my* details, what made me smile, everything… He knew.

It was as though things were falling back into place; like time had stopped and I wanted it to desperately start again. I wanted to know what happened next. With this newfound understanding and my sarcasm intact, I started to laugh saying, "I do have a few questions."

"I would imagine," he cracked a smile and began to laugh. He looked down between his polished shoes before sitting straight-backed. "Ask anything," he offered with open hands.

"Cole and Gracie?" I questioned after hearing the pitter-patter of little feet somewhere nearby.

"Are foster children," Andrew answered. "From time-to-time, Charles and Abby take in children who need a stable home while it's determined if their biological parents are deemed fit to get custody back." I nodded understanding. Charles and Abby were good people. It didn't surprise me that they opened their home and lives to children in such circumstances.

"And they are teachers?" I asked a few seconds later trying to get reacquainted.

"Yes, but Abby also takes on 'restoration' projects whether it be nineteenth century art, furniture or clothing. Charles became a medical doctor after we first left Ellsworth but he hasn't practiced in years. Instead, he uses his education and experience to head up hospital boards. He has a great understanding of what the medical professionals need and combines his business background to effectively advise higher level administration."

"And you?" I asked pulling my hair over my one shoulder and subconsciously wrapped it around my fingers. It was an innocent and simple habit but it caught his attention and he grinned and shook his head. With his reaction, I stopped twirling the ends of my long locks – his distraction – and encouraged him to continue.

"I attend to institutional investments, conservative financial expansion, risk assessments, consulting..." he rattled off uninterested by his impressive career path.

"High school student... quarterback?" I teased.

Smiling, he answered, "No, high school student and quarterback... those are first's."

"You have trouble with history and English too?"

"Yes," he responded wearing his boyish grin. "You'll find that attitudes towards events and *certain* people are encapsulated differently than how they were back then. As for writing, well, we're all accustomed to an older style."

The room was silent but the feelings between us were loud. It was because of this that my mind picked up again and I started to panic. There were so many things I didn't remember, so many more important questions to ask and the madness that kept checking in with my rationality. My hand began to nervously trace my collarbone.

Seeing this, Andrew slowly got up from the sofa he was sitting on and not breaking eye contact, got on his knees in front of me. He was the calm in the storm of emotions that were plaguing me. Drew placed his hands on the cushion on either side of me. Just his presence made me feel safe. I smiled at him and his eyes smiled back. Not needing to trace my collarbone, my fingers found his chest and moved up behind his ear. His eyes were absorbed with mine; soft but still strong. As my fingers ran through his hair, it occurred to me for the first time the ability my hands had with sharing memories with him, Charles and Abigail.

Not really knowing how it worked, I thought of last night after the game as I slid my hand under his. I worried that I hadn't done it correctly until his eyes became unfocused and blinked out of rhythm. The connection was made.

I thought about the football field, the stadium lights and hearing him call my name. I remembered the butterflies as he walked closer, how he put his jacket over my shoulders and the pull I felt towards him. I remembered the kiss… I needed him to know that even in the ambiguity, even when I didn't know what I knew now, I was called to him.

The exchange ended. Drew no longer had to worry how things would unfold with me finding out the truth or how I would handle the initial shock. He didn't need to pretend; he was no longer at bay. He didn't have to think about what could have been anymore and no words would ever go unspoken. Softly, he kissed me like he thought I would break. My hands touched his chest again but this time, I pulled him closer. After that, our lips intertwined and there was no room for space or time.

The door to the office opened a few seconds later. "My apologies," Charles said walking in on Andrew and I.

"It's okay, Charles." Andrew breathed pulling back slightly but didn't look over his shoulder. Instead, Drew ran both his hands through my hair and pulled my face closer to his, brushed his nose with mine and smiled.

"We should get going," Charles cleared his throat uncomfortably from the doorway.

"Yes," Andrew stood and I did too. Drew stayed close to my side and his hand politely found the small of my back.

"Where are we going?" I asked looking from Andrew to Charles.

"The hospital. I want to check out that heart of yours," Charles answered.

"My heart? But it's fine."

"Just to make sure, Beths," Andrew said as we walked out of the office.

"No really," I reassured them as I passed Charles and into the hallway ahead of the men. "I take my medication religiously," I added and heard Andrew and Charles stop dead in their tracks. I turned. "What?" I shrugged when they shot each other concerned looks.

—

After my revelation about taking medication, Charles and Andrew basically carried me to Charles' Bentley which he pre-started. On our way to the hospital, I kept looking out the side mirror watching as Andrew followed behind in my car. Charles floored the Bentley which rode smooth and soundlessly over the wet pavement; classical music was playing from the speakers.

"He was nervous, you know," Charles said noticing that I had checked the mirror again. Sure enough, there was my Corvette easily keeping pace. I looked over at him as he continued, "That you would not be *his* Bethany."

"*His* Bethany," I repeated, squinting in thought, glaring out the windshield. "And if I wasn't?" I asked tensely.

"Abby and I had assured him that it was in fact you, but he was skeptical. However, once he saw for himself, there was not a doubt in his mind."

"I still don't remember everything..." I prompted and began to tug worriedly at my dress.

"Truthfully, I didn't think you would remember much at all, but after today, it wouldn't surprise me if it all comes back to you," Charles said skillfully steering the powerful car, not sacrificing speed.

"I *feel* it more," I tried to explain, recalling how the once puzzling emotions had stayed with me after every dream.

"Sometimes it's good not to remember everything," he smirked from the driver's seat. At this I wondered what tragedies had met him over the past century and which he'd like to forget.

"Where was Andrew before he became the 'new' student?" I asked thinking about the logistics of all of this.

"Colorado," Charles answered and knowing that I would have a million more questions about how everything had evolved, he placed his hand out on the center console for me to take. I put my hand in his and just like that I was in a different place.

"Are you sure we shouldn't have called first," Abigail asked Charles whose eyes were closed. His hand was covering them.

"Abby, I'm certain," Charles said reassuring his wife as he squeezed his eyes tightly before pinching the bridge of his nose with his thumb and index finger. When he opened his eyes, the scene came into view.

"Here we are," the cab driver said pulling up outside a row of ideal brownstones in the early hours of a Colorado morning.

"Thank you," Charles said paying the driver and then helped Abigail out of the cab. "Would you mind staying for a little while," he requested and when the man cringed, Charles encouraged him with monetary reinforcement.

"What are you doing," Abby asked when he was back at her side.

"Nothing," Charles said putting out his arm for her to take. They had no bags – they had gotten on the first flight out and Charles wasn't expecting that his and Abby's visit would be a long one.

Walking up the few steps to Andrew's door, Charles knocked firmly. "Why did you ask the driver to stay?" Abby asked again looking over her shoulder but before Charles could reply the door opened. Drew was getting dressed for work and was tying his tie when he saw who was standing on his stoop.

"Charles. Abigail. Is everything alright?" Drew asked immediately. "Is it Cole? Gracie?"

"The children are fine," Abigail smiled at the sound of their names.

"May we come in," Charles respectfully requested.

"Of course," Drew said kissing his sister's cheek as she stepped inside while he flipped the tail end of his finished tie and readjusted his collar. Charles kept both of his hands in his pockets avoiding a handshake; an exchange between the two of them would certainly reveal the cause behind this unannounced trip.

Charles watched his wife take off the decorative, satin scarf she wore around her neck as she looked around her brother's living quarters. There was a large stone fireplace to the left where a 'L' shaped couch, a coffee table and an area rug differentiated the living room from the open layout kitchen. To the right was a wide hallway with a bathroom to the left and at the end was Andrew's room; his bed was partially covered with unmade linens. The walls were painted in hues of dark blues and accent pieces were in complimentary creams. The residence was established, simple and amiable – it suited its tenant.

As Andrew closed the front door he asked, "Can I offer you something to drink?" Charles who never underestimated Drew's intelligence or intuition knew that his brother-in-law would suspect that something serious must have occurred for them to show up unexpectedly at his door. His offer of a beverage was a result of his good manners.

"No, no thank you," Abby shook her head as did Charles. Drew eyed them both and crossed his arms warily.

With this Abby suggested, "Maybe we should sit down." Andrew gestured for Charles and Abigail to take a seat while he chose to remain standing.

"How are things at the hospital?" Charles inquired.

"The hospital is doing well; increasing its margin," Drew reported. "Forgive me, but I don't believe you would have come all this way for an update which we speak of weekly over the phone. So," Andrew half-laughed, his youth perfectly frozen like his charm showed on his face and in his eyes. "Not that I am not exceedingly happy to see you both, but if you don't mind, to what do I owe this pleasure?"

Abby looked out of the corner of her eye at her husband who took in a deep breath. Charles was tired – physically, emotionally and mentally. However, it was of the utmost importance that he kept it together not only for his own sake but for Abby's and Andrew's. It had always been his role.

What Charles hadn't thought through was how he would start the conversation; the beginning seemed like a good place. "Three days ago, someone moved into town but it didn't come to your sister and my attention until that person was enrolled at the high school two days ago."

"Someone we know?" Drew questioned. It was a constant reality for the three of them that they could potentially run into someone who knew them from years ago and would see that they *hadn't aged. It was atypical but it was a possibility. They had to be cognizant as to which professional and social circles they associated themselves with and mindful of people's varying degrees of separation.*

"No," Charles answered extinguishing his fear. "Well, yes," he then amended realizing that technically, the three of them did know the person who had moved to Ellsworth but not for the same concerns Andrew was addressing.

His eyes narrowed, "Who then?

"This is going to sound…" Charles began to warn.

"Who is it, Charles?" Andrew asked with his lips cracking a smile at the corners. He had no idea the blow that awaited him.

"Andrew," Abby said also trying to brace her brother. Hearing the caution in his sister's voice, Drew's eyes shot to her and then he looked slowly back at his brother-in-law, as ready as he could be for whatever it was.

Charles, terribly conflicted, hesitated. While he was elated over the miracle that literally walked back into their lives, he knew that the initial breaking of the news to Drew would trigger a deluge of emotions, reopening wounds that never healed.

He swallowed hard. "Drew, it's Bethany," he said and waited, watching as his words reached Andrew. Drew's composure did not break at the sound of my name. No, his reaction was far worse – worse than Charles had anticipated. Andrew was crumbling; his mind was refusing to comprehend the craziness Charles spoke while his heart embraced it instantly. After nearly a hundred years, Andrew was at war again. Knowing his window to explain was small, Charles continued, "I was introduced to her… re-introduced to her, by her grandfather, Coach Taylor… whose first name happens to be Jonathan." Andrew's eyes widened at the unrelenting insanity.

"The football team coach that you assist – his name is Jonathan Taylor?" Drew asked with a dry mouth and stared down at the hardwood floor under his feet.

"Yes," Abby said softly. "We didn't tell you his first name because we didn't think it was of any importance. We believed it was just a coincidence and an unnecessary detail. Neither he nor his wife, Claire, has ever spoken of a Bethany; we didn't see why we would need to inquire." Charles nodded in agreement of his wife's account. For the past two days she had been second guessing every interaction they had had with my grandparents over the past two years. They had come up with nothing.

Charles and Abby intently watched Andrew; the walls he had built up were cracking at their foundation. "Andrew," Charles said calling for his attention. Drew looked up at his brother-in-law and Charles saw the torment stirring in his friend's eyes. It was the calm before the storm.

"What are you telling me?" Drew asked as rationally as he could. "Are you saying that there is a girl in Ellsworth who happens to resemble…"

"No, Drew," Charles cut in knowing exactly where Andrew was trying to take this. "I am saying that right now, the new girl **is** Bethany."

Like a strike of lighting, Andrew's defense mechanism was up but this was something Charles had anticipated. Drew began to rub the back of his neck. "You flew all the way out here to tell me that Bethany Taylor," his voice broke at my name, "is alive and well?"

"Andrew," Abby whispered desperately.

"No," he defiantly scowled at his sister.

"I had her stay after class yesterday, Drew. I talked to her," Abby tried but Drew interrupted her once more.

"You two should have seriously reconsidered... Do you even hear yourselves?" Andrew began to pace. Charles hadn't seen or heard Andrew this way for over a century; not since the last time Drew was in Ellsworth.

"Andrew," Abby begged.

"No, Abigail," he barked with ferocity.

A little dazed but steadfast, she persisted. "Her name is Bethany Ann Taylor. She is seventeen years old. Her eyes are incredibly green. She's prettier than I remember; she's funny and irrefutably intelligent... she traces her collarbone when she's nervous," Abby paused and let out a sigh like a cry describing her sister-like best friend.

Silence, that's what there was in the room. There was complete and utter silence as Andrew's world was shaken.

Knowing him as well as he did, Charles took a step closer to his brother-in-law. Reinforcing the fact, he said point-blank, "It's her, Andrew." Bewildered, Drew shook his head but quickly, his guard was back up and with it, his anger.

"How can you say this to me? You, of all people, Charles, Drew said breaking more and more. "After losing her... what it meant... she... I... It took me so long to just get to a place where I could breathe again without it hurting."

Drew was right – Charles knew what this would do to him. Charles put his hand on Andrew's shoulder and locked eyes. "Andrew, if I wasn't absolutely certain that it is Beths, I wouldn't have come." There was no doubt in Charles' mind that it was really me and the only thing he could do for Drew was to offer him logical stability. "Abby and I both understood and respected your decision to not move back to Ellsworth with us two years ago. Remember that; remember that we know, I know, what it would do to you if this wasn't the truth. But Drew, it's her." There was a mix of utter disbelief and confidence in his voice that did not go unnoticed by Andrew. Finding the ledge of the fireplace with his hand, Drew sat down and buried his face in his hands trying to take it all in. Abby sat at her brother's side and without invitation, gave more details. "There was an announcement over the PA system Monday morning for a Bethany Taylor to report to Coach Taylor's office. I heard it and Charles found me in my classroom shortly afterwards having heard it too. At first, neither of us believed our ears," she said looking up at her husband.

Charles then continued, *"After that period I walked down to Coach Taylor's office...Jonathan's office. I wasn't expecting anyone to be there apart from him. I thought I would ask him questions about the final roster or whatnot and casually inquire about a Bethany Taylor but when I got to his office, she was there, sitting across from him,"* Charles took in a slow breath, still taken away by the scene.

"Did you speak with her," Andrew asked wanting to know more but was not sold.

"Very little," Charles answered. He recalled how his composure had been tested in the wake of our re-acquaintance. *"I was caught off guard. I didn't know if she would know who I was... but I believe she does."*

"We didn't sleep that night," Abby said abiding to the timeline. *"We didn't know what to do; I thought it best to see for myself before we acted. The next morning, the attendance for one of my physics classes had her name added to it. Our paths would cross without me having to do anything. When I got to the classroom, she was already sitting there,"* Abby stopped herself trying not to cry. *"She looked like Bethany, exactly,"* she let out a moan, *"beautiful like she always was,"* Abby said pushing away falling tears. Andrew didn't flinch; he was stunned. *"I kept her after class to speak with her. She, in every way and in every sense..."* Abby expounded. Drew folded his hands in front of him and he bent his head down, his jaw tightened.

"Andrew," Abby said concerned. "Please Drew," she said as more tears fell down her face. Andrew stood. He looked down at her, then at Charles and, finally, at the door. "Get out," he whispered. Horrified, Abby looked at her husband who remained calm. Charles saw this coming, that's why he had asked the cab to stay. When neither of them moved, Andrew repeated, "Get out."

"No Andrew," Abby appealed desperately.

"I'm begging you to go," Drew ordered.

"We wouldn't have come if it weren't true," Abby tried again but Charles stepped towards her and shook his head silently. Understanding that there was nothing else she could say, she got to her feet, walked back to the couch, picked up her bag and scarf, and then headed to the door. Her heels were the only sound in the apartment and they echoed coldly.

Charles turned to Drew. "I would never," he emphasized, repeating firmly, "I would never lead you back down the road you have come so far on. You know that." With this Charles started towards the door. Drew stepped in front of him with an outstretched hand wordlessly asking for Charles to show him the memory of meeting me, to show him something.

Charles looked at his brother-in-law's hand refusing to share any memory of me with him; it was something he had promised himself he wouldn't do on the flight here. "NO," Charles said flatly. "You are going to have to see for yourself." He added before joining his wife at the door, opening it for her and waiting as she stepped out onto the landing. Turning, Charles said with one last look at Andrew, "Drew, you can tell yourself that your sister and I have lost our minds, but if there is a plane leaving Fort Collins tonight, I hope you're on it." Closing the door, Charles led his wife to the parked cab. "Back to the airport, please," he said to the driver when they got into the back seat. Abby leaned her head on her husband's right shoulder as he put his arm around her. Resting his left elbow where the glass met the door, he covered his eyes with his left hand. He exhaled, letting go of the breath he had held in.

Quicker than a blink, Charles' memory fast-forwarded. He and Abby were back at the Estate, the kids were in bed and he was in the office working into the night. Abby was leaning on the doorframe with her arms loosely folded in front of her. "Hello," Charles smiled at his wife noticing her presence.

"Do you think he'll come," she asked point-blank. "It's been a day and we haven't heard anything from him."

"He'll come," Charles responded, while putting his pen down and leaning back in the chair.

"How are you so certain? And why go through the trouble of making the arrangements – buying clothes, the cars…" she asked but Charles cut in.

"Abigail, he'll be here."

"Fine," she shrugged. "I'm going to go to bed. Will you be up soon?"

"In a little while," Charles nodded and smiled at his wife who covered her yawn with the back of her hand and grinned with her eyes at him. He got up from the desk, went over to her, kissed her forehead and they parted way. He stood in the same spot until he heard her climb the stairs and close the bedroom door. Then he found his seat again. Checking the old faced clock at the other side of the room above the second fireplace, he picked up his pen once more. As though on cue, headlights flickered outside of the office windows, illuminating the grounds on the side of the house as a car pulled down the long drive. Charles didn't waste time getting to the front door.

When he opened it, Andrew was walking up the stairs looking up at the Estate, a place he had once known as his home. Seeing Charles in the entryway, Andrew looked painfully back at him. Drew was still dressed in the suit from yesterday, the tie was missing and his collar button was undone. He had no bags with him, only the clothes on his back.

Charles waited patiently as Andrew took in the entryway. The last time he had been here was the night after I had passed. Charles quietly closed the front door as the taxi pulled away, driving back down the dark, single lane cobblestone driveway with only headlights to guide.

Drew stopped at the top of the staircase that led down into the dimly lit, empty ballroom. Charles imagined how haunting this place must be for his friend and how many unhealed wounds were being ripped open.

"Did you eat," Charles asked presuming that Andrew had not.

"No," Drew replied as he turned and looked up at the chandelier overhead.

"There are leftovers from dinner in the refrigerator," Charles offered.

"Thank you," Andrew said now running his hand over the table underneath the chandelier.

"The keys, there," Charles said pointing to the two sets on the table, "Those are for you, your pick. They're in the garage… the old stables," he corrected realizing Andrew had not seen the updates he and Abby had made. The changes were modest, of course, keeping true to the Estate's timelessness. When they had converted the stables into the multicar garage, Abby joked how their horses had become horsepower; part of the coping mechanism they had developed as the world passed them by. "And there are clothes, toiletries and anything else you would need in your old quarters." Andrew looked at his brother-in-law thanking him for the provisions he had prearranged. Nodding solemnly, Charles excused himself and headed up the stairs. He looked back over his shoulder to see Andrew walk towards the hallway off the main entrance towards the office, unhurriedly reacquainting himself with the house.

Charles knew things would get much worse before they had a chance of getting better. The pain this place held for Drew was great and Charles had experienced it too on another level when he *and Abby first moved back two years ago. At first, the memories came like a flood and pulled you under. Charles knew that in the next few days Drew was in for the fight of his life.*

"He's here," Charles whispered as he got into bed next to his wife.

"What," she asked shocked, rolling over to face Charles.

"He just got in," Charles said pulling the blankets over himself and moved closer to his wife.

"He's here…" Abby said, "and she's…"

"Yes," Charles smiled.

"Will he go to her? Should we check on him," Abby began to panic, sitting up and leaned against her pillow. Charles had already given thought to the scenario.

"He won't go to her, not tonight. Perhaps not for a few days," he said closing his eyes.

"What? How can you be so sure," she asked turning to him.

"I'm sure," he answered keeping his eyes closed.

"But," Abby started.

"Abigail," he said opening one eye and finding her waist with his hand. She laughed as he playfully rolled her to the other side of him and engulfed her body in his. There was silence until she broke it.

"You knew he'd come. How did you know he'd come?"

"Abby," Charles yawned.

"How did you know?"

"I bet he could have told you that I would have things ready for him."

"You're probably right," she laughed at their strong friendship and brotherly bond.

"Probably?" Charles smirked. "Probably," he repeated and tickled her.

"Fine, yes! Yes, you were right," she laughed as she turned into his chest and he stopped. Calm, she whispered, "Charles, this is really happening."

He smiled staring up at the ceiling and pulling her closer to him, he softly answered, "Yes, it is."

"Beths," Charles said after breaking the hand connection still driving down the rain stricken streets. As my senses realigned I was taken by what he had revealed to me. Catching the Corvette in the rearview mirror again, I looked at the archangel behind the wheel. Then I looked at the man next to me.

"Thank you."

"Of course," Charles said looking over at me and then back at the road. "You should know that Abigail, Andrew and I aren't able to *share* this hand connection or memory exchange with other people. It was something that has only worked between the three of us."

"That and the age thing," I added.

"Yes, that too," he grinned making a right onto the road the hospital was on. He then inquired, "Your heart…"

"I have a Ventricular Septal Defect."

"VSD," Charles said aware of the medical condition. "When were you diagnosed?"

"Two years ago." The routine physical for my admittance to Columbia resulted in more than I had bargained for. Michael was actually the one who went with me to the specialist appointments which followed, once again going above and beyond the duty of an agent.

"Two years ago?" Charles asked disgusted. "That should have been detected at birth if not your infancy."

"That's what the specialists said too."

"So what was their prognosis?" he asked mentally streaming through what he knew about the congenital heart disease from his education along with the medical assumptions he had made over the years about the cause behind my untimely passing.

"I'm on medication and do the recommended cardio. I visit the cardiologist every three months. According to him, although it was caught late, it's not significant and as long as I keep doing what I'm doing, there shouldn't be a need for surgery."

Charles didn't say another word as he pushed his foot down on the gas pedal. I knew he wanted to see for himself; he had the curiosity of a doctor and the concern of a dear friend. Strangely enough, in telling Charles about my condition I felt as though a weight had been lifted from my shoulders. When I had been diagnosed I didn't want Ryan or my grandparents to worry so I didn't tell them. My mother didn't need to know that I had a weakness; she would have been 'too busy' to sit with me in waiting rooms anyway.

The Bentley pulled into the hospital parking lot and Charles parked in one of the first spots that read, 'C. Landon', a perk of being a trustee. Andrew parked my car a few spots away and was at my side while we walked towards the emergency room doors. I was now more aware of the strength the man standing next to be had, what it meant for him to come back to Ellsworth. I wanted my mind to work faster in recalling the past I had with Drew, Charles and Abigail, but I knew it would take time.

The entire nurses' desk looked up as Charles and Andrew walked in. "Good afternoon, ladies," Charles said to the scrubs wearing army. I looked for Kate knowing she had a shift this evening but I didn't see her.

"Good evening, Dr. Landon," most of the women smiled as we walked by. Charles, Andrew and I continued to the elevators and stepped onto one that opened. Inside, Charles pressed 'four'. I moved closer to Andrew who touched the small of my back as the compartment filled with people. I looked up at him and it caught him off guard but a smile quickly washed over his face. Sliding his hand into mine I was instantly hit with images that did not belong to me.

We were in my grandparents' dining room only a few short hours ago. I had just come downstairs and he stood, turning to see me. I smiled surprised, innocent and blushed. In that instant he felt a piece of him fall into place.

I heard the elevator chime at the second floor as my eyes refocused. His emotions still lingered in me and I welcomed the elation he felt. Everything about him was right and I hadn't understood why until now. He was perfect to me because he was everything I remembered – everything I wanted… the way he looked, the way he looked at me, the way he spoke, his mannerisms, his smell, the way he held me... We hadn't just met, we had a history together and it seemed we were picking up right before it went horribly wrong.

When the doors opened at the fourth floor a gurney surrounded by a medical team rushed passed us. I overheard something about ICU and was distracted momentarily. Charles held out his arm directing Andrew and I to the right. We walked down the hallway and Charles opened the last door on the left.

This room, unlike the rest of the building, looked and felt like a typical hospital. The walls were white and the fluorescent lighting gave off a dull glow. There was a big machine against the right wall. Opposite it was a wall made of glass which revealed another room where Charles was now turning on monitors. An intercom clicked on, "Bethany, you are going to have to take off any jewelry or metal that you have on," Charles instructed. I took out my earrings and took off the long key necklace over my head and handed them to Andrew who held his hand out. Then the large machine made a noise and a door–like panel clicked open. I looked at it skeptically. Andrew kissed the side of my head before I stepped inside the small space and closed the panel.

I could hear Charles' voice through an intercom say, "There are going to be a few noises as the machine makes its rotations. Hold the handles to your sides and try to stay as still as possible." A clunking but rhythmic noise surrounded me as the machine began the scan. I closed my eyes and focused on my breathing. It wasn't uncomfortable being in the small space rather it gave me time to think about what the day had brought. This was all really happening… Thoughts pounded my mind. The dream and flashes – they were memories from my past. The unexplained feelings I had been having for Andrew were finally exposed and with it came a love story.

"Alright, Bethany," Charles said over the speaker as the machine quieted. The panel popped open again. I stepped out and walked into the glass room where there were monitors, and a central computer. Charles, sitting by the main screen, was analyzing the three-dimensional picture of my heart, making it bigger and bigger as he zoomed in. Andrew's hand found the small of my back again as I put my jewelry back on and Charles examined the image. "Your heart rate and pulse are normal," he said selecting a particular angle on the screen. The lines and numbers on the side of the image kept moving as the recording of my heartbeat grew then deflated. He moved his fingers in a straight line and the three-dimensional image split into two halves. With another tap, he zoomed in on a selected part of the image causing the readings on the side to turn red and flash a warning of an abnormality.

"What does that mean?" Andrew questioned leaning closer to the screen.

Charles stared at the picture and sat back in the swivel chair. "That's her congenital heart defect," he said looking up at Andrew. It was a condition the two had hypothesized I had over the years as the medical field developed. In that moment, their assumptions were proven true. "Beths you've been taking the Digoxin and increased your cardio correct?"

"Yes."

"Good. That's good, Bethany." Charles said encouragingly.

"Is there anything more we can do?" Andrew asked Charles, not satisfied with anything less than complete certainty that everything was being done.

"Since she wasn't diagnosed until fairly recently, tracking changes since the introduction of the medication will tell us if something as invasive as surgery should be considered."

"Surgery," Andrew asked anxiously.

"The size of the hole in the wall of the heart and its placement are not disturbing the heart's overall function. But surgery is not out of the question. I'll have to see a copy of the cardiologist's notes starting at her initial diagnosis up until her last appointment in order to monitor the treatment and see if it's making any headway. We'll keep a close eye on it," Charles said swiping the screen clean of the image of my heart.

Ryan was leaning up against the nurses' station talking to Kate when the elevator doors opened and Charles, Andrew and I stepped out. My brother turned his head carelessly and took a double take, surprised to see me walking towards him.

"This is not good," I said so only Charles and Andrew could hear.

"Bethany?" Ryan said straightening up with a puzzled look on his face. "What are you doing here?"

"Hello Ryan," Charles said interceding for me. Quick on his feet he explained, "My brother-in-law and I were just showing Bethany around the hospital. She has generously offered to help with the charity fundraiser."

"Bethany?" Kate said coming up behind Ryan in her scrubs. Kate looked at Charles and then at Andrew standing next to me. "Hi," she said letting a smile slip onto her face at the up close encounter with the archangel.

"Hello," Andrew politely responded.

"Ryan, Kate," Charles said courteously, "this is my brother-in-law, Andrew. Andrew, this is Ryan Taylor and his fiancée, Kate Connelly."

"We met earlier," my brother informed Charles but he and Andrew still shook hands.

Drew then greeted Kate with a polite nod. "A pleasure," he added and Kate grinned at his subtle chivalry. Ryan watched Andrew's behavior out of the corner of his eye as he asked me if I needed a ride home.

"My car is in the parking lot," I said remembering that Drew had followed behind the Bentley.

"Andrew," Charles started, "we should get going."

"Thank you for the *tour*," I said looking at Charles.

"I will see you in class," he grinned. I then turned towards Andrew who had reached into the back pocket of his jeans and handed me my car keys.

"Thank you," I said but could not hide my disappointment in leaving his company. He heard my discontent and matched it with his own, proving that the feeling was mutual.

"You had a great game last night," my brother complimented Drew of his quarterback appearance. "St. Anthony's next week, right?"

"Yes sir," Andrew nodded.

"We should get going," Charles said not wanting to push their luck.

"It was nice to meet you, Kate." Drew smiled at my future sister-in-law and shook my brother's hand again, then turned to me. "I'll see you soon," he said with searing eyes.

"Until next time," I sweetly quoted and he smiled knowingly. With that, Charles and Drew walked away, through the Emergency Room doors.

"Weird," Ryan speculated as he watched them reach the Bentley through the automatically sliding glass doors.

"Not weird… charming," Kate corrected.

"Not you too," Ryan complained.

"What? He's handsome," she giggled.

"Please," Ry said shaking his head as the two of them turned back to the nurses' station while I continued to watch as Charles and Andrew got in the car. "I'm handsome," I heard Ryan add after rethinking what his fiancé had just said.

"Yes you are," she laughed and kissed him lightly on the cheek. With Ryan's attention now on one of the flat screens in the waiting room reporting football standings, Kate whispered to me girlishly, "Sooo?"

"Sooo?" I grinned back at her.

"Do you have a thing for him?" Kate asked wide-eyed tilting her head towards the doors. My immediate blush gave away any chance I had at dodging the question. "Ah!" she squealed. Ryan looked over his shoulder at us but we acted like nothing happened. "Good choice, Beths," she said softly after my brother turned back around. "Andrew's got that mysterious thing going for him, don't you think?"

'If you only knew,' I thought to myself sarcastically.

Following Ryan back to our grandparents' I became aware that the love I had for the town was much deeper than its country ways. I had a bond with this place, a past. At the stoplight I closed my eyes, mentally tired from what the day had brought. My past and present, two worlds, were colliding. It explained why Andrew was the gentleman that he was. He was raised in a time when a man's word meant everything and etiquette wasn't compromised by social convention. His manners had stayed with him, having been instilled in him on the basis of morality. A smile crossed my face. Then my own flashes, unburdened by the anxiety that once plagued me, flew in front of my eyes.

There was a small, wooden, white Church, a courthouse with horses out front and a long dirt road which I knew now as a paved Main Street.

I opened my eyes, sitting in my car, on that once same dirt road which was now paved and had double yellow lines. The light turned green and 'the tank' continued towards our grandparents' house. As we rolled into the driveway, it occurred to me that I had fallen into a Romeo and Juliet 'might-have-gotten-it-right-if-they-had-a-second-chance' story. More images and memories flooded me, and with them the emotions that were so closely attached. I was slow to get out of my car, slow to walk up the porch steps and slow to answer Ryan when he asked if I was feeling alright. "I'm really tired. I think I'm going to go lay down," I answered as I climbed the two flights of stairs. With my head finding my pillow, Drew's face, etched in my mind, was the last thing I saw before I drifted off to sleep.

Sunday, September 20th

'Buzz, buzz,' I heard the annoying vibration coming from my nightstand. The morning light shone in my eyes as I grabbed the dancing phone and answered it groggily, "Hello?"

"I just saw Kate and she told me that she saw you and Andrew at the hospital yesterday, TOGETHER! Tell me everything!" Olivia squeaked over the phone.

"Um..." I said sitting up in bed rubbing the mascara from the corner of my eye.

"Did he say anything about why he kissed you after the game? How long did you talk for? Did he kiss you again?" she asked rapidly. "Beths, are you there?" she said when I didn't answer.

"Ugh, yeah," I said looking around my room. I had slept through the rest of the afternoon into the morning.

"I'm going to stop by before work. I'll be there in a minute," she said eagerly before hanging up. I put the phone back on the nightstand and checked the clock. I had slept through my morning run due to the exhaustion from the mental marathon I had run yesterday and decided that I would go out later after Church. Tossing the covers to the side, I made my way sleepily down the stairs to the bathroom to get ready for Mass.

I snipped off the tags of the dress I was wearing and stared into the mirror, leaning up against the armoire to steady myself. I was still witnessing the sporadic flashes of an older time and as another few left me, I looked down at the wooden floor under my bare feet. My imagination was not creative enough for this; that much I knew. As my rational mind tried to disprove what had come to light, my soul stood firm.

With one hand on my dresser, I put my country boots on one foot at a time. My hand lost its hold and slid along the top of the furniture with a piece of paper underneath it. The message was written in my grandmother's handwriting.

Beths,

Found these on the porch...

Next to it were beautiful, fresh peonies tied with a brown string. I picked up the bouquet and breathed in the floral aroma. There was a small brown envelope stuck between the stems. My hands shook slightly as I opened it. In Andrew's perfect penmanship it simply read my name. I smiled and twisted the brown string that held them together.

Liv's feet pitter-pattered as she sprinted up the stairs. When she got to the top she stopped and said, "Um..." pointing to the flowers I was holding.

"Um..." I said pointing at Bobby's letterman jacket which she was wearing. We both beamed. "You first," I said striding towards my bed.

"Okay!" Liv wasted no time as she sat down beside me. "So, Friday after the game Bobby and I went out with everyone. We got something to eat at the diner and Christina was there and you should have seen the look on her face when I walked in with him! Anyway, Bobby and I talked the whole time and when he dropped me off he kissed me," she swooned. "So, it's official and everyone in town knows that WE are a couple!" Liv said flopping back onto the bed. "After work yesterday, he came to pick me up. We hung out but couldn't go to the park like we wanted because it rained so hard. Then we watched a movie at my house and when he went to leave, he left his jacket which I think suits me," she said popping its collar and giggling.

"Liv, I am so happy for you!"

"Thanks," she said blissfully. "Okay, your turn," she adjusting herself so that I had her full attention.

"Yeah," I started as I put the bouquet and note down next to me. I hesitated. What I was about to tell her was a lot... I hadn't even fully comprehended it myself. I was scared she would think I was crazy. If the roles were reversed, I would think she needed her head examined. But, I decided that if Olivia was the friend I thought she was, I'd rather her think that I was crazy then wonder what I was holding back. I took a deep breath...

"Bethany, you've lost it," Liv said putting her hands up when I finished, "like you're a hundred percent off your rocker.

You actually expect me to believe this?" she asked looking insulted. I was hurt even though I understood her reaction.

"I…" I fumbled.

"Maybe you dreamt this," she offered as she stood up but I knew that I was telling her the truth – no fabrications, nothing but the facts. I handed her the note.

"This could be from Jackson… or from any guy in town," she said passing it back to me.

"It's not," I promised. I knew it was Andrew's writing. Plus, Jackson and I didn't have that type of relationship – he liked Olivia – but I couldn't say that.

"Bethany," Olivia groaned when I began to pace back and forth, rubbing my collarbone anxiously.

"You don't believe me?" I finally asked.

"I just think you've been under a lot of stress lately and that your imagination is getting the best of you… I mean it could be worse," she said flipping her hair over her shoulder. "You could be hallucinating about Oompa-Loompas or something."

"Oompa-Loompas," I asked putting my hands out at the outrageousness of her comparison. "Really Liv," I said covering my face with my hands and laid back down across my bed.

"I don't know! All I'm saying is that you probably should take it easy for a while. I mean if the heart thing is true…" she trailed. Reaching into my nightstand drawer, I pulled out the orange medication vial she had the pharmacist fill for me the first day we met. "That's what these are for," I said handing it to her.

"Oh," she said looking worried, "so you do have a heart condition?"

"Yes," I said softly.

"Does Ryan know?"

"No."

"What about your grandparents?"

"No."

"You didn't die Beths! See this is exactly what I'm talking about," Liv stated rolling her eyes.

"I know it sounds crazy," I whined covering my face with my pillow.

"Just do me a favor. Make sure you take the medicine. I don't need you croaking on me." She jabbed my side and I moved the pillow away.

"Thanks Liv," I laughed and lent up on my elbows adding, "And thanks for this."

"For what?" she asked.

"For being my dear diary, talking mirror, best friend..."

"Um, let's see. That would make you mine... We're sort of like each other's fairy godmother," she smiled. Trying to make light of the situation she shrugged, "Besides, life was boring before you got here." I grinned and happened to look next to me at the beautiful peonies. I was certain my life would no longer be boring – time would make sure of that.

—

Liv left for work shortly after our talk, still wearing Bobby's letterman jacket which she wasn't going to willingly take off. It made me smile that she had a Romeo. Distracted by the morning, I took my time doing my makeup, but was running late for Church, still finishing my hair.

Ryan, Gramps and Grams were waiting for me patiently in 'the tank' when I came out of the house. "Finally," Ryan said as he turned the key in the ignition.

"Sorry," I apologized fastening the end of my elaborate, lose, country inspired braid in the truck's side rearview mirror.

"I love your outfit, dear," Grams said from the back seat as I buckled the passenger seat belt.

"Who's D & G?" my grandfather asked behind me.

"Designers," Ryan smirked over at me, impressed with himself.

"Dolce and Gabbana," I expanded.

"Doll Chee and Gabanzo," Gramps tried to replicate and nodded his head looking out the window thinking he had said it correctly. I shook my head and Ryan smiled at the road. I loved my family and moments like this; and just like that, another piece of me fell into place.

—

Around noon, after brunch, I made my way up to my room to change into my running clothes. Ryan came up the stairs while I tied my sneakers. I could hear Chris and Gregg out in the backyard throwing a football around. They had made it a point to mention that I had missed yesterday's football 'date' and they expected an apology. I offered them freshly baked cookies and my transgression was forgiven.

"Hey," I said putting my earphones next to my phone so I wouldn't forget them. When he didn't answer, I looked up. He was acting strange.

"So..." he started. I grinned at his lack of grace in situations that made him uncomfortable, such as this. "How ya doing?"

"I'm doing well, thanks," I smirked.

"Good. That's good," he crossed his arms in front of him.

"Is everything okay, Ryan?" I tried helping him.

"Yeah, I just wanted to talk to you about something," he said collecting his thoughts.

"Shoot," I encouraged.

"Okay," my brother said leaning up against one of the floor to ceiling posts. "I wanted to know if you and that Wicks kid were like, you know, hanging out or whatever?"

"Like going out?" I asked.

"Yeah... Seeing you at the hospital yesterday with him and his brother-in-law... the flowers on the front porch," Ryan motioned to the bouquet I had put in a mason jar from the kitchen.

"No," I answered honestly. My 'relationship' with Andrew was much more twisted or, according to Liv, 'a possible figment of my imagination'. I wasn't lying by saying that Drew and I were not dating.

"Oh okay. I was just wondering," he added paternally. I was lucky to have him as my older brother. He always watched out for me and I wanted him to know that I appreciated it, even if he wasn't the best when it came to talking about it.

I walked over to him and gave him a hug, "Thanks Ry."

Putting his arms around me, he hugged me back and said, "Of course Beths. Now, if he does ask you out…"

"Ryan," I laughed.

Monday, September 21st

I had stayed up the night before to finish my English paper which kept my mind preoccupied. Thanks to Charles, Abby and Drew, I now knew why I had such difficulty following the writing guidelines. It made perfect sense and was pretty comedic.

Admittedly, I had never wanted to go to school as much as I wanted to today and physics class could not come fast enough.

As I walked down the locker lined hallway, I saw Drew waiting outside the classroom with his hands in his pockets. A fellow student stopped to congratulate him on his performance in Friday night's game and I watched, closing from a distance. Drew's demeanor – collected, confident and kind wasn't something only I took notice of. Other girls did too; they paraded by, flirting as best they could. He politely smiled but did not fuel their advances.

When I was a few feet away, Drew turned his head and looked in my direction. Seeing me, a boyish grin grew on his face. "Good morning," he said standing tall and strong.

"Morning," I replied with a shy smile.

"My name is Andrew Wicks," he said putting out his hand facing upward.

I laughed nervously and asked, "What are you doing?" as I placed my hand in his. It was an old kind of handshake between a man and a woman and as our hands touched, sparks didn't fly, but memories did.

Fleetingly, a whirlwind of colors and promises swirled in front of my eyes.

Coming out of the exchange, I felt his lips kiss the top of my hand as we refocused on each other. "I'm courting you, Miss Taylor." Drew winked and walked into the classroom leaving me breathless in the doorway as he took his seat in the back right corner of the room.

"Hey Beths," Jackson called as I haphazardly tried to find my way to my seat.

"Hey Jackson," I said stopping by his desk. "Great game Friday," I added as the butterflies settled.

"Thanks. I saw you with your brother. How was your first small-town football game experience?" the Captain asked.

"I'll never forget it," I laughed. It was true – I would not forget the game or the experience, especially the part after the game where Drew kissed me on the fifty yard line. With a growing confidence I said to Jackson, "I'll talk to you later."

"Sure thing," he said opening up his textbook. I then walked right over to Andrew and when I got to his desk he looked up, surprised.

I put out my hand for him to take and nodded saying, "Bethany Taylor," playing along with his 'I'm courting you' comment. He stood and took my hand in his.

Again there was a connection between us but this time I narrowed in on the potent emotions the weekend had brought. They were feelings of excitement, intrigue, happiness... an echo of our time years ago. The feelings lingered after our hands left one another's. They confirmed that even as he and I were meeting for the first time, a second time, love never fails.

"It's a pleasure to meet you," I said enticingly.

"The pleasure is mine, Beths," Drew eyes melted into mine.

"And thank you for my flowers," I smiled and tilted my head in sincerity. "They're beautiful."

Andrew kissed the side of my head and whispered in my ear, "A small token of my affection." As we leaned back from one another, our smiles aligned.

The classroom door closed and he and I both looked towards the front. Abby had walked into the room and as the rest of the class turned in their seats, she saw Drew and I standing together in the back. The euphoria on her face was easily visible, humoring to Drew and I as I found my seat.

Abby handed out papers, placing them upside down on everyone's desk. "Since, most of you didn't do as well as I know you can on the last quiz," she started, "this quiz will hopefully allow you to redeem yourselves." When she placed my quiz on my desk she didn't express any special treatment towards me; it was as if Saturday and its revelation had never occurred. I knew this was a show but a necessary one. "Okay," Abby said after she handed out the last paper, "you may begin."

I flipped over my quiz and was caught off guard by the questions waiting for me. These problems were complex and beyond any high school curriculum. I looked up and found Abby watching me with a devilish smirk on her face. I looked back down at the paper and reread each quantum physics question. I shook my head and smiled before picking up my pencil. Accepting the friendly challenge, I dug into my personalized handout.

When the bell rang, the classroom had mostly emptied with only a few other students mulling over their standard physics quiz. I was content with the answers I had come to for mine but if I would have known about her scheme, I would have liked to use a calculator this time. She was still proctoring the last few students when I put my paper on her desk. Catching sight of one another we wordlessly enjoyed our lightheartedness.

"Abby's not taking it easy on you?" Charles asked when I passed in front of his desk before the start of biochemistry.

"No," I chuckled as a few students around me found their seats.

"Sorry about that. I saw her making your quiz last night," he grimaced jokingly.

"This might turn ugly," I teased leaving Charles laughing at his desk as I walked to my usual seat in front of Jackson and next to Drew. They were discussing football stuff when I put my things down.

"How'd you think you did on the physics quiz," Jackson asked looking up at my arrival.

"It was okay," I gave my opinion over my shoulder not wanting to interrupt the two guys. Judging by Andrew's slight grin, he too knew of Abby's 'specialty' quiz for me. Charles had walked up on the other side of Andrew handing him a playbook which made Drew turn his attention away from Jackson and I. A second or two passed before Jackson leaned over his desk. "So Bobby and Liv," is all he said and I understood.

"Yeah," I twisted around, verifying that I knew about her and Bobby being 'official'.

"You know," Jackson said changing the subject, unaware that Charles walked back to the front of the class leaving Andrew with unoccupied ears. "I could really have used some back up at the party after the game Friday. I don't like those things to begin with. You should come out next time."

"I don't really know if those kinds of things are something I would feel comfortable going too," I laughed truthfully. I had never been a partier; I didn't enjoy the atmosphere that came with them and this made sense to me now too. It wasn't that I was antisocial, rather, socially speaking, I was better acquainted with a realistic definition of a 'good time'.

"They're not that bad and it's not like I'd leave you standing alone. Think of it as an opportunity for you to work on being more observant," he grinned and added jokingly, "I mean it would also be a night Zach, Duke and the guys would probably never forget." Then two things happened simultaneously: Charles was bringing the class to order, calling for attention while the pencil Andrew had been holding snapped in his hands at Jackson's innocent words. Even though the more prominent of the two events had been Charles' request, I was always effortlessly aware of Andrew and his reaction did not escape me. I shook my head with a smile on my face and turned back around in my seat, trying not to burst out laughing.

I watched the clock in front of the room, patiently waiting for the exact moment the bell would ring so I could jet out of the classroom. I could not afford to have a single word exchanged without laughing uncontrollably at Andrew's pencil snapping. As I walked to my car I heard Andrew calling my name. I turned to see him jogging up behind me. "Hello," he said coming to a stop.

"Hi," I said running my fingers through my hair after the wind had tangled it. He watched as I pulled it over my shoulder and curled the ends, taming it.

"Would you like to go out sometime?" Andrew asked unswervingly and as dashing as ever.

"Like on a date?" my mind hiccupped.

"Yes," he smiled.

"I, ah, yes."

"Good, tonight then? I'll pick you up at seven," he asked stepping closer to me. With the distance between us lessening, I nodded trying to break through the sudden haze I felt. "Later then," he said running his thumb over my lower lip. Andrew stepped back and walked away looking over as he got into his black Camaro. I somehow unlocked my car, got in and closed the door, placed the key in the ignition but knew I wasn't capable of driving anywhere until my feet hit the ground… figuratively. I watched his car pull out and followed it with my eyes as far I could see until it was out of sight. I jumped, startled when I heard someone knocking on the passenger window. I hit the unlock button and Olivia got in with her mouth wide open. "WHAT was that?" she asked moving her hands in front of her in no particular direction.

"What?" I asked trying to ground myself.

"I just saw Andrew Wicks run up to you and then he did that…that thing when he leaned in, did that lip thing," she paused half-swooning herself. "What did he say!"

"He asked me out… tonight," I said staring down at the Corvette's insignia on the steering wheel.

"What?" Olivia shrieked.

"Yeah…"

"Are you nervous?" she asked turning so that her left side was against the back of the passenger seat.

"Yeah," I replied again.

"Feel like you're going to throw up?"

"Yeah," I began to giggle.

"Want me to come over and help you get ready?" she continued excitedly.

"Please," I said breaking out of my mindless stare. Then I turned the key in the ignition and she clapped her hands with that best friend exuberance.

—

I had run up the stairs after I had taken a long, feminizing shower. Olivia was doing her homework waiting for me. She already picked out three possible outfits for me to choose from, including accessories for each option. After trying on all three, we had both agreed upon the simple, yet classic, little black dress.

Olivia did my hair in large, loose curls as I gave myself a French manicure/pedicure during which she talked about today's gossip at Ellsworth High including the news about her and Bobby.

"How do I look?" I asked as I put in the last elegant earring that she said was the 'finishing touch'. It was getting darker outside; a reminder that fall and its shorter days were coming.

"Wow," she said shaking her head. "And that is why you are the supermodel."

"You like it?" I asked taking a look in the full length mirror. I had to admit, Liv did good work.

"Yes. I love it and I'm sure he will too," she grinned back at me in the reflection. A car door closed out front and Olivia ran to the window to see who it was. "White Mustang, white Mustang!" she eagerly announced. I felt my heartbeat accelerate and my breathing picked up. The door bell rang and we both looked at one other. Then there were footsteps on the flight below and Grams called up the attic stairs sounding pleasantly surprised, "Bethany, Andrew Wicks is here."

"Go!" Olivia said pushing me towards the stairs. When we reached the last flight I stopped and adjusted my dress, straightened my shoulders and took a deep breath. Liv handed me my clutch. We could hear Andrew and my grandmother talking. "Ready?" Liv whispered and I nodded.

As I took those first few steps, I could see Andrew slowly coming into my view. I saw his polished black shoes, then his black pants, belt, up to his white, crisp shirt, black tie and black jacket. His broad shoulders, framed with strength, stood wide while his hands were clasped behind his back; he was truly a sight to be seen. Drew's eyes were focused on me as I came into his view. I only hoped I looked half as good to him as he looked to me. His lips moved faintly when I reached the last step. I turned to see Grams grin as she put the dish towel she was holding over her shoulder. "Have a good time."

"Thanks Grams," I answered shyly.

"I'll have her home by eleven as promised, Mrs. Taylor," Andrew said to Grams, but didn't look away from me.

"I'm sure you will, dear," she said appreciatively.

Looking back over my shoulder, I saw Liv leaning on the banister. "Good evening, Olivia," Andrew said catching her off guard as he acknowledged her presence, and at the fact that he knew her name.

"Hi," she said embarrassed, "Ugh, have fun."

"Thank you," he smiled before turning to get the door for me. I looked back at my best friend and she mouthed, 'OH MY GOSH,' to me before I stepped onto the lit porch. Andrew closed the door behind us but paused, looking to his right. "Coach Taylor, thank you again, sir."

"Just have her home by eleven, Wicks," Gramps nodded. I smiled at him and he smirked back at me before returning to his paper.

Drew and I walked side-by-side to the white Mustang, he opened the passenger door for me and I slid inside. My heart raced as I fastened my seatbelt and he got in on the driver's side, starting the car. As we pulled out of the driveway I could barely make out where the sun had set. The evening sky was intruding on the slight brighter shade of blue over the trees. It was an exceedingly clear night and with the city lights far away in every direction, the view of the stars wasn't interrupted.

I pressed my shoulders back against the cradling sports car seats and turned my head slowly to the man sitting next to me. I steadied myself for the butterflies that would follow but I was helpless when I caught him glancing over at me. He said, "Hello," again but this time it was different.

"Hi," I whispered back, smitten. I didn't know the exact protocol for a date let alone one with a man who already knew everything about me. It was rather unfair that my memories were coming back gradually, but I knew with time the blanks would be filled in, including the details about Andrew. In the meantime, I didn't mind relearning them firsthand.

We sat in silence as we past the entrance to the driveway of the Estate. He continued down the road in the darkness, the headlights were the only source of light. Drew had his left hand on the steering wheel, right hand on the gear shift and sat relaxed, looking out the windshield. I shook my head as my own thoughts sabotaged me. 'I'm not even in his league…' I whined internally. Fretfully, I began to rub my collarbone. He noticed.

"Are you alright?" he asked. I nodded my head and forced a smile. "Convincing," he said sarcastically.

"I might be a little…" I started not wanting to own up to the fact that I was petrified by this whole date thing.

"Apprehensive?"

"Nervous," I admitted.

He turned his right hand over so that the back of his hand rested on the gear shift and his palm faced upward. "Go ahead," he welcomed, wanting me to see a memory. I slowly placed my hand in his. Our fingers laced…

The flashes were quick, sharp – bulleted. They were short and to the point, purposefully done for comedic relief.

Andrew knocked on my grandfather's office door early this morning before homeroom. He asked Gramps for permission to ask me on a date. The quarterback asking the coach about his granddaughter… Drew's nerves were radiated through him.

Next, in a situation of misfiled rage, Drew snapped a pencil in his hands after hearing that other guys in school would appreciate my company at a party. Anxiety pummeled him like a tackle from behind.

Then fear is what he felt jogging up to me in the parking lot before asking me out. What if he wasn't the man I remembered? Or what if he wasn't the man I wanted anymore? Fear…

But all of these paralyzing emotions lost their hold as he watched me walk down my grandparents' stairs and were replaced by a blissful, wide-eyed, hold-on-as-tight-as-you-can kind of feeling. My black heels showcased my long legs which met the hem of the flattering, simple, tight waisted, black dress I wore. But it was my faithful, emerald eyes meeting his that made him not want to blink.

"Are you still nervous?" he asked looking over at me with a reserved grin.

'No' I shook my head bashfully. His hand returned to the steering wheel needed for the curving road that passed underneath us.

There was an intimacy in him sharing those memories. Drew unguardedly showed me his worries and stresses in order to relieve mine; there were few things sweeter or kinder. Only adding to the beautiful moment, he looked over at me. With a heavenly sincerity he spoke, "By the way, you look absolutely stunning Bethany."

A breath escaped my lungs at the sheer elegance and charm. "Thank you," I blushed.

His eyes returned back to the road as he flipped the Mustang's high beams on, and the engine picked up as the car climbed a hill. "So," I breathed in, "where are we going?" When he didn't answer I guessed, "A restaurant?"

"No, but if you would prefer that…" he started, concerned.

"No. No, whatever you have planned is great. This is a first," the words slipped out.

"First?" Drew caught. "This is your first date?" he swiftly reworded his question. "Oh," he said sounding surprised. Somewhat mortified, I nodded my head. 'Was it bad to say that?'

'Had he expected me to be a pro?' 'Was I as big of a hermit as I labeled myself?' These were all questions I thought in the seconds of silence.

"Is that… a problem?" I asked.

"No," Drew said letting out a little laugh. My eyebrows rose at whatever humor he found in this.

"Why are you laughing?" I asked somewhat wounded by his reaction.

He stole a look at me and saw the hurt. "If I have offended you in any way, I do apologize. And before I put my foot in my mouth, would you do me a favor?"

"That depends," I answered folding my arms.

He smiled as he stared up the narrowing path and then requested politely, "Would you please close your eyes?" I couldn't deny his angelic face, deep, ocean eyes and the striking smile which lured the response he wanted to hear.

"Fine," I huffed, closing my eyes even though it was not necessary. I had no idea where this road led and it was so dark that I couldn't see beyond the headlights. "But you have to tell me why you laughed?" I countered.

"I merely assumed it wouldn't be… I don't know much about your life before you moved back to Ellsworth."

"You assumed that this wouldn't be my first date?" I inquired.

"Beths, a man would be a complete fool if he did not ask for an overture with you," Andrew spoke fluidly.

"Wow," escaped from my lips not having expected such a response.

Andrew drove a little farther and finally slowed to a stop. I heard the engine calm and his door open and close. Keeping my promise, I kept my eyes shut tightly. I felt safe with him even when everything else around me was a variable. I heard my door open and felt his hand on my elbow. He led me out of the car and stood close beside me as I clung to his masculine arm while he escorted me over the uneven earth.

"Is this the part when you kill me?" I asked kiddingly.

"Hardly," he laughed. I knew he was smiling and I was upset that I couldn't watch the expression cross his face. Drew's pace slowed. "Okay, you may open your eyes now." I didn't know what to expect but I opened them anyway.

An old barn which had been forgotten for some time overgrown with trees and foliage was illuminated by the Mustang's headlights. Drew walked forward and pulled open the huge wooden door with little effort. Inside, the light from little white string lights threw dim shadows over a rustic table for two. It was picturesque. Perfect. Taking a step or two into the barn, I was in awe. "It's not a restaurant but if you would like to go to one, I know a place close by…" he suggested.

"No," I said mesmerized by the setup. "This is amazing," I added meeting his timid eyes. I continued to look around the barn at the thousands of lights above not realizing that Andrew had gone back to the car to turn off the headlights and took a basket out of the trunk. "Drew," I said turning to find him setting the table for dinner. "You did all of this?" He grinned and shrugged as though it was nothing. "This is incredible," I said taking my seat.

"I'm glad you like it," he smiled sitting across from me. I shook my head still trying to grasp everything. "What," he asked interested to know what thoughts were running through my mind.

"I just never thought my first date would be anything remotely close to this," I girlishly beamed, captivated by it all.

"Well, what did you expect?" he asked playfully.

"To be honest, I guess I never really thought much about it."

"Well, this is my second first date and I never thought it would be like this either," he smiled placing a cloth napkin over his knee.

"Second, first date?" I asked.

"Yes," he said pouring our drinks into two fine crystal glasses. He took a sip before looking across the table at me. "A century or so apart, he smirked, "with the same girl."

I knew my face had turned a shade of pink as my fingertips straightened the utensils next to my plate. I wasn't sure how exactly I had gotten to this point – how I had gotten in this chair sitting across from him. I understood that today I woke up, went to school, he asked me out, it took hours to get ready, he picked me up and now, here we were in this enchanting barn with a picnic basket and he was smiling back at me in the glow of string lights. My eyelashes innocently fluttered as I looked away from him and down at the table; my hand finding my collarbone.

"You…" I swallowed then looked up at him. "No one?" I asked. In between our time together, a century's worth, there had been no one else? No other dates?

"No one," he said as though it wasn't daunting.

"But," I started, "I was gone. It would have been okay… I would have wanted you to be happy, even if it was with someone else."

"No one," he repeated with softening eyes.

"Andrew?"

"Are you hungry," he asked changing the subject; I nodded in response.

He had filled each of our plates with an array of savory foods. The serving ware of fine china and crystal was a far cry from paper plates and plastic utensils. I brought the cold glass to my lips, sipping slowly while meeting his eyes from across the table.

As our second, first date unfolded, a wicked smile crossed my face and his as well. Fate had been our enemy but tonight it was our friend.

We were quiet as we ate, stealing glances of each other in between bites, not saying a word, but having a complete conversation. Even though I had so many questions and felt there was so much that needed to be said, this wasn't the time or the place.

He took his last bite, wiped his mouth with his napkin and returned it to his knee. "So, the weather," he said sarcastically looking up at the starry, night sky through the holes in the old barn roof.

"Are you making fun of me Andrew Wicks," I asked giving him my not-so 'evil eye'.

"Perhaps," he chuckled.

"That's great," I said amused by his amusement. "On a more serious note, dinner was delicious. Thank you."

"You're welcome," the handsome man sitting across from me nodded. I was undeniably taken by him, his features, his mannerisms, his personality… everything about him appealed to me; even his flaws. He didn't know the power he had over me or how I could watch him all night long.

I ran my hand through my hair, pulling it over my shoulder and caught him watching me as I did so. "What?" I asked self-consciously.

"Nothing," he answered, leaning back in his chair with a pleasant smile on his lips. We wordlessly acknowledged the childish captivation we had for one another.

"So, the weather," I said taking a deep breath and looked up at the sky through the space left by the missing boards.

"The weather," Andrew reaffirmed tilting his head up. My eyes trailed back to him and my desire to be closer to Drew was undeniable. Ignoring the impulse to override my instincts, I stood up. He stood as well, the gentleman that he was, and looked confused as he watched me place my napkin on the table and move my chair next to his. Seeing what I was doing, he smiled and turned his seat so that we were face-to-face. He waited until I sat back down before he found his seat again, grabbing it with his hand between his legs and sliding it under him.

Drew then pulled my chair closer to his so that my legs were in between his. Like he had taken pleasure in my longing to be near to him, I enjoyed his display of strength.

In our rearranging of seats, the bottom of his tie had flipped over. Intuitively, I reached out and turned it back to the way it should lay, touching it lightly to his chest. He looked down at my hand and then at me with a raw happiness in his eyes at the simplest gesture of caring for him.

I looked down at the dirt barn floor attempting to hide my nervousness. Andrew's shoes were so perfectly polished that I could see the reflection of the string lights above us. "Don't look away," he said as his hand ran into my hair, under my ear, lifting my chin up to his. His piercingly blue eyes seared into mine. I wanted to hold his hand but knew that flashes would be a side effect and taint the undemanding moment. So instead, I placed my hand on his extended forearm. Turning it over and resting it on my knee, I slowly traced his exposed wrist, playing with the invisible line right before his hand. I moved my forefinger and middle finger gently under the cuff of his sleeve and back out again. There was no pattern, no rush, just softly touching his skin. His eyes closed and his breathing slowed. I grinned to myself and daringly reached for his tie again, pulling it towards me. His eyes opened and Drew leaned in and put both of his hands on either side of my exposed legs, touching right above my knees and below the hem of my dress. He looked down and quickly took his hands away.

"My apologies," he repented. Dresses use to be longer, thicker; different than the one I was currently wearing. His awareness of coming off too forward at a simple, unconscious touch was both noble and adorable.

I moved his arms so that his hands were back where he had placed them. Andrew had done nothing wrong and there was no doubt in my mind that he would continue to be a gentleman; failsafe, I knew I was a lady.

My skin was soft in his strapping hands. "I've missed you," he whispered so low that I barely heard him. My shoulders caved and my heart was in my throat. "Don't," he said not wanting to upset me.

I would never be able to comprehend everything that he had gone through; our story had turned so cruel. I wanted no part in the hurt that was hellishly inflicted on him – I only wanted to be a blessing.

"You don't have to miss me anymore, Andrew. I'm right here," I said bringing my hands up to his face, running my fingertips along his jaw line. His lips parted slightly and he looked down, overcome by the miraculous truth. "Drew," I said fighting for his eyes. "I'm right here."

"I know. I know you're here. I'm just," he stammered.

"Happy to see me," I shrugged and grinned trying to ease the weight of reality.

"More than happy," he played along with a boyish smirk.

"Delighted?" I teased, touching the collar of his shirt, flirting or trying too.

"More than delighted."

"Umm," I said thinking of what else I could come up with.

"Taken… I am taken by you," he said as he ran his hand through my hair. "Taken by your smile, by your laugh, by how you look at me… and how you make me want to be a better man."

"Taken," I repeated finding its perfection.

"From the first moment," he avowed. Our lips lingered dangerously close, our eyes longingly pulling us to the other. Invitingly I brushed my nose against his and with that he closed the space between our lips until there was none.

In one quick motion Drew's arms wrapped around me as we stood. He took a few steps forward, leading me backwards knocking over my chair. I pulled his shirt under his jacket closer to me as he felt for the barn post behind us which he then carefully pushed me up against. Drew's hands moved along my waist up to the sides of my face, tangling into my locks with every mounting kiss another piece of me fell into place. We knew each other's ways; as the passion built I realized we were making up for lost time.

Finding each other again and again, we rediscovered one other. Drew pulled me in at the small of my back and I ran my nails up and down his neck, softly scratching with every draw. Our kissing softened and when our lips separated, we stood motionless. There was so much attraction, so much… but it was complimented by patience.

I leaned into his embrace and rested my head on his shoulder. I felt him nestle into the crease of my neck, smelling my mint shampoo, hugging me tighter in his strong, protective arms.

With a restoring breath, Drew kissed the top of my head and led me back to the table. He picked up my chair which had fallen over and waited as I sat back down. He took his seat and then pulled mine closer to his again, mirroring the way we had been sitting before our impulsive make out session.

Andrew and I talked about the weather. We talked about school and about classes. We were becoming reacquainted. He and I found humor in the struggle we shared with history and English and talked about football and about our lives now, in the present.

We laughed – a lot. Nothing was forced. Nothing was fake. Everything was wonderful.

"May I show you something?" he asked placing the empty dessert plate on the table. I nodded, taking the last bite of chocolate cake from my fork, slid it clean out of my mouth and placed it next to it.

Drew moved his napkin from his knee and stood up. I watched as he walked over and picked up an old wooden ladder and leaned it up against the loft above. He had climbed to the fifth prong before grinning back at me to follow which I did without hesitation in my high heels. Trustingly, Drew helped me onto the loft and walked towards the back, opening two large shutters, revealing a breathtaking view.

"Ellsworth," he said answering my question before I could ask it. The lights from the town were few and far between like the stars in the sky, making it appear as though the night sky and the town were one. A slight breeze blew and the sound of rustling leaves from the trees surrounding the barn applauded together in the darkness.

Andrew came up behind me and wrapped his arms around me. I could feel the warmth coming off of him and felt his lungs rise and release as we took in the view together. I wondered what was going through his mind, what he was thinking. Stealthily, I moved my hand keeping my intentions unknown until they touched. The emotions and images that flashed in front of my eyes told me that I had been successful.

Drew had a firm hold on a book at his side. His other hand tightened into a fist and then his fingers spread out repeatedly as he walked down the high school hallway following behind the principal. He was as composed as he could be externally, but internally his anxiety and skepticism had been escalating for days. Even though Drew had returned to the place he thought he'd never come back to, the town of Ellsworth – more specifically the Estate, it had taken him four days to get himself to this point.

Charles had started the ball rolling on Andrew's cover as a high school student. A few fake transcripts and a vague conversation with the administration, and Drew was enrolled as a twelfth grader. Charles had also taken care of getting the essentials as well – the cars, the clothes... As for getting things in order mentally and emotionally, that was another matter entirely. Scars from wounds of days gone by were ripped open when Drew returned. Any progress he had made over the years was washed away.

Since his return to the Estate, he slept very little and walked the corridors and rooms that had gone unchanged, much like the man who passed through them. Charles, Drew's loyal friend and constant companion, checked on him frequently. Drew had held himself together quite well over those four days and gladly immersed himself in work Charles left him on the office desk. Taking on the distraction, Drew re-outlined Ellsworth's hospital's strategic plan, evaluated their investments and suggested changes to the business portfolio. But as soon as Drew looked up from the papers, he was once again faced with reality. But yesterday it all caught up to him and came crashing down; Sunday.

It was the first time he left the grounds; Charles, Abby, Cole, Gracie and Drew went to early Mass. Knowing that Charles and Abigail were smart enough to anticipate his breakdown, he was grateful that they brought the children to the babysitter's, Claire Taylor, so they did not have to witness it.

The spectrum of emotions was still tight in his chest as he followed behind Mr. Donovan. However, Drew was prepared as best he could for either possibility: that the new girl in town was in fact 'his Bethany' or that I was just a girl fortunate to resemble me. Regardless, Andrew was steps away from finding out for himself.

Mr. Donovan knocked on Abby's classroom door and they both heard her answer, "Yes." The principal turned the doorknob and even though Abby had advised Drew that I sat towards the middle of the classroom, his eyes needed no instruction. He found me, instantly.

At the sight of me, his heart raced and his eyes felt starved seeing me now after all of this time. I was wearing a short, white, summer dress which was cinched at my waist by a brown braided belt. The neckline cut straight across my shoulders, showcasing my collarbone and sun kissed skin. My complexion was natural, rosy from the summer months and my long, dark brown hair was soft and feminine in big, loose curls. My legs were crossed under the desk, long and lean, finished with brown country boots. He saw a flicker of the emerald green of my eyes which were focused on Abby. Drew thought to himself how his memory had somehow failed to capture my beauty to its full capacity. Without even knowing, I stopped him in his tracks.

He, Charles and Abigail had decided that they would take no action until after Drew made his own determination and spoke about it. Having given his word to Charles, Andrew focused on getting to his desk in the back right side of the room when he heard Mr. Donovan say, "Take a seat." Walking through the classroom door Drew exchanged a glance with his sister – one that confirmed to her that Drew knew it was me; he didn't need any more proof. 'It's her' echoed in his mind as the weight of this understanding began to sink in.

He had prepared himself for both outcomes. If he had any doubt that it wasn't me, he would be on the next flight out of Ellsworth and back to Colorado. But if it was me, the very small percentage that it was, he would under no circumstances leave town.

Drew walked down the row watching me out of the corner of his eye. He noticed that I blinked wildly looking down at the pencil in my hands as he passed; confused, perhaps. But he knew the reaction was promising and that's all he needed. His heart raced with unmatched exhilaration.

A few desks behind mine by the window, Drew sat down and literally lost the breath in his lungs when he saw my right hand reach my collarbone and trace it unconsciously. It was a habit of mine, one that he used to tease me about. A grin washed over his lips and he sat fascinated, watching me, feeling things that he hadn't in such a long time.

As the period ticked by Andrew watched me undisturbed and complexly consumed. He would smile to himself as he observed me taking notes, holding the pencil the way I did, writing in an elegant fluidity. He did not need to see my penmanship to know what it looked like. He had it memorized from old handwritten letters we had exchanged with one another. They were some of his most cherished possessions and he read and reread them over the years. The lacy cursive strokes I was taking now were the same as the ones on a folded letter he had carried with him in his wallet even until today. Taking his wallet out of his back pants' pocket, Drew slid the cream colored folded paper out. It had turned darker over time, but still read 'Drew' in black ink. He turned it over, slid his finger under the blue wax wafer which had once sealed it. The letter was neither the longest nor the shortest we had exchanged but it had been the last.

As he looked up, it was amazing for him to see me in this time having known me in another. My habits and mannerisms were not of this era and yet no one around me noticed. He, however, along with Charles and Abigail picked up on the subtle elegances immediately. It was like a breath of fresh air for them, a safe place to land, home.

I pulled my hair over my left shoulder and mindlessly twirled a strand before letting it bounce with the rest of the curls. It drove him crazy... that along with my bare skin, the curvature of my bronzed shoulder, my toned leg muscles showing below the hem of my dress... But it was the longing to hear my voice, to speak with me, that was making him feel like a caged animal. He put the note back in his wallet and caught Abby's eye a time or two. He could imagine what she was thinking. 'Patience, Andrew,' 'Don't scare her,' and 'You're not the only one who wants to talk to her,' were all things that brought a brotherly laugh out of him.

He looked back over at where I sat and noticed something strange; I was surrounded by letterman jackets. A primitive reaction made him extremely territorial and the realization that times had vastly changed in the realm of courting caused heat to rise in him. My sweet disposition was something he had treasured protecting and now inflicted with a form of jealousy Drew sensibly realized that others would bid for my affection. And he didn't like it.

When the bell finally rang, Drew watched me as the rest of the students filed out of the classroom. He stood up when Abby walked towards him, her heels loud and evenly spaced. He could not bring himself to look away from me and saw me get to my feet and put my bag over my shoulder. 'You shouldn't have to carry those,' he thought to himself wanting to hold my books for me, but knew he couldn't propose the offer.

"Are you alright?" Abigail asked in a low voice as she came to a stop in front of him with her back to me.

"Yes," he answered looking at his sister momentarily but was not quite sure that he was. When he looked back over at where

I was, I was looking at him and our eyes locked. For the first time in over a century, he and I made eye contact. For the first time in a long time he wasn't thinking about himself. And for the first time in forever, he knew the better half of him was standing only a few feet away. Witnessing the exchange and knowing that her brother wanted to go after me Abby reminded him, "Andrew, don't." Drew watched as I broke away unsure and nervous.

"Abby, it's her," he said watching as I headed for the door.

"Yes," her breath caught as she held back tears from the rawness in Andrew's words. "It is." There was awe and a hope in him, there was life.

"She remembers," he said sounding more like a fact then like the theory her and her husband had. Before Abigail could answer the two looked up at the commotion of Charles and me colliding by the door.

"Pardon me," his brother-in-law said as he caught me, surprised by the scene he had walked in on. Andrew was certain that Charles had only anticipated finding him and Abby there after class. It had been part of the plan; to see what Andrew thought – if it was really me. "My apologies, Bethany," his friend said as we settled.

"It's alright," I blushed.

It was seeing Charles and me standing, talking with one another that made Andrew forget his restrictions. He moved passed Abigail and began to push the desks out of the way wanting nothing more than to be by my side. It was Charles' voice saying his name and his hand around Andrew's bicep that broke Drew's trance. He regained his composure only a few feet away from the woman whom he loved. His heart felt as though it might implode in his chest as he watched my right hand find its way to my collarbone again.

"Charles," he heard his own voice say in disbelief.

"I know," Charles whispered looking from him to his wife who was still standing in the back of the room.

Andrew heard his sister speak feebly, "Beth... Bethany, you should get to your next class." I looked away from Drew, nodded at her, turned to go, but stopped to look over my shoulder at him. He nodded his head at my hesitation, almost saying 'it's okay'. He saw a smile break over my lips, a reflex to his gesture. He felt like a part of him was reawakened. It was an innocent, beautiful exchange and he heard his brother-in-law, who was standing next to him let out a breath of air having witnessed the unbelievable moment.

There was a loud noise in the hall behind me which broke the trance I had on him and he watched as I left the room.

Abby walked to the door and closed it. Andrew slid into the closest desk and sunk his head into his hands. "Are you alright?" Charles asked placing his hand on his brother-in-law's shoulder. Nothing could have prepared Andrew for this. Nothing. "Drew," Charles said when he didn't answer. Andrew's eyes began to burn and fill but he would not let the tears fall.

He got up and turned away from Charles and Abby as his mind raced. Pacing, Drew walked along the front of the classroom, holding onto the chalkboard ledge knowing that he was breaking inside. His left knee hit the floor and his right hand clamped on the metal ledge as his right knee gave way too. Slowly, he sat back against the cinderblock wall. "Give it time. Give her time," Charles said, squatting down in front of him. Abby stood next to her husband with her hand over her mouth, tears falling down her cheeks.

"Charles," Drew croaked in bewilderment looking back at him. "It's her."

"I know," a smile washed over his friend's face.

"But how," Andrew began to almost laugh at the insanity.

"I haven't the slightest clue," Charles smirked.

"Why are you two laughing?" Abby all but stomped her foot as she continued to sob.

"Oh, Abigail," Drew said standing up and hugging his sister.

"Don't 'Abigail' me," she huffed into his chest and Drew handed her to her waiting husband's arms.

"You are convinced then," Charles said to Drew.

"Yes."

"You're staying," Abby asked as Charles offered her his handkerchief. Andrew nodded as he placed his hands in his pockets.

"Bethany Taylor, Bethany Taylor, please report to Coach Taylor's office. Bethany Taylor, Coach Taylor's office," the loud speaker rang out. Charles and Drew looked at each other as Andrew shook his head. Ecstasy continued to fill his body, a lightness taking over his being. I had always caused his calculated mind to go blank and I still had that effect.

"Now what," Abby looked up at Charles who deliberated.

"We wait. We give her time." That was the last thing Andrew wanted. "Time," Charles repeated letting Drew know that even though his balance was off, Charles had his best interest in mind. With a silent look, Andrew thanked him.

"Whatever she needs," he said looking over at the closed door. "Whatever she needs."

It wasn't the images ending that made my vision blurry; it was the tears that had filled my eyes from the memory I had just witnessed, felt and relived his second, first impression of me. I was overcome with his feelings, something that he could not fake in the connection we shared. "Don't cry," he said stepping in front of me drying my tears with his thumbs as they fell. "Beths," he whispered. I looked back at him – he had swept me off my feet not with his charm, his looks or the way he looked at me, but by his humble heart and relentless faith. "You know, you're even pretty when you cry," he tried to make me laugh. Shaking my head I stepped back to get a better look of the man in front of me.

"The hurt… the YEARS," I began to cry.

"*Time* creates wounds of regret and despair but you, you have taught me that love can heal." I placed my hand on his cheek and he turned his head into my palm, kissing it. He closed the space between us and I felt my eyes wanting to shut as his lips were about to touch mine. However, I moved my hand up to his lips. Pausing, he looked down at my steadied obstacle. With as much strength as I could afford, I stared at my fingertips and said quietly, "I don't kiss on the first date. Even though we just kind of did earlier," I finished with an enticing smile.

"Well," he leaned back. "I suppose I have no choice other than to ask you on a second date," he grinned appreciative of my principles. I blushed and he welcomed me into his awaiting arms, holding me as we looked back out over the small town on our second, first date.

Tuesday, September 22nd

Emergency practices were called for the football team which included morning, afternoon and evening sessions. The only emergency was that the quarterback was interested in the coach's granddaughter and Gramps denied it as ungracefully as any guilty paternal figure could. I loved that Gramps cared for me as much as he did. However, it did mean that today I would only get to see Andrew in class.

Liv found me at my locker before homeroom which gave me time to tell her about the date. She put aside her issue with the whole 'you died' and 'they haven't aged' thing momentarily in order to enjoy the date description. 'Utter perfection' is what she called it, from the string lights to the way I handled myself.

Walking down the hallway to homeroom I passed Charles, Abby and Drew. Abby spotted me first and grabbed her husband's arm excitedly before returning to her teacher-like demeanor. Smiling, Charles nodded slightly as I walked by and Andrew made me want to stop in my tracks with his ridiculously charming grin.

I acknowledge them all as I passed by pretending as though everything was normal, like Dr. and Mrs. Landon were just regular teachers and Drew was simply just another new student. The charade was necessary and I knew that but every ounce of me wanted to join them.

—

After the final bell rang, I found Olivia by my locker dressed in her cheerleading practice clothes. "Hey, what's up," I asked putting my books away except for my history textbook. I was unfortunately going to need that for homework.

"Want to go on an adventure?" she asked with sneakiness in her tone.

"What kind of an adventure," I laughed with narrowing eyes.

"An undercover one," she said with bright eyes. Closing my locker, I agreed and she happily locked her arm in mine leading me down the hallway.

"Where are we going," I asked when we turned down the hallway where my grandfather's office and the locker rooms were.

"You are walking me to practice, however we are taking an unchartered way," she smirked at me.

"Ugh," I sighed and looked up at the ceiling dramatically as she pulled me along.

"Oh, puh-lease," Liv shot back in a girlish gasp. "Did Magellan's first mate ask him where they were going? Umm, no!"

"I'm sorry, when did this 'adventure' grow into circumnavigating the globe?"

"That's not the point and you know it," she said whipping her head so that her ponytail flipped behind her and accidentally hit my face.

"Ouch," I said covering my eye with my free hand and laughed at her.

"Sorry," she apologized and then jokingly added, "That's an occupational hazard of being friends with a cheerleader."

"Yeah, yeah," I laughed. "Lead the way, Magellan," I continued my sarcastic jest. Liv stopped at the boys' locker room, cracked open the door and then proceeded to walk inside. I had no choice but to follow her.

"That's his locker," she said touching the ends of the letterman jacket that was hung inside. Sure enough above it read 'Thompson'.

"Olivia Thompson," she swooned.

"Liv, this is the 'adventure'?" She bounced her head up and down.

"Yes," she smiled and focused back on his locker. I looked around at the other lockers and read the names above them stopping at 'Wicks'. Inside were the clothes he had worn today hung neatly and on the shelf above the hooks were a few books and his car keys. I stood there reading the label with his last name on it over and over again. "Bethany Wicks, you're just as pathetic as I am," Olivia chimed in, reading my mind. I shook my head and smiled at her – I was caught. Armed with another comment, I started to speak but was interrupted by the doors of the locker room opening. Liv's eyes widened and we both looked for an escape.

We found temporary refuge standing on a toilet bowl in the locker room bathroom. The football team had unexpectedly come back in to go over the mechanics of a new play on the whiteboard. I could hear my grandfather bringing order to the team and through the slit in the door I saw Jackson, Zach and Dr. Landon watching with the rest of the guys around them as the play was talked through. "Ew, ew, ew," Liv whispered in a panic as she tried not to touch anything she didn't have too.

"Shh," I whispered back warningly.

"This is by far the most disgusting," she began saying so low only I could hear it. She stopped talking when the stall next to us shook as a player slammed the door shut and proceeded to use the facility. Liv looked up at the ceiling and closed her eyes as though she was in severe agony. "I'm going to throw up. I'm going to throw up," Liv said bringing her fist to her mouth trying to convince herself not too.

"Don't you dare," I glared at her pointing my finger. 'It will be over soon,' I mouthed and then the player flushed his toilet.

I was trying to move so that I could see more people through the tiny slit, in particular, Andrew – just one glance. I finally found him amongst his teammates. He was sitting by Jackson and Duke focusing on the board blocked from my view. Dressed in his practice uniform, I temporarily forgot that I was standing on a dirty toilet in a boy's locker room. A couple of times Jackson and Andrew leaned closer to one another discussing the play, while Gramps broke it down player by player.

My grandfather and Charles, 'Coach' Landon, had left the locker room for a few minutes. The talking switched from football to other topics like reports that were due soon, girls and plans for the weekend. From what I could make out through the noise, a couple of guys were going to a party at a nearby college Saturday night, Duke had failed his math test and Cunningham was still grounded by his parents for his shenanigans two weekends ago. Liv and I both perked up when we heard the mentioning of my name.

"Bethany Taylor," one of the deeper voices said and a few others joined in on the conversation, making it easier to follow.

"I could stare at her *all* day," another guy's voice added.

"I would do anything to get a date with that girl," I heard from a more familiar voice, belonging to Clifton who I had a few classes with. Liv hit my arm and grinned at me at the gossip we were overhearing. I rolled my eyes and looked back through the slit unable to see Andrew's reaction blocked by another player.

"Jackson, you seem to be best buds with her. Think you could help a guy out; put in a good word for me?"

"No way," Jackson shook his head.

"Oh come on man. We're teammates – help a brother out."

"Leave Turner alone," Duke said. "He's working his own angle to get her." At this Jackson threw a towel at Duke and rolled his eyes.

"We're just friends," he said clearly.

"What about you, Wicks?" Duke questioned.

"What about me?" Andrew asked and the player who had been blocking my view of him thankfully moved so that I could see Drew again. He looked up from the floor leaning forward with his forearms resting on his knees. He didn't like that I had become locker room conversation and it bothered him but he couldn't say anything without bringing attention to his invested interest in me.

"What do you think about Bethany Taylor?"

"She's beautiful."

"See," Duke said then looked back at Jackson and continued, "What's wrong with you, Turner? Why haven't you tried to make a move yet?"

"Dude, she's not my type," Jackson said looking at Andrew out of the corner of his eye. Had Andrew told Jackson about our date? They were friends… or had Jackson caught on to something Andrew might have said? The teenage girl in me was freaking out.

"So you are saying that perfect isn't your type?" Clifton asked not understanding Jackson's excuse.

"No, I just have my eye on someone else," Jackson half-whispered before adjusting his pads.

"Who?" Duke asked in a high pitched voice.

"Alright, let's see what the play looks like," I heard my grandfather say as he walked back into the locker room with Charles. The doors to the field were pushed open as the noise of cleats marched back out and dissipated as the doors shut again.

"OH THANK GOD," Liv said throwing open the stall door and with her feet safely back on the floor, she rested her hands on her knees and breathed deeply.

"Yeah," I said following her out of the stall and flipped the hair out of my face, not touching anything until I scrubbed my hands with bleach. Feeling as though we were being watched, we glanced at one another and then slowly looked around. My grandfather, holding a clipboard, was standing next to Charles who had his hands on his hips.

"Hi Coach," Liv said to my grandfather, standing up as if nothing was wrong.

"Hello Olivia, Bethany," he smirked and then asked good-humoredly, "Did you two get lost?"

"Very," I said beginning to laugh at the awkward scene that had unfolded.

"It was my fault. It was supposed to be an adventure and I was Magellan..." Olivia started. Charles looked down at the floor biting his tongue as he held back his own laughter.

"Come on Liv," I giggled taking her arm.

"On your way, girls," Gramps said nodding towards the door, cracking up as well.

—

Liv and I were still in hysterics hours later as we retold our locker room episode to Kate. We had picked her up from the hospital after her shift was over. The plan was to meet Ryan back at the house and go over possible floral arrangements for the wedding. Kate, Liv and I walked through the front door and I froze at the sight of my grandfather and mother sitting in the living room across from one another in the armchairs.

Having already witnessed my mother's wrath once before, Kate bravely stepped forward and put out her hand. "It's a pleasure to meet you Mrs. Taylor. I'm Kate Connelly, Ryan's fiancé and your future daughter-in-law."

Standing, my mother replied coldly, "It is Ms. Reid," and ignored Kate's generously outstretched hand. My grandfather simply shook his head and looked over at me and nodded towards the dining room table. Kate and Olivia started up the stairs, most likely out of sight but within earshot. There was a folder set on the table, two glasses of untouched water and a blank check. My grandfather sat in his normal chair at the head of the table, my mother sat at the other end and I sat in the middle. Once settled, my grandfather opened his mouth to speak. My mother cut him off. "Independent?" she asked irate. I said nothing. "Well, that's fine *Bethany*. I see how it is," she snapped.

"See how *what* is?" I asked just as angrily as she had sounded, turning my head to meet her eye-to-eye. I had met my limits with her; enough was enough. So much had happened in my life over the last month; things that I had no control over. But this, my mother and the imminent conversation, I could take control of and, by all means, I was going too.

"Brainwashed too, just like your brother?" she sneered in her rage giving her father-in-law an evil glare. For such a pretty woman she looked possessed with the attitude she had. Gramps, a solid, even-tempered man, refrained from giving her the pleasure of showing how he really felt about her.

"I am not 'brainwashed'," I responded. "And neither is Ryan."

"What else would you call wanting to live in this God-forsaken, redneck town?" she said lifting her hands from the table.

"I don't know," I retorted, "Maybe a home?" She started to laugh wickedly but I paid no attention to it.

My grandfather reached for the folder and opened it, moving things along. "Bethany, the paperwork was filed for your emancipation. However, your mother is now threatening to," he paused, "has now threatened to sue you…" I watched him as he continued disgusted, "claiming that you owe her living expenses and monetary compensation."

"You want money," I said looking back at her surprisingly not surprised.

"Compensation," she corrected.

"For… existing?" I added sarcastically. "Does that include rent for the nine months you were pregnant with me too?" My grandfather snorted at how I was playing this.

My mother eyed him momentarily and then continued in her demeaning and callous ways, "Don't be ridiculous. The… my penthouse," she said pulling out a pen from her couture purse and placed it on the blank check. Although I could feel my hands shaking, my gut was strong and set. Not loosing an inch of ground that I had gained against her, I pushed forward confident.

"Gramps could you please read the name on the penthouse billing address?" I asked.

He flipped through some documents and said, "Mr. Jonathan R. Taylor." He looked up and a small smirk broke across his face. Having to care for myself for the past two years included having to complete paperwork and forms for a variety of things. I had learned a thing or two. I also sorted the mail making sure that there was no trace of my attending Columbia for my mother to come across. Sadly, I was sure she wouldn't care enough even if it were staring her in the face. However, every time I came across a piece of postage with my father's name on it, it stuck out because it brought a smile to my face.

"And could you tell me the date the lease was signed and paid for in full?" I bulldozed.

"Almost sixteen years ago," Gramps said reading off the agreement, "by Mr. Jonathan R. Taylor," he finished with a sound of relief in his tone.

"In case you didn't catch that Ms. Reid, the penthouse is in dad's name," I said reiterating what Gramps had read. Taking the pen I wrote out the check and handed it to her. "This should be enough for your plane ticket back to New York," I said standing with my hands firmly on the table. "Come at me again, and you'll be hearing from my attorney." I warned as I walked out of the room, flung open the screen door and stepped onto the porch. My hands fell to my sides after I quickly dried infuriated tears from my face. I turned around, intending to join Kate and Olivia upstairs when I noticed Ryan sitting on the rocking chair next to the open door. He had seen her rental car parked on the street, parked behind it and had listened to the heated discussion out of sight. Ryan was trying to remain calm, his shoulders bent forward. He, like I, was at a loss for words at our mother's behavior. The door swung open and my mother brushed passed me turning on her heals right before the steps. "You ungrateful little…" she started but my older brother stood with a broad chest and took a step forward. Noticing his presence she backed down and marched heatedly towards her rental car. I folded my arms as Ryan and I watched her pull away.

"Take a ride with me," Ryan said walking down the steps towards his truck. Without saying a word, I followed him.

—

Both windows were down and music was blaring as we drove on the highway away from Ellsworth. It was getting darker out as dusk gave in to the night.

"I'm sorry you had to go through that… again," my brother finally said when his hold on the steering wheel became more of a hold and less of a death grip. "She is a real piece of work."

"Thank you for bringing me to Ellsworth," I said for the first time. He looked sideways at me. I could see his face in the fleeting light of headlights passing in the opposite direction.

"I really didn't give you a choice, Beths," he smirked and looked back at the road.

"No, you didn't." I smiled but continued seriously, "I know that you regretted leaving me with her." My brother didn't say anything; these were words we had never spoken. "But I'm happy that you did... You met Kate, you got closer to Gramps and Grams, made great friends, you like your job… you built a good life for yourself. I'm really proud of you, Ry."

"It means a lot to me for you to say that, Beths." Catching my eye he continued, "What you just did back there with her and how you carry yourself… You're stronger than I give you credit for… and you have a good head on your shoulders. Dad would be so proud of the woman you are." I bit my lip hard hoping that my brother's heartfelt words wouldn't make me cry.

We were both silent for a few minutes until he put his directional on which prompted me to ask, "Where are we going?"

"Coverly. I meant to drop a contract off earlier," Ryan said reaching into the backseat with one hand feeling for something. Finding his clipboard, he put it on his lap. Stopped at a red light I saw the familiar Lumberyard logo that was on Ryan's shirt and jacket on the top of the order form. But in the glow I saw the heading read, 'Taylor Lumber'. My eyes widened as I looked back up at Ryan's t-shirt making sure that the symbol was a definite match. It took me a few seconds to speak.

"Ryan…" I started.

"Yeah," he said looking at the road and then down at the order again.

"Do you *own* the Lumberyard?" I asked.

"Ugh," he said glancing over at me as the light turned green.

I turned in the passenger seat fighting my seatbelt as my back leaned up against the passenger door so I could see him fully. He was caught. "Were you ever going to tell me?"

"Ugh…" he said looking back out the windshield as 'the tank' accelerated.

"Were you going to tell me?" I asked again.

"It's not that big of a deal," he tried to play it off.

"Does everyone else know?" I questioned.

"Yeah, of course," he said flipping a page of the clipboard and glanced down.

"Chris and Gregg," I asked knowing that they were involved at the Lumberyard.

"Chris works for me. Gregg has a job in finance but is a shareholder at the lumberyard and helps out on the weekends if we're busy," Ryan admitted.

"And you *own* it," I said as more of a statement than a question. When he didn't answer I went to my next question. "Ryan, on a scale of one to rich, where are you?" My brother tried to avoid answering so I cut in, "You're rich aren't you!"

"I'm comfortable," he said modestly, finding the address he was looking for then tossed the clipboard into the backseat.

"I can't believe you didn't tell me you owned the Lumberyard," I said turning forward almost laughing.

"Listen BETHANY REID, it's not that big of a deal," Ryan sarcastically commented.

"Not that big of a deal?" I asked.

"Not in comparison to you," he laughed and in an old western accent he joked, "Let's just hope Ellsworth is big enough for the both of us." I broke out laughing as he rested his right arm along the top of my seat. A cool, damp breeze whipped through the open windows.

Changing the subject entirely I asked, "So… are you excited for the wedding?" I couldn't wait for him to see his bride in the gorgeous gown she had chosen. The look on his face when she walked down the aisle was going to be priceless.

"Yeah," Ryan said halfheartedly and cracked his neck.

"What?" I said confused by his deflated reaction.

"I love Kate. I've known I was going to marry her the moment I met her," he smiled at the memory. "It's just been really busy the past few weeks at the Lumberyard. I've been stretching myself too thin," he said and I understood. Ryan had been MIA; working early, staying late… but then again the hours he had been putting in made more sense now that I knew he *owned* the Lumberyard. "I'm sorry if I haven't been around much," he finished looking over at me.

"It's okay," I said playing with the radio.

"I've been meaning to tell you something, since New York," he blurted. Ryan had been looking for an opportunity and he was choosing now to do it.

"Shoot," I responded and sat back.

He moved his hands along the steering wheel and unnecessarily looked in his rearview mirror. "'Operation Bethany' wasn't entirely my idea. I thought that your escape from the penthouse would be when you went to college," he admitted still unaware that I was technically two years into a degree. "But, the day before I showed up in the city to get you, I had a dream about dad."

"Dad," I repeated.

"Yeah," my brother said not voluntarily elaborating.

Intrigued, I asked, "Well what happened in the dream?" Until recently, I thought dreams were just dreams and nothing more but my opinion on them had completely changed. Case and point: Andrew.

Ryan slowed 'the tank' as we came to a flashing railway light. "I don't know," he said coming to a stop behind the lowered bar. I could hear the train whistle and the train's bright light was coming around a bend in the tracks a good mile away.

"Ry, you can't tell me you had a dream about dad and not expect me to ask you about it," I tilted my head.

"Fine," he said taking a deep breath and hesitated. "He looked good... happy I guess. It was weird."

"How was it weird?" I pushed.

"I was on the front porch steps, sitting, twirling a football in my hands. Dad came out of the house and sat down next to me like Gramps would. He was wearing weird clothes but it was definitely him. I mean from what I can remember of him... everything," Ryan grinned at the comforting recollection, "even those eyes of yours." The emerald greens were distinctively his and were a giveaway that I was his daughter. Ryan wavered before continuing, "It sounds strange but he even *smelled* like I remember. He told me it was time for you to come home to Ellsworth." Ryan smirked, looked over at me and then back at the first cars of the train rushing by. "Dad said that you needed me and that it was important." Ryan finished, "That's it."

The rest of the freight blew by and the train was a dark shadow headed away in all its glory. The bar lifted, the lights stopped and Ryan crossed the tracks. "I know it's weird," my brother said uncomfortably a few minutes later.

"No it's not," I answered looking straight out the window. It might not make sense to Ryan but he wasn't seeing all the pieces to the puzzle like I was. Streetlights and commercial businesses illuminated Main Street. Able to see his face clearly, I looked over at my brother and gratefully said, "I'm glad you listened."

"Me too," my brother smiled as we drove into the heart of Coverly.

Wednesday, September 23rd

I didn't sleep, not even for a minute. I was wired. The conversation I had with Ryan played and replayed in my mind all night and into the morning leaving me with an incredible urge to be at the Estate.

—

"Where are you going?" Ryan groggily asked as I passed him in the hallway.

"Running an errand before school," I whispered back not wanting to wake up our grandparents. Not coherent in his sleepy state, my brother nodded and continued to the bathroom to get ready for work while I headed downstairs.

—

Dressed, prepped and feeling alive, I didn't really know what I was doing. I just *had* to be at the Estate. The connection here to my father was undeniable. I saw that now. But also the connection I had to the people there – Abby, Charles and Drew… how could I not be there.

The sun was hinting at the horizon as I pulled onto the cobblestone path. Underneath the oak alley the Estate came into view. It was breathtaking – it was home. Emotionally triggered, a single flash hurried in front of my eyes.

I saw the house through older eyes, a memory, but it looked exactly the same.

As my eyes adjusted, I knew at that moment my parallels were no longer parallels, but one line.

I pulled up next to the black Bentley and climbed out of my car. I caught my reflection in the driver's side window and smiled at the maxi dress blowing in the breeze. It had a soft pattern, was feminine and complimented my figure. My hair swirled around my face as the wind picked up as I turned the corner and walked alongside the Estate.

I didn't stop walking until I reached the spot on the grounds where I had my very last memory from. I didn't know why I needed to be there; it should be the last place I should want to be but I suppose it made the most sense. I was facing a dark memory by overriding it with light.

I watched as the sun rose above the tree line in the distance. It was a beautiful morning; quiet and calm with a brilliant sky. I was surprised to find Charles standing ten feet from me when I turned. He must have seen me and waited, giving me the solitude I needed. When our eyes met I smiled and looked down at the grass between us feeling as though I had been caught with my hand in the cookie jar. "Good morning," he spoke recognizing the irony of where I stood, knowing its history. Charles crossed his arms behind him, true to his turn of the century manners.

Freely using his first name I grinned in a childlike way saying, "Hello Charles." His ageless eyes that had seen so much and held so much wisdom, smiled back at me. He looked as young and carefree as I remembered him, sending shivers down my spine. The excitement between us, the two of us, two friends being reunited after the dust had settled, fueled the moment. Playfully, I ran towards his waiting arms. He spun us twice, laughing. "Hi," I said almost giggling when we had calmed.

"Hello Beths."

"Miss me?" I joked.

"More than you know," Charles said before leading us to the Estate, arm-in-arm.

Charles and I were talking at the kitchen counter when we heard Abby coming down the stairs in the entryway. We both waited and watched as she paused at the bottom of the stairs and suspiciously looked down the hall. When she saw me her eyes narrowed, but her lips smiled. "I thought I heard you," she said gracefully fluttering towards us.

"Hi," I said hugging her and she didn't let go. Charles took a sip of his coffee momentarily blocking the smile on his face. When Abby pulled back I couldn't help but notice that she too looked somehow younger in her enthusiasm, just like her husband.

"What are you doing here?" she asked excitedly holding my wrists at my side.

"I don't know," I said shaking my head. "I just needed… wanted to be here," I shrugged and looked over at Charles who understood.

The pitter pattering of two sets of little feet could be heard on the servant stairwell behind me. Sure enough Cole and Gracie came down one right behind the other. "Bef-fany," Gracie said pushing off the wall as she took the last big step and then crossed the kitchen attaching herself to my leg.

"Hi Gracie," I laughed as Abby picked her up into her arms. "Hi Cole," I added.

"Hey Bethany," he said giving me a high five as he walked through to the dining room where he plopped himself into one of the chairs. It was breakfast time.

"You'll eat with us," Abby invited before I could say anything. I started to shake my head because I didn't want to intrude but Charles' hand was on my back leading me into the dining room; he was not taking 'No' for an answer. I helped Abby move stacks and stacks of paper scattered around the dining room table to the hutch under the windows. I noticed that the letterhead read 'Ellsworth Hospital'. In the margins and on separate spreadsheets Andrew's penmanship was crafting and tailoring the reports – both financially and clerically. "He's still a work enthusiast," Abby said placing another stack on top of the pile I had just put down. Charles, of course, was the front man because to everyone Andrew was just a high school student, busy with football and not some business intellect. I smirked at the mastermind's detailed work running my fingers over it. Abby set the table while I looked around the room more closely. I couldn't help but take it all in.

"Bethany," Charles said from the kitchen. I could hear a skillet sizzling and he was mixing batter in a bowl.

"Yes," I said looking back at him.

"Would you mind telling Andrew it's time for breakfast?" he asked with a smirk on his face. He knew that Andrew would enjoy my surprise visit.

"I'll do it," Gracie said standing on her seat ready to jump to the floor.

"I think we should let Bethany do it today," Abby said sitting the little girl down and pushing her chair in some before kissing her on the top of the head. Abby looked up and smiled at me, tilting her head towards the stairs.

I climbed them with my hand gliding up the banister; it was all so familiar. When I reached the top, I looked down the hallway to the left and then to the right. 'Right,' I thought and started to walk quietly. The door straight ahead at end of the corridor led to my old quarters – my old bedroom. I was not ready for something like that and was thankful when I heard faint noises coming from the room next to it; the door to the left. It was open an inch or two and I touched it so that it moved a little more.

I saw Andrew cross the room, shirtless and perfect. His hair was wet as he ran his hand over the back of it; he had just gotten out of the shower. His packed practice football attire was in his bag on the floor at the foot of his bed. With his back towards me I opened the door and stood watching him as he took a shirt from the dresser – a solid white v-neck t-shirt. His back was tight, strong and muscular as he put the shirt on over his head and turned with it halfway over his chest. I was leaning against the door frame when he saw me. Shock took him first but it was quickly replaced with a broad, immaculate smile, one that, again, took my breath away.

There we were standing, looking at one another. I felt giddy, electrified. I smiled and then ran to him; he swept me up into his arms as I wrapped mine around his neck.

"Hi," I whispered into his ear as my hands ran through his damp hair. It was like they knew what to do – a detail that came naturally to the surface.

"Hmm," he moaned deep in his chest enjoying my touch and my lips that teased at the corner of his ear. "Good morning, beautiful," he sighed as he opened his piercingly blue eyes looking back into mine.

—

My feet still hadn't hit the ground as I turned the combination to my locker before the homeroom bell sounded. A note fell out when I finally got it open.

Bethany,

Looks like you may be right about the secretaries becoming annoyed with me over the announcements. I'll have your grandmother bake cookies as a peace offering.

I spoke with Mr. Donovan - you can skip afternoon classes today. The hospital's Board of Directors are meeting to discuss the fundraiser. Dr. Landon is expecting you.

Thanks again.

Love,

The Old Man

P.S. Word of Advice: I'm sure he'll save you a seat so you don't have to hide in the bathroom stall.

I laughed as I made my way to homeroom at my grandfather's sense of humor. The meeting didn't come as a surprise to me, having spoken about it over breakfast at the Estate. Charles had told me that he had talked it over with Gramps after football practice last night and to expect it.

Over coffee and pancakes Charles, Abigail, Andrew and I truly enjoyed the morning. I felt so at home, so comfortable in my own skin there. Their voices were like echoes finally reaching my ears and stimulated more and more memories and emotions to reveal themselves. I was finally finding a place in this world where my past intertwined with the present.

—

I was relieved to see Kate in her scrubs sitting at the nurses' station when I got to the hospital. "Hey Beths!" she said somewhat surprised to see me. "What are you doing here? Is everything okay?" she asked concerned.

"Everything's fine just here for the meeting," I nodded.

"Oh. They're meeting in the conference room; top floor. Make sure you find me before you leave. I want to show you a picture of the bridesmaid dresses," she beamed.

"Will do," I said as I made my way to the elevator. As the doors shut, I touched my chest and felt my heart beating. Everything was fine – there was nothing to worry about. I mean, medicine – check, cardio – check, doctor watching it – check. What else was there to do? And then there was Andrew... the reason for it figuratively skipping. I had never heard of anyone dying from being completely and irrevocably smitten before.

The doors opened to a deserted hallway and I read over the sign with directing arrows; the conference room was to the left. Three doors down, I could see the Board of Directors sitting around the large, mahogany conference room table through an etched glass wall. On display, I knocked softly before opening the door. Charles, sitting at the head and in the middle of speaking, pointed, acknowledging my arrival. Eyes which had already latched on to me through the glass in the hallway followed me now as I scanned the room. Abigail, who was sitting to her husband's right smiled when our eyes overlapped. Soon whispering and nodding in my direction avalanched as the 'Bethany Reid' domino effect infected the esteemed members. I glanced around the room once more looking for a space to sit when I noticed the archangel stand up from his seat at the other end of the table.

Andrew held the back of the seat for me as I sat down. I felt a faint blush rush to my skin as I looked up at the thirty prestigious doctors and investors who were still watching me closely. Drew pulled over another chair for himself a few people away; I couldn't help but notice how tired he looked, a result of yesterday's rigorous marathon of 'emergency' football practices *and* late night paperwork. I wondered what the Directors would think if they knew that the high school quarterback was the one calling the shots when it came to the hospital's finances. Instead, they were under the impression that Charles had invited Andrew to the meeting to give him a taste of the business world.

"Bethany," Charles said politely calling for my attention and continued professionally, "has graciously offered to donate her time to help promote the fundraiser." A few people smiled graciously in my direction but most made curious side comments at the announcement. Ignoring the 'Syndrome' I noticed an agenda on the table; there were check marks next to topics which had already been covered. My introduction was the last bullet – my timing was impeccable.

"Minerva, you were saying," Charles said giving the floor to an older woman who sat towards the middle of the table. I instinctively looked over at Drew and found him not paying attention to the woman speaking either; instead, he was looking at me and smiled. 'Hello,' he mouthed.

'Hi,' I mouthed back but before another exchange could be made, Minerva finished and Charles was reiterating some specifics about the Gala; the date, December 11th, and the location, the Estate. It seemed that the Board was skeptical if the venue could hold the anticipated number of guests. Obviously, they had never been to the extensive, elegant home. Seeing that his colleagues were somewhat doubtful, Charles reassured them that there would not be an issue in accommodating the guests. I watched as he crafted his way into everyone's confidence never once sounding smug. Charles was far wealthier than any of the people present could imagine but you wouldn't know it. He was kind to the withdrawn, gracious toward the absurd and didn't have ears for gossip or slurs. It was clear that over the years he had truly mastered the art of conversation, a gift.

As the meeting came to an end and the room began to break up, I took the opportunity to read over the agenda more closely. It appeared that my purpose: Publicity/Promotion was going to include participating in some sort of press release. I couldn't imagine what good it would do. According to Olivia, the tabloids' most recent claim was that I had been abducted by aliens. Regardless of whether or not I thought I would be helpful, I would offer both Charles and my grandfather the help I promised.

"Thank you for coming," Abby said sliding into the empty seat next to me.

"Of course," I shrugged and she handed me a folder. Opening it I realized that it was a press release she had prepared which I would submit as my own. "Please don't argue with me. You have plenty of other things on your plate. It's the least I can do…"

"You didn't have to put it together. I would have," I started.

"But now you don't have too and you can worry about more important things like physics homework," she finished sarcastically and I shook my head. Charles leaned over the chair next to Abby and asked, "Would you mind if I checked your heart again?"

"Sure," I said getting to my feet and followed behind Charles and Abby. Andrew was left to talk to Board members who were interested in the upcoming football game and how the team was doing. He played his role by answering their questions but I couldn't help but notice that his eyes watched the three of us as we left.

After a few minutes of standing in what felt like a padded closet with humming walls, the intercom chirped in, "Okay Beths,"

Charles' voice said giving me the heads up to step out – which I did gladly.

"It appears that it has been dissipating," Charles said comparing notes back and forth between an open chart and the images on the screen.

"Is that my chart?" I asked taking a closer look at the name on the cardiology report and other medical documents. Sure enough 'Bethany Taylor' was on the top of every one. "But how did you get this?" I asked looking up at Charles who turned to Abby for the explanation.

"A phone call," Abby answered unaware that she had an audience. "I pretended to be you." I watched as she bit her fingernails nervously, fascinated by my heart beating on the screen even though she didn't know what any of it meant. When she turned her head, she saw my shock at her disclosure. "Alright, so I did something illegal but it's the first time I've done anything like this," she defended herself. Abby then looked at Charles who was holding back his amusement. "I don't see what the big deal is. *You* and my brother have been falsifying birth certificates, driver's licenses and everything else for decades," she rationalized. Charles looked back at his wife lovingly, observing how endearing she was to him in her rant.

"I appreciate it, Abby." I assured her. She huffed not totally convinced herself. "Really," I laughed at my friend who moped from the weight of a guilty conscience.

Charles finished scribbling his notes in my chart before standing and shutting off the high-tech equipment. "It looks like your condition has been improving slowly. Keep up with the cardio and continue with the medication. We'll perform these scans regularly but other than that, I think you're heart is in far better condition than it was when it went untreated."

"Thank you," I said relieved as he motioned towards the door. Abby and I both reached for the door knob; her hand unintentionally covered mine.

Flashes flew in front of my eyes faster than any I had ever experienced before. Her mind was racing over good memories that her and I had shared – happy moments.

We were walking in town together, then we were picking out new ribbons for our gowns; another and we were telling each other secrets that we hadn't told anyone else – they were like keys and we trusted each other with them.

Again, another memory of her and I silently communicating with one another by a simple look as we stood in a group of women. More flashes and she and I were giggling as my father, Charles and Andrew joined us in the study after a long day of work. I was the sister she never had…

Out of nowhere the images changed – it was the night of the accident. She sat motionless staring out my bedroom window into the darkness as Charles paced nervously in front of the fireplace.

He had just received the news that there had been one survivor, only one, and no one knew if it was her brother or my father.

Abby loved my father; I could feel that. He was dear to her heart. It was too complex to understand in the swiftness of the scene but it was true and deep. That night she knew she had lost a family member. Now, she urged Charles to tell me what they had learned and not keep it from me because if she were me, she would want to know…

I thought I knew what was coming, I thought I'd see Charles bringing me into my room and helping me onto my bed and Abby would try to come to my side but instead, she flashed forward.

Abby was in the dining room in the early morning hours. The sun was coming through the curtains and reflecting off the polished oak table. She sat with a cup of tea in front of her, untouched. Her focus was on her brother sitting across from her with his head in his hands. He was cut and bruised but Abby knew that the real pain he was experiencing was not physical, it was emotional. Drew was devastated by the loss of my father and overcome by the guilt he felt even though it was unwarranted. Charles, standing behind Andrew, went to put his hand on his brother-in-law's shoulder but Andrew moved away from him, not wanting to be consoled. Drew paced in front of the empty fireplace, stopped, rested his palms on the mantle and bent over. She and Charles exchanged a look of concern that was interrupted when the doors to the room opened. Abby watched as I walked into the dining room with red, tired eyes. She watched me look from her to Charles and then to Andrew. Stopping a foot away from Drew, he turned his head, expecting it to be Charles. When he realized it was me, he swallowed hard and turned completely. Abby looked up at Charles, neither of them knowing what to expect and her heart sank as she saw me take the step into Andrew's chest weeping, wanting nothing more than for him to hold me. Andrew slowly put his arms around me, the remorse evermore manifesting; something only Charles and Abby saw.

As Drew held me, he leaned his cheek on the side of my head and a few silent tears fell from his eyes as he tried to remain strong. Abby's eyes began to fill but beyond her blurred vision I could see Charles walking over to her, touch her arm and then led her out of the room to give Andrew and I time alone.

I was hit with the next emotion before the scene. The stabbing ache identified what I was about to witness for the fourth time, however, the nightmare was from Abby's point of view.

She woke in her bed having heard me yelling Andrew's name in the hallway but when she came into the hallway, I was nowhere in sight. But soon thereafter she heard her brother yelling for Charles on the grounds. She rushed to the window to see him running towards her brother who was holding my body in his arms. Abby rushed down the servant stairwell and out the kitchen doors onto the grounds. Charles was looking for a pulse and Abby was only a few feet away from my motionless body when her hand clamped over her mouth. Charles turned and held her back in his arms as she cried out. But she knew. She had known when she looked from the window but now it was confirmed.

Strangely, it was the calamity of losing both my father and me that lingered vividly.

I could feel reality as my knees hit the hard hospital floor but the connection was still made; the flashes were not affected.

Andrew had his back to Abby. He had packed his things and was leaving the Estate in the middle of the night. Charles was trying to talk some sense into him and reached out to stop his hand from picking up his bags. 'STOP IT! NO!' Andrew shouted with refocusing eyes. He looked petrified at what had just transpired not knowing what it meant. Charles too looked down at his hand and then back up at his friend unable to explain the connection and whatever memory of me he had unknowingly shared for the first time.

Andrew threw Charles up against the wall distraught and enraged at the recent discovery of this gift and curse. Charles didn't fight back knowing Drew meant him no harm. Panic-stricken and not knowing what else to do, Abby reached for her brother's arm. Irate he bellowed at her as well. Stunned, drained and completely defeated, Abby stepped to the side and only turned her head with the slamming of the door. Andrew was gone.

'Just let him go. Just let him go.' she kept repeating to herself. Her mourning was plagued with sadness and, behind that, was a building anger. However, her anger wasn't because of Andrew's leaving; rather… it was because of mine.

I felt both of my hands hit the cold floor and the flashes finally stopped. "Bethany, are you alright," Charles dropped to my side.

"I…" I said blinking wildly trying to see straight. Abby stood motionless next to me as Charles put his arm under my arm, steadying me as he brought me to my feet.

I looked straight into Abby's eyes. Aware that his wife and I had exchanged strong memories, Charles silently left the room giving us privacy. "I'm sorry, Abby," I said faintly, still dazed by her recollections.

"Me too, Beths. Me too," she said sifting through rehashed wounds as I hugged her.

"My father," I began to ask as we stepped into the empty elevator a few minutes later. Knowing that there were still gaps in my memory, Abby tried to help. "You and your father moved to Ellsworth after the Estate was finished. That's when we met."

"What about my mother and… other family?" I questioned.

"No, it was just you and Jonathan. You were all each other had," Abby said as the doors closed. She put out her hand for me to take but I refused. Talking about my father had always been a soft spot of mine and I wasn't sure if I would be able to handle seeing him through someone else's memories.

"I don't want to see or feel it. It's too much," I admitted.

"Beths, trust me," she encouraged.

The flashes were selective and moved on to the next hastily to prevent me from getting completely nostalgic. Abby's third party view had encapsulated the sweet father-daughter relationship affording me to detach myself and simply watch.

A calm smile crossed my face as she let go of my hand. Abigail had left me with a peaceful feeling, an emotion that I hadn't felt quite worthy of. "Although your time with one another was cut short, you did have time with him and you have those memories," she said as the elevator doors opened. My eyes released a few silent tears before I took a deep breath knowing that she was right. Deep down I did have recollections of the handsome man who was my hero and whose world I was the center of.

—

Abby and I decided to get coffee and tea in the cafeteria, talking a mile a minute about the Board and the plans for the Gala. It was so easy to be around one another that it made it difficult to remember we were teacher and student to the outside world. We were like two peas in a pod and our friendship had withstood the test of time.

After we got our drinks, we walked back towards the elevators and as if we had planned it, the doors opened to Andrew and Charles stepping out. By the look on Andrew's face it was clear that Charles had told him about the intense memory exchange between Abby and I which had literally brought me to my knees. "Are you okay?" Drew asked me then glanced warily over at his sister.

"Drew, she's fine," Abby said crossing her arms. "Would you stop acting like she's made of glass?" Andrew took a deep breath and tilted his chin down fighting the urge to bicker back at his sister which would only escalate the small, sibling battle. It was comedic to see them this way.

"Return to your corners," Charles kiddingly refereed standing next to his wife and kissed the top of her head. "We should be going," I heard him say as Drew looked down at me and I blushed. "We will see you later," Charles said kindly giving Andrew and I some time alone.

Abby kissed me on the cheek and then Andrew. She looked up at her brother and continuing to taunt him chimed in, "I was thinking Drew, Bethany might just find the whole chivalry thing suffocating."

"Suffocating," Andrew injected. Her eyebrows rose as she added, "I'm just saying that sometimes you can unknowingly be a little… pretentious."

"Pretentious! Me?" Andrew said pointing to himself. A sarcastic smile washed over Abby's face unable to keep it straight through the ruse.

Realizing this, Drew patted Charles on the arm, "Please remind your wife that humor should not be used as a weapon unless provoked."

"You are dangerous," I heard Charles say to her as they walked towards the Emergency Room doors.

Andrew and I laughed at the two of them as he pushed the elevator button and held the door. It wasn't until after the doors had shut that Drew's concern became prevalent again.

"How are you feeling?" he asked.

I took the opportunity to channel Abby's wit. "Not well, under the current circumstances," I said taking a sip of coffee.

"Circumstances?" Drew asked worriedly.

"Well, I went on an amazing date with this guy and haven't heard back from him," I giggled taking another sip.

"What a fool," Drew's smile widened as he now played along folding his hands in front of him as the elevator doors opened and a few people got on. When we had reached the top floor Drew led me back to the conference room which was now empty. He collected his papers and belongings while I looked at a packet from the meeting of a thorough analysis of the hospital's current financial situation.

"Do you think that they can reach the goal?" I asked flipping through the charts and suggestions he made for the Board of Directors.

"Between you and me, they already have. An anonymous donor will be sending a blank check. Whatever money the Gala brings in will pay for utilities and other expenses," Andrew said adding the last of his papers to his pile.

"Anonymous, huh," I laughed taking another sip of coffee; my bones were still cold from my early run this morning in the chilly autumn-like weather. "So that's what you do? You save hospitals?" I inquired wanting to learn more about him.

"Yes. I make sure that people have a place to go, that the institution is financially stable and sustainable. No one should lose the person they love because they didn't have the means to save them," he genuinely answered. "By the way," he continued, causing me to look up at him alerted by the change in his tone, "I'm leaving tonight for Colorado. I have to wrap things up out there on the project I was working on before I make the move back to Ellsworth permanent," he finished turning towards me.

"Out there," I asked wanting to know more.

"Yes, Fort Collins, Colorado. I was working with a few hospitals in the area; Charles was here, working on Ellsworth's. I just need to finish tying up some loose ends," he nodded, "but I'll be back for Friday night's game," Drew grinned as he took the cup of coffee out of my hand and put it on top of his papers. He leaned in, placing his hands on the table behind me and whispered unexpectedly in my ear, "And if it's okay with you, I was hoping you would give me the pleasure of a second date afterwards."

"Oh," is all I could muster.

"Would that be okay?" he asked and I felt his breath on my neck.

"Uh huh," I mumbled aware of his close proximity even though our bodies were not touching.

"Very well then," he said tilting his head, lingering close to my quivering lips.

"Are you only asking because you don't want to be considered a 'fool'," I joked trying to use his own words.

"That and because I want nothing more than to spend time in your company," he brushed a piece of my hair behind my ear. "And because I would like to kiss you," he finished before taking a half-step back and smiled. I shook my head slowly at his teasing.

Putting my hands out on his chest I smirked, "I'm guessing Charles told you my heart works so now you're going to try and make it stop."

"Not stop, skip," he corrected with a grin, kissing the side of my head.

Thursday, September 24th

After my run I was making my way up the driveway and saw Ryan getting out of his truck in the same Lumberyard clothes he had left in the day before. As a result of a surplus of orders and the already long days, Ryan was a little distracted – it was a good thing, seeing as my worlds had collided.

"Hey," I said sweaty and panting, taking out my earphones coming up alongside him.

"Hey," Ryan yawned rubbing his forehead with the sleeve of his t-shirt.

"You look like hell," I said walking backwards in front of him. He reached out to grab me but was too slow. As we walked into the house he proceeded to throw himself onto the couch. "Tired much?"

"Eh hmm," he said into the pillow before turning on his side. I sat down in one of the armchairs, taking off my running shoes.

"How's the Lumberyard?"

"Busy," he said groggily.

"That's a good thing though, right?"

"Ah hmm," Ryan said and then like a light switch, he was out cold, fast asleep. I smiled at his inability to keep his eyes open even long enough for me to take my shoes off. I tossed a blanket over him before heading upstairs to get in the shower and ready for school.

I knew Andrew wasn't going to be in school so I was anticipating that it would be a long day of daydreaming. But, I was wrong. As I got out of my car, Olivia ran over to me and pulled at the passenger door. "Open it," she said urgently. I obeyed and got back in on the driver's seat.

"What's wrong?"

"Two things: one, the bridesmaid dresses Kate picked out for us are hideous." she started.

"They're not that bad. She showed me yesterday…"

"Beths, they're ugly," Liv said flatly. The topic was obviously non-negotiable in her mind. "Don't worry. I've convinced her to look at a few I picked out. But anyway, more importantly, the second thing: I ran into Andrew Wicks."

"What? When?"

"Yesterday, he came into the drugstore with that little blonde girl…"

"Gracie," I answered.

"Yes," Liv nodded. "He was picking up a few things… he said hello when I was ringing him up and we got to talking."

"And?"

"And I don't think you're crazy. He's like not human," Olivia said, her head leaning back against the headrest; she was completely enamored by him.

"What did you talk about?" I asked eagerly.

Throwing her hands up she said, "I can't even tell you. All I know is that there is something about him that is… like… majorly old school. I wouldn't have caught it if I wasn't looking for it though."

"So you believe me?"

"If I say yes, does that mean I'm crazy too?"

"Yes," I responded.

"Then by all means, yes, he's some timeless frozen dude…"

I put both hands on the steering wheel and leaned my head against them. "Thank God."

"This boat of insanity has just launched into the great unknown," Liv said flattening her shoulders against her seat and tilting her head back.

"You have a way with words, Liv," I smirked sideways.

"It's a gift," she nodded.

"While we are accepting insanity…" I turned wanting to tell her about the meeting at the hospital, the memories Abby had shown me and about Andrew asking me out on a second date.

"Tell me everything," Liv said propping herself against the door, bracing herself for my latest entry to my real life, human diary.

"Hey," Jackson said coming up beside me at my locker.

"Hey," I responded taking out my biochemistry books.

"Ready?"

"Yes sir," I smiled. Since Jackson and I had the same schedule, we walked to almost every class together. It had become another routine.

"So, I heard about you and Wicks going out the other night," he said looking out of the corner of his eye. My face flushed and he restrained a smile.

"What?" I said trying to recover from my initial, unguarded reaction but was unsuccessful.

"Well, the truth is I've been waiting for you to mention it but I gave you two days and now your time is up," he laughed as he held the classroom door for me.

"Oh," I said making an 'I'm sorry' face at him as we found our neighboring seats.

"I'm also guessing that I have you to thank for those 'emergency practices'," Jackson challenged and I bit my lip.

"Sorry about that."

"Yeah, yeah," Jackson chuckled and handing me a small stack of papers said, "Here are the notes from yesterday's classes."

"Great. Thanks."

"Oh, and we got our English papers back. Yours is mixed in there." My face cringed when I flipped through and saw a 'C'.

"You know if you ever want me to read over your paper before you hand it in," he offered. My eyes perked up.

"Really?"

"Sure. You seem to be a genius in calculus. I could use some help…"

"Deal! How are you in history," I bartered.

"As good as you are in physics," he countered.

"Just a recap, you'll help me in English and history in exchange for calculus and physics?"

"Sounds good to me," he said putting his hand out to shake on the agreement. When I placed my hand in his I half-expected flashes to pass in front of my eye; oddly enough, I had to remind myself that it wasn't normal to exchange memories. "Just do me a favor and spare me from any more of those insane practices," the Captain requested.

"I'll try my best," I shrugged.

"So, your date with Wicks... how'd it go?" The happiness on my face answered his question. "Good. Wicks is a good guy." Then Jackson asked, "Have you heard anything about Olivia and Bobby?" I shook my head having nothing to offer him. Liv and Bobby hung out with the rest of the cheerleaders and football players – something Jackson already knew. "She seems happy," he speculated.

"I guess," I agreed but felt horrible for him.

"Well," he said taking a deep breath and looked up at me with forced eyes, "what's a guy suppose to do, right?"

"Focus on something productive?" I tried.

"Distractions... Football does kind of consume my life and there's always school."

"And me... I mean I could always go for another tour of Main Street," I smiled at him.

"Thanks Beths," Jackson said understanding that he had me to lean on in moments of weakness; that it was safe. Just then the classroom door closed as Charles walked in behind the last few students. I turned around in my seat and caught the smile Charles sent me inconspicuously as he began his lesson.

"Beths," Charles called out as I walked by his desk after class. Wordlessly, he asked for me to stay behind.

"What's up?" I asked when the last of the students left.

"I have something for you," he said reaching into his leather briefcase next to his chair. He pulled out a package wrapped in brown paper tied with string.

"What is it?" I smiled looking up at my old friend.

"It's from Andrew," Charles said folding his arms in front of him. "He said to tell you that flowers alone are not the only gift to be expected from him. Now, he could have written that in a card, I suppose, but he was clear in making sure I handed it to you, personally. My guess is that he wants to *see* your reaction. This hand connection…" Charles said holding up one hand, "does have its perks when it comes to replaying memories."

Shaking my head, I smiled and put my bag down. Pulling the string, I untied it and then unfolded the brown paper. In my hands was a book that I had not held in over a century; it was the one I had been reading when my father walked into the study and told me that there were other books in this world but none quite as full of adventure. The lack of binding was evidence that I took part in that adventure as often as I could. It was also the last memory I had of my father – the night before Coverly.

Drew had it all this time. He knew that it was my favorite. I sat down in the closest desk holding it as tears began to fill my eyes. Looking up at Charles, he nodded, acknowledging that he knew the significance and the connection. Opening the pages slowly, there was a faded green ribbon holding a place.

"You must have left the book in his coat pocket before the day on the grounds because he found it one evening after we had left Ellsworth. He's clung to it ever since." I swallowed and flipped through my markings which still lined the margins of the pages. "At first the book became his comfort – he could read the words your eyes once read over. But then it became more to him." My fingertips brushed over my lips as I saw markings that did not belong to me, but were Andrew's. I looked up at Charles, searching for what to say. I had nothing. I was moved, I was comforted and more in love.

Chapter Four
Friday, September 25th

Friday was on the horizon, literally. It was warmer than it had been but it was still a fall day. The anticipation of seeing Andrew after tonight's game almost propelled me during my morning run. I felt like I was flying. However, at school, classes dragged on. Liv and I had passed a record number of notes to one another throughout the course of the morning and afternoon. As soon as the bell rung for dismissal, we were in my car heading to my grandparents' house.

"YOU READY LIV?" Ryan yelled up the stairs after he got home.

"YEAH, I'M COMING!" Olivia said getting to her feet. "Is my bow on straight?" she asked me, twirling so I could see the back of her ponytail.

"Yup," I grinned.

"Alright, I'll see you at the game. And please don't forget this," she said putting a bag with an outfit she had picked out for herself for the after party on my bed.

"I couldn't even if I tried," I said truthfully. It had taken her hours to decide what to wear. She hugged me and then she was off, halfway down the stairs.

"Oh!" she ran backup the few steps. "And you look beautiful. Andrew is going to love it," she added before bouncing down the stairs.

I laughed and looked down at the clothes Liv had dressed me in which were not only for the football game but was also the outfit for my second date with Andrew. Hearing Liv on the first floor, I then heard Ryan yell up, "I'LL BE BACK IN AN HOUR TO GET YOU, BETHS!"

"OKAY!" I shouted back down. Getting to my feet I closed the armoire doors and looked around my spotless room. Over the past two days my nerves had taken their toll and as a result, I had cleaned and organized feverishly.

Looking in the mirror, I smiled at my reflection. Liv was really good at this fashion thing.

Ryan, Kate and I sat on the bleachers at the fifty yard line waiting for the game to start. The announcer's voice echoed throughout the stadium. "Give it up for the Ellsworth Sparrows!" Olivia was cheering her little heart out on the sidelines as the crowd roared. I saw Andrew jogging next to Gramps in the back of the pack onto the field. "Who are you watching?" Kate asked trying to follow my eyes. "It's that Wicks boy isn't it?" she whispered excitedly. I smiled and she patted my leg, smiling too. "Good choice," she winked. Ryan was too distracted checking out the competition to notice our little conversation. I think Liv likes forty-two," Kate said looking at the beast of a player.

"Number forty-eight," I corrected, "Bobby Thompson."

"Oh thank God," she said as she compared the two, making us both laugh. When I looked down at the Sparrows' sideline,

Andrew was looking up into the crowd at me, holding his helmet in one hand and taking a drink of water with the other. Our eyes met and he smiled as he put the cup down and put his helmet on, heading onto the field with Jackson and another player for the coin toss.

The game had a lot of contact. There were a lot of loud hits, a lot of yellow flags and a lot of shouting coming from Ryan. "Are you kidding me!" my brother hollered as Kate and I pretended not to know him.

"At least it shows he's passionate," I kiddingly commented at the show Ryan was putting on.

"Yeah," she eyed her fiancé apprehensively and tugged his shirt hoping he would settle down.

After the final whistle blew, the sidelines roared for their hometown heroes. The final score was thirty-four to thirty-two, Sparrows; a hard-earned victory. As the stadium emptied Kate stood and stretched. "Are you ready to go?" she asked.

"Actually, I'm getting a ride." I said looking down at the field.

"From who?" Ryan asked turning towards me. I hesitated but Kate took the lead.

"Have fun," she said kissing my cheek, understanding that I was being vague for a reason. Thankfully, she walked away pulling Ryan with her before he could ask me any more questions.

A few minutes later Liv made her way up to the stands. "Hey," she said when she reached me.

"Here you go," I said handing her the bag I had promised to bring.

"Thanks!" she smiled.

"Have fun!" I yelled back down to her as she headed towards the bathroom, trying to take the ribbon out of her hair on the way.

"You too," she twirled.

The stadium had slowly cleared out. The parking lot was finally empty except for a black Camaro. The Friday night lights glowed over the stadium as I waited and decided to sit down closer to the sidelines in the first row and look up at the stars. It never ceased to amaze me how clear the sky was here in Ellsworth.

I heard a rhythmic pounding on the metal bleachers and when I turned my head Andrew was walking towards me with his equipment over his shoulder. He had a grin on his face that would stun any woman. I stood up with my hands in my jacket pockets.

"Hello," he said as he stopped a foot in front of me.

"Hi," I smiled.

"How are you this evening?" he asked properly.

"I'm well. How was your trip?"

"Everything's settled," he nodded with a smirk.

"I'll see you later, Wicks!" I heard a man call out from the announcer's box.

"Thanks Mark!" Andrew shouted back. After Mark made his way down the ladder, there was a loud sliding noise and then the only light came from the moon. Andrew opened the gate that separated the stands from the field and I followed behind him. He put down his equipment and pulled a bag out from under the bleachers, throwing the strap over his shoulder and led me to the center of the field.

"What are you doing?" I asked.

"It was here," He said as he put the bag down and started to open it. He took out a blanket and laid it on the field. Then he took another smaller blanket and wrapped it around me. Andrew stepped closer and said softly, "I kissed you here once without permission and I won't apologize for it. As for tonight, well, it's our second date so I can kiss you," he smiled and his lips met mine again.

He stepped back and sat down with his one knee up and his arm resting on it, waiting for me to join him. I sat down cradled by him, my back leaning against his chest. I took a deep breath and looked up at the night sky.

"I missed you," I whispered. He kissed the side of my head.

"What's your favorite color?" he asked a moment later.

I paused and then answered, "Blue." He contemplated it and then went to ask another question. "What's yours?" I asked cutting him off out of my own curiosity.

"Green. What's your favorite book?"

"*First Impressions*... And thank you for holding onto it for me," I grinned.

"You're welcome," Drew exhaled and I could hear the smile on his lips and felt him pull me closer. I was positive that Charles had shared the memory of when I opened the gift. "I do believe it is more commonly referred to as *Pride and Prejudice.*"

"But," I shook my head.

"I know," he laughed. He and I had argued about the title change even back then.

"What is your favorite book?"

At the same time we both answered, "*Great Expectations.*"

"Some things never change," I joked and he smirked as he pulled me closer. I turned completely around trying to make sure his hold on me wouldn't be sacrificed in exchange for seeing his handsome face. Very calmly, very openly, I brushed my hair over my shoulder and my eyes narrowed as I studied his face. In the moonlight, he watched me, unsure of what I was doing. I nervously bit my lip. "Please don't do that," Drew said running his thumb over my bottom lip. "It's tantalizing," Drew breathed and leaned back. I smiled and playfully pushed him back. He landed controlled with his left hand behind his head and his right hand pulling me with him. Now lying side-by-side, I giggled as he adjusted the blanket so we were both covered. I cuddled closer next to him. He breathed in and looked up at the stars. I smiled at the moment, and propped myself up on my elbow. He looked over at me and I lightly touched my nose with his before kissing him, going in and out without any sort of pattern or rhythm. He enjoyed the random yet building passion between us.

"You," I said between kisses.

"I," he repeated me mockingly.

"Stop," I laughed and put my hand on his chest and his arms wrapped tightly around me. I looked down at my hand and stared at it.

"What is it?" he asked concerned.

"Nothing," I shook my head and curled into him. His arms wrapped tightly around me.

"Bethany," he said a few moments later. "Please tell me what's on your mind." I knew that I could not respond to him with words.

I placed my hand over his and not choosing any particular memory, I recalled every moment that he had taken my breath away. In those memories, both new and old, was my affections for him; feelings that were felt when there was no known reason to feel them; they were pure.

I left him with the most recent memory I had of him from seconds ago. Being in his arms, being here with him…

I watched as his eyes blinked rapidly with the exchange and when they had focused, he didn't wait to kiss me. When he pulled away, there was only enough room between our lips for a breeze to pass through. He was looking into my eyes, longingly; his hand brushed my neck and his lips were slightly separated, ready to speak.

"What are you doing tomorrow… and the following day… and every day after that…" Drew asked sweetly. At this I rested my forehead against his and closed my eyes. I felt his hand on the side of my face again. I looked up smitten and slowly ran my hands into his playable hair and trailed my fingertips down his cheek and followed his jaw line. He unhurriedly leaned in and we both closed our eyes. His lips touched mine as our second date melted into our second chance.

Saturday, September 26th

The next morning I gracefully skipped down the stairs and into the kitchen wearing a dress with a long, flowing skirt. Ryan looked exhausted leaning up against the counter as Chris and Gregg filled their plates with the breakfast Grams was cooking. "Where do you think you're going?" Ryan yawned at my entrance.

"Ugh…" I started knowing that momentarily Andrew would be here to pick me up; plans we had made last night.

"You're going to miss our Saturday football date?" Chris whined. I tried to get a cup out of the cupboard but Gregg blocked the way.

"Gregg," I sighed trying to maneuver around him. Grams smiled as she attempted to hand me a plate of food which was intercepted by Gregg.

"It's that Wicks boy isn't it," Ryan said pushing himself up off the counter. I shrugged and couldn't help but let out a smile. Chris and Gregg both shook their heads at Ryan's paternal reaction. Ryan, realizing what he sounded like in front of his buddies, relaxed and surrendered, "Well do I at least get to meet him?"

"You already have," I said getting a clean cup from the drain board and pouring myself a glass of orange juice.

"Not as your potential boyfriend. That's a totally different introduction. It includes a strong handshake, the sinister glare and a short speech," my brother listed.

"A short speech?" Gregg questioned and Ryan shot him a look. Gregg returned to his pancakes, stabbing them with his fork.

"Okay, I promise that the next time you and Drew..." I started.

"Wait! Who's Drew? There are two guys? Bethany, that's not cool." Chris interjected.

"No," I laughed as I put the orange juice back into the refrigerator, "Drew is his nickname... its short for Andrew. Andrew's last name is Wicks..." I explained so that Chris could connect the dots.

"Oh," Chris said after pondering it for a minute. "Then I want everyone to call me... Lumber Man," he said putting his fists on his hips and turning his head up and to the side.

"You're an idiot," Ryan said throwing the dishtowel at him. "If anyone is Lumber Man, it's me," Ryan finished copying his friend's pose. Grams, Gregg and I laughed as I put my empty cup in the sink. Without getting out of his Lumber Man character Ryan said, "I think I'll use my superpower strength," picking me up over his left shoulder. My feet were in the air before I had time to try and defend myself. He walked us through the swinging door into the dining room as Gregg and Chris followed, then through the screen door and onto the porch where Gramps had been sitting all morning. We were all laughing at each other and while still upside down, I saw Gramps stand and shake Andrew's hand. The two of them looked amused at the scene that had just interrupted their morning greeting. "Hi," Ryan said putting out his right hand.

"Hello," Andrew responded, accepting Ryan's handshake and then looked at Chris and Gregg who were staring him down like two additional protective brothers. "Hello," he nodded to the both of them, properly acknowledging their presence. They nodded back at Andrew and Chris crossed his arms.

"Um, now would be a good time to put me down," I said to Ryan helplessly.

"One minute," Ryan said as if there was more important business to take care of.

"Ryan," I said when he completely disregarded my request.

"So, you and my sister," Ryan started. At this I began to punch his back.

"Okay, okay, there's no need to get violent," he said putting me down next to Chris and Gregg. With my feet firmly on the ground, I saw Gramps smirk and put the newspaper under his arm, ready for whatever Ryan was about to make awkward. Andrew stood straight with his frame square and his arms crossed behind his back.

"You and my sister are… going out or something?" Ryan asked with his chin up in peacock mode.

Andrew grinned at me and answered my brother's question, "If she'll have me." My heart skipped.

"Well," Ryan said clearing his throat, "What are your intentions?" my brother asked folding his arms in front of him, standing as tall as he could. I poked his side at the unnecessary probing. Chris and Gregg were getting a kick out of the entertainment.

"I think that's enough," Gramps cut in.

"No, it's fine," Andrew assured him. "I've already asked your grandfather if it was alright that I see Bethany."

"Really?" Ryan asked shocked, looking at my grandfather who nodded in confirmation. It was another sign of Andrew's traditional upbringing; a true gentleman in his time made him unable to mold to current societal conventions. Dwelling on the notion, I thought it was ironic how people today thought it was odd to ask such a thing when it used to be unheard of not to a couple of decades ago.

"Yes, Wicks asked," Gramps said looking at Ryan, then at me.

"Oh," Ryan answered. I smirked and looked down at the porch. I loved Drew's sense of proper courtship. "Well, then…" Ry said looking for what to say next.

"I do apologize if I have offended you," Drew said. "You are her older brother…"

"No, nah, don't be silly. I'm just watching out for her. Right, Beths?" he said putting his arm around my shoulder. "But I will warn you, as her older brother… if you hurt her, I will have to hurt you."

"Yeah," Chris added and Gregg nodded towards Drew.

"I can respect that," Andrew grinned and laughed when my grandfather rolled his eyes.

"But you two have fun," Ryan said as Gramps herded Ryan, Chris and Gregg back into the house.

"Move along," I could hear Gramps say as the guys made their way back into the kitchen.

When we were alone I turned to Andrew and said sheepishly, "Sorry for that."

Andrew smiled, "It's good that he is so protective of you." Raising his eyebrows he grinned, "Who exactly are the other two…" I laughed as we walked towards his car.

As we made our way out of the driveway towards the Estate I asked, "So, is the white Mustang the car of choice?"

"Only when I'm with the princess," he smirked as he ran his hand down my forearm and our fingertips interlaced. "I do miss the horse though. I've been left with no choice but to settle for horsepower," he grinned putting his foot down heavier on the accelerator to hear the engine roar.

Pulling onto the cobblestone drive I looked out the window seeing the morning sun through the old oak trees which lined the path so beautifully. In many ways it was like driving into a time warp. The grounds isolated from the outside world allowed us to be unscathed by everything else. As we slowed to a stop in front of the Estate I looked over at him when he didn't move to get out of the car.

"Is everything okay?" I asked as I unlocked my seatbelt.

"Yes, I was just... I was wondering if I could ask you something," he said nervously turning towards me, making sure he had my full attention. "I was hoping I might... I want to discuss a topic of utmost precedence," he paused. I enjoyed watching how his nerves directly affected his tone and his choice of words which was now becoming more and more formal. Andrew continued, "Bethany, by asking your grandfather for his consent to see you exclusively, I have made my intentions known to your family." After a brief pause Drew continued, "Now, I am asking you... to accept my advances to gain your affection, exclusively."

I was silent for a minute as I held back a few giggles while translating his words. His handsome face quickly changed from a determined demeanor to one of confusion; that's when I realized I had not given him an answer to his offer. "Is 'exclusively' not the right word?" he questioned.

I burst out laughing at his antiquated vernacular that he used so naturally. His proposition of us dating sounded so much more complex but his upbringing would not allow him to skip over such an important step. "Well, I'm not an expert but I believe people just say, 'Would you like to go out with me?' but I would be more than happy to… how did you say it?" I stopped and then mimicked, "Accept your advances to gain my affection, exclusively."

Leaning his head back against the headrest he said, "I knew I didn't word it correctly. It's difficult, you know," sounding exacerbated. "I mean it's English but the way some people speak… do they converse with their parents with that grammar?"

"Wow," I said now bending over in hysterics. Andrew was laughing his nerves away too.

"Am I giving myself up?" he asked rubbing the back of his neck, anxious because of his inability to adapt to the current times.

"Yeah, I mean yes." I corrected with a smile making eye contact with his ocean blue ones.

"Well then," Drew said now playing along. "Hmm," he considered something then started, "Will you go steady with me?"

This time I controlled my laughter and said, "You're getting warmer."

"Okay," Andrew said attempting to redeem himself. He looked out the windshield considering something for a moment and decided to try again. For the first time, he let his shoulders fall slightly breaking his impeccable posture – completely unnatural for him, and casually ran his fingers threw his hair messing it up like other guys our age wore theirs. Then Andrew reached into the backseat with a slight smirk on his face. Holding his letterman jacket, he returned his attention to me impersonating an average teen and asked, "So, do you feel like being the luckiest girl in Ellsworth and wearing the quarterback's jacket?"

Armed with a quick sense of sarcasm I played along replying in my own impersonation of an arrogant girl's voice saying, "You would be the lucky one." Taking the jacket, I continued, "I should warn you, Bethany Reid is a much bigger deal than some quarterback from a small town. You might have to adjust to living in *my* shadow."

Andrew laughed at my wit and 'valley-girl' charade and admitted, "Alright that was scary." His stature broadened again, as he naturally returned to the Andrew I knew.

"Thanks," I smiled as I too dropped the abnormal act and looked at his letterman jacket. Glancing back up I saw his waiting eyes and I answered his question seriously, "I would be honored to be your girlfriend, Andrew."

He brushed a bang to the side as I wrapped his letterman jacket over my shoulders and looked at him giving me a wicked smile. Opening his car door, Drew walked around the front and helped me out of the Mustang. He started to walk up the steps toward the front door and stopped when he didn't feel me next to him; I was still standing by the car. "Is everything alright?"

I put my finger up and motioned for him to walk back down the steps. He did so suspiciously. "What is it?" he asked when he stood in front of me.

"I would like a kiss from my *boyfriend*, please." A grin grew on his face and he looked down at the ground and then back up at me.

"I like the way that sounds," he said sliding both of his hands into my hair.

"Boyfriend," I repeated again, bashfully.

"*Yours*," he said in a low but clear voice.

"Mmm," I moaned as the space between us got smaller, our eyes closing, entranced by the almost kiss.

"Mmm," he echoed as his lips breathed in mine.

—

He and I spent the day at the Estate. Every second we were together was perfect. We fell right back into where we had left off, as if nothing had torn us apart. Charles and Abby seemed to grow more and more elated as they checked in on us throughout the day. Walking the grounds with Andrew, he asked me questions that he didn't already know the answers too – questions pertaining to my life over the past seventeen years in New York. He was curious to know what I had done and what I had experienced. I didn't feel weird talking to him about it. The hard part was trying not to become mesmerized by such a noble man. I wanted to ask him questions about his life over the years but every time I tried to he would say it was unimportant and request that I continue. What I was able to get out of him was that he had moved every two to three years with Charles and Abby to a new place, a new town. He had taken what he learned from my father and applied it to new ventures and investments.

Drew was successful at what he did and that didn't surprise me. When I asked him if he ever got tired of business or thought of switching fields like Charles did with medicine, Drew simply smiled and said, "If understanding the finer points of business is my talent and I didn't use that gift to help other people, then I would be a fool. Charles is a brilliant doctor. Abigail found that she enjoys the natural sciences. But I never strayed from numbers or the economy because I found as industry developed, its fundamentals reaffirmed my methods and proved my theories. It was always fun. I still enjoy what I do."

—

I didn't want the day to end but it did. Without saying a word, Andrew walked me up my grandparents' front porch steps and kissed my forehead, smiling at me before turning and walking over to my grandfather who was sitting on the porch swing reading. Andrew shook his hand saying, "Goodnight, sir," before making his way back to his car. Gramps didn't look like he would ever get use to the idea of me, his granddaughter, dating even if it was with the perfect gentleman.

Somehow this had become my life, my story. Luckily, I didn't know differently than to believe like a child.

Sunday, September 27th

I smiled nonstop as I ran through the town of Ellsworth before the sunrise. My music was on shuffle but it seemed to be playing all the right songs. I knew I wouldn't be able to see Drew today; more 'emergency' football practices had been called. But there was tomorrow.

"Ryan, seriously, you have to get up now or we're going to be late for Church," I said already dressed for Mass standing over my brother's bed as he rolled over mumbling that he just needed five more minutes. "Fine, five more minutes but then I'm coming back in here and taking your pillow hostage," I warned. Turning to leave the room, I felt his pillow hit the back of my head. Picking it up I laughed, "Cute, Ry, real mature," and threw it back at him.

"I wasn't going for maturity," he yawned stretching to the four corners of his bed.

"Well, consider this your wake up call," I said as I folded some of his laundry, cleaning as I went around the room.

"Yeah, yeah," Ryan said slowly getting out from under the covers and to his feet. He was still wearing his Lumberyard clothes.

"You didn't change?" I asked pointing at his disheveled state.

"I was tired…" he said as though it were an excuse for poor hygiene and yawned again.

Handing him a towel that was over the back of a chair I pointed towards the hallway, "Shower." Ryan took the towel, rolled his eyes and walked to the doorway before I heard the towel snap and felt the burn of it on the back of my left leg.

"Ouch!" I said rubbing the spot and turned to see him snickering. We looked at each other and then I lunged as he ran for the bathroom door, closing and locking it just as my hand touched the door knob.

"Ha!" I could hear him say from the other side.

"Fine!" I yelled after hearing the shower turn on. I marched down the stairs with a mischievous smile on my face and into the bathroom below. Waiting a few seconds, trying to time the moment Ryan would be in the shower, I then flushed the toilet.

"SHHIII… REAL MATURE BETHANY!" I heard him bellow as he was scalded in the shower above.

"I WASN'T GOING FOR MATURITY!" I yelled up the stairs and I could hear him laughing as I walked into the kitchen.

"What's going on?" Grams asked as I kissed her cheek and said good morning.

"Oh nothing," I smiled as I poured myself a glass of orange juice.

It was the fifth Sunday Mass that I had been to in the small, white church and finally, people seemed to be warming up to me or the idea of me. My politeness, even in the face of their coldness, had not gone unnoticed. After the congregation recessed through the Church doors, a few parishioners stopped to talk with me. They saw that I was human and that I truly wanted to get to know them if they would let me. I had weathered the storm and was overjoyed that I was now able to make progress. I happily answered questions they asked – some were about New York, while others asked if I liked living in Ellsworth.

On the drive home Gramps, Grams and Ryan concluded that after much speculation and skepticism, people were now in love with me. I thought my family was being a little ridiculous. However, I found relief knowing that I could say, 'Hello,' to familiar faces on a regular basis. I cherished how safe this place let me feel. After all, it held the things I loved, both new and old.

Sunday's talk with Grams was centered on Mr. Wicks. My grandmother was happy to hear that we were officially a couple. I couldn't tell what she liked more: the fact that he was a strapping, young man or that he was a strapping, young man related to the Landon's. Her liking for that family was obvious and she cared for Cole and Gracie as if they were her own.

Olivia came over after work. She brought with her the last few magazine covers I would be on the cover of, her homework and my refilled prescription. While flipping through the magazines, Liv and I exchanged stories of the past two days and the boys that we had spent them with. Liv described everything down to the last detail, completely smitten by Bobby. They were the two high school teenagers who finally admitted to liking one another. I was happy that her crush had turned out to be somewhat of a decent guy knowing that most girls choose the wrong person to play the role. I did cringe though thinking about Jackson and how his feelings for her were unknown. However, I was no matchmaker and Liv was smart enough to make her own decisions. When it was my turn to talk about my weekend, Olivia listened like a kid does when a mother reads a bedtime story – open to the impossible.

Having caught up with each others' 'diary entries' which included a high-octave squeal when I showed her Drew's letterman jacket that now hung on the chair next to my bed, Liv dove into my armoire. She was on a mission to pick out my outfits for the week as well as her own. In return, I checked over her pre-calculus homework with her favorite purple pen. "OH MY GOSH!" I heard her say and looked over. She was kneeling by one of the drawers, cradling something in her hands.

"What?"

"You seriously have THE coolest things," she said digging through more of the drawers for new discoveries.

"I'm glad you think so," I laughed returning to her assignment.

"Can I borrow this?" she asked holding something up.

Without looking I answered, "Yeah, sure."

"You're not even looking," she caught me.

"Liv," I said turning my head towards her, "You wear my clothes, take care of them and return them in perfect condition... you can borrow whatever you'd like. Plus, if it weren't for you, I wouldn't be wearing half of the things I own."

"This is like a dream come true," she said looking in the mirror holding up a statement necklace, another freebee for being Bethany Reid.

"Good," I smiled. "Your homework..."

"Pre-calculus is so boring. I wish it was history or something," she said plopping next to me to see the corrections I had made. I gave her an 'are you serious' expression at her comment. She knew I was horrible in history... and the reasons behind it. "Oh sorry," she said catching on to how funny her remark actually was. "You are the one who has the century old roots. By the way, I have to pick a topic for my paper in that class. Do you think Andrew could give me some firsthand accounts of..." Liv began to crack herself up.

"Do not finish that sentence," I laughed as she rolled away from me as I pretended to push her.

Monday, September 28th

"You, Ryan Taylor, want to go for a run?" I whispered in disbelief as my brother sat on the couch tying his sneakers. The only morning light was coming in from the stained glass window on the platform halfway up the stairs. I was dressed in my running clothes and had my music in hand when I came across my brother who was also in sweats ready for a run.

"Yeah," he said as if running recreationally was something he did normally. "Don't look at me like that. I used to run for football."

"Ry, that was at least two years ago," I continued to whisper, not wanting to wake up Gramps or Grams.

"We'll see," Ryan smirked as he passed me, walking onto the porch. When I followed behind him, he was stretching his arms behind his head. Looking down at me, he asked, "You ready?" with a smirk on his face. I put my earphones on the swing, not needing them today. Ryan and I looked at one another before pushing each other out of the way, trying to get down the porch steps first and then we were off on our run.

"Who won?" Gramps asked over the top of the *Ellsworth Edition* almost an hour later. I smiled sweaty but victorious, climbing the steps and sat next to my grandfather. Ryan, however, leaned against the banister completely winded and looked up at Gramps.

"I might be," Ryan tried, "a little," he said sitting on the steps, "more out of shape," he continued with a deep breath, "than I thought."

"And what gave you that idea?" Gramps kiddingly questioned Ryan's breathless attempt. He and Ryan grinned at one another as my brother sat on the steps, leaning his head back on the railing. The screen door opened and Grams came out holding a cup of coffee for Gramps and a cup of tea for herself.

"Good morning," she said to her grandbabies before sitting in the chair next to her husband.

"Thank you, dear," my grandfather said taking his coffee. There the four of us sat together, talking and laughing as the sun came into full view.

—

Drew came up behind me at my locker, his nose nestled at my neck. "Hey you," I said turning and wrapping my arms around his neck.

"Morning," he said with a grin across his handsome face. A forced cough caused me to turn my head. Jackson stood next to his friend looking adorably awkward.

Blushing I closed my locker and kept a safe distance from Andrew for Jackson's sake but Andrew also had a natural rush of pink in his cheeks. We were not the 'public display of affection' sort, especially with our old-fashioned manners but when Drew and I were together it was as if everyone else disappeared.

"Turner," I heard a guy's voice call over the morning crowd by us. Looking up I saw a letterman jacket making its way over. "What's up, Wicks?" the redheaded, ball cap wearing, football player said as he put out his hand, which Andrew shook. Jackson was a good foot taller than Bobby who was wearing baggy jeans, a stupid logoed t-shirt and a navy blue baseball hat.

"Hi Beths," I heard Olivia say as she came up behind Bobby, holding his hand.

Surprised, I smiled, "Hey Liv." I stole a look at Jackson who had breathed in slightly when he saw Olivia. My heart sank.

"Hi I'm Bobby," he introduced himself.

"Bethany," I said returning his handshake.

"Yeah, I know," he answered. He seemed like a decent person but with Jackson standing there I just couldn't let myself like him. I knew it was wrong but I had sort of an allegiance to Jackson and his unknown feelings for Olivia.

"The guys and some of the cheerleaders are planning on taking you out to dinner like an official 'welcome to the team' thing," Bobby said turning to Andrew. "Since Coach is giving us off Friday we were planning on going to Bryant Square."

"Beths, you'll love it there," Olivia added.

"Oh," I said a little taken aback at the invite. "You don't have to invite me because Andrew and I are together," I said and saw Andrew's lips grin at how sweet it sounded.

"No. Actually, to be honest, the girls are using it as an excuse to hang out with you," Liv explained.

"Oh," I laughed, "That would be cool. Thanks."

"So, Bethany's in. What about you, Captain?" Bobby asked.

"I'll be there," Jackson nodded and looked at Andrew who also nodded.

"We're taking four cars. Zach, Donahue, Clifton and I are driving."

"Sounds good," Jackson responded looking away from Olivia and Bobby's intertwined hands.

"Cool, well I better get to class," Bobby answered giving Liv a kiss on the cheek before leaving the group.

"Later," Jackson said quickly before walking in the opposite direction. With a quick glance at Andrew, I knew that he also was aware of Jackson's feelings towards Olivia – most likely the bond they had formed.

"See you later," I said hurriedly leaving Andrew and Liv and followed Jackson. "Hey," I called out, "Jackson, wait up," trying to catch up to him with his large stride. Reaching out, I grabbed his arm and he looked down at me, his eyes narrowed. Without having to ask him if he was okay, I let go and put my arm around his as we walked into history. He seemed better when we took our seats and he grinned at me thankfully. I didn't know what I could do to help him but I would not let him wallow alone.

By biochemistry, Jackson had recovered completely and I was relieved that Andrew would be around for him. I saw Drew outside of the classroom before class started. Zach and Duke had called out his name and his open hand was met with slaps instead of a typical handshake in return. It was a barbaric gesture compared to how Drew was use to being greeted by another person, but it was another facet of societal 'evolution' if you can call it that. Two more football players had made their way over toward the small gathering. "Clifton, Tyler," Andrew added as they too slapped hands. Every teammate respected Andrew not only because he was best friends with the captain but because he was a good quarterback and they truly liked him and respected him.

As I walked in front of the teacher's desk I heard Charles' voice, "Good afternoon, Beths."

"Hi Ch… Dr. Landon," I said trying to recover the minor blunder.

"Everything okay?" he smiled.

"Yes sir," I assured him.

"How are you feeling?" he asked standing up.

"If you are referring to my heart," I said whispering, "I'm fine." He smiled at my response.

"Have you been taking the medicine?" he inquired like a concerned parent.

Putting out my hand, looking like a handshake he took it with a smirk on his lips. He knew what I was about to show him; recollections of all the mornings I had taken the medication as soon as the alarm sounded. "I believed you before…" he said releasing my hand.

"Oh, I know," I interrupted. "I just figured that when Abby asks you later…you could pass along the message with some proof," I smiled and heard him chuckling to himself as I found my way to my seat.

After hanging Drew's letterman jacket on the back of my desk, I looked forward, waiting for class to start. I felt a tap on my shoulder and saw someone slide into Andrew's chair. As I turned my head, I was surprised that Courtney Sanders was the culprit. She was a pretty girl, petite, with blondish hair and brown eyes. She was one of the most popular girls in school but looked nervous now talking to me. "Hi, I'm…" she started.

"Courtney Sanders," I smiled happy that I had taken Jackson's advice. This making it a priority to know everyone's name and a little bit about them was handy in these situations.

"Yeah," she smiled, relief washing over her.

"Hi, I'm…" I said putting out my hand.

"Bethany Taylor," she copied. "I love your dress, by the way. Listen, I was just wondering… some of the guys from the team and some of the cheerleaders are going to Bryant Square on Friday..."

"Yeah, I'll be there. Bobby mentioned it this morning."

"Oh, great," she said gleefully. "I guess I'll talk to you then?" she said looking up at Charles who was ready to start the class.

"Today we are going to pick up on page one-seventy," he began as he eyed Jackson and Andrew who were coming in to the classroom late. He glared at them and shook his head. I had to restrain myself from laughing out loud watching as Andrew walked passed his brother-in-law with a mischievous expression. "Page one-seventy," Charles repeated as the two players slid into their seats.

—

Class ended and Clifton pounded Andrew's fist before leaving; an exchange that Drew had yet to adapt too. I shook my head back and forth, biting my tongue. When I looked sideways at Andrew he was shaking his head too, humorously disgusted at how etiquette had changed and how he hadn't kept up as well as he thought. It was times like these I wasn't sure who was better off – Andrew for living so long or me for getting a fresh start seventeen years ago.

"You are an old man," Charles blurted to Drew when the classroom had completely emptied causing my pent up laughter to release.

"Charles," Andrew broke out laughing.

"What was that?" Charles said trying to imitate Andrew's unnatural reaction.

"Alright," Drew said standing from his desk with his book at his side. He reached down and slid my books into his hands, carrying them for me without a second thought. "I'll admit that maybe I need to catch up a bit on things like that..." Andrew started.

"And terminological phrases," I jokingly added, "Like how to ask out a girl for instance." Charles not knowing what I meant touched my hand and I recalled the scene. He was in hysterics when the images stopped and our hands separated.

Andrew looked at me with an embarrassed grin crossing his face. "Okay, that as well."

—

I had one more class before the final bell – English. As I clicked my pen and touched the clean page in my notebook, I smiled to myself. Not everything had gone out of style; I would write Andrew a letter… and what better class to do it in. I spent the period drafting what I would say. I knew that in his wallet, he kept a letter from me from years ago. I made sure to mention that and how this letter, this note, was written by the girl who thought even more of him now than she did then.

Wanting to present it the way I would have, in an envelope, I stopped at the Main Office and asked for one and wrote his name on it. Thanks to Liv and our previous 'adventure' to the boys' locker room, I knew where Drew's locker was. Waiting in the safety of my grandfather's office until the football team took the field for practice, I then slid into the testosterone chamber. I put the envelope underneath Drew's car keys on the shelf above his neatly hung clothes and smiled all the way back to my car.

—

"CHRIS!" I yelled over the sound of a loud saw outside the barn shaped workshop. Chris and another guy he was working with looked up, cutting the power to the saw and took off their safety glasses. "Hi," I started embarrassed at the now awkward silence. A group of workers off to the side who were going over at an order looked up at the abrupt quietness.

"Bethany? What are you doing here?" Chris asked giving me a quick hug and continued, "And why aren't we married yet?" I shook my head and Chris smirked, "I see how it is. You're leaving me for that Wicks kid…" He let out a breath of air for dramatic effect, "Well, I can't say I didn't see this coming. Bethany, I'll let you down easy. It's not you. It's me," he sighed.

"I was never good enough," I played back sarcastically to which he laughed, appreciative of my sense of humor.

"Hey Bethany," I heard Gregg call out as he walked down the path towards us. Gregg was not dressed like the rest of the guys at the Lumberyard; he was wearing a suit and tie.

"Are you on lunch?" Chris asked shaking his buddy's hand.

"Yeah," he said looking sharp in his dress clothes.

Chris, returning his attention to me, questioned, "What brings you here, Beths?"

"Is Ry around?"

"Sure is. He's up in the office," Gregg said pointing up to a nicer, newer looking barn where he had just come from. "So… you and Wicks?" Gregg asked.

"Ah hum," I nodded as a shade of pink touched my face.

"What's his favorite team," Chris asked curiously.

"Not blue," I said with a distorted expression and shrugged.

"Then he's okay in my book," Chris joked.

"Up the path, to the other barn," Gregg directed me after punching Chris in the arm.

"Thanks guys. See you later?" I hoped.

"Yup," they said as I turned and started towards the newer, nicer barn.

Once inside, I looked around. It was beautiful. Unlike the work barn, this space was finished and professional. The area was both warm and welcoming and had awards, achievements and recognitions displayed, showcasing the quality workmanship the Lumberyard had done. The lighting in the open rooms was soft and the amenities were high end. It was impressive, especially to clients who would come in to go over plans and finalize proposals.

"Bethany?" I heard from above me. I looked up and Ryan was looking down over the banister from the lofty second floor. "What are you doing here?" he asked walking down the wooden stairs.

"I came to visit. I thought you'd want dinner," I said as I held up a big brown bag.

"Thanks. I'm starving," he said taking it and tilting his head back up to where he came from.

The second floor was my brother's office which had a view of the entire Lumberyard. Ryan placed the bag on his old, wooden desk and sat down pointing to the chair on the opposite side. As he started to dig into the dinner Grams had packed, I took the seat across from him, "Ry, this place is really nice."

"Thanks," he smiled as he looked around.

"So what do you do besides sit up here and look pretty?" I asked sarcastically.

"Looking pretty is what I do best," he touched his chest kiddingly but then continued, answering my question. "This place was strictly a supplier but after Mr. Manahan retired and sold it to me, I started doing some subcontracting work. That took off," he said taking a bite.

"So you build things?" I asked standing up and looking at blueprints that were laid out on a drawing table behind me to my right.

"Aha," he said. "That is a headache," he gestured towards the blueprints I was reviewing.

"Why?" I asked as I took a closer look at them.

"The architect is off his rocker. The engineer will never approve it. I'm going to have to call in another guy," my brother said shaking his head in frustration.

"It's the support beam. Move and brace the columns to prevent further fatigue and go with synthetic wood beams to create the truss design," I recommended mechanically as if it were a word problem. I then snapped my head up hoping he hadn't heard what I just said. No such luck. Ryan was looking at me stunned. I quickly added, "I mean…"

Ryan stood up, abandoning the food on his desk and walked over to the blueprint. I frantically looked around the open office. He traced his finger over the support beam line, considering my suggestion. Then he looked up at me suspiciously. "How did you…" he started to ask.

"Ryan," I said touching the table lightly, "Is there any possible way you could forget the last minute or two?"

"Not a chance," he said flatly and a smile broke over his face and his hand rested on his hip. "Where did you learn that?" he questioned, crossing his arms in front of him.

"I, ah, I saw a special on television?" I fibbed pathetically.

"Bullshit. Bethany, where did you learn about support beams and truss designs?" he challenged, stepping closer to me still smirking.

Taking a step back and not making eye contact because of my inability to successfully lie, I answered, "At school."

"Oh really? Last time I checked, Ellsworth or Saint Hale's Academy for Girls didn't offer engineering classes…"

"Ryan, there's something I probably should have told you awhile ago…"

Ryan turned the seat I had sat in moments ago around and pointed, "Sit!" Listening, I sunk into it as he leaned against the drawing table and said, "Explain."

"I have an interest in that kind of stuff," I pointed to the drawing.

"Engineering or Architecture?" he asked.

"Both," I nodded.

"How much of an interest," my brother grilled.

Defeated, I looked down at the floor and said softly, "Enough to start a degree in it."

"A degree," Ryan said in a tone higher than usual.

Trying to get myself out of the secret I had kept from him and from everyone I added sarcastically, "You know the thing that you get at college."

"Bethany Ann," he said not amused by my attempt to use humor during this conversation.

But Ryan would not gain ground by using intimidation from the use of my middle name. "Ryan Jonathan," I retorted, crossing my arms and then looked dramatically around his office. He had failed to mention that he owned the Lumberyard until I put two and two together.

"It's not the same. We're talking about the fact that you have a COLLEGE DEGREE," he said putting his hands up in the air.

"Started… started a college degree," I corrected.

"How did you not tell me this?" he said walking over to his desk, touching his head. "How could I not know…"

Turning my chair around to its original direction, I teased him by using the same line he had used about not telling anyone about me, "It's not easy to bring up in casual conversation."

"That's not funny," he said pointing at me but began to laugh.

"Dude, you own your own business and you didn't tell me," I said trying to even the playing field.

Plopping down in his chair, he leaned back and ran his hands through his hair roughly. "I just can't believe you're in college… you're seventeen!" I shrugged and leaned back, sitting comfortably. "How far into it are you?"

"Two years."

"Two years," he breathed and rolled his eyes. "Does mom know?" he asked and I answered his question with a roll of my eyes. "What school?" was his next question.

"Columbia."

Ryan snorted. "She would LOVE that," he said pushing back in his chair laughing and put his hands behind his head. Our mother's infatuation with prestige was one of the many reasons her and Ryan did not get along. When she found out that he had no plans of attending an elite university, because he had his eyes set on a state school for an associate's degree, she nearly lost her mind. She surely lost her voice the night she found out. Our mother yelled and screamed at him and it wasn't too long after that Ryan moved in with our grandparents. If she only knew that her 'dead beat' son, as she referred to him, was an owner of a successful business and that her 'career killing' daughter was halfway through an Ivy League degree, she might have a stroke.

"Columbia, geeze Beths," he smiled but with pride at me. Leaning forward on his desk he asked with a growing curiosity, "Engineering?"

"No," I answered playing with one of his paperweights.

"Architecture?" he then assumed.

"Nope," I replied and he looked up at me puzzled. "Architectural Engineering," I said focusing on the paperweight in my hands but watching out of the corner of my eye for his reaction. He hit the top of the desk with his hand and his mouth opened.

"You're ridiculous. Do you know that?"

"Ryan…" I shook it off.

"No, seriously," he started, "What were you modeling by day and a bookworm by night?"

"Mostly bookworm," I said unimpressed and returned the paperweight back to his desk. It was true. There was nothing glamorous about sitting in an empty penthouse alone. I would never forget that lesson. It had humbled me.

Handing me a fork from his desk drawer, he slid the rest of the dinner over for us to share. "You know, now that I think about it, I can't say that I'm surprised," my brother said taking a bite. "I mean you've always been smart."

"It's not because I'm smart, it's because I had a lot of time on my hands." I corrected after swallowing a mouthful of Gram's delicious baked ziti.

"Does anyone else know?" he questioned.

"Mrs. Landon," I said and he gave me a confused look as to how and why she knew. "She gave a physics exam. I finished it way too fast and forgot to use a calculator." I shrugged knowing that I was really, truly horrid at the fibbing thing.

"You *forgot* to use a calculator?" Ryan laughed.

"I know," I shook my head.

"So how are you at sketching?" he asked.

"Pretty good," I downplayed. Sketching was something I knew I was exceptionally good at.

"You're not licensed yet, right?" he continued.

"Not yet... I'm only two years into my degree," I said taking another bite of dinner.

"Hmm," he said and I could see that he was scheming something. "Want to do me a favor."

"That depends," I speculated light-heartedly.

"Oh, come on!"

"Yeah, fine. What?" I laughed.

"Sketch a house – for Kate and I. Think of it as an audition."

"An audition for what?" I asked taking another bite.

"Well I need an in-house architect... and wouldn't mind replacing the current engineering firm eventually. Plus, you could work here part-time while you finish up your degree and then full-time once you graduate," Ryan negotiated as he passed me a bottle of water.

"Are you serious?" I asked with a raised eyebrow.

"Very."

"As long as my two year head start stays a secret..." I stipulated.

"But," my brother tried but I tilted my head. "Fine. Deal." As I stabbed another forkful of food Ryan said, "You know dad was really good at that kind of stuff." His statement caught me off guard. We never spoke about dad but this was the second time he brought him up. Lately, I was learning more and more about my father and from different angles too. They were things that I always wanted to know the answers too.

I took a deep breath and figured now was as good a time as any to bring up the question that was the hardest to form. "Can I ask you something?" I asked bravely.

Ryan nodded his head and said, "Shoot."

"It's about dad," I warned.

"Okay," he said remaining serious.

"How did he die?"

"Beths…" Ry started.

"Ry, please," I begged.

Ryan wiped his mouth with a paper napkin and then looked across at me. "There was an accident…" My heart ached at the words Ryan chose. They were hauntingly familiar to the ones Charles, Abby and Andrew had spoken. It didn't matter how my father had passed in this lifetime. I knew an eerie parallel would be the answer. I put my fork down and leaned back in the chair as Ryan continued. "Dad was just in the wrong place at the wrong time." I felt a pain that throbbed as the words Ryan unknowingly used fit into the definition of the phenomenon.

—

My windows were wide open letting the cold breeze whip through the car. It felt good on my face since I felt sick after hearing Ryan tell me details of my father's death fifteen years ago.

The music that was playing was interrupted by an incoming call. I pressed the phone button on the steering wheel.

"Hello?" I answered.

"Hey Beths," Olivia said over the speakers.

"Hey, what's up?" I said pulling onto Main Street.

"So what did you think about Bobby?" she giggled excitingly.

"He seems nice, Liv," I answered.

"I knew you'd like him! I'm so excited for Friday. You are going to love Bryant Square and the restaurant we're going to is so nice. It's like," she paused and then finished with, "upscale."

"Cool," I said coming to a stop, letting familiar faces cross in front of my car. They waved and I waved back.

"We're going to have so much fun. All the girls are freaking out that they get to hang out with a famous model. They're hoping for some beauty tips."

"My tip is to not wear too much," I laughed.

"Yeah, well I'm sure they'll want to hear about New York and have other questions for you but don't worry. I already told them that you're super boring," Liv said jokingly.

"Thanks Liv," I chuckled as I continued to drive down Main Street.

"Yeah, yeah," she teased. "Well practice just ended and," Liv said becoming distracted. Seconds later she said, "Andrew wants to talk to you," I could hear the smile in her voice.

"Sure," I said feeling instantly giddy at the surprise. I heard Liv hand the phone off.

"Hello?" his voice said, warming my heart.

"Hello," I answered, biting my lip.

"There was a letter waiting for me in my locker. You wouldn't happen to know who it is from, would you?" Drew asked and I could hear him smiling as he spoke. I knew he had stepped away from the football and cheerleading crowd he was with.

"Perhaps," I flirted.

"Perhaps," he laughed. "Well, I do recognize the handwriting on the envelope. It belongs to that of a young lady who has my heart." I touched my chest and shook my head. He was perfect.

"Does she?" I asked not knowing what else to say.

"Yes, she does." The noise from the people around him got louder as everyone got to their cars and said their goodbyes.

"Have you opened the note yet?" I inquired.

"No, I've been in other people's company but soon enough," he said and I could hear the echoes of an older time in his words. I could hear car doors closing and engines starting. "Have a good evening, Bethany."

"Good night, Drew," I said and heard him hand Olivia back her phone.

"Hey," she said and I heard Bobby's voice close by. "I have to go. Bobby's giving me a ride home but I'll see you tomorrow?"

"Yes," I confirmed as I turned off Main Street and onto my grandparents' block.

"Later Beths," my best friend said and the phone disconnected. I was still blushing from my short conversation with Andrew as the music in my car resumed over the audio system.

Tuesday, September 29th

If crazy could be defined, I was pretty sure my picture would be next to it. But the crazier my life got, the more it made sense and I would rather be in a straightjacket than question the chain of events. And truthfully, why would I?

After my run with Ryan, I showered and headed to school. Abby was in the hallway standing amongst the students' morning buzz. She was waiting close to my locker dressed in a high waist skirt with a cream colored blouse and her hair was neatly twisted and pinned back. Even though her outfits clearly reflected an earlier era's inspiration, it could be viewed as just being 'vogue'. I smiled knowing the real influence behind her wardrobe selections where her impression from an older time and how the irony was overlooked by people who passed by her. "Good morning Mrs. Landon," I grinned when I reached her.

"Good morning, Bethany. May I see you for a moment?" she nodded towards the empty faculty lounge with a smile.

After she closed the door behind us, she wasted no time. "Charles will be quite angry when he finds out I pulled you aside…" Abby would be unable to hide this memory from him when their hands met next time; a slight drawback in the luxury of their 'gift'.

"What? Why?" I asked concerned.

"He doesn't want us to overwhelm you," she explained.

"Well, I love Charles for being so protective," I said sincerely, "but I am fine, really. I know it might be hard to believe."

"That's what I said," she smiled, pouring herself a cup of hot water from the small kitchenette. "If you aren't doing anything later, Charles and Andrew have practice until seven and are picking up Cole and Gracie from a play date afterwards. I was hoping…" she started.

"I would love to keep you company," I answered excitedly. Abby and I would have time together at the Estate to 'catch up' even though a hundred years was a lot to crunch into one afternoon. But then again, time was insignificant when it came to understanding our friendship and, of course, we had the advantage of sharing memories without a single word.

"Wonderful," she smiled widely. The homeroom bell rang and morning announcements followed over the PA system. "You should probably get to class," she frowned before steeping her teabag.

"You're not planning on springing any quantum physics questions on me today, are you?" I asked jokingly as I reached for the doorknob and so did Abby. Our hands touched unintentionally and the connection was made.

Flashes of Ellsworth flew in front of my eyes. The currently paved Main Street was a dirt road with few storefronts on either side and there were no stoplights.

Then I saw the curved road which led to the oak alley but it was a one lane path which made the cobblestone entrance stick out unlike its hidden appearance now. As the flashes of the drive leading up to the Estate revealed much younger oak trees, it was amazing how the house looked exactly the same, relatively unchanged. Even with the renovations Charles and Abby had made to the stables, now the multi-car garage, the Estate maintained its charm. It had been something important to the two of them, almost like an ode to my father – the man who designed and built the home.

"Sorry," Abby apologized as the images stopped. "We really have to stop doing that," she said motioning to the door knob where my hand still was.

"It's okay," I said honestly. I loved how we could communicate so much so quickly and accurately, especially since I could feel the emotions and understand them more fully.

As Abby and I walked down the now deserted hallway, I asked her, "When did you come back to Ellsworth?"

"Charles and I left the Estate shortly after Andrew did. The three of us made sure we stayed together moving from town to town and eventually state to state before our agelessness could be recognized by the people we knew. But every couple of years Charles and I would leave Andrew and visit the Estate for a week or so making sure that the house was cared for, whether it needed updates or cleaning. About two years ago though, when we visited, neither Charles nor I wanted to leave after the week was over, so we didn't. The three of us were up for another move anyway and Charles and I always considered Ellsworth our home and missed it, I suppose. Andrew finished up in California and went to the next place we had previously decided on, Colorado… It was the first time we had separated since the night he stormed out of the Estate. It was strange not being together, the three of us…" Abby trailed off.

"Drew *never* visited?" I asked.

"No, and Charles and I didn't expect him too either. We flew out to him for holidays and visits. Charles spoke with him every other day over the phone about the hospitals and other things," she explained.

"What about…" I started, interested in learning the finer details of their story.

"Homeroom," Abby pointed towards my classroom door with a smirk on her face.

"Yes, ma'am," I groaned.

"We'll continue later," she grinned knowing that I had a plethora of questions. I pouted childishly, not wanting to leave the conversation. "I have plenty of questions for you too," she added with a smile and took a sip of her hot tea.

"Good," I grinned happily as I walked into homeroom.

"Hey Beths," Jackson said handing me a piece of paper as I sat in my desk.

"Hey," I said taking it. It was his calculus homework.

"Do you mind looking it over?"

"No problem," I said and glanced down at it.

"Do you want me to read over your history answers?" he offered.

"That would be awesome," I said pulling out my notebook and handed it to him. When we both had finished reviewing and correcting each other's work, we swapped them back. Then Jackson handed me something else… a note… from Andrew. A smile broke out over my face and Jackson, not completely anticipating my girly response, laughed and shook his head.

"I had strict orders to make sure you got this before physics."

"Thanks," I somewhat squealed, looking at my name on the front of the envelope and opened it quickly.

Dearest Bethany,

I have seen ink wasted on numbers and needless matters but fear that with your last letter, you have given it more worth than any ink deserves. Absorbed by your affections for me, I must admit that you are the only thing that my forever battling heart and mind have ever truly agreed upon. The impression your life has made on mine is that of the simple truth, that love is a gift.

I will be waiting outside of Abigail's classroom. I ask that you save your fingers from scripting a response and, instead, let them rest in my hand.

Yours *always*,

Andrew

—

He was waiting outside of our physics classroom. He smiled at the sight of me and I blushed as the distance between us closed. Drew's hand reached out for mine and thinking of this morning's conversation with Abby and the plans we had made for this afternoon, I laced my fingers with his and the images passed in front of his eyes.

He saw my conversation with Abby and felt my excitement for the plans to catch up with her and to be at the Estate. It would give him comfort like it did me. Then I turned my thoughts over to reading his letter and the longing I had felt since this exact moment.

He placed his other hand on the small of my back and pulled me closer to him enticingly after the flashes stopped. As I ran my fingers up his wrist to his forearm, I stood on my tippy toes and whispered into his ear, "We're going to be late for class."

"I know the teacher," he whispered back and grinned as he spun me so that my back was up against the lockers.

"If you kiss me, I will have a hard time stopping," I said as his lips moved dangerously close to mine

"I just can't be late for practice," he said sarcastically.

"Don't worry, I know the coach," I giggled. He laughed as he ran his thumbs down my waist, to my hips. Andrew leaned in and my hands grazed the sides of his face as our lips met.

"Mr. Wicks, Ms. Taylor," we heard Mr. Donovan's voice say a few feet away and stepped back from each other, having been caught. Mr. Donovan was walking down the hall with another teacher. "Shouldn't you two be in class?"

"Yes," Andrew and I both answered somewhat embarrassed. Drew held the door for me as we walked into the classroom. Abby had already started her lecture and watched us as we found our seats, red-faced. I looked over my left shoulder and Drew shook his head, still laughing and smiled at me. I grinned as I opened my textbook and turned back around to listen to today's lesson.

—

Gramps, Liv, Bobby, Charles and Drew were off to their respective practices. Kate was busy at the hospital while Ryan and Chris were working late again at the Lumberyard with Gregg's help and Grams was spending the afternoon at the Ladies Guild meeting for the upcoming annual County Fair on Saturday. I had stopped by the house, leaving a note for Grams saying that I went to the Landon's and would be home later. I was now on the once dirt, now paved, curved road looking for the hidden cobblestone that was once so prominent. The autumn breeze rushed in my open windows as I turned and went up the path. The scent was crisp and fresh; a mix of floral aroma and fall leaves.

Putting my car in 'Park', I slowly got out and took a closer look at my surroundings. The trees were thick, old. The cobblestone was worn against the perfectly manicured grounds and the Estate itself was majestic, historic, but most of all, timeless.

"What are you looking for?" Abby called out from the doorway.

"Nothing," I said starting my way up to her, "Everything," I added, laughing.

"Where to begin…" she exhaled, putting her finger to her chin. We both giggled as we made our way into the kitchen.

It took three hours for Abigail and I to pretty much cover a hundred years worth of time. She highlighted moments in our memory exchanges keeping her emotions honest and open.

Places and decades evolved as her story, their story, unfolded in front of my eyes. It wasn't always glamorous and it wasn't always safe but it was true and it was very much a part of who they were. However, Abby's mind always seemed to bring her back to Ellsworth. With the last few images of her and Charles' return to this old town two years ago, my vision cleared and my eyes refocused on the room we were in.

"So," she said filling my empty cup with more coffee as we sat around the wooden island in the kitchen.

"So," I repeated rolling my shoulders, stretching my back, "Do you miss it?" I asked.

"Miss the one horse town? I guess in a way. I miss its rhythm – but some days are very reminiscent, kind of like today," she smiled at me as I brought the rim of the cup to my lips.

"How have you stayed the same and no one has noticed?" I asked still perplexed by the feat.

"In those days, in that time, there wasn't exactly the same census system that there is today," she smirked. "Charles and Andrew have become very well-versed in staying under the radar. And we make sure never to stay in one place long enough for anyone to notice that we don't age."

"Do you like moving all the time," I asked tilting my head.

Contemplating the question for a second Abby finally answered, "At first it was exciting, moving to new places, seeing different things but just as we made deep relationships with other people, we would have to leave and we couldn't stay in touch without the risk of exposing our secret. Unfortunately, it became routine to meet people and become numb to the idea that we couldn't build long-term friendships. That becomes depressing." She was troubled by this but when she looked up, she smiled. "Until you and all of this happened. I can't wait to see what your life has been like... It's your turn," Abby said placing her hand out for me to take.

"Alright but there's really nothing to see," I warned.

"Let me be the judge of that," she grinned.

"Okay," I shrugged and placed my hand in hers.

I thought as far back as I could in my seventeen years and worked my way forward. I started with Ryan and I, and our relationship before he moved out. Then I showed her how difficult it was for me the night he left but that his happiness was more important to me.

I grazed over the days that followed not wanting to dwell on the emptiness I felt without him being part of my day-to-day life or how it amplified my desire to know my late father. That was something that I had always felt but now longed for in the loneliness of the penthouse.

I recalled how my life changed when my mother's idea of pageants and modeling became her ambition for my life. The memories from hundreds of photo shoots and PR functions I had attended were superficially significant but emotionally empty; more now than they had been then.

I had few and far between glimpses of my mother's presence so I didn't have to go into detail about her lack of maternal instinct or care. However, I did throw in a few of her most memorable episodes where she knowingly or unknowingly inflicted psychological scarring. But, I didn't dwell on them. Instead, happier times of Ryan and my grandparents' visits flooded my mind all at once. The drastic change in emotion from when they arrived to when they left emphasized the extreme boredom that followed which, in turn, gave light to my devotion to schoolwork.

I had kept my academic successes to myself and recalled how my life had changed when I received my acceptance letter from Columbia. The next images were of my visit to the doctor and how I had learned about my condition, very much alone. As a result of the diagnosis I had become a dedicated runner and the running, along with classes pulled me through that season of my life.

The last thoughts I revealed were that of Ryan's unexpected visit and his intentions to take me back to Ellsworth with him. I concentrated hard on the memory because it was the moment everything changed for the better and the first page of a new beginning.

Abby was quiet for a minute after the flashes subsided. She took a long sip of tea with both hands and then looked back at me.

I was looking passed her and out the large double hung window into the backyard toward the darkening evening sky. "I'm sorry," Abby said.

"For what?" I asked.

"I don't know," she said placing her elbow on the back of the chair and leaned her head against her hand. "I don't know what's worse: us frozen, waiting unknowingly or you alone, unknowingly waiting."

"It sounds the same to me," I said in jest as the sound of tires on the cobblestone came from the front of the house.

"Right on time," she said getting to her feet and turning off the oven. The delicious smelling dinner we had prepared was ready to be served. Abby turned around before opening the oven doors and said, "Thanks for this," gesturing between the two of us.

"You're ridiculous," I laughed getting to my feet, taking the fine china plates and silverware out of the cupboards and drawers.

"I know but it's just that..." she began.

"You could get used to it?" I finished her sentence.

"Yes," she smiled.

"Abby," I said turning to her, "You better get used to it." Her smile widened as she slid oven mitts on and took out the tray. Following me into the dining room, we heard the front door open. Cole and Gracie ran towards the bathroom to wash their hands. When everything was set, we both looked up at the dining room doorway, noticing that Charles and Andrew were silently watching us.

"Hi," Abby said and the two of their smiles grew as they entered the room, each walking towards their other half.

"Good evening, ladies," Charles addressed before kissing his wife on her cheek. Andrew put his right hand behind my neck and softly kissed my forehead. Abby and I looked at one another warily and then back at our respective men. Drew, still in his practice uniform, was dirty but handsome in the rugged sense. His lips were red from the cold wind and, once again, I found myself mesmerized. I heard Charles say to his wife, "Supper smells amazing."

"Good. It's Beths' favorite," Abby said and skeptically stepped away from her husband and looked over at Andrew. "What's gotten into you two?" she asked looking between them

"Nothing," Charles said devilishly stepping toward her. Abby took a step and Charles countered. She took another step and he would not let her pass. He and she acted so differently behind closed doors. They seemed much younger and much less reserved than when they were in public. They were very much still young and in love.

"How was practice?" I asked Andrew as I watched Charles teasingly follow Abby into the kitchen.

"It went well," Drew answered as he also enjoyed Charles' mimicking of Abby and the laughter that was now coming from the kitchen.

Andrew looked down at me and asked, "How was your afternoon?"

"Quickest century of my life," I said sarcastically and he innately held my hand. The unintentional connection was made and with it, my mind became polluted.

There were no images; only hues of grays and blacks as Drew tried with all his might to prevent the century old memory from surfacing but it was too late. The emotions were uncontainable and transferred into me like a bolt of lightning. A stomach turning, empty, bottomless ache ignited for a fraction of a second before we could release our hands.

Drew's arms were around me, holding me up in the seconds of weakness that followed. "Are you okay?" he asked panic-stricken.

"Yes," I said stretching the truth because hell had just passed through me. But I would not let this man feel guilty over such raw emotions, emotions that he didn't intentionally want to share or for me to know he had lived with. Drew was upset and angry at himself for the mistake that had taken my knees out from under me. I would never forget that pain; it still radiated through me, trying to latch on.

He fought with words he wanted to say but before he could, I kissed him fervently with every ounce of my being. He had to know how sorry I was for both then and now. I hated the thought of him wrestling with the worst life had to offer. In time, with me here with him, he would get over the guilt and see passed the hurt.

Andrew had been caught a little off guard by my reaction and hesitated before kissing me back but when he did, it intensified the passion between us. I pulled his jersey closer to me and breathed only out of necessity. My lips traced his as his tongue found mine.

"Ah hmm," Charles coughed intentionally, having entered the dining room with Abby who then elbowed him in the side for disrupting Andrew and I. We slowly pulled our lips from one another's and turned our heads towards Charles' voice but did not let go. "We can't leave you two without a chaperon for a minute, can we?" Charles joked and crossed his arms but was smiling. Abby, standing beside him, looked like she was going to explode with happiness. Proper etiquette would have it that an unmarried, courting couple would not be left in each other's private company. This was one of a few things that Andrew and I didn't mind society changing its view on.

"Drew, shower?" his sister asked placing another prepared dish on the table.

"Yes," he said kissing the side of my head before jogging up the stairs to his bedroom to wash up before dinner. Charles opened the lid of the dish Abby had just put down. She tapped his hand away from trying to steal a bite and closed the lid.

"You too," she motioned for her husband to wash up before the meal.

"Yes, dear," he breathed but stole a bite when she had turned away. She heard the glass lid close and watched as he slid out of the dining room.

"Charles!" she laughed and then turned back to me. "See! They aren't perfect," she humorously exaggerated.

After dinner I helped Abby in the kitchen. It gave us more time to talk about the past, try to figure out the present and even daydream about the future. I enjoyed every second. She was thrilled to learn that Ryan had learned of my high education and he had 'proposed' that I sketch his future house. She basically pulled me out of the kitchen, through the entryway and into my father's old office where Charles and Andrew were working. They were sitting on the couches facing one another and stood when we entered. "Carry on," she said not paying them much mind and opened my father's desk drawer. She took out sketching tools, placed them on the desk and pointed at the leather seat for me to take, encouraging me to draft the house plans for the soon-to-be married couple in the place my father once sat. Abby now understood my feelings for Ryan and the bond we had, and she was grateful that he played the role he did in my life. I relished in the connection this place had with my father and even to Ryan, in some weird way.

Abby left soon-there-after to care to Cole and Gracie, leaving me to work. I quietly worked, getting my ideas down on paper and out of my head. It was a creative release and I added to my vision, oblivious to the world around me.

Abigail checked in on my progress, peaking over my shoulder at the sketch of the custom designed home that would hopefully meet and surpass my brother and sister-in-law's expectations.

"Wow," she whispered so that Charles and Andrew couldn't hear.

"I think I'm done with the rough draft," I said standing up and taking a step back so she could get a closer look. The layout and the details would come to life with each board they laid down. I had infused the design to reflect my brother's personality and was amused at how easily it came together. Of course, I added facets that Kate would appreciate if it were to ever be built.

"It's beautiful," Abby said trying to imagine what it would look like. "I'll have the architect who helped us with the renovations to the Estate draw up and sign off on this tomorrow," she said taking on the responsibility. Due to my limited education and not being licensed, I appreciated Abby's offer and the connections she had to expedite the plans. Sketching was the easy part compared to the actual construction timeline. The deadline was approaching quickly – the wedding was less than two months away, but Ryan had a tendency of waiting until the last minute for matters concerning him; he always put everyone else first. However, the fact that he owned the Lumberyard meant it wasn't too much of a stretch that he would be able to pull it off once the plans were filed. "Really Beths, it's great," Abby said looking up from the desk.

"Thanks," I said as I looked down at my pencil smudged hand before rolling up my work and quietly leaving the office.

Once back in the dining room, Cole handed Abby his completed homework pad and was focused on his handheld game.

"Bethany, do you want to play?" he asked as he leaned to the right, enthralled by the false reality.

"No thanks, Cole. I'm not very good," I said as Gracie got out of her chair and sat on my lap. I played with her blonde pigtails as she watched over her brother's shoulder.

"I'm only good because we don't have a television," he explained.

"I would try for the computer if I were you," I laughed.

"No television and definitely no computer," Abby said as she looked over the letters Gracie had traced in her book.

"You, Charles and Drew are eventually going to have to accept the fact that…" I started.

"It's not worth it, Bethany. Trust me. I've tried," Cole advised as he leaned to the left, still heavily concentrated on his game. I stood and walked over to the window; I could tell that the sun was making its way to the horizon on the other side of the house.

"Cole, I wasn't allowed to use those things when I was younger so you don't need to either." Abby said handing Gracie a crayon.

"That's because…" I whispered so only she could hear.

"Don't you finish that," my friend said under her breath trying to hold back laughter. "Cole, Gracie, why don't you go get that present you've been working on for Bethany?"

"Sure!" Cole jumped up and grabbed Gracie's hand.

"Presents," Gracie yelled excitingly as they ran out of the room.

"Presents?" I asked.

"Cole made a small box out of popsicle sticks and Gracie made a finger painting," Abby smiled as she picked up the rest of the scattered books and placed them back into the children's schoolbags.

"You know Abby, technology isn't…." I began.

"Please…" she started, "We use telephones and we adapt accordingly. Plus, not having some popular luxuries keeps the children out of trouble. Cole plays that one racing game but that's where Charles and I draw the line."

"Not all advances in technology are bad," I tried.

"I know. We use a lot of them, like air conditioning, washing machines, blow-dryers… deodorant," she grinned. "There are moments when I think we should adapt a little more. Maybe one of us would have seen you in one of those modeling photos.

We've just lived so simply for so long, that everything else just kind of whisks by."

"You put the popular world on a back burner, I understand that. I was in it and I know that there is always someone prettier or something nicer or the latest 'gadget' to want… It's never ending. No one ever 'wins' but everyone wants to play."

Charles, Abby and Drew's conscious decision to not allow themselves to be inundated with what the popular world had to 'offer' limited them far less than it would have impacted them. Education was still education and people were still people; I could see how they lived all these years, day by day, without the purposeless noise that so many were fascinated with.

—

Being Andrew's girlfriend was something that came easily. I never had to think of how I should act or not act – it all came naturally. We were completely old-fashioned, logically I suppose. No line was crossed, no tension felt. It was like we were living a love song. My life was fine without him and he had his life together too. We were the *icing* on the cake for one another – not the cake. That's why we saw each other as the blessings we were in each other's lives. "What were you working on before?" he asked as we walked out onto one of the many second story balconies of the Estate.

"Just sketching," I grinned, flattered that he had taken notice. Andrew understood that sitting at my father's desk alone would be comforting to me. He didn't press the subject any further.

The sun was meeting its second golden hour: sunset. He and I sat down on one of the lounge daybeds on the balcony and watched as the sunset's gold and reds illuminated the horizon with its refractions. It was getting colder out as the looming night carried a cool breeze passed us. Without a word, Drew pulled me closer so he could share his warmth with me. I rested my head on his chest and his hand played with my hair, long on my back. Moments like these I felt like I missed him, missed the time he had spent all those years without me. He kissed the top of my head and I looked up to meet his piercingly blue eyes. He was thinking hard about something; not at all relaxed as I had been. Drew slowly pushed himself up and I placed my hand down, next to his to support the change in position. With his right hand he took my head in his hands and kissed me fiercely, passionately. I pulled back slowly and tried to read his eyes but I wanted nothing more than to spend my time kissing him. As our lips met again, he moved his left hand to my back making sure that as he turned me, it was graceful. He was over me now, holding himself up with his arms as his lips kissed mine. I felt like I was breathing him in with every embrace. My hands ran up his back and then back down before I traced his jaw with my fingertips. Waves of emotions made my legs feel unsteady even though I was lying down.

His lips traveled to my neck and then up to my ear. His hands ran through my hair as I turned so he could lie next to me. Kissing, we ran our hands over each other's sides, never crossing the line, but tempting enough. I felt so absolute; there was a freedom in his arms. Our bodies were close to each other's, there was no space unused. He ran his hand along my waist and pulled out of a kiss. I watched as he opened his eyes looking the way I felt; longingly and blissful.

I looked down at his chest and my hand grazed where his skin met his gray t-shirt. He kissed it before brushing disheveled hair away from my face and behind my ear, and kept it there. "You are beautiful," Drew said meeting me eye-to-eye not regretful for the road that led us here. I bit my lip and he brought his fingers up, tracing them and whispered, "You must know that I am completely enamored by you." I slowly reached for his hand, anticipating the emotions that I wanted to show him. But just before our hands touched, his lips found mine again. When our fingers, met flashes erupted.

Bright and clear as a movie, they were intense, almost over-powering emotions that swept over us. But they weren't just mine, they were his too. It was as if our feelings for one another combined as our history intertwined with our present. I felt Drew's lips harder on mine, kissing me more ardently and only slowing when our hands let go of one another's.

The emotions which had come quickly and intensified as they collided now lingered as Drew and I stared into each other's eyes. There we lay under the unfolding night sky, star-crossed; something time couldn't touch.

Wednesday, September 30th

"That last mile was not a mile," Ryan argued, winded but not completely out of breath. With his next sentence he spoke in a southern accent, "That was a *country* mile."

"A country mile?"

"Yeah, longer than an actual one," my brother explained. I rolled my eyes as we walked up the driveway. "I'm telling you," my brother said sitting on the front porch steps, untying his sneakers.

"Fine, but I still kicked your butt," I teased. Ryan mimicked me and then stuck out his tongue.

"You are improving," my grandfather said to Ryan from behind his paper. "I didn't feel the need to call an ambulance for you this time."

"Thanks for the support, Gramps," Ryan shook his head. My grandfather put out his hand as I passed, giving me a high-five for my winning streak as I headed inside to take my shower and get ready for school.

—

With the end of class came a homework assignment. I heard Jackson moan as I copied down the instructions. We had been given homework in every class today and had other assignments that were piling up too. "Are you doing anything after school?" Jackson leaned over and asked.

"No," I exhaled. "I mean homework obviously," I shook my head while looking over the long list.

"Do you want to do it together? Coach gave us today off because of the game tomorrow..."

"Yeah, that would be great actually," I accepted as we walked out of the classroom and into the hallway.

"I have a Student Government meeting now but can we meet at the coffee shop on Main Street in about a half hour?"

"Sounds good to me," I smiled and Jackson nodded.

"Cool," he said and walked towards the Main Office as I headed towards my locker.

Liv was waiting for me there, her foot was tapping and her eyes widened when she saw me. "Thank God," she said and grabbed my wrist.

"Hey, what's up?"

"I have an emergency," Olivia said as she led me towards the ladies' room; a tiled haven. "The guys don't have practice today and I was supposed to have cheer practice but that just got cancelled and," she continued jittery. "Bobby just asked if I wanted to go the movies after school since I don't have practice or work and I said, 'Yes', but I clearly wasn't thinking because..." she took a deep breath so she could finish her story, "I wore my cheer practice clothes to school and don't have cute clothes and he looks nice and I don't and..."

"Okay," I said connecting the dots; she didn't have time to go home and change before their impromptu date. "Go," I said pointing to one of the toilet stalls.

"What?"

"Trust me," I said and went into the stall neighboring hers.

"Beths, what," she began to say as I locked my door and took off my blouse, then handed it over the divider. "Here," I shook my hand waiting for her to take it.

"Seriously?" she asked.

"Yes," I said and took the t-shirt she gave me in return.

"You are my hero," Olivia said not having taken this possible solution into consideration.

"Yeah, yeah," I laughed now taking off my skirt and handing it over to her.

"No, really," Liv said exchanging her black yoga pants in the clothes swap. We opened the stall doors and stood by the sink as we exchanged jewelry and shoes. Her feet were a little smaller than mine but not by much. "This is one of those best friend moments."

"I would say so," I smiled.

"Well not that I think you'll need my services, but if you ever need help carrying a dead body across the floor, you know who to call."

"Thanks. I'll remember that," I said shaking my head. When I looked back up she had taken her hair out of her braid and was adjusting the skirt. She looked adorable but I wasn't surprised.

After all, she had been the one to set the outfit aside for me to wear.

"How do I look?"

"Awesome," I smiled and then turned to my reflection. A plain dark pink v-neck t-shirt, black yoga pants, leopard patterned flats, a long gold necklace, gold bangle and some loose waves in my hair… It was simple but it worked.

"You're a life saver and I love you," Liv said clutching my arm.

"Just have fun," I said opening the door for her as we walked back out into the busy hallway. She floated away and I walked back to my locker. Andrew was waiting for me there and his head tilted when he saw that I was wearing a different outfit from the one I had been wearing in biochemistry. His eyebrow rose when I started to laugh.

I walked up to him and rested my forehead on his chest. "Hello Houdini," he said wrapping his arms around me. "What's with the wardrobe change?"

I pulled away and looked down at my 'new' outfit and began to explain, "Bobby asked Liv out after school and she didn't think her outfit was cute enough…"

"Well, you look stunning."

"Thank you," I smiled and opened my locker, taking out the books I needed for the coffee shop get together with Jackson. Andrew moved behind me, wrapped his arms around my waist and kissed my neck softly, sending chills down my spine.

"May I just say," Charles grinned as he came up to us standing flatfooted and crossed his arms. "You two make a beautiful couple. It's barely tolerable." Charles' tone was different than his own; they were not *his* words, rather he was reciting them. I noticed Drew push his tongue against his lower lip and shook his head.

"What?" I asked picking up that something was going over my head.

"You'll have to pardon my brother-in-law. He is ecstatic that he can finally say the very thing I have teased him and my sister about for quite some time."

"Aw," I sighed. It was true. Charles and Abby made a beautiful couple. With Andrew being Abby's brother and Charles' brother-in-law and best friend, he knew how the two complimented one another and how they lit up when the other was around. After years and years of witnessing it, the 'barely tolerable' part was clearly out of jest and not jealousy.

"I have been holding that back," Charles laughed.

"Oh come off it, Charles," Drew laughed as the three of us walked towards the parking lot.

—

Both gentlemen were off to the hospital to review the strategic plan and the Board's progress, Abby was taking the children to a play date. My grandfather was taking my grandmother out to lunch. Kate was working and so was Ryan. Liv was on a date with Bobby... and I parked my car on the side street by the coffee shop. The weather couldn't decide if it should rain or not. It was not partly cloudy out – it was completely cloudy.

The door to the corner coffee shop was made of small, glass panes with an old, wooden frame around them. Painted a teal color, it was chipped and old but it added a charm to the place. Inside, the walls were exposed brick, the floor was wooden and the tables were mismatched along with the chairs that went with them. The front wall was one big window where you could watch people pass by, up and down Main Street. Along the back of the storefront was a high counter and there was a wall of baked goods. Placing my belongings down at one of the tables by the large, front window, I took out my wallet and got in the short line to get an iced coffee and maybe a chocolate croissant.

Jackson and I had put in a solid three hours of work before we took our first break. With our history papers outlined, physics chapter summaries done and calculus questions finished, we sat back in our seats and took a deep breath. "Only biochemistry and English to go," Jackson said putting his pencil behind his ear and ran his hands from the back of his head to the front. "I need a refill," he smirked and stood up with his paper coffee cup.

"Me too," I followed. It was getting darker outside and the lanterns along the street had flickered on. Inside the coffee shop, the lights overhead illuminated the small business as other people came and went.

"I have to tell you, Beths," Jackson said once we were in line. "If it wasn't for you, I think I would have lost my mind by now."

"You would have been fine," I grinned.

"No seriously," Jackson said looking over at me. "I'm not just talking about homework. This whole Olivia/Bobby thing..."

"I think I know what you mean," I interrupted. "You give me hope that there are good guys out there who are worth the wait."

"Thanks," he blushed.

"Bobby is..."

"Coarse and unrefined," Jackson grinned.

"Yeah," I said bewildered that he had taken the words right out of my mouth. Jackson continued to laugh.

"That's what Wicks said to me earlier. Not the exact words I would have used but it works," Jackson said before handing the barista his empty cup. In Andrew's defense, he didn't mean to give away his old ties to a different time, but the style in which he spoke was such a clear reflection. Jackson was mistaking it for a proper upbringing; perhaps, writing it off as etiquette acquired from a boarding school. Nevertheless, it was something that I had to make sure did not come out of me when Jackson and I worked on our English assignments. The way I wrote was very similar; a dead giveaway.

"Iced coffee," Jackson said handing me a new one as we walked back to our table.

"If they broke up… Olivia and Bobby… would you ask her out?"

"No, not at first," he said placing his drink on the table. "I wouldn't want to be *that guy*."

"The rebound," I tilted my head as I took a sip out of my straw.

"Yes."

"Gotcha," I said watching as Jackson opened his biochemistry notebook. I sent up a quick little prayer for the guy sitting across the table from me. I knew that he deserved someone great and that moments like this, even as insignificant as they may seem, were the perfect opportunity to remind him to stay strong.

"What about you and Wicks? How are you guys doing?" Jackson asked.

"We're doing well," I smiled.

"You two are great together."

"It's barely tolerable," I laughed replaying what Charles and Andrew had joked about before.

"Yes," Jackson chuckled in agreement.

"Thanks Jackson," I nodded back at my friend.

Thursday, October 1ˢᵗ

"Wicks, let's go!" one of the football players yelled from the charter bus outside the front of the school. Most of the team was ready to leave for their friendly scrimmage scheduled for tonight a few towns over. Even though it was a bye week, Gramps had set it up to keep his team focused and prepared. Andrew waved in the direction of his fellow teammates as he closed the trunk of his black Camaro.

"Good luck," I said looking up at him.

"I'll see you tomorrow," Drew said putting his bag across his shoulder, leaning in towards me.

"Yes," I nodded. I knew it was ridiculous but I didn't want him to leave. It was hard enough to part ways at curfew. Putting his hands in the side pocket of his black, game day, dress pants, he took out his car keys and placed them in my hands causing me to look up at him.

"Take care of her for me?" he requested motioning towards his car.

"What about the Mustang? I joked.

"You were never good at riding horses. I figured the Camaro would be a safer bet," Drew grinned at his sarcastic remark.

"Oh thanks," I said giving him the best evil eye I could.

"Don't give me that look. We both know it's true," he laughed.

"Wicks," another player called out from the bus. It was obvious we were being watched now. Andrew looked down at me and my feelings about his departure must have read clearly on my face. I wanted him to stay – even if it meant sitting next to me in biochemistry in silence. I was selfish wanting him close to me.

"I'll see you tomorrow," Drew repeated adjusting his bag on his shoulder.

"I know," I said taking a deep breath and forcing a smile. "Be careful," I added.

"Me? I'll be fine. It's you…" he began.

"Eh, me," I asked tilting my head while sarcasm oozed out of me, "I'm the cat with nine… eight lives."

Andrew didn't find this amusing, "That's not funny, Bethany."

"I'll be careful," I promised giving him a look of obedience and added terminology that registered with him, "I give you my word."

He smiled at my attempt of submission and took one last long look into my eyes before kissing me softly on the forehead and turned to walk toward the bus. I watched him as he was greeted by the guys while I made my way through the front doors of the school to my locker only to find Olivia and Bobby lip-locked next to it. Spinning my combination and clicking the door open, Bobby turned his head slightly at the closeness of the noise. Liv, reacting to his change in focus, turned her head and saw me.

"Hi Beths," she said looking around the now buzzing hallway. They truly were unaware of the crowd that grew as time for the homeroom bell ticked closer and closer.

"Hey," I smirked.

"Ugh, we should probably get going, babe," Bobby said looking at the large analog clock above a nearby bulletin board.

"Yeah, I'll be there in a minute," she said as he picked up his football bag and pads and walked out to the bus.

"I would say have fun," I started.

"I swear I didn't have any intention of a public display of affection," she said leaning up against the lockers.

"Been there," I laughed to myself recalling Charles' not-so-quiet 'coughs'. "How was your date yesterday?"

"It was great. We had a lot of fun," she beamed. "So what are you going to do tonight?"

"Well while you cheer your head off in the cold, I will be home doing one of our bridesmaid duties – making favors for the wedding," I said getting my books out for morning classes.

"Oh right. Have fun with that," Olivia said remembering that Kate wasn't too pleased that her sister was missing it. "Since the buses aren't getting back until super late I switched my days at the drugstore so I'm free all day Saturday."

"Great, you should come by and experience a Ry, Chris and Gregg 'football event' if you're up to it," I suggested.

"Okay," Liv smiled, "Afterwards we could walk to the fair."

"Great," I said closing my locker. All of Grams' hard work preparing for the County Fair would not be missed by any of us.

"I should go. I'll see you tomorrow. I can't wait for tomorrow night!" Liv said excitedly as she started to walk away.

"Me too! Have fun!" I yelled after her and she twirled in her cheerleader uniform, with a ponytail ribbon and all, before opening the doors.

No sooner than the doors closing behind her did the PA system ring out with one of the secretaries' irked voice, "Bethany, your grandfather would like to see you in his office." I laughed hoping Gramps would make some sort of peace offering soon before the secretaries refused to take anymore of his requests.

"Shouldn't you be on the bus with your team?" I asked as I walked into my grandfather's office.

"I am waiting for the last possible second," he laughed, collecting his leather bound playbook. There was a knock on the door. Since I was standing next to it, having just entered myself, I opened it.

"Coach," Jackson said leaning his head in. Upon seeing me he stepped into the office. "Hi Bethany," he said distracted.

"Hey Jackson," I smiled.

"What is it Turner?" Gramps asked.

"Everyone is accounted for," Jackson reported, "Except for you," he finished with a huge grin.

"Well done Turner," Gramps chuckled before Jackson took my grandfather's briefcase and jacket for him. "I'll be out in a minute.

"Good luck tonight," I wished the Captain.

"Thanks Beths. Do you think I could get your notes from class?" he asked concerned about his strong 4.0.

"Of course," I nodded.

"Thanks. See you later," he said as my grandfather shooed him out and closed the door. Gramps had high hopes for Jackson and had taken him under his wing. They had respect for one another and at the same time, they shared an unannounced humor.

With a seriousness taking laughter's place, Gramps pointed for me to sit in one of the chairs while he took the seat behind his desk. "Unfortunately, I don't have much time before my players will become bored in the parked buses out front so I will try to make this quick," he paused folding his hands. "Charles, Coach Landon... Dr. Landon," he corrected himself three times, "and I had an interesting conversation earlier this morning regarding your health." I shifted in my seat becoming uneasy. I looked around the room knowing I was unable to fib especially to the man across from me. "Dr. Landon has explained the... diagnosis," Gramps said having some trouble saying it aloud but continued, "and informed me that you have been well aware of the seriousness of your condition for some time now." I sat in silence as my grandfather leaned on his desk, hands still folded. "Bethany," he began and I expected him to be angry but his tone was the complete opposite; instead he sounded disturbed. "Why did you feel you should keep this a secret when there are people who love you and would want to know this so they could help you through it?"

I bit down on my tongue somehow trying to control the burning in my eyes at my grandfather's heart tugging, heartfelt words. "I didn't want to trouble anyone," I admitted.

"Trouble anyone?" Gramps repeated letting out his breath. He knew that I was referring to my mother, the only family I had when I lived in New York. "Bethany, I just wish I would have known. If I did, I could have acted sooner to get you away from there," he mumbled to himself.

"It's not your fault," I said flatly and he looked up at me and forced a smile. "It wasn't a foreign prison, Gramps," I teased. "Plus, I'm here now," I added optimistically.

"Yes you are," Gramps said leaning back in his chair. "The only reason the topic came up at all was when I questioned Charles on why he was not joining the team on the bus ride. He told me he was going to drive up after his appointment with you at the hospital. I had to pull it out of him what appointment he was referring too. When he said it was a heart scan… well, he was kind enough to share with me that he has and will continue to keep a close eye on you and that heart of yours. After this discussion I hope *you* will be the one to update me on a regular basis."

"Yes," I agreed.

"Good, now that that's settled," he said standing up. I copied him and got to my feet too. "You should get to class," he said putting his hand on my back, leading me to the door.

Stopping I said, "Gramps, I'm sorry I didn't tell you…"

Interrupting me he smiled, "It's okay my dear, I'm just happy you're alright."

"I love you, Gramps," I said hugging him as if I were a little girl again.

"I love you too," he said hugging back. "I love you too."

—

To the class' surprise, Coach Landon was seated at his desk as we filed in. Everyone assumed that he would be at the away game with the varsity team but I knew that he was sticking around for one more heart scan before he left. I was not feeling resentful towards him for telling my grandfather about my condition but it also did not appease me. I sat through the entire class taking notes for Jackson. With the bell ringing for the final time today, I closed my books, collected my things and waited for the class to empty out.

"I understand if you are upset with me," Charles began and I rolled my eyes. "But we both know you would never have told your grandfather otherwise."

"Charles, if you are watching my heart and it's under control then why would I want to worry him with something like this," I countered.

"Bethany, I can watch and analyze all I want; that doesn't mean there aren't risks, possibilities..." he offered grimly. "Besides, as an assistant coach, I did have to offer an explanation as to why I was not going to be able to be on the bus." My eyebrows furrowed as I tried unsuccessfully to dismiss Charles' rationalization; but he was right. "He cares for you and as sorry as I am that I was the one who told him, I will not apologize for caring for your personal wellbeing."

"I know," I nodded.

"Now, as for that heart scan," my old friend said tilting his head towards the door.

"How's it look?" I asked looking over his shoulder as he clicked over the 3-D image. He was thorough in comparing the scans he had in my chart with the newest one. About a hundred clicks later, Charles shut the monitor off and turned in the swivel chair with my chart in his hands.

"There is no change," he said.

"Good."

"Not necessarily," Charles said and it caught me mid-step. I turned my head at the undertone in his voice.

"Not necessarily? What do you mean?"

"It's not bad, Beths, it's just that there has been no significant change since the original diagnosis. Do not be mistaken, the ventricular rate through the quadrant…" he began but I cut him off.

"Charles," I interrupted nervously. I had no real knowledge in the field of medicine and needed a translation. Looking up at me from his chair, he placed my chart on the counter and leaned back in his chair, folding his hands.

"You haven't shown improvement." When I didn't answer he continued. "It's just that I would have hoped that there would be some sign of progress from the documents in your chart but there is none. It hasn't gotten worse but it hasn't gotten better either."

"But I'm okay, right?"

"You're fine," Charles said standing up and putting both of his hands on my arms. "We'll give that heart of yours another month with the same cardio regime and medicine. If there is still no change by that time, then we'll make some adjustments."

"Adjustments?" I asked.

"I would do a heart cath," he answered. I nodded feeling slightly better that Charles had years and years of experience and would stop at nothing to make sure I was okay. "It's invasive but that would be my next step," he said looking into my eyes. "Relax, Beths. Worrying won't help."

—

"It's really not that difficult. See, loop, swoosh and curl," Chris said tying a ribbon on one of the favors trying to teach Ryan. Ryan rolled his eyes and pushed back from the dining room table. "I don't 'loop, swoosh and curl'," my brother said going into the kitchen to retrieve another beer.

"That's why yours look like crap," Chris yelled after him. "Sorry, Mrs. Taylor," Chris apologized when he looked back at Kate, Grams, Gregg and I realizing that we were an audience to his last comment. Our palpable skepticism caused Chris to put his hands up and in his own defense, he said seriously, "I'm straight. I swear!" We all started to laugh as the favor chain continued in its production line. Gregg and I were filling the lace bags with bits of chocolates while Grams and Kate slid the labels onto the ribbon, followed by Chris and Ryan who had been slowly tying them together. The last duo was far behind because Chris had basically been working by himself.

"I wonder how the game is going," Grams said as I passed her a filled bag. She looked at me with a grin, knowing that by the mention of the team the thought of Andrew would catch my attention. Kate checked her phone with her sister's cheerleading updates and read, "They are winning but it's physical," before texting a response back.

"Bedford was always a rough team," Gregg said reflecting on his glory days as an Ellsworth Sparrows' fullback. Chris, a former Sparrows receiver, nodded in agreement. The television in the living room turned on and Ryan sat down on the couch. Gregg and Chris exchanged a look and followed their friend's lead, finding spots on the couch next to him. I shook my head and slid into Chris' seat taking over the 'loop, swoosh and curl' station while Kate took my job of filling the bags.

"Are you starting to get excited?" I asked my soon-to-be sister-in-law even though by the look on her face I already knew the answer.

"I am, just a little nervous. I don't want to forget anything," she said handing the next bag to Grams.

"You won't dear," Grams said kindly, patting Kate's hand before she slid a label onto another favor and added it to the pile I had inherited.

"It's going to be beautiful," I encouraged and Kate smiled. Grams and I looked at each other and grinned, happy that she would shortly be officially part of the family.

As the last favor was placed into a cardboard box the ESPN recap ended and the boys stood stretching before turning back to the dining room to find that it had been cleared. "You're finished?" Ryan asked innocently.

"Ha, please," I said handing him a full box. He smirked while taking it and motioned for Chris and Gregg to get the others. Grams spread the tablecloth over the table and returned the floral centerpiece to the middle. Kate was taken by surprise when my brother handed her the box to hold. He then placed both of his hands on the sides of her face, kissed her and then took the box back, leaving his fiancé breathless. "That was adorable," I shook my head and Gregg and Chris agreed. Kate's phone beeped and she looked down at it.

"It's the third quarter. We're winning but Finn is hurt and Duke is trying to make up for Clifton who is being double teamed," Kate read.

Ryan, holding the box, read the message over her shoulder. "That's their offensive line..." he started but stopped himself realizing I knew what it meant. Andrew would be under a lot of pressure from the other team's defense. I found some comfort in knowing that Andrew would not suffer any broken bones no matter how hard they hit – a side effect of being 'frozen'. But what did worry me was that he would bruise and could feel the pain like everyone else.

"He'll be fine," Gregg said reassuringly. "One thing Bedford has never had is your grandfather coaching them." I grinned at Gregg appreciatively as he followed Ryan and Chris out to the truck.

Kate put on her jacket saying, "Thanks for your help."

"Of course Kate," I responded. Then she kissed my grandmother's cheek and opened the screen door saying over her shoulder, "See you tomorrow."

"Beths! Can I PLEASE drive it! Just once," Chris yelled as he admired the Camaro parked next to my car.

"No Chris!" I said for the zillionth time tonight.

"How about that one?" he asked pointing towards my Corvette which was across from Ryan's truck and Gregg's Jeep. I grabbed my keys from the center table and threw them to Chris. His face lit up in the porch light as he and Gregg looked at each other. Chris jumped into the driver's seat and Gregg got in the passenger side like a chaperone would. My car roared to life, the windows were rolling down and the speakers played with the change in radio station. Ryan looked up at me on the porch and rolled his eyes, laughing as he opened 'the tank's' passenger door for Kate. He walked around and closed the hatch of the truck, securing the boxes of favors one last time and he stopped in front of my car and stared down Chris and Gregg.

"YOU TWO BETTER BE BACK HERE BEFORE I AM," he yelled over the music before getting into his truck and starting it. Pulling up next to the driver's side window he yelled, "FIFTEEN MINUTES... TOPS!"

"FIFTEEN MINTUES," Chris moaned over the volume but quickly added, "FINE!" as Gregg decided on a station. Ryan pulled out of the driveway and made a right while Chris and Gregg headed left. Grams and I laughed as we walked back into the house and closed the front door behind us.

My car was back, safe and sound when I looked out the attic window before turning off the lights. I smiled to myself as I threw the blankets over me and nuzzled the side of my face into my pillow. The house was quiet and the only light came in from the window; the source: the front porch light, three stories below. Tonight, in its tranquility, not even the crickets felt like singing. I breathed in and out trying to learn a thing or two from my surroundings but I was wired; I felt like I had just drank a pot of coffee, had a candy rush or was on the verge of an anxiety attack. However, my eyes closed and just like that, I was in a different place.

I was looking at Abby through the mirror in front of me as she pinned a strand of my hair to the side so that my loose curls would not fall on my face. The two of us had been talking for some time and I could feel the stitch in my side from laughing. My father had brought Abigail to my room at the end of the long North Corridor to introduce us to one another and also to help me get ready for the welcoming party which I was not aware of until I had arrived at the Estate mere hours before. Luckily, my father had ordered a dress for me for the occasion and Abby was more than willing to help me. She had mentioned more than once that she was still surprised that I was not much younger than seventeen because my father's description of his daughter had placed me closer to thirteen. Nevertheless, she was happy how things had turned out because now instead of babysitting, she would actually have someone to talk too.

As we laughed about different things and talked about topics one discusses when first meeting someone, like where they were from or things they liked to do in their spare time, I couldn't help but try to take in my new chambers. Upon entering the room, to the left was a fireplace with a thick, carved, wooden mantle. At the moment the fireplace was lit and was giving off the majority of the room's light. To the right of the fireplace was a small room or a large, walk-in closet with a window on the far wall. There was another to the right showing off nothing at the moment as it was dark outside, but I knew the grounds were extensive. With the morning light I would see what seasonally changing scenery the windows framed. Back in the main room and opposite the fireplace was a cushioned bench at the foot of an equally impressive, carved four posted bed with nightstands on either side. Set high, I would need to jump onto the bed in order to get in, and after the long trip I had, that is all I wanted to do. Across from the doorway were two large windows separated by a wooden vanity with the oval shaped mirror and oil lamp that was feebly trying to give off light. The floors were made of a hard oak and each wall was lined with crown moulding, suitable for royalty but to my eyes it was just a fun facet of the room. And that was it – that was my new room; cozy and safe and mine.

I suppose Abby caught sight of me in the mirror looking around my new quarters as she continued to lose-curl my hair to perfection. Being as polite as she was, she allowed me to soak it all in. "I cannot wait to see the expression on people's faces when they meet you," she broke out causing me to look sideways at her upturned lips.

"Why is that?" I asked.

"You are not what your father described."

"Oh," I said not knowing what to make of her comment.

"Not to fret," she quickly added assuring me that the night would not end in disappointment. "You will see what I mean," she finished with a smile.

"Is there anything I can do?" I shrugged.

"Can you turn into a thirteen year old?" she joked.

"Afraid not," I laughed and she did too. There was a soft knock on the door and Abby called out, "Come in." Having expected my father, I was surprised to see through the reflection of the mirror a thirty-something, tall and handsome man with dark hair and equally dark eyes standing in the doorway. His profile was classic and his posture, strong. Feeling nervous like I always did, I restrained myself from touching my collarbone by keeping my grip on the ledge of the vanity.

"Charles…" she said also surprised that it was not my father. "Bethany," Abby continued, "This is my husband Charles Landon. Charles, this is Bethany Taylor."

I stood from the seat and turned in my ivory gown which flowed to the floor; the corset was tied tightly around my waist and chest. Charles, still looking intently at me bowed slightly and I returned the gesture with my first true curtsey of the evening. Looking back at his wife, Charles did not say a word but she answered his question. "I know," Abby laughed and walked over to his side. "Not what you were expecting."

"No, not at all," he smirked and then looked back at me, "But it is a pleasure to meet you, Bethany."

"A pleasure," I smiled back and then looked at Abby understanding what she had warned me about seconds ago. Exchanging a look with one another, we began to laugh again.

"Shall we," Charles asked as held the door for us as a gentleman does. Nodding slightly, I picked up my gown at its sides and made for the hall, passing the two of them.

"Do you know where my father is?" I asked nervously as the noise from below became louder the closer I got to the top of the second floor staircase.

"He went to change," Charles assured me. Smiling sheepishly, I slowly walked down the stairs into the entranceway overwhelmed by the magnitude of guests.

"Would you like to come with us?" Abigail asked, motioning to the grand staircase leading to the ballroom.

"Thank you, but I think I will wait for my father," I smiled kindly at both her and her husband.

"Alright," Abby nodded and then turned.

"Abigail," I called out causing both of them to look back. I took a step forward and touched Abby's hand lightly saying, "Thank you." She had been so nice to me and had calmed my unease as though it was nothing at all, when to me, it had meant so much.

"Of course," Abby said a little taken aback. "I'll see you later on," she added as she took her husband's waiting arm and they walked down the majestic marble staircase into the grand ballroom.

The front door opened behind me and carriages with guests arriving could be seen in the light of the lanterns. Turning back towards the party, I studied the ribbons and flowers that were twirled together along the banisters, competing with one another. Turning once more, I saw my father coming down the second floor stairs to the crowded entranceway were I waited.

"Bethany," he said as he walked across the way, passing guests who turned to look at what caught his attention. "You look beautiful," my father added in a whisper and smiled down at me.

Putting his arm out, he asked, "Shall we?" I took his arm and looked up at him as though I was a little girl. He was my world.

"You didn't have to do this you know," I said feeling embarrassed as I now became aware of the stares.

"I knew you wouldn't be fond of a gathering welcoming you to Ellsworth, therefore, I selectively chose to leave that out of the letters," he grinned.

"Wonderful," I whispered back. Admiring the majestic archways above and around us I added seriously, "The Estate is amazing."

He too looked around at his newly built masterpiece and then down at me, "This home is for us, Beths. This town, these people, this place is home." Looking around the bustling ballroom I couldn't help but notice that my father had, in fact, invited everyone; there were hundreds of guests comfortably mingling in the ballroom below us. Unknowingly, my anxious hand was at my collarbone as my nervousness about meeting all these people set in. However, before I could slightly irritate the skin, my father, who was familiar with my habit, took my hand in his and said lovingly, "You were born to stand out, Bethany; it is about time you accepted that. In fact, if anyone should be nervous it is me. With your wit and beauty," he sighed, "Well, let us just say I will go gray from fighting off your suitors." Looking up at him, I rolled my eyes and he laughed as a blush rose to my face along with a wide smile. Before we started down the steps, an older gentleman's voice called from behind us at which my father turned.

"James," my father said putting out his hand.

"Brilliant event, truly brilliant," the man complimented, taking a quick look around at all the happy guests. "And is this the lady of the hour?"

"Yes. Bethany this is Mister Hughes. James, this is my daughter, Bethany," my father said proudly.

"I have heard so much about you. Your father has been anticipating your arrival for some time now, as has the town. Although, I imagined you to be quite younger than you are."

"That is my fault James," my father smiled at me and continued. "As I am sure you can relate too, in my mind I froze my little girl at thirteen."

"Yes, yes, well with four daughters of my own, I can certainly understand that," Mr. Hughes said patting my father on his shoulder. "Well, don't let this old man stop you from much more important introductions," Mr. Hughes insisted.

"You are the first, actually," my father smirked.

"Oh, well then, I thank you for the honor," he nodded with a smile and then stepped aside, cane in hand.

"Thank you, James," my father said leading me down the elaborate staircase into the ballroom.

Faces passed in front of my eyes like a blur; curtsey after curtsy, and introduction after introduction were too numerous to count. I watched my father as he walked up to each person, greeting them, welcoming them to his home, making sure they were *enjoying themselves and then lighting up as he introduced me. I spoke briefly to each group, answering the same initial questions. By now I had my responses down so well that I had to be careful I answered the right question. There was no way to remember everyone's names or even their faces. Only time in this town could do that. Nevertheless, everyone was pleasant and it was nice to be around people from the town which I would now call home.*

There came a point in the evening when neither my father nor I, didn't notice a waiter passing by with a tray of food. It was then that we graciously bowed away from the overwhelming number of guests and made our way to the head table where our supper was waiting for us. Distracted halfway there, my father watched as two familiar people, Charles and Abigail Landon, walked up the grand staircase. With this, my father redirected us; we were headed back through the crowd in pursuit, laughing as we climbed. Once we were back in the entranceway, we turned left and walked down a hall which led to a closed door. The room was my father's office and both fireplaces at each end of the room were lit. There was a sitting area with two sofas separated by an impressive coffee table at one end and at the other stood a strong, large, oak desk. The wall opposite of the doorway consisted of windows and French doors that led to a small terrace level with the grounds. Ornamental décor in the room matched the rest of the Estate but was much simpler in style – much like my father. "You do know that there is a celebration going on," he joked patting Charles on the back, leaving me in the doorway.

"And that is why we are here," Charles said pointing towards his wife who I could not fully see as my father's back was blocking my view. *"We've come to reclaim the work enthusiast,"* Charles added which led me to believe that there was another person in the room also blocked by my father.

"I see," my father said letting out a laugh and then reached back at me so that I could walk into the room and at his side. Nodding at Charles, I then acknowledged Abigail as well and that's when I saw someone standing across from her. He was younger than she, tall, broad and strikingly handsome. Even in the dim light of the fireplace and single oil lamp, his ocean blue eyes pierced through the room and left me with weakened knees and a stomach full of butterflies. *"Andrew, this is my daughter Bethany. Bethany, Andrew Wicks – Abigail's brother,"* my father spoke. Curtseying without taking my eyes off of him, he too returned the gesture with a bow. Although I had been given introductions for hours, this felt like the first time. My father continued to talk as he crossed the room to his desk but Andrew didn't break the stare we shared until my father asked, *"What is it that you are working on?"*

"Nothing really," Andrew responded distractedly and I shyly looked down at the floor.

"I daresay it is nothing," my father said as he enthusiastically turned one of the papers so that he could examine it better. "You've reworked..."

"Enough!" Abby said putting her hands up. "Enough business discussions... tonight we are celebrating the newest addition to Ellsworth," she said walking to my side and smiling at me. Grinning back at her I still felt the blush in my face from meeting her brother.

"You are right, Abigail," my father smirked and moved back towards the doorway. "After you," he smiled down at me as I carried the skirt of my gown in both hands. The noise from the entranceway and the ballroom returned to my ears and helped me wake from the cloud I had floated to after meeting my latest acquaintance.

"Do you really think that could work," Abigail and I both heard my father ask Andrew from behind us. Turning, we saw the three men still in the doorway as Charles inquired, "What exactly?" Abby stepped closer to them and at her reappearance they hurriedly filed out of the room, chuckling all the while.

Back in the entranceway and headed towards the ballroom staircase, a young man walked up to my father saying, "Pardon me."

"Good evening, Nathan," my father replied with an outstretched hand.

"Mister Taylor... Charles, Andrew," he nodded and then asked, "Mister Taylor, I was hoping for your permission to have a dance with your daughter." Wide-eyed I looked up at my father who did not seem surprised and then back at this stranger.

"That is very kind of you, Robert, but I am afraid Bethany's supper is waiting for her. Perhaps another time." Understanding, Nathan excused himself from our company.

"How many is that?" Charles asked. My father's nostrils grew entertainingly as he took in a deep, steady breath. Slightly confused, I listened as the conversation unfolded.

"Too many," he answered and readjusted his stance looking at Charles with a defeated expression.

"How many?" Abigail laughed.

"Thirty-six," my father said and then looked back at me as Charles patted him on the back.

"THIRTY-SIX," Abby repeated. "But the night is not even halfway over," she almost snorted with laughter. "Impressive," she added looking at me as I felt the shock hit me, not having the slightest inkling of any requests.

"No worries, my dear," my father smiled at me. "You are a rose among thorns and I have had seventeen years to prepare for this evening," he laughed.

"I... he... he was the first one that has asked..." I started to say not having known of the evening's undertow. And yet, before we could turn to walk down the steps, another young man approached my father asking for a dance with me. Postponing any sort of courtship at the unrelenting male population, he declined the request.

"Thirty-seven, ah," Abigail breathed jokingly.

"Thank you, Abigail," he said tilting his head comically as he put his arm out for me to take. I had been subconsciously rubbing my collarbone and hesitantly looked down into the ballroom looking at it quite differently.

"I think I need a little fresh air," I said not ready to enter back into a game I did not want to play.

"Would you like me to go with you?" Abby volunteered.

"No, that's alright," I smiled shyly. "Go on ahead," I encouraged my father too. "I'll be down in a few minutes."

"Alright," he nodded and then casually spoke, "Andrew, go with her." It was not a question or an order but somewhere in between. This caused Andrew and me to look at one another timidly. He took in a breath and blinked quickly for a moment as I too got my bearings and smiled slightly. When the pair of us looked back at our families, they had already begun to walk down the stairs, leaving us. Andrew put out his arm for me to take.

"Thank you," I said as my arm intertwined with his and my other hand held my gown as we walked towards the large, rounded, oak door. Like a gentleman, he held it open for me and I stepped out in the cool night. The air reached my lungs as the sound of the door closed behind us. The noise on the other side sounded more distant than it actually was. I felt his hands brush the outside of my arms as he placed his jacket over my shoulders. Turning my head slightly, I pulled my hair to the side and wordlessly thanked him. With his hands in his pants pockets, he *stood next to me on the steps of the Estate as the oak alley moved in the wind.*

"You don't have to stay out here. I'm sure you have work to do, people you should be talking with…" I said in my true, foolish fashion, but hating it as soon as I had spoken.

"That's alright," his masculine voice said rather calmly.

"You could at least be dancing," I offered him one last chance to not feel obligated by my father to stay outside with me. Andrew's stance and confidence changed with the next words, "To be honest, I feel like I already am." Completely taken by this stranger, we both smiled bashfully at one another.

The world did not stop and it was not love at first sight but it was an 'I-want-to-know-more-about-you' kind of feeling; one that I later realized was my first impression of love.

I awoke, motionless, in my bed. I closed my eyes again at the sweet memory that had surfaced. I lay awake enchanted by the recollection of meeting Charles, Abby and Drew for the first time. They had been just another moment, another introduction expected that night. It was ordinary, typical, plain and simple… yet, it echoed. Like a single, insignificant drop, it rippled through time.

I looked at the clock. I had not been asleep for more than twenty minutes. Sitting straight up in bed, I knew where I had to be…

—

"Where are you going?" Ryan asked as I passed him on the porch after dropping Kate off.

"I, ah, I, ah," I said looking for anything to say.

"I'll cover for you as long as you're in before one," he whispered tilting his head towards my car.

"Thank you," I said hugging him quickly and then I was off.

I accelerated as I pulled out of the sleepy town and roared down the open road. I pulled onto the cobblestone and saw the Estate lights glowing in the distance. At the front door, I turned the knob and walked into the entranceway. The chandelier was lit overhead but there was no sign of life. I placed my keys on the round table and started towards the staircase when something caught my attention down in the ballroom. Abby was lying on her back looking up at the archway ceiling with Cole and Gracie who were sleeping under blankets and had pillows under their heads.

Abby sat up slightly at my entrance and I walked silently down the stairs to where they were.

"What are you doing?" I whispered.

"Gracie likes to look at the 'pretty ceiling'," Abby quoted the little girl. "And Cole, as much as he'll deny it, enjoys it too."

"Oh," I said lying down too and looked up. It was entrancing; the architecture, the detailed craftsmanship and the pure magic that could inspire a little girl to feel like a princess. Abby put her head back on a pillow and was quiet, too quiet.

"Everything okay?" I asked softly, watching her out of the corner of my eye. She took a calm, deep breath and her eyes narrowed. "Abby," I said turning on my side. "Abby," I said again and reached for her hand to get her attention. Our hands touched. Knowing that I had been thinking about the dream I had just had, the one of our first meeting still vibrant in my mind, I looked at her and expected that she would see it as well. However, she continued to stare up at the ceiling, unaffected. I sat up, crossing my legs and stared at my hand as though it were broken. I tried again; still, there was nothing. Abby turned her head sideways at me with slow tears coming down her cheeks.

"Abigail," I said slowly and her eyes closed as she pushed herself up off the floor.

"I don't know how Charles and Andrew haven't noticed yet," she whispered as she dried the tears. I hugged her tightly. I knew she was scared.

"When?" I asked wide-eyed. "When did it stop?"

"I don't know... maybe yesterday?" she said looking down at Cole and Gracie.

"Are you okay?" I asked concerned.

"Yes, I think so. I mean I feel fine," she said shaking her head.

"Well what do you think it means?"

"I don't know," she said looking up at me. "This has never happened before."

"Here," I said placing my hand out, palm side up, "Try again." Against my own liking, I recalled the strongest memory I had – the one on the grounds, the nightmare. Abby touched my hand and shrugged when nothing happened.

"Nothing?" I asked already knowing the answer; I could *feel* when a memory was passed.

"Nothing," she said taking her hand back.

"And both of them haven't noticed?" I asked for clarification.

"No."

"Okay, well maybe…" I started, trying to come up with some kind of reasoning.

"Beths," she paused and her hand touched her stomach as she looked down at it, "I think it might have to do with the fact that I'm pregnant."

"What!" I whispered back in shock.

"I'm pregnant," she repeated with a short breath as she looked up at me with a smile crossing her tear stained face.

"But Abby, I thought that…" I started.

"That it was impossible?" she said looking around the empty ballroom. It was one of the drawbacks of not aging physically; she had been left barren because of it.

"Abby," I said reaching out for her hand this time, not for a memory but for support.

"I've felt different for a while now. After seeing you… I just wrote it off as anxiety and stress I guess. But when it didn't subside I thought maybe something was wrong. I mean, I haven't been sick or felt different for quite some time," she shrugged. Reaching into her pocket, she pulled out a piece of paper and handed it to me. As I took it in my own hands I saw the hospital's name on top. I skimmed to the bottom and read the findings, 'PREGNANT'. I looked up at Abby with my jaw open, speechless. "I didn't want to worry Charles..." she said taking the paper and placing it back in her pocket. "I had one of the nurses do a workup on me just out of curiosity. They say I'm about a month along."

"A month?" I asked doing the math in my head. It had been almost four weeks since I had arrived to Ellsworth.

"Yes," she said staring back at me, "And I don't believe in coincidences."

The front door opened and we both looked up. We could hear Charles and Andrew laughing about something as Drew put his bags down. "I won't say a word," I promised in a soft voice.

'Thank you,' she mouthed. Charles and Andrew spotted us at the top of the staircase with the sleeping children. A surprised but happy smile crossed Andrew's face as he started down the stairs towards me.

"Hi, how was the scrimmage?" Abby asked as her husband bent over and kissed her on the forehead.

"It went well," he answered looking at Cole and Gracie with warm eyes.

"Hello," Andrew said as he bent one knee on the floor, touched my face with his one hand and kissed me lightly. He lingered as our eyes opened.

"Hi," I whispered.

"Drew," Charles said nodding towards Gracie as he picked Cole up in his arms. Andrew picked Gracie up and followed Charles up the stairs to the little ones' bedrooms. When the two men were headed up the second floor staircase I looked over at Abby.

"Abby," I said continuing with our conversation, "You said you think your body 'changed' about a month ago but you still had the memory connection for a little while afterwards?"

As she got to her feet, Abby answered, "After you passed, it was a few nights later that Charles and Andrew experienced the first hand connection. We believe we gradually stopped aging after that. What's happened to me now is the same, only reversed."

"You will... age?" I asked knowing that no words could justify her situation.

"I believe so. That's the only way that this could have happened," she said touching her stomach. My mind was contemplating the current revelation. Abby was pregnant and would no longer be 'frozen' as time passed. Could Charles and Andrew have changed and not known it too?

"Abby," I said taking her hands in mine and making her look into my eyes. She was scared, that much I could see. I took a deep breath and smiled for the excitement she should be feeling but wouldn't allow herself. "You're pregnant. Do you know how amazing that is? How happy Charles is going to be?" Instead of a smile more tears flowed out of her eyes. "Abigail, you will enjoy this moment," I demanded from her.

"I know," she said as her hand was at her stomach again. "I'm pregnant," she said smiling through her tears.

"Yes!" I smiled back wiping them from her face.

"But," she said as her eyes wandered around the room again.

"Abby," I said finding her eyes. "In this moment there is nothing to be afraid of." She took a deep breath and swallowed back the tears. "Abby, you have to tell Charles," I said as I heard the two men coming down the second floor stairs and into the entranceway.

"Soon," she said looking at him as he walked next to his brother-in-law down the ballroom staircase. They were laughing with one another, animated and enjoying each other's company.

"Soon?" I gasped. "Are you serious?" She looked over at me and I put my hands up, palms facing her and wiggled my fingers. "I can't hide this," I said referring to the memory connection. Her face lit up when she realized her secret wasn't exactly 'safe'. Nothing was really with such a connection.

"Please Beths," she begged wide-eyed.

"How?" I asked both knowing that there was no way of avoiding it, "and more importantly, why?" I added, "Why not tell him? He's going to be beyond elated." I put my hands on her arms and said seriously, "Abby, honestly, you being pregnant is absolutely amazing. You and Charles deserve this moment." She knew I was right and as the men walked over to us, still wrapped up in their football recap, they did not notice Abby's confidence falter before she found it again in her husband's presence.

"Charles," she said but her husband and brother hadn't heard her, caught up in their own conversation. "Charles," she tried again.

"Then when their defensive line," Charles continued as he recalled the opposition's blunder.

"CHARLES," Abby said again but this time impatiently, causing the both of them to look at her.

"Sorry," she apologized for the tone that had come out. "I just wanted to," she said focusing in on Charles, "say that I," she paused looking over at me.

"What is it?" Charles asked looking between us.

"Maybe you should sit down," Abby said and he looked at her in confusion.

"You want me to sit down?" he asked looking around the empty ballroom and then back at his wife. A worried expression then crossed his face and he took a step closer to her. "Abigail," he said wanting to know what was causing her uneasiness. Abby looked back at me and I looked at her. A smile, the smile, I had been waiting for from her finally came to her lips. The deafening silence in the room ended as she started, "Charles, I'm... we're pregnant."

Charles' eyes narrowed and he repeated softly, "Pregnant?" Andrew turned, listening to see if he heard correctly, surely taken aback. He looked away from his sister and towards me to verify that he had. I nodded at him and watched as Charles looked into Abby's eyes, initial shock wearing off. Without having to ask again, Abby answered reassuringly, "Yes."

"Abby," he said looking intensely at her.

"Charles. I'm pregnant," she said and this time with jubilance as she told the love of her life.

He leaned in and kissed her avidly, holding her in his arms. Andrew and I looked away and smiled at one another in the craziness of the moment. Still holding her face in his hands, Charles pulled away. "You…"

"I'm about a month along," she said slowly so he would be brought up to speed. Charles turned and looked at me with widening eyes, and then back to Abby. Andrew had looked over at me too; however, he didn't turn away. Drew was staring at me thinking what I thought when Abby had entrusted me moments ago with her secret. One month… the timing was perfect. This could change everything.

We were in the dining room and Charles hadn't taken his eyes or his hands off his wife. He was bewildered, excited and full of questions. What did this mean? How had Abby changed? Was he and Andrew going to change too? No one saw reason why they wouldn't be far behind. After all, they had all become frozen around the same time. It didn't make sense that Abby would be an exception to their anomaly. The confirmation of whether they'd changed or not would be the loss of the memory connection; a gift/curse they believed they acquired before they became physically ageless.

"The most logical reasoning is that the memory exchange was the beginning of the 'change' but we didn't know what it signified or what we were in for. If you take into consideration what has happened to Abby now, I would guess that the reverse is applied when we 'change' back, *if* we change back. The memory connection was the first indicator to me that something wasn't right when we changed and now, the lack of the memory connection confirms that you're not ageless any longer," Charles hypothesized aloud. I watched as Drew stared into the burning fire under the mantle.

"I just think that The Grander Plan is fixing itself," Abby said simply.

"Do you really believe in a 'The Grander Plan'?" I asked not knowing where Abby stood on spirituality.

"Absolutely, try telling a century old woman differently," she smirked and then looked down at the table, thinking. "There is a reason why people aren't supposed to live as long as we have. In a way I guess I am grateful that I was given the chance to see life without having to worry about the finish line," she said letting out a breath but then seriousness washed over her young but wise face. "There are certain things, little things, which people miss everyday which is evidence that someone else is in control. I've learned that time is nothing more than the space needed for events to come to their fulfillment. There are days you live through; mediocre days that people may see as a waste or even boring. But they are each days that get you to the days you live for; the moments that you never forget." Staring at nothing in particular, she was lost in the decades that had passed her by and the moments that stuck out. Shaking her head she smiled over at me. "Let's just say all the doubts I had about God went out the window when all I could do was watch life unfold," she finished as she looked up at her husband who was smiling down at her. He took her hand and he stared at them intertwined with his and realized that there was no memory exchange, no connection. "Sorry," she sweetly apologized.

"You would say that," he laughed and kissed her on the top of her head before he placed his hand over her stomach like any expecting father longs to.

Knowing that change was a possibility for them, Charles and Andrew thought it best to test the hypothesis – if they had changed, like Abby had, then there would be no hand connection. So, being the catalyst, I put my hand in Charles' first.

"Okay," I said as Charles let go of my hand a few seconds later, "Got it! Thanks! And I don't appreciate the selection." I joked. Out of all of the memories he could have picked from, he had chosen one that made me feel a little uncomfortable. He smiled wickedly teenage-like, very out-of-character for him.

"What was it?" Abby asked.

"The first night you two met," I said looking at her out of the corner of my eye and shaking my head trying to get the feelings and images out.

"What's so wrong with that?" she asked defensively.

"Bethany feels emotions clearer than the actual images of the memories," Andrew explained with a smirk on his face knowing what Charles had revealed.

"You can't blame me!" Charles said looking at me. "I was young." Then laughing he added, "And slightly intoxicated." Abby hit his arm. "Your turn," Charles said to Andrew whose expression changed. He was skeptical, nervous. His forehead was creased in thought as he decided on which memory to focus wholly on. I put my hand out and he slowly put his hand in mine.

We were on the balcony two nights ago... his body was aching and he could tell mine was too.

Then my hand was back at my side and my eyes refocused on the dining room. I nodded my head, signifying I had seen, and certainly felt, the memory.

"Maybe you just need more..." Abby started.

"Time," Andrew finished in an aggravated tone.

"Something triggered Abby's change," Charles said touching the small of her back and kissing her lightly. Feeling as though we were intruding on the moment between the couple, Andrew and I left the room and walked down the staircase into the ballroom. Drew was deep in thought over what Charles had just said. Wanting to know where he was and what he was thinking, I slid my hand into his.

Andrew was sitting in the corner of my old chambers. He had his elbows on his knees and was leaning forward looking around the empty, cold room. He could hear murmured voices from people who had come to pay their respects after my passing but Drew did not want to be around anyone. For once, he didn't care if his behavior was rude – he felt incredibly alone even when surrounded by people. I had left and he felt as though I had taken a piece of him with me. I was his treasure and now that I was gone, so was his heart. The emotions ached through him, only reminding him that he was alive. His legs were weakened and his eyes heavy. He was waiting for me to come through the door but knew I wasn't going to. "Please," he cried out. "Please," he began to sob deeply as his eyes closed.

My eyes readjusted and he was looking back at me. "You can't just do that," Andrew said infuriated that I had made the connection without warning or approval. "You can't just use it like its normal. It's not normal," he added agitated. Drew was very much still in that memory, still in that room… desperate.

"Hey," I said trying to get him to look at me. "Hey," I said again this time moving so I was in front of him.

"You shouldn't have seen that."

"Well I did," I swallowed distraught at the idea that he had experienced that personal hell. I kept eye contact so that he would know that I would not waver while his temperamental mood persisted. "But it is nothing more than a memory."

"No, it's not just a memory – you were never *just* a memory," he said sternly back at me. I was taken aback by the depth of the rage but knew that living in the past was not the answer. Hurt, I saw the doors to the veranda thirty yards behind him which led out onto the grounds. I needed the fresh air – I needed a minute to escape and refocus. Walking around him, I was halfway across the floor when I heard him call, "Bethany, Beths," he said reaching for my wrist and stepped around me so we were face-to-face.

"I was out of line," he apologized but he was still evidently flustered.

"Yeah," I answered looking sideways around the ballroom recalling the dream I had of our first meeting. I felt his hand slide into mine and knew instantly what he would now see.

My dream played across his unfocused eyes. I knew that the emotions I had that night were strong yet innocent and he would, for the first time, understand.

As his eyes refocused he shook his head and smiled down at me. "I hate it when you do that," he said letting out a breath.

"Do what?"

"Make me feel like an absolute fool."

"Then stop acting like one," I answered with a laugh.

"Easier said than done I'm afraid," he breathed jokingly. Looking up at him, a smile crossed my face and I took his arm and pulled him to the exact spot where we would have danced if music played. I coughed in a fake/serious way and taking the hint, he stepped forward in time for me to follow his lead. We twirled as he hummed a melody. I rested my head on his chest and our patterned footwork slowed. I looked up at him when he ran his hand down my arm and stopped at my elbow. "I have to admit," he whispered, "that was not the first time I saw you."

"What?" I asked surprised. A smile washed over his face as his eyes looked to the left and were off somewhere beyond this ballroom, remembering what they had seen once upon a time. "Please tell me," I begged, wanting to hear the memory but he grinned and shook his head.

"May I keep that from you?" he asked

"Keep it from me?"

"For now at least," he added. I knew that all it would take was the touch of our hands for me to see the memory he was speaking of but I also realized how few secrets there were between the two of us because of the hand connection. It was important to have something that he could call his own; it was because of my respect for his privacy that I did not persist. Drew kissed my forehead and a devilish smile crossed his face, making me take a cautious step backwards.

"Andrew, what are you planning?" I questioned his mischievous expression. He did not answer but the next moment I was in the air and he was swinging me around in his arms. I clasped my hands around his neck and we laughed as he sped up and then came to a stop, placing me back down. I curtseyed and he laughed but reciprocated with a bow.

Drew then sat down on the marble floor, lying with his hand behind his head, wordlessly asking me to follow. We laid there for a long while looking up at the ornamental ceiling. My head rested on his chest while his other hand played with my hair. We were together and happy. I knew time wouldn't stop for me or let Andrew go, but in the moments that we shared, everything was right; I could live from one to the next.

Chapter Five
Friday, October 2ⁿᵈ

"Christina, Kerry, Nicole, Tina, Kim, Jessica, Becks and, of course, Courtney are coming. As for the guys, I'm pretty sure Clifton, Duke, Joe, Ben, Zach, Jackson, Bobby, and Andrew are all definite," Olivia listed as she tried on another outfit in front of the mirror. It was almost five o'clock and Bobby was picking Liv and me up at six. The plan was for everyone to meet at *Amelia's* in Bryant Square by six-thirty.

"Sounds good," I said brushing on my mascara while sitting cross legged at my makeshift vanity.

"Yeah, it's going to be a lot of fun. You are going to love Bryant Square. It's like Princeton meets Rodeo Drive meets Stars Hallow," Liv tried to explain.

"Interesting," I laughed.

"And the restaurant we're going to is so good but it's kind of expensive," Liv said finally deciding on a light yellow, ruffled dress with neutral toned wedges. "What do you think?" she asked for my approval.

"Very nice," I smiled spinning my mascara closed.

"Now, what are you going to wear?" my 'stylist' asked aloud looking through the armoire.

"Actually Liv," I said standing, "I have kind of been thinking all week of what I want to wear."

"Really?" she asked turning around. "You're taking my job away?"

"No," I laughed, "Please, it took me a whole week to pick out one outfit." The truth was I had been anticipating the trip since the invite because it was sort of a big deal to me. Not only was I going to hang out with a group of my peers, which was a rarity in itself, but it would also be the first time Andrew and I would be out in public as a couple – other than in school. I wanted to look nice for the personal milestone. Smiling, Olivia retreated to the seat I had been sitting in and waited for the unveiling of my selection. I slipped the green silky top over my head, stepped into a tight, black pencil skirt, then reached into the back of the closet and pulled out a dangerously high pair of stilettos that I had only worn once before. Adjusting myself in the mirror I turned and asked, "So, what do you think?"

"I'm so proud!" Liv jokingly held her hand over her mouth and waved her hands as if she were going to cry.

"I'd like to thank the Academy…" I played along.

Walking over to me, checking out the heels, Liv made me spin slowly so she could get a look at the whole outfit. "It's simple but you look hot!"

"Hot?" I asked.

"Well you look classy too." She reassured. "But I'm pretty sure you'll knock the socks off of everyone."

"Maybe I should change," I said with wavering self-confidence.

"What? Are you nuts? No!" Liv said grabbing my hands. "You look gorgeous!"

"In case you haven't noticed, I'm not a fan of sticking out," I said sliding out of the shoes and losing four inches in height.

"And in case you haven't noticed, you stick out with baggy sweatpants and a t-shirt. So, put those back on!" Liv demanded.

"You're scary when you talk like that," I said doing as she commanded.

"I'm petite AND blonde, I need something in order for people to listen," she smiled innocently. "Plus, as your small town stylist, I have a reputation to uphold and Andrew will thank me."

Liv's phone chimed. She quickly scooped it up and read the new message. I knew her well enough to know that something was wrong. "What is it?"

"Bobby can't pick us up. He has no more room in his car," she said rereading the text.

My eyebrows rose at the surprise that Olivia's boyfriend would first of all, not reserve a seat in his car for her but also tell her via text message.

"I'll drive, Liv. It's okay," I said not wanting her to be upset.

"Yeah, it's fine," Liv said only fooling herself.

We were running a little behind – there was a curling iron catastrophe but Liv and I were finally headed out the door. Walking onto the front porch, we both looked up to see Gramps sitting next to two of his players. They were both well-dressed and were, of course, wearing their letterman jackets. Coincidentally, they just so happened to be my favorite players: Wicks and Turner. I don't know who stood up first, Jackson or Andrew, but my grandfather was the first to speak. "Well, don't you two ladies look nice," he complimented.

"Thanks Gramps. What are you guys doing here?" I asked looking from one to the other, smiling.

"Turner heard that your ride might have fallen through," my grandfather said looking at Jackson who hadn't taken his eyes off of Olivia. I walked over to Gramps and kissed him on the cheek. "Have fun," he said aloud and held me back so that Olivia and Jackson could walk next to one another. Only Andrew and I were close enough to hear him say, "My work here is done. You two have a good evening," before putting his newspaper under his arm and walking towards the front door. Andrew smiled at me and I put my arm around his. My grandfather added over his shoulder, "Oh and Wicks, I expect to see Bethany home before curfew."

"Of course," Andrew nodded as we walked down the front porch steps.

I had caught Jackson looking in his rear view mirror at Olivia who was clueless about his feelings for her. He wouldn't make any sort of move because he respected the fact that she currently had a boyfriend. He was too noble to mess with that… further proof that he had been raised right.

—

Bryant Square was as charming as Olivia had described. She pointed out boutiques and shops that she loved while Andrew and Jackson talked about football. "That's *Amelia's*," Liv said, pointing to a corner property with elaborate overhangs and strategic lighting.

"It's pretty," I said as we drove by the restaurant, around the shopping square, towards a parking garage.

"Wait until you try the food," she raved.

Jackson pulled his Silverado next to the other cars our group were standing around. Andrew opened my door and helped me out of the modern 'carriage'. "Thank you, sir," I whispered causing a smile to wash over his face. Jackson had held the door for Olivia too, but unfortunately, Bobby had strolled over to them. "Hey, you made it," Bobby said kissing Liv and put his arm around her. Just like that, Liv forgot what Bobby had pulled. It was as if she didn't see the signs that were in front of her eyes. Both Bobby and Jackson had offered a glimpse of their true colors but somehow Liv was colorblind. With time, I hoped she would learn for herself.

The eighteen of us were not quiet as we walked through the Square but we were not the only people out and about on such a lovely evening. Liv had put her arm in mine and walked next to me surrounded by the other girls while the guys dillydallied behind us. "That is so cute!" Nicole said pointing to a window display. It was almost impossible to follow one conversation because they all seemed to talk over one another. The girls had graciously welcomed me into the group and weren't at all distracted by the

'Reid Syndrome' which had once plagued them. It had worn off by seeing me at school every day.

Approaching *Amelia's,* Jackson took charge without a second thought and approached the hostess podium. "Good evening. Welcome to *Amelia's,*" an older man dressed in a suit said eyeballing our large party.

"Hi, we have a reservation. It's under 'Turner'," Jackson said.

Looking down at the guest book the host said, "Yes, if you will follow me, please." We followed him through the cozy restaurant before entering a sectioned off room with a long table already prepared for us. The walls were exposed brick adding to the rustic décor and there were small votive candles lit on the table, completing the warm ambiance. In typical high school fashion, the girls chatted at one end while the boys sat at the other.

The conversation, the company and the food were all perfect.

Andrew was laughing, joking and listening along with his teammates. They had all welcomed him as their friend and he was able to channel in on how he had once felt at the age he was frozen in. I enjoyed watching him enjoy himself and the high school experience.

It was evident that Jackson had become closest to him. They had developed a friendship much like Olivia and I; it was real and lasting.

I looked around the table as the waiters took our plates away and couldn't see how the night could possibly be spoiled. When the waiter came back with the bill, Andrew imperturbably slid his card into the holder. I saw Jackson take the leather receipt holder from him and shook his head, saying, "You can't pay. We were supposed to take you out." As he opened it, Jackson's eyes widened and Duke, who was sitting next to him then took it out of his hands. Duke's jaw opened as he pulled out the credit card Andrew had slid in.

"Is this the American Express Centurion?" he asked examining it. Andrew didn't respond and I could tell he wasn't too thrilled at the attention it would bring him.

"Let me see," Bobby said taking it from Duke's hands. "Dude, this is awesome," Bobby said flipping it back and forth examining the card. Whispers quickly rippled down the table as Bobby handed it back to Andrew.

"Bethany," Courtney said touching my hand. "You are so lucky. Not only is Wicks good-looking but he's rich too."

"I am lucky," I said but for reasons that weren't as superficial as the ones she had mentioned.

"Have a good evening," the host said making sure to shake Andrew's hand as we left, having been informed by the waiter of his possession of the elite card.

"Good night," Andrew responded as the eighteen of us walked through the doors back to the Square.

We walked around the Square for a couple of hours, laughing and talking with one another.

I had patiently waited all night to get Jackson alone. When the opportunity presented itself, I walked up next to him and whispered, "You did the right thing, Captain." He looked down at me and then over at Bobby and Olivia who were hand-in-hand.

"I know," he nodded and added, "but it doesn't change the fact that I'm not holding her hand."

"I'm sorry," I said.

"Don't be. He's the guy that you should feel sorry for. He doesn't know what he has."

"He'll mess up and she'll realize what kind of guy he is,"

"Well, if he does, it would be the last time I would ever let her get hurt," Jackson said and my heart fluttered at his words.

"Are we ready to head back?" Zach said to the group spinning his keys on his finger.

It was a quiet ride back to Ellsworth. There had been some rearranging and Olivia ended up driving back with Bobby. So, it was just the three of us – Jackson, Drew and me. "Did you have fun?" Jackson asked Andrew once we were on the highway.

"Yes," Drew smiled truthfully.

"Good," Jackson nodded, "And you?" he directed to me in the reflection of his rearview.

"Congratulations, Jackson, you got me out on a Friday night. Does this mean I'm one of the popular kids now?" I asked kiddingly to which Jackson and Andrew laughed.

"If we say, 'Yes' will she believe us?" Jackson asked his buddy pretending to whisper.

"I'd say there is a good chance," Drew grinned, peaking over his shoulder.

"Okay," Jackson said like they were breaking from a huddle. He turned his head slightly and said, "Yes, Bethany, you are *now* popular."

"Funny, guys. Very funny," I mocked.

Saturday, October 3rd

"Twenty-four, thirty-six, hut, hut, hike!" Olivia called as Gregg and I took off towards the rose bushes, also known as the end zone. Ryan, Kate and Chris converged on us as Liv threw the football like a girl, lobbing it to Gregg who somehow still caught it. No sooner, though, Chris two-hand touched him.

"What? How do you like that?" Chris said talking smack.

"Nice," Gregg said rolling his eyes after acknowledging Chris' little dance and strongly handed the football into his stomach, causing the rest of us to laugh.

"Chris, we're the ones who are down fourteen points," Kate said putting her hand on his back as he made his way to their huddle.

"Yeah and if we weren't playing two-hand touch, Gregg would have dragged you to the end zone," Ryan laughed.

"Hey Andrew," Liv waved and I turned my head to see him walking from the side gate in his small town costume of jeans and a navy blue v-neck sweater over a white button up. Shaking Ryan's hand, then Gregg's and Chris', Drew nodded towards Kate and Olivia before smiling at me.

"How was the team meeting?" I asked.

"It went well," Drew said kissing me on the cheek.

Kate had stolen the ball from Ryan while pretending to kiss her fiancé. "Hey!" he said looking at her and then began to chase his soon-to-be bride while she held the ball away from him.

"Five bucks on Ryan," Chris said tilting his head to Gregg.

"You're on," Gregg accepted.

"See you at the Fair?" Liv asked me as she rocked on her toes.

"Yup," I grinned as I locked arms with Andrew's.

"Later," she said twirling away and joining Chris and Gregg. "Slap bet... Kate over Ryan," Liv upped the ante.

Drew and I had walked a block or two in silence as my curiosity caught up to me. A lot had happened in the past two days: Abby's pregnancy, our night out in Bryant Square with friends from school... I had almost forgotten the conversation I had with my grandfather in his office before the away game. "Andrew," I began. He looked sideways at me, responding to his name.

Unruffled I asked, "By any chance did Charles tell you that he spoke with my grandfather about my heart?" We walked the length of an entire front yard and under the shade of a tree before I noticed Drew still hadn't answered. His silence caught me off guard so I turned seeing that his jaw was clenched. "You knew that Charles was going to tell him?" I asked surprised. Andrew turned his head but kept his eyes on the setting sun behind me; he was hiding something. "You knew?" I asked again.

"Yes," he answered, "I knew."

"He told you he was going to say something?"

"Actually, I'm the one who insisted that he speak to your grandfather," Andrew admitted.

"YOU asked him too," I retorted, trying to keep my voice even.

"Yes, Bethany, your grandfather has a right to know," Drew defended his request.

"Don't you think I should be the one to decide something like that?" I challenged.

"Of course," Drew nodded and continued, "but we are talking about you and we both know you wouldn't have."

"Well, maybe I don't want to cause him pain with something that is out of his control," I shrugged slightly angry.

"If it had been a possibility, your father would have liked to have known," Andrew argued giving me a serious look, "especially if any preventive measures could have been taken." Looking back at him, I knew he was right and I looked down at the sidewalk.

After a few silent steps I mumbled, "Thanks."

"You're welcome," he laughed with his hands in his pockets.

"Is there anything else you think I won't do that you've asked Charles or Abby to take care of for me?" I asked sarcastically.

"No," he said letting out a breath. "But I never really know what Abby is up too," he grinned.

"Yeah," I laughed. The noise coming from Main Street was growing as we got closer but my mind couldn't be farther away. "Can I ask you a question," I asked in an almost warning-like tone, "You're not going to like it."

Sensing my unease, Drew readied himself and replied, "Okay, let's have it."

"I have to ask you," I tried explaining why I was about to ask what I was about to ask.

"You *have* to?" he grinned.

"Yes," I nodded seriously.

"Alright then," he encouraged. There were so many questions that I wanted to know the answers for that I didn't know where to begin.

"I've been trying to piece together all of the memories… in sort of a timeline. Some of the memories are from you, Charles and Abby but others are mine… I just need a little help placing them," I said gazing ahead at the wall of people we were approaching.

Andrew, half-expecting my request took a deep breath and offered, "Maybe, if I explain some things, it could help."

"Okay," I nodded.

"The memory of you in your father's study... When he told you he was going to Coverly. That was eight months after you arrived to town. Your father... there was a last minute business trip," Drew said becoming tense. "The dream, the one where Charles brought you to your room where Abigail was, that was two nights later. Your father and I were in Coverly and there had been an accident on the way back," Andrew recalled and swallowed hard. Over a hundred years had separated the hours we were thinking back on but time didn't care because yesterdays are all yesterdays and Andrew still felt its sting. "Charles had been notified. He only knew that one of us had survived. When I got to the Estate, I went to find you – I had to find you, to tell you myself. I owed it to Jonathan to be the one to tell you that everything had been done to try and save him," Andrew paused, choked by emotion but pushed onward. "I knew he was all you had."

Andrew and I made eye contact and I could see the agony this was putting him under, but he was right, I needed to know. "Your father had left Charles his business in his Last Will & Testament which we didn't know until his burial. Without question, you would have remained at the Estate never having to worry about money with the substantial means your father had left behind. Charles would have taken you as his ward." Understanding what was being told to me, I examined Andrew's expressions and knew that the worst was yet to come as his eyes narrowed, "I made the biggest mistake of my life separating myself from you. I was incapable of facing you as you rightfully mourned the loss of your father. I blamed myself for your pain, wishing it had been me instead…" Drew said staring blankly as if he could see the rooms and recollections. "The worst of the guilt got the best of me," he confessed. Andrew was now at a loss for words trying to describe his hours of desperation.

"No," escaped my lips as my eyes moved from side-to-side as my own memory caught up to me.

"A week later," he began not wanting to say it aloud.

Connecting the timeline, I interjected, "The nightmare, the one on the grounds…" Andrew looked up at my utterance with a pained expression, still not having forgiven himself.

"I was angry with you… I knew that you…" I started.

"That I was being a coward," Andrew finished disgusted by how he had let things unfold.

I took over the conversation now, not needing him to tell me how or why things transpired the way they did. "I didn't mean it when I said that I hated you. I knew it was the only way to make you *hear* me. It was the only way to make you see how ridiculous you were being," I said owning the emotions that I had once let tear through me.

His jaw clenched and his face sickened. Then he mumbled, "I did eventually see how ridiculous I was being but it was too late; you were gone." My eyes burned before the archangel as tears fell down my face. Drew wiped them from my eyes and whispered sincerely, "Don't cry." His hand gently raised my chin so I was back in his eyes.

"What if..." I said thinking of the hundreds of things that should have gone wrong or could go wrong causing me to drop my head as he put his arms around me.

"You can never win at that game," Andrew spoke from experience before kissing the top of my head and holding me closer to him. I knew I was safe. Andrew and I stood on the sidewalk in each others' arms with time surrounding us, and in that moment I understood how my future was very much tangled with the lessons from the past. I didn't quite understand everything but I knew it would be different this time. It had to be different.

"It was Charles who was supposed to go to Coverly with your father that night. I used to think about that quite often," he said and I looked up at him. "It should have been Charles with your father that night but it wasn't. I am grateful for that. Trust me when I tell you, I have run every possibility for the way things should have gone... Yet, the only solemn conclusion I have come to is the 'What if' mentality is the devil's snare."

I could hear a family walking on the opposite sidewalk which made me aware of my surroundings. Composing myself, we started walking again towards Main Street. The crowd bustled around us. There were table displays and gaming booths set up all along the street, plenty of rides and numerous kinds of food vendors. It was the worst place to continue our unfinished conversation. "This way," Andrew said leading me through the crowd towards an empty gazebo which was forgotten with the party buzzing around it.

When Drew and I sat down, I watched him anxiously flex and release his fist as he concentrated and deliberated silently. Then without looking up he reluctantly put his palm up for me to take. When I didn't he said, "I'll show you everything. Go ahead."

"I don't think I could," I said looking away from him and back out over the crowd. The ability to share memories was not normal and if we were like 'normal' people, we would be left with only words to express the feelings and describe the places captured in our memories. It was then that I realized the true power of words.

"Before you, I was a man devoted to work and finding purpose. When we met, I felt as though I was found. Bethany, you never *haunted* me… you were never a ghost to me. I haunted me. My pain was not caused by you nor did any of this happen *to* me. It happened *for* me. I can see that now more than ever."

Drew took a deep breath and continued, "I missed you. I missed your smile, your laugh and *everything* about us." The seriousness isolated us as if no one else existed. "I was so angry with everything that had happened. It wasn't how it was supposed to be and I fought it... I fought it," he exhaled. "When Jonathan passed I watched helplessly as the only family you had was taken from you. I couldn't look at you without feeling somehow responsible," Drew said and shifted forward. "I tried to separate us like a coward and then… you were gone. I was beside myself. I would sit and pray waiting for you to come back through the door. I begged to have you back even if you hated me; even if you blamed me for everything. I needed to explain myself… that I didn't try to push you away because I didn't love you," he said firmly. "That was never the case. I needed you to go on and to be happy again… to finish your story, even if it didn't include me. I couldn't understand why I was being given so much time and you were given so little." I held my breath at his words. "You were it for me, Beths – the one, my one, *always*. You see me for the man I am and the man I am not." Andrew was quiet for a moment trying to calm his breathing. "For some time I resented my memory for keeping you around because while my body and memory were frozen, I was dying inside and my soul was trapped. I became so angry – angry at life, angry at death, angry at you..." he said straightening his back but continued to look down at his hands. "I reached a point where I came to terms with what had happened and however much time I had, I would spend it trying to save someone else's Bethany."

"You could have moved on," I said knowing that he had been alone and was burdened far longer than any person should be.

"Move on?" he asked as though it was an outrageous statement.

"You could have given someone else the privilege to love you."

"I did," a thoughtful smile crossed his lips. "I loved through my work."

I took a scattered breath trying to hold back the tears. "Andrew, if another woman came along I would have wanted you to be happy. It would have been okay."

"No," he answered absolute.

"Never Drew? There was never someone else?" I asked.

"No," he said shaking his head. "Bethany, there are loves of your life and then there is the love of a lifetime. You were that for me and I was perfectly content with that," Drew said with his ocean blue eyes piercing into mine. I knew he was telling the truth.

"I'm sorry I *left* you," I whispered as the tears welled up in my eyes.

"I'm sorry I pushed you away. I am *so* sorry for that," he said still angry about it and stood walking towards the railing, grabbing it tightly. I came up next to him. "I didn't want to push you away, Beths," he said looking down at me. "You have to know that."

"Why did you? Did I do something to make you feel like it was your fault?"

"It was a last minute trip and…" he said still stuck in the memory.

"Drew, my father wouldn't want you to feel this way and I forgive you for whatever you feel you need forgiveness for." "Andrew," I said so he would look up at me. When he did I grinned and said, "Forgive yourself."

"Forgiveness?" he repeated and let go of the railing and turned to me.

"*Take it*," I said placing my hands on his chest desperately hoping he would.

"Take it," he breathed as he ran the back of his right hand over my cheek. He knew the meaning behind these words. They had been the last I had spoken to him on the grounds. Finding solace in my eyes, he whispered, "I thought the years without you were like a sentence, a punishment for hurting you the way I did."

"But now?"

"Now… now I see how it opened my eyes and shaped my life. It broke me in every way it could, but it brought me to my faith," he exhaled. "And I'm starting to see how it was preparing me for the day that I would find you." Drew ran his hands into my hair and our eyes were locked on one another. "I'm a different man, a better man – one that stands a chance of deserving you and someone who would have waited forever for this." I closed my eyes and I felt his lips touch mine. When our lips separated, I opened my eyes. I saw a smile wash across his face before his eyes opened to meet mine.

"Wicks, hands off my sister!" I heard Ryan yell out and looked over fast enough to see Kate elbow my brother. They were walking up to the gazebo followed by Olivia who was holding a pink cotton candy, fighting off Chris who was trying to steal a piece.

"Can we please do the bumper cars?" Gregg begged not too far behind.

I rested my head on Drew's shoulder and he wrapped his arm around my waist. "Shall we?" he asked gesturing for us to join them.

—

After experiencing my first, good ole County Fair and the chaos of town tradition, Andrew and I pulled up out front of the well lit Estate a few hours later. Walking wordlessly up the steps, the bright entranceway was welcoming and warm.

"How was it?" Charles greeted us while holding a sleeping Gracie.

"It was nice," I answered as Andrew took a few steps toward the dining room.

Charles warned his brother-in-law, "If I were you, I wouldn't go in there."

"Why?" Andrew asked in a hushed voice so he wouldn't wake Gracie.

"Abby graded the physics tests…" Charles began and Andrew's face contorted. Drew then continued hesitantly into the room. Charles and I waited and heard whispers which escalated until what they were saying was clear as day.

"Don't give me that, Drew!" I heard Abby snap.

"But when will I ever use this? My profession has never and will never call for me to be proficient in it!" I heard him slam a book shut. I bit my lip and Charles shook his head, laughing quietly at the teacher/student dispute with sibling-like warfare.

"Good luck," Charles said slowly turning towards the staircase to put Gracie in her bed. I quietly walked into the dining room and saw Abby standing next to Andrew trying to breakdown a physics problem for him. I knocked on the door and they both looked up.

"Thank God," Abby said. "Maybe you can explain a thing or two to Mr. Thinks-He's-Above-High-School-Physics."

"Oh please, Abigail," Drew said to his older sister.

"It's not brain surgery, Andrew," she rolled her eyes.

"I wish it were – at least then Charles would be able to explain it," he said sarcastically looking at the book. Abby hit his arm with the back of her hand before clearing off the rest of the dinner plates and walking into the kitchen. I stood by the fireplace which lit the room and threw off comforting heat.

"That bad?" I asked pointing to the red-inked test next to the open textbook.

Raising his voice so Abby would hear him, he answered, "Yes, it's that bad."

Abby came back through the door and said, "Beths, please help him with that? I wouldn't want to think of having to give my own brother an 'F'." she jeered.

"Oh come on, Abigail," Drew protested.

"Just because you're a business prodigy doesn't mean you're a genius OR that you'll get a free ride in my class."

Picking up the test paper Drew said, "You're the teacher. If I don't understand it, imagine how many of your students don't either."

"Ha, okay," she said smiling at the challenge and looked at me. "Bethany, what is the answer to number five?" she said pointing at the large 'X' over his work. Studying the paper over, I read the question and answered, "6.41 meters per second."

Abby smirked and looked at Andrew, "*My* students," she said mockingly, "do understand."

"How did you do that?" Andrew asked baffled. "You didn't even pick up a pencil."

"I have a good teacher?" I shrugged playing along with Abby's unfair set up. Without a word, Andrew sat down in the closest chair now inspired to learn it. Abby and I laughed as I followed her into the kitchen.

"Think he'll figure it out?" she questioned as she started to wash the dishes.

"Are you referring to him learning the material or my education?"

"Both?" she shrugged.

"Someday," I laughed and picked up a towel and dried what she cleaned.

Abby and I watched Charles and Andrew through the opened kitchen doors as we drank our tea and coffee. Charles, who was sitting across the dining room table from Drew, tried to teach himself physics so he could then, in turn, try and help Andrew. It was priceless. Abby and I spent the next hour discussing anything and everything, old and new; especially about the baby she was already in love with.

Gracie came down the servant stairwell rubbing her eyes. "Gracie," Abby said walking over to her and picking her up.

"I had a bad dream," the little girl's voice waivered.

"It's okay," Abby held her tighter and asked, "Do you want me to come lay with you?" Gracie shook her head and looked through the double doors and pointed. Abby put her down on the ground and watched as the little one marched over to Andrew and tugged at his arm.

"Gracie," Drew said putting down his pencil and pulled her on to his lap. She whispered something in his ear with the saddest eyes.

"Okay," Andrew answered and stood up with her in his arms. Charles looked back down, referencing the physics' textbook again as Andrew left the room and walked back into the entranceway. I watched down the hallway as he carried her back upstairs.

About ten minutes later, I left the dining room as Abigail attempted to explain to her husband one of the laws of physics the doctor could not seem to grasp. I climbed the stairs, laughing at the two of them and saw light coming from Andrew's room.

I stopped in his doorway and saw him lying on top of his covers with his arm around Gracie as he read a fairytale to the sleeping girl. Cole was lying at the foot of the bed also having joined them but had fallen back to sleep. I crossed my arms and leaned against the door frame. Drew was perfect in my mind. This was such an adorable moment I thought I might explode. I watched for a second or two before he felt my presence. 'Hi,' he mouthed and closed the book, placing it softly on his nightstand. With ease, he picked up Gracie and tapped Cole's shoulder, waking him up. "Come on, pal," he said and Cole followed Andrew sleepily out of the room and down the hall to his own room. I stepped inside Andrew's quarters and smiled when I saw his letterman jacket hung in his closet next to his business suits. I walked over to the far end of the room and looked out the large windows at the dark grounds. The half moon gave only a little light to the vast acres but I could see that the light was on in my father's office the floor below, shedding some immediate light on the stone terrace. I yawned and covered my mouth, tired from what the day had brought.

"You too?" Andrew said walking back into his bedroom.

"Yes," I nodded and smiled. He sat back down on his bed and put out his arm. I climbed onto the bed and curled up next to him, his shoulder welcoming me, acting as my pillow. He kissed the side of my head and reached with his other hand for Gracie's storybook on the nightstand and opened it. I smiled and wrapped my arm around his chest as my head rose and fell with the air that passed in his lungs. "In every age," he began and I closed my eyes as his voice soothed a part of me I didn't know existed. "There are times of war and times of peace. This was the time in between."

Sunday, October 4th

Hours had passed since I left the Estate but I couldn't sleep. My bedroom lights were still on, my music played low, set on shuffle, and I was tangled up in my blanket, staring at the roof's wooden eaves. It was the early morning hours of Sunday and I knew I would have to be up for Church soon. I could hear crickets two stories down and the breeze caused mayhem to the still unchanging green leaves. Everything was quiet, still and peaceful. I heard footsteps on the stairs that were cautious and climbing. "Hey Ry," I said when I saw his head pop up over the banister. I adjusted my pillows so I sat up a little.

"Can't sleep?" he asked.

"No. What about you?" I questioned pulling my hair up into a messy bun.

"Too much candy," he joked. "The door was open and I saw your light on," he explained, pointing to the chandelier hanging in the middle of the room.

"Oh," I said looking down at one of the seams on the blanket.

"What's on your mind?" he asked not buying the 'can't sleep' bit.

"Nothing," I tried to convince him. "Are you okay?" I asked knowing that he needed sleep more than anyone.

"Yeah, I'm good," my brother said looking around the attic.

"Nervous about the wedding?" I asked.

"Nah," he shook it off.

"The Lumberyard?" I tried again.

"Nope."

"Ugh, you're going to have to help me out here," I laughed. Ryan grinned before fiddling with things on my makeshift dresser. "Ryan…" I started.

He picked up my desk chair, spun it around and sat on it backwards, leaning his arms on the top and resting his chin on them. Whatever was bothering him was serious. I waited for him to start.

"I know I've already told you this but you know I love you right?" he asked.

"Yeah Ry," I said sitting up completely, giving him my full attention. I wrapped the blanket over my legs as the nighttime breeze washed through the window.

"Like take a bullet, get hit by a moving bus, walk on hot coals, watch a chick flick if you wanted to…" he listed.

"Yes Ry," I smiled, "and I would do the same for you."

"I know," he said looking away from me and I watched as his eyes traveled back. Opening his mouth, he said, "I'm getting married in like a month."

"Yes," I nodded quietly. Ryan paused again formulating his next words.

"I won't be living here anymore," he continued.

"I know," I shrugged.

"We," he said motioning in between the two of us, "won't change. Our relationship and stuff," he finished.

"No," I grinned.

"Just making sure you know that."

"I know," I said looking down at the floor.

"So, this Wicks kid, Andrew," my brother said changing the subject. I felt a lump in my throat. "He's a good guy. You like him…" he said with it sounding more like a statement than a question.

"Very much," I answered. Ryan was quiet again. "Don't you?" I asked nervously, wanting his approval. Hoping beyond hope that my brother and protector liked the man I loved.

"Yeah, he seems like a great guy. He has his head on straight, has a good family, Gramps can't find anything wrong with him…" Ryan shrugged and we both smiled. "It's just that…" Ryan stopped.

"What?" I asked troubled that he found a flaw.

Ryan looked at me and said, "I watched you two together during the Fair. How he looks at you… how he acts…" A grin washed over my face. I knew Ryan couldn't be close to understanding half of the craziness of Drew and my relationship but he saw the change Drew made in me. Ryan and I exchanged an unspoken understanding of the affection I had for Andrew. "You love him don't you?" Ryan asked well out of his comfort zone. I nodded my head slowly but whole-heartedly. "Does he know?" Ryan inquired.

"I'm pretty sure," I smiled.

"I'll tell you one thing," Ryan said standing up and putting the chair back. "He's in deep for you."

"Yeah? You think so?" I asked girlishly.

"Ugh, yeah Beths," Ryan huffed.

"What makes you say that?"

Ryan turned off the music and walked back over to my bed, taking my blanket and tucking me in. Standing above me he looked down saying, "The way he looks at you... the world could stop and the kid wouldn't know it." My heart fluttered at the choice of words Ryan had chosen which were unknowingly accurate. Kissing my cheek, Ryan said, "Night, Beths."

"Night, Ry," I said as the initial shock of his words wore off. Ryan shut off the light switch and made his way down the stairs. My mind echoed my brother's observation. Andrew loved me and I, him. It didn't matter what time we were in or what the world around us was like. Our feelings were real and stronger than the hands of time.

Time Elapses

Chapter Six
The Wedding

"Kate," Olivia started, "Are you ready?" she asked as the beauty dressed in stunning white turned to meet her sister's anxious eyes. Kate smiled and took her bouquet from her Maid of Honor. The organ was playing as the ushers opened the doors only letting me exit, never revealing the waiting bride.

My brother was standing at the end of the aisle. The little Church was filled with familiar faces belonging to family, friends and people from weekly Mass. As I walked slowly towards Ryan, I smiled at Andrew as I passed him about halfway. He was sitting next to Charles and Abby and we somewhat blushed at one another before I focused my attention back on my brother and his groomsmen.

Ryan and I communicated wordlessly as my eyes met his; he was looking for a calm in the midst of his nerves and he found that in my reassuring smile. My brother looked handsome dressed in his suit. Gregg and Chris were standing alongside him also looking sharp, having cleaned up for the occasion. For once the three guys were not joking around for more than five minutes; it had to be a new record. I found my place next to two of Kate's friends from college who were also bridesmaids and watched as Olivia made her way down the aisle. She and Ryan exchanged a smile as the organ changed at the pinnacle of excitement before the doors opened one last time.

The congregation stood and Kate, a gorgeous bride, was led by her father. The light behind them glowed, emphasizing the picturesque moment and gown's silhouette. While all eyes were on Kate, mine were on my brother. His breath caught in his lungs at the sight of her; he was completely and utterly spellbound. The closer she got to the altar, the more emotional my brother became. Having seen him cry only once in my life, I was moved that he was moved. Mr. Connelly kissed his eldest daughter's cheek and shook his son-in-law's hand. In the front row, my grandmother dabbed her eyes with my grandfather's handkerchief.

As the ceremony began, I looked over at Drew – Charles had leaned over and was whispering in his ear. Andrew sat straight-backed, his eyes were glued forward. I thought nothing of it as the pastor made the Sign of the Cross.

The bells rang out as the newly married couple walked out the front doors as husband and wife. Liv and I followed giggling, happy for our siblings.

The reception was set underneath a large, white tent on the back lawn of the Church's property nestled between bordering trees. There were white linen tables set with candles, flowers and decorative centerpieces. It was simple and elegant, and the weather was cooperating.

"Want to dance, Beths?" Gregg asked as most of the bridal party made their way to the dance floor. I put my bouquet down on the table when a familiar skirt suit walked up behind him. I didn't need to look up to know who it belonged too. Her cold voice caused a shrill to go down my spine as she spoke my name. Gregg turned to see who the woman was and he looked apprehensively between her and me, feeling the instant tension.

"Mother," I replied in a respectable but resilient tone. I knew our paths would cross again but I just hadn't anticipated that it would happen at Ryan and Kate's wedding reception.

"What are you doing here?" Ryan sneered as he came up beside me.

"I was invited," she said not breaking eye contact with me. She was a pretty woman; I could not deny her that.

I was sure that from an outsider's point of view there was no need for my brother's callousness towards her... that is until you actually got to know her.

"Mrs. Taylor." Kate said joining her husband. "I'm glad you could make it." Ryan looked at Kate bewildered but she continued, "It means a lot to me... and Ryan that you could be here to share today with us."

"*You* invited her?" Ryan asked confused to which Kate nodded. Her intentions were from her heart of gold; Kate hoped that her gesture of inviting her mother-in-law to the wedding would be seen as a peace offering. Unfortunately, that wasn't how my mother worked. Ryan and I had enough experience with Dana Reid to know that.

"I *am* the mother of the groom," our mother barked at Ryan. "If you can call this a wedding," she added and Kate flinched at the malevolent remark. Kate's olive branch and kindness was wasted on someone who would not welcome or reciprocate any such gesture. Gregg, who had never met Dana Reid, looked disgusted within the first two minutes of being in her company.

"Glad you could clear that busy schedule of yours," Ryan seethed.

"It was not easy," our mother said looking into her pocketbook. I knew that I needed to get her attention so that she would aim her callousness towards me, not at Ryan and Kate. My plan was to distract her and get her away from the reception at any cost, even that of my own happiness.

"You do know that just because your calendar is full it doesn't mean that your life is," I said as I adjusted the pretty belt at my waist. The bridesmaid's gown I was wearing did not appropriately dress me to match the path that this conversation was going to take; it was far too frilly.

"And what have you been up too? Barn raising? Cow tipping?" she retorted and continued her rant, "I'm sure the locals," my mother said looking at Gregg who was the newest and closest victim, "loved that a washed up celebrity rolled into town." My blood was boiling as she insulted everyone around her; everyone that I cared about.

"Dana," a familiar voice said coming up behind her. Drew was holding two glasses of champagne in his hands and Olivia had her arm around his.

My mother changed her demeanor immediately at the sight of him. Andrew nodded toward Ryan and Kate. I did not miss the flicker in his eye in the momentary overlap when our eyes met. Ryan gave Olivia a strange look, not understanding why she clung so closely to *my* boyfriend's arm. I tilted my head, also confused by what they were playing at. Handing my mother one of the champagne glasses, they tapped the fine crystal and took a sip. My mother was eyeing Drew as if he were a prize to be won.

"You and your brother-in-law are the only refuge for decent conversation in this town, Andrew," she said waving her over-jeweled wrist in the direction of my brother and me.

"I'm not quite certain about that," Drew said before adding, "Congratulations again, Mr. and Mrs. Taylor," with a kind smile to my brother and Kate as he lifted his glass once more. Ryan wrapped his arm around Kate and she placed her wedding banded hand on his chest, smiling up at him. They were smitten.

"Now then," my mother said ignoring the sweet moment, "please continue telling me what it is exactly that your family invests in." Andrew looked down and then up at my mother with a grin hiding at the corner of his lips. In that moment I knew what he was doing – I knew that grin. He knew exactly who my mother was. The memories I had shared with Abigail of this woman and my life in New York weeks ago were very present in Andrew's mind. Abby had shared them with him. He recognized my mother and was very aware of the role she played in my past. My eyes shot around the tent looking for Abigail. Sure enough, she stood off to the side, watching the scene unfold.

When she saw me looking for her, she smiled and nodded confidently before taking a sip of her ice water. Charles, standing next to her, was watching Andrew, waiting. I returned my attention to Andrew but Olivia caught my eye. Standing next to Drew, she smirked devilishly. This was going to be amusing.

"Charles mentioned that he is the owner of the Bentley," my mother said eyeing the luxury car parked a few yards away.

"Our family is very fortunate…" Andrew began humbly.

That's when Olivia added fuel to the fire, "Drew's family owns extensive properties and they've also invested some of their assets in lucrative businesses for generations."

"You and your brother-in-law come from old money?" my mother inquired, placing her hand on Drew's forearm shamelessly flirting. "It's so kind of you, really, to take time to be *here*. Where is Charles?" she asked looking around. Charles, however, was already in route. She was pleased when he joined the circle.

"Pardon me, I wanted to congratulate the newlyweds," Charles said with an outstretched hand to Ryan. I watched as my mother took notice of the well tailored suit Charles wore. His polished manner and cultured tongue were additional indicators of his wealth. If my mother was a money detector, she would have started beeping.

"Have you two met?" Ryan asked our mother, afraid of the impression she might have made.

"Yes, well Charles and Andrew have been keeping me company for the past half hour. They are refreshing, really. I enjoy their company. It's stimulating," she gloated. Charles' eyes found mine as he was offered a glass of champagne by a passing waiter. He glanced back over at me as he took a drink and then subtly raised his glass in my direction; whatever was about to happen, I was ready to enjoy it. "They live in a turn of the century Estate… How is it that you know the bride?" my mother questioned Charles curiously.

"I am a member of the hospital board where Kate works. However, it's through Jonathan Taylor that I met the wonderful couple."

"Jonathan?" my mother's head turned at the use of my father's name.

"Yes, Jonathan Taylor and I coach football at the high school together."

"Oh," was all she could manage realizing he was referring to her father-in-law. There was no love lost there.

"And Ryan's business has done some fine work at the Estate."

"Ryan's *business*?" she asked in a pitched voice.

"Yes," Charles continued unaffected, "He is very successful." My mother looked at my brother taken aback by the news.

"How again is it that you know Ryan and Kate?" Charles asked as though he didn't know who she was.

"Ryan is... my son," she said with some difficulty, recovering from the fact that he was doing well for himself.

"He's your son?" Charles repeated acting surprised. Ryan nodded confirming the fact and then looked back at our mother. "Well Dana, you must be proud," Charles declared openly.

"I, ah," she said looking away from my brother. Kate's arm hugged around him tighter; she loved him unconditionally – something our mother never showed him.

"Would it be right to assume then that you are Bethany's mother as well?" Charles questioned. My mother nodded still somewhat dazed.

"Dana, I must apologize," Drew said as Olivia loosened her hold on his arm and he extended his hand towards my mother. "I have introduced myself to you under misinformed pretenses."

My mother looked down at his hand and took it slowly not understanding what he was referring too. Andrew looked over at me saying, "Bethany and I are…"

"Dating," Olivia finished with a 'rub-it-in-her-face' tone. My mother's eyes widened and her neck snapped in my direction. Her mouth was slightly opened in shock from the revelation. Gregg, who had stayed quiet the entire time, spoke up, "Drew is also the star quarterback for the *local* high school football team," he said making sure he stressed the word 'local' since my mother had used it derogatively moments ago.

"I am sorry that I didn't introduce myself properly. Bethany has never spoken of you, and you don't resemble each other in the slightest…" Drew said moving next to me. He kissed the side of my head and then placed his hand on the small of my back. I smiled up at him and he grinned. Looking over at the horrid woman, Andrew continued, "You didn't say that your last name was Taylor, correct?"

"Reid," Ryan added glad that they didn't share a common surname.

"You?" she stuttered to my handsome, wealthy and intelligent boyfriend. "You two are dating?"

"Yes," Drew said firmly. In response to my mother's reaction, Olivia let out a laugh, Gregg was fighting back a smile, and Charles took another sip of champagne to hide the grin on his face.

"Didn't see that one coming, huh, mom?" Ryan chuckled, enjoying her warranted humiliation more than anyone else. Kate tried to restrain her laughter but failed and joined in with her sister.

"If I'm not mistaken, according to you, Andrew and Dr. Landon's zip code would technically make them 'rednecks', wouldn't it?" Ryan continued.

Charles' head tilted and Andrew's eyes narrowed as my mother's level of discomfort grew. "That's not what I meant when I said…" she tried to backtrack on what she told Ryan when he first moved to Ellsworth.

"No, you were clear when you said I was a redneck for living in this town."

"Is that right, Madam?" Charles inquired; his southern roots were equally as deep as his refined temperament.

"This is some sort of joke," my mother said, attempting to redeem any shred of dignity she thought she had left. She had found these two 'perfect' men who she thought she had won over and then, in a rapid turn of events, she found herself the fool.

"This is not a joke," Ryan assured her, rocking happily on his heels with his hands in his pockets.

"I'm just glad my daughter is keeping with good company," my mother said to Charles and then looked at Andrew. She wasted no time trying to weasel her way back into my life so that she could reap any benefit she thought there might be. Knowing her tricks, Ryan put a stop to it immediately.

"Mom, you have always reminded me that you think it is 'unfortunate' that I'm your son. But let me remind you that Bethany," my brother said looking across at me, "Beths is *legally* not your daughter anymore." We smiled at one another.

"Bethany…" she started, trying to muster an ounce of maternal instinct. When she took a step towards me out of desperation, Andrew protectively stepped in front of me. Ryan, too, was ready to take a step forward between my mother and me if necessary. However, Drew had the situation under control. Gregg grabbed a feisty Olivia who was not hesitating to defend her best friend.

"I would try and restrain yourself, Ms. Reid," Charles interceded.

She had lost all of her demeanor in the unfolding of the truth. "What is that suppose to mean?" she snapped, turning against the trophy she thought she had won.

"It means exactly how it sounds," Charles said with unwavering composure, never creating false allusions. Charles was, after all, a full-fledged gentleman.

"It means shut up and get the hell out of here," Liv deadpanned and all of our heads turned in surprise at the petite, frilly dress wearing, blonde.

"Well, I've never..." my mother started as she placed her champagne glass on the table. She turned and never looked back. After seventeen years, her useless conditional love was finally put in its place.

"Having fun?" Ryan asked as he and Kate twirled towards Andrew and I, and Chris and Olivia, on the dance floor about an hour later.

"Yes," Drew replied and his arms held me tighter.

"Good, good... Did you see the look on mom's face," Ryan asked me and laughed for the hundredth time. "It made my day!" Kate purposefully stepped on his foot. "I mean besides the fact I married my best friend and the love of my life," he amended and kissed his bride.

"Nice save, Romeo," Liv said at our impromptu 'meeting' on the dance floor.

"*It means shut up and get the hell out of here*," Ryan mimicked Liv's voice and laughed louder at the comment she had made.

"I can't believe I missed it," Chris shook his head. "I go to the bathroom and all the good stuff happened." Kate eyed him and Chris added, "Other than the vows part."

"Her face... was priceless," Ryan said looking up at the tent above us.

"Good. I hope you took mental pictures because I didn't get you a wedding gift," Olivia smirked.

Ryan looked at Liv and asked, "Seriously, you didn't get me any presents?" as if he was a young child.

"Oh please, cry me a river, build me a bridge and get over it," she shot back.

"Aw, how sweet," I narrated their constant childlike bickering.

"It's some sort of brother and sister-in-law love-hate relationship," Kate grinned.

"You should be thanking Andrew," Liv said motioning towards him. "He was the one that got the ball rolling." I knew Drew had done it for me – much the same as Charles' motive.

"I appreciate it," my brother said to my boyfriend.

"My plan was to take her out before you noticed she was here," Liv added aloud. "What?" she said when Chris looked down at his dance partner uneasily.

"You're very intimidating for such a small person," Chris explained, holding her a little farther away as they danced. She rolled her eyes. Chris added, "You're cute, blonde and… lethal." We all laughed as we danced back into the mix of other guests.

I looked up to mention something insignificant to Andrew only to see his eyes focused to his right, beyond my shoulder. I turned my head slightly to see Charles and Abby dancing with one another, smiling and talking as the music swept around them. They were a stunning couple and stared into each other's eyes, seeing each other for the souls they were. How they stayed in love after all of these years was incredible to me. But then again, they didn't complete one another, they complimented one another. That was something I saw the first night I met them and was still true to this day. My eyes traveled back to Andrew who still wore a troubled expression. His eyebrows were furrowed in response to whatever taxing thoughts his mind was reeling over. Whatever it was, it was weighing on his appearance. Without noticing me examining him, his eyes moved to my other side, to his left. I followed his line of sight again and watched as he observed my brother and his wife laughing and twirling around their reception. Drew's eyes narrowed even more. "Everything alright?" I smiled. He looked down at me and sheepishly nodded.

Andrew led and I followed. We fell into a pattern and it wasn't until Drew caught Charles' eye that he, for the first time in our dancing history, misstepped. I ran my foot over Drew's polished shoe and scuffed it in exchange. He was flustered and I looked up at him and then at Charles who turned with his wife so that I could not see his face. It was odd but Andrew was quick to recover.

"What was that," I giggled, laughing it off.

"Nothing," Andrew said. With this response, I knew it was definitely something.

I sneakily moved my hands from around his neck and put one out in another dance pose, one we were more familiar with. Not realizing what I was doing, Andrew naturally put his hand out for mine. It was only an instant but the flash was crystal clear.

Drew was sitting in the pew and his eyes moved from me standing beside Olivia down to his lap and then up again but straight ahead. His eyes were not focused on anything in particular. He was simply trying to live through the moment. Panic, anxiety and fear were all very relevant in his consciousness. Charles, who was sitting next to him, leaned over. "Please Drew," he whispered. "Think about this. Please, I beg of you." The desperation in Charles' voice was raw, leaving a hollow ache in Andrew's chest.

The flash ended as soon as Andrew realized what I had done. A look of terror was in his eyes as mine refocused. I was confused and couldn't understand what I had just witnessed. Staring into his amazing ocean blue eyes, I let the waves hit me as the radiating emotions from the exchange subsided.

"I'm going to step inside," Drew said tilting his head towards the Church. "Just for a moment," he added as he stepped back and walked off the dance floor. I watched as he made his way to the open doors. His back was the last thing I saw as he ducked inside.

Chapter Seven
Antebellum

It was another Monday morning in the hallways of Ellsworth High School. Every corridor encompassed bustling students finding their way to their lockers.

A lot was going on. The Ellsworth Sparrows had clinched their spot in the playoffs, Jackson and I were study buddies and met at least once a week at the coffee shop after school. Bobby and Liv were still dating… it was over two months now that they were together. There were moments when I couldn't understand why; for example, Bobby flaked on being Olivia's date to the wedding. Instead of calling him out on it, Olivia made up an excuse for him and acted like it was okay. Hopefully, time would show her what kind of person Bobby really was.

Charles and Abby were busy organizing the Gala which was next week and were enjoying being expecting parents. I had never seen someone more excited about morning sickness than Abby. Charles was that husband who didn't want his wife to pick up anything heavy or do anything too strenuous. It frustrated Abigail but was funny to watch.

As promised, I reported to my grandfather every time I had a heart scan. Gramps was always happy to hear that there were no negative changes. As for my brother and his bride, they had left for their honeymoon but would be back in time for the Gala.

I turned the locker-lined corner and saw Andrew spinning his combination. There he was, collecting his morning books in the midst of the crowded hallway, standing out over everyone else. I don't think he noticed, and even if he did, he couldn't help it. After all, he really wasn't your typical high school student. He could pass for a mature looking eighteen year old. However, he was actually twenty-two... well, more like a hundred and twenty-two give or take a few years. There was no inkling of his secret unless he spoke when he was tired or when his guard was down. Then words from an older time would slip out.

Drew was taller than the average Ellsworth High male student but average for the football team, standing a strong six-four with a muscular build. His chiseled seraphic face was handsome and matched his heavenly body. I smiled as I made my way closer to my boyfriend.

Andrew didn't turn at my arrival but I already knew what his amazing, piercingly blue eyes looked like and hoped that they were less troubled than when I last looked into them. Over the past two months, he and I fell into place. We didn't spend every second together. He had his time for football, his friends – especially Jackson, classes, hospital work; and I had mine. I think that's what made the moments we spent together more special. We were happy with our own lives and doing our own thing. When we did spend time together we could share more and better appreciate the precious moments.

The Estate was where we felt most at home. There were so many rooms and spaces to enjoy. It was as though our past started to melt into our present. I found myself blending new memories with old ones. I actually had a simple life, once you got passed the complexity of it. There was nothing missing from my life in Ellsworth, my life with Andrew, and there was nothing more I could ask for.

I was smiling, waiting for him to turn, smile back, and kiss me lightly like did every morning. Today, however, he slowly turned, closed his locker and even though I didn't know what was about to happen, my stomach sank instinctively. Something was wrong. I didn't have time to ask because without hesitation, he began to speak harsh, callous words. "I can't do this anymore," Drew said with an unforgiving face. "I thought I'd give it a fair try, but I just can't pretend any longer. It's over."

"Pretend?" I swallowed and my eyes blinked. "What?" I felt like I was dropped into a haze and struggled to regain my composure. This was the same man who waited and loved me for over a hundred years... the one who said there was no one else for him... What was he saying?

He continued to speak words that would later haunt me. It was like the noise from the hallway became muted in the background as I tried to focus on the meaning of what he was saying. He was breaking up with me. "I can move on now. And I'm going too," he finished.

My clear skies blackened as the blow hit me but I somehow felt nothing. I didn't recognize the possessed, unfeeling man in front of me who blindsided me. The seconds of self-preserving deafness passed and the world was still. I felt everything that we had built up come crashing down. I tried to take a deep breath as my heart, burdened but strong, continued to beat inside my chest.

The homeroom bell rang above us and with his remorselessness towards me – towards us – Andrew walked down the hallway to his first class. He didn't think twice of the devastation he left in his wake or the memory he left me with.

I stood lost in the crowd, fading in the swarm around me. 'This can't be happening. Wake up, wake up!' I shouted in my head. I turned confused with the passing students until my back found the lockers. I leaned against them for support as the second bell rang overhead causing me to jump. I was awake – this was real. In the empty halls, I was alone. He was *gone*.

The day went on and I went with it; my mind did not feel like my own. The almost out of body experience detached me from feeling anything. I was silent in all my classes and walked passed Charles after biochemistry, not making eye contact. This wasn't real. I was very much in shock.

Olivia stood at the top of my steps when I looked up from my vanity. "No! Is it true? You actually broke up with Drew?"

"What?" I whispered out, speaking the first word since the last time I spoke to him.

"I overheard at practice," she said, walking closer to me and sitting cross-legged at my feet.

"I didn't…" I started and licked my lips, shaking my head. "He," I tried to say the sentence aloud. Olivia's eyes widened as she understood what I was about to say.

"What happened?" she asked, placing her hand on my knee concerned.

"I don't know," I looked down into my lap as my fingertips traced and retraced my collarbone.

"There was nothing he said or did… no signs or warnings?"

I thought about her question for a moment and my mind focused on the only oddity I could not define. "He acted strange at the reception… when we were dancing."

"What did he do?"

"He was looking at Charles and Abby, then at Ryan and Kate. He was upset so I did that hand connection thing and," I hesitated recalling the sudden flash that had only revealed anxiety and a pleading Charles.

"And what?" Olivia asked, listening intently.

"And he said that he needed a minute and went into the Church." I didn't make eye contact with Liv.

I was deflated and lost in my own mind.

As the night came not a single tear fell.

—

Shock had preserved me and denial had acted like a steadied shield. I walked up to Drew much like the day before. He didn't turn at my arrival and ignored me as though I wasn't standing next to him. My stomach sank further as embarrassment took the form of a blush that rushed to my face. His behavior and my unwillingness to accept the truth was heartbreaking. Turning away, mortified by the stares from passing students, I became fully conscious of the finality in the words that he had spoken the day before. Somehow, it, we, were over.

The strength in me was disintegrating as those first few hours of comprehension came. With every tick of the clock the sinister break deepened with no indication of a bottom. I dwindled further and further, shutting down completely; if breathing wasn't an involuntary action, I'm sure that would have stopped too. What happened in the time that separated when Andrew and I both believed that we were meant to be, and what we had now become?

It was dark and had been for a while but I didn't move from the foot of my bed. The first tears trailed down my cheeks.

This was real. This was happening.

My hands started to shake and I took a deep, sharp breath. Mentally exhausted, I closed my eyes. As soon as my eyelashes touched, I was bombarded by memories.

I pushed my eyes open and placed my palms on the hardwood floor, steadying myself as I broke out into sobs. Stomach turning memories that I had once cherished as a gift were now nothing short of a curse. The flashes and the recollections of days gone by, forced me to face the truth, we, he and I, were a thing of the past. My time with Drew, once little tastes of heaven, were now hell's playground.

The morning would come whether I slept or not – I didn't. I dressed without thinking as regret burrowed into my chest; 'could have been' and 'should have been' have a way of doing that. However, exhaustion was favorable compared to the pain I felt when my eyes closed and my mind played over the past.

Unable to hide the visible toll my breakdown over the breakup was taking on me, I put on one of Ryan's Lumberyard baseball hats. I wore it low over my face, offering coverage and blocking my red eyes – a symptom of heartache. With my brother away on his honeymoon, I easily made it passed Gramps and Grams to my car.

I was at my locker when I saw Andrew from under the rim of the hat, and quickly looked away. My eyes whelmed again and with shaking hands, I exchanged the books I needed for my morning classes while staring blankly into my locker. I needed to be somewhere else. I allowed myself the mistake of retreating to the security of frozen, unharmed memories when I was his and he was mine. I let myself remember what it was like to be in his arms. I knew I would regret it and as soon as the images left, I did.

There were only a few people in the hallway when my eyes refocused. Everyone was filing into their homeroom classrooms as I shut my locker but didn't make to move. My emotions were adjusting from my past to my reality and it left me worse off than before.

"Beths," Olivia said for the second time even though it was the first time my ears let me hear her. I turned and she was looking back at me. My tears poured down my face at the sight of my best friend in the now empty hallway. She hugged me as I cried silently on her shoulder. I could hear her crying too.

In physics, I avoided eye contact with Abby by pretending to read my textbook. All the while, I was wondering when Andrew had decided that we weren't worth everything that he had been through. Even worse were the thoughts that I had fallen short of the woman that he had remembered. Unwilling to accept these possibilities and unable to block them from my mind, I became crazed in my own body. I left class using the bathroom as an excuse, seeking refuge.

Closing the stall behind me, the pain proved to be just as strong as the love I had for him.

After the bell, I walked back into the classroom which should have been empty but Abby was sitting at her desk, waiting for me to get my books.

Not having heard her call my name even in the silence of the room, she grabbed my elbow. Completely clueless but seeing my face from under the baseball cap, Abby's eyes widened in shock. "What's wrong?" she asked. "Beths, are you okay?" I shook my head unable to answer without my voice cracking. "What is it?" she asked panicked, sitting me down in a desk. Not knowing how to sum up the past forty-eight hours into words, I shook my head again. "Beths," Abigail said desperately, "What's wrong?" Did she not know that Andrew broke up with me? He must not have told her. Taking a deep breath, I composed myself as best I could for the mess I was.

"How are you feeling? Any morning sickness?" I tried diverting the attention. Abby wasn't showing yet but it was only a matter of time before she would have the baby bump her and Charles were happily anticipating.

"I'm fine," she said not fooled by my attempt. "What's wrong?"

"I, ah," I stuttered not wanting to say the truth aloud. My heavy eyelids closed as my shoulders fell. I grabbed onto the desk chair as though it was the only thing holding me to this world. My head was pounding, and I swallowed hard as I looked back up at Abby. "Abby, Andrew and I," I began and my eyes were whelming up again. Her eyes widened and she leaned back slowly.

"No," Abby said as denial replaced fear. "No, no," she repeated shaking her head. She had seen me like this before – once before – and her ability to recall it was not lessened by all those years in between. "He," Abby said touching her chest. I silently nodded, assuring her that it was true. "What? When!" she asked panicked. "How did this happen?"

"I don't know," I moaned unsure of how much time separated his feelings for me. Not wanting to talk about it I stood up and walked towards the door.

"Bethany…" Abby said but I couldn't have this conversation here. I turned and walked into the crowded hallway.

"Beths, Beths, wait up," I heard Jackson calling after me as I headed to my car after the final bell. "Hey," he said coming to a slow jog. I opened my car door and threw my books into the passenger seat; books that I had been carrying all morning, not once going back to my locker. "Bethany," Jackson said again, seeing that I was avoiding him.

"Hey Jackson, sorry I have to run I have… plans," I said sounding more like a question than a lie. I looked up when he put his hand on my door. With one look, Jackson nodded.

"You didn't break up with Wicks," he said sounding angry. I shook my head back and forth. "Are you alright?" he asked taking a half step closer to me dressed in his practice uniform. I shook my head again. "Is there anything I can do?" he offered sweetly.

"No," I swallowed and looked up at my friend.

"He told the guys that you broke up with him," Jackson said, repeating the locker room talk. I was more confused now than before.

"Why would he do that?"

"I don't know," Jackson shrugged. "I just wanted to make sure that you're okay."

"Thank you," I said and the tears took over. Liv had walked up to us and took my keys from my hand.

"I'll drive," she said and Jackson stepped away. Liv was skipping cheerleading practice, and knowing that I wasn't alone anymore, Jackson made his way towards the field.

Olivia didn't say a word; she just sat in my room doing her homework while I stared off into space, letting the relentless pain barrel through me. Into the night, Liv studied as I held onto the story of Drew and I that I so desperately wanted to live in again. As the hours passed there were minutes that felt like forever and then there were hours that felt like seconds. I became so sick of myself that I would have screamed, but I had neither the air nor the energy.

My best friend stayed the night without a word needing to be said. She was sleeping as I stubbornly refused to succumb to the agony that came when I closed my eyes. If the pain from the past wasn't bad enough, the realization that there was no future with him was worse. Not being able to see passed this was my weakness and it was gaining strength, overtaking me without a challenge.

As the light crept over the horizon, I sat up in bed. My swollen, overworked eyes felt heavy and the ache in my chest was tight with a delirious longing. I knew then that I was not the healing kind.

In the shower I closed my eyes as I rinsed my mint shampoo out of my hair. That's when a flash from an older time threw itself to the front of my mind.

I could hear the carriage wheels against the cobblestone. I could smell the fall morning breeze and felt the waking sun reaching through the trees. The leather straps snapped as the sound of the horses' hooves clattered rhythmically in the quietness of the early hour. I was sitting next to him with my head resting on his shoulder and a smile crossed my lips when he laced his fingers with mine.

"No," I groaned, forcing my face into the stream of water and put both my hands out, feeling for the sides of the shower walls. "No," I cried again as my tears mixed with the streaming water.

Charles was at my locker waiting for me when I walked through the front doors of Ellsworth High. "Bethany," he said motioning towards an empty classroom amidst the morning rush. Charles closed the door behind us and stepped toward me. I was certain that the slim chance that Abby hadn't told him about Drew and I by now, he would have heard the rumors going around the school. I met my old friend's intense look with emotionless eyes from under the cap. Even prepared, he was taken aback by my appearance. Wanting to know what had happened, he held out his hand requesting to see. I unhurriedly placed my hand in his.

The connection was made and with it, images along with their allotment of emotions was transferred. Charles saw everything, even the few times I had let my eyes close and what come with it. He too felt the tortured pain and devastation. The world hadn't ended but mine felt like it had.

Charles' hand twitched in mine as my heartache defined my days and nights. His hold on my hand got tighter so that the connection would not break. When the last few images crossed from me to him, he let go.

"Beths," Charles choked as soon as his eyes refocused. Grabbing my shoulders he attempted to make eye contact with me under the Lumberyard logo. He now knew how far I had fallen inside of myself. "It's going to be okay."

I looked back at him – a sign that I was buried somewhere inside the shell of a person I was becoming. "Drew has been coming home late from practices and I've been busy at the hospital. We had no idea that he..." Charles trailed off. His normally controlled composure was rattled. He looked down at me and I looked back at him. We both knew that if Andrew didn't want Charles or Abby to know about something, they wouldn't. Drew was not imprudent. I stared off as another wave of pain washed over me.

Charles took a step back, rubbing his hand over his mouth fervently, unable to grasp the current reality and also dealing with the remnants of distress from the exchange. He looked at me like he wanted to heal the invisible wounds but there was nothing he could do. The bell rang and Charles looked up at the clock and took my shoulders again. Calmly, collected and authoritatively he said, "It will be alright. I promise you."

After a blur of morning classes and a silent lunch across from Olivia who had skipped class, I found my way to biochemistry. As I walked through the classroom door I saw Drew already standing by his desk, smiling and surrounded by his fellow teammates and friends. Sliding into my seat and pulling my cap lower over my red eyes, I went unnoticed, invisible.

I sat a foot away from him for an hour and a half. Not once did he turn from Charles' lecture which ended with the bell ringing in its full glory. Andrew left the classroom with everyone else as I stayed in my seat. I only got up at the sound of the final bell a few seconds later. I hadn't realized I wasn't alone until I saw Charles sitting at the teacher's desk, watching me helplessly. I wiped a falling tear from my face and said nothing as I walked by.

Back in the hallway, I saw Andrew at his locker. I wondered how many times my heart could break before it shattered.

I had made it to the exit doors with my car in sight, when I heard a friend's voice call my name. As I turned, I saw Jackson jogging up behind me, unaccompanied.

"Bethany," Jackson started, "I, ah, do you want to go to the coffee shop without the studying part. Just to talk about... everything. If you want..." I bit down on my lip and looked back at him. Jackson was an angel without wings. Not wanting him to see me cry but knowing that I was falling apart, I hugged him and he pulled me into his chest.

"It's alright," he whispered as more tears fell down my cheeks. After a few moments, he asked, "Did you eat anything today?" I shook my head back and forth. "Yeah, that's what I thought," Jackson said more to himself than to me. "We'll split a donut... or a dozen," he tried to make me laugh.

Pulling away from him, I dried my eyes with my fingertips and looked at his shirt which now had tear stains on it. "Sorry about that," I apologized.

"Are you kidding?" he said glancing down and then up at me. I shrugged and looked down.

"I am really sorry Bethany," Jackson said sincerely. "I don't know what he's thinking. I don't know where it came from. I was under the impression that everything was great."

"So was I," my voice broke as I turned for the door which Jackson held for me. The two of us made our way across the parking lot towards Main Street.

I didn't cry while we were at the coffee shop and part of that had to do with the fact that we were in public. The other part had to do with Jackson distracting me from thinking about Andrew by talking about school and topics unrelated to my ex-boyfriend.

I made it into my grandparents' house and up to my room before I started sobbing uncontrollably again. While I was crying, I felt like I was waiting for one of two things – for something to make sense or to feel nothing at all.

Olivia came a little later on after she got off from work. We talked a little bit. I asked her how Bobby was, how her math test went… She asked me if I wanted to talk about Drew but I didn't have the energy. "Thank you," I said when we had laid down in my bed.

"Of course," my best friend said knowing that I appreciated her being around even if that meant it was in silence. I realized that the different relationships in my life, friendships, bonds between siblings, grandparents… were love stories too. Sometimes the best relationships and the best stories aren't just the romantic kind.

Liv had been studying and drifted off to sleep before her textbook slid onto the floor with a thud. Looking up at the ceiling, my mind was in a different place. I replayed the day in the middle of the night and the prayers I used to pray had become a tirade of frustration. I basked in anger, convincing myself that there was comfort in the pain. After all, it was half empty – the cup, the metaphor, and me. With another day gone, grief's shapeless form found a new home.

Where did the man I had known go? Should I have planned for this? But *he* took the step back. *He* walked away. Everything he said, everything he did, never gave any inclination that there was a doubt in his mind that we weren't meant for one another, or that it wouldn't work. With every question I posed, there was a reason to argue against it. I was conflicted. I was confused. I was lost.

Then the worst feelings came with thoughts I now dared to contemplate. What girl would benefit from the lessons of our past? This question wreaked havoc on me, tearing through my mind and into my heart. I felt like I was trying to stop myself from drowning but had nothing to hold on too. It was senseless to entertain the thought, but I did.

Getting up quietly from the bed, I walked down the stairs to the bathroom and closed the door before turning on the light. I heard a soft knock seconds later and opened it slowly. "Can't sleep?" my grandmother asked and I nodded. With her index finger she gestured for me to follow her.

We walked down the stairs to the first floor and into the kitchen. She turned on the light and put a pot of tea on the stove. Dressed in her nightgown and me in my pajamas, we sat at the kitchen table. It was two in the morning.

"Olivia told me, dear," she said breaking the ice.

"You don't have to stay up with me, Grams," I offered.

"Hush now, that's my job," she lovingly grinned from across the table and patted my hand.

—

"Bethany Taylor, Coach's office," the PA system sounded halfway through biochemistry. Closing my textbook, I accidently dropped my notebook on the floor in the space between my seat and Andrew's. It was Jackson, however, who picked it up and handed it to me.

'Thanks,' I mouthed as he adjusted in his desk eyeing the stone-cold quarterback.

"Come in," I heard my grandfather's voice say from the other side of the door. Turning the knob, I stepped into his office and took what had become my designated seat across from him.

"Hello," he said watching me carefully. My grandfather had his hands clasped in front of him so that his elbows rested on either side of his chair.

"Hi Gramps," I breathed and stared into my lap, avoiding his paternal eyes.

"Bethany," he said calling for my attention. I looked up at him only to find in his expression that he knew about my breakup. He looked apologetic and worried, leaving me at a loss for words. "You're safe here, Beths. Let it out," my grandfather said. The warmth in his words reached me. I did let it out until there was nothing left.

—

I was at my locker putting my books away when I turned and saw Drew walking down the hallway next to Jackson. Both dressed in game day attire, they were headed towards the locker room. Drew did not stop smiling or laughing next to his friend. When he was only a few feet away, he suddenly slowed in passing and turned towards me. I looked up from under my baseball cap and my heart caught in my throat at the unexpected moment. For a second the thought crossed my mind that maybe, just maybe, this had all just been a nightmare. "I'll need my letterman back," Andrew said as cruel and damaging as his initial goodbye. Walking alongside him, Jackson looked at me over his shoulder and then at Andrew in shock at how icy, rude and heartless Andrew had acted. It was not something that Jackson or I thought Drew was capable of. As Andrew's words echoed in my mind, I looked away as the two of them went through the next set of double doors.

I was back at the top of the attic stairs again, not remembering having climbed them. Drew's letterman jacket was on the back of my desk chair where I had put it before everything had fallen apart. It had stayed untouched but it no longer belonged to me. I gently grazed my fingertips over it and picked it up from its temporary home. My head found my pillow and I put the jacket over me and closed my eyes. His lingering scent fueled the rush of anguish but I shut my eyes tighter. I welcomed the suffering because it was proof of a 'Once upon a time'.

—

Liv came over not too long after the game had ended still dressed in her cheerleading uniform. Even though the playoff game was a big deal, Olivia was back at my side as soon as she could. She was like my shadow, watching me every second she was given and at times, powerfully silent. Tonight though, she looked afraid. I rolled over as she got into bed on the other side. "Beths," she said finally.

"Yeah Liv," I mumbled back.

"It's going to be okay," she whispered as she pushed a piece of hair out of my face.

"Yeah," I breathed as another piece of my heart broke; the part that still hoped.

It had been a while since Liv had turned off the light. I stared blankly into the darkness and knew I shouldn't let myself relive the memories that my mind was pulsing through me. But, they kept me company. They had the makings of a brilliant story but I knew that the ending had been ripped out.

Drew was fine from what I could tell. He was laughing in school, focused on football, and I was certain he was busy with work for the hospital. Maybe if I knew why he broke things off I could try and accept it... Maybe then, I could begin to pick up the pieces.

—

According to the newspaper on the table in the living room it was Saturday and the Ellsworth Sparrows had won the division playoff game. They would play Friday for the state championship.

I was surprised when I saw Charles on the front porch with my grandfather who had taken the liberty of arranging for me to have an unscheduled heart scan. It was something that Charles gladly agreed too. Charles would miss the mandatory football meeting this afternoon where my grandfather and the team would review their performance from last night's game. They would also discuss strategy for Friday's opponent who stood in between them and the championship title.

The scan showed no marginal changes and Charles seemed more relieved than usual. As we got back in his car, he asked if I would come over to the Estate – Andrew would be at practice; it would just be me, Abigail, and him. I agreed but asked that I pick something up at my grandparents' first and follow behind him in my own car.

When we pulled into my grandparents' driveway I went inside, got Andrew's letterman jacket, and told my grandmother that I would be back in a little while. She nodded and watched as I got in my Corvette and followed behind Charles' Bentley.

At the stoplight, I looked over at Drew's jacket on the passenger seat. Remembering when he gave it to me, I wiped the tears from my face before gripping the steering wheel tighter. The thought of having to hand the jacket back to him was gut wrenching. I would leave it at the Estate instead.

It was more difficult than I thought walking up the Estate steps. It was even harder to be in its rooms. The Estate was haunting. It was a physical reminder of everything I had once had, and moreover, everything there would never be. It was as though its purpose was a testament that happy endings are moments and not lasting, that people die, and that second chances don't guarantee a different outcome.

"BETHANY'S HERE!" Gracie yelled when she saw me from the kitchen. Abigail and Cole peaked from behind her as the little girl rushed in my direction and I bent down to give her a hug. She clung so tightly around my neck, giving love so freely. It should have made me smile but it made me hurt just a little bit more.

"Cole, Gracie, why don't you go play outside while we talk with Bethany?" Abby asked as she joined us in the entranceway.

"Yeah sure," Cole said taking Gracie's hand as the two skipped down the ballroom staircase towards the doors.

"Not beyond the trees," Abby yelled reflectively in her motherly voice.

"Okay!" Cole yelled back as he closed the doors to the veranda with a bang. Without a word Charles stepped to the side and gestured to my father's office. I clenched my hands around the letterman jacket. Like those months ago, I felt like a stranger in this house.

"Please, sit Bethany," Charles said as I looked around the office and then sat on the very edge of one of the sofas by the fireplace. This had been the room where I had first laid eyes on Andrew. It looked so different in the sunlight. With two sets of eyes glued on me, I glared back at them.

"I wanted to leave this," I creaked, looking down at the jacket in my hands. "I shouldn't even be here. If he comes home early…" I said as my eyes jumped from inanimate object to inanimate object.

"Here," Charles said, taking the jacket from me and threw it over the back of the other sofa.

"We're glad you're here," Abby spoke on behalf of both of them. I nodded shyly, trying to breathe steady breaths. "Beths, you have to understand that we did not know. We would have…" Abby began but stopped.

"Bethany," Charles said, sitting on the coffee table in front of me.

"Charles," I smiled through the welling tears. My old friend placed his hands over mine.

Emotions from better times flooded. Charles was comforting me and reminding me that not everything from the past was tainted.

"I don't want to feel anymore!" I said pulling my hands away. I heard Abby begin to cry as I covered my face, exhausted.

"Look at me," Charles said and I shook my head as the tears poured silently down my face.

"Beths," Charles pleaded and I unwillingly looked up at him. It was clear that I wasn't the only one that the breakup was taking a toll on. Charles looked worn but still very much in control.

At the end of my rope and completely drained, I spoke before he could, "Maybe it was suppose to end this way. Maybe it should have ended this way last time. Maybe…"

"This is not what was supposed to happen!" Abby interrupted passionately, looking for support from her husband but none came. Charles, rubbing his hands together, was staring down at the floor. "Charles?" Abby questioned.

"He's a grown man, Abigail," Charles said calmly over his shoulder. "He is fully aware that his actions have consequences."

"Like hell he does!" Abby said outraged. She now directed her aggravation at me. "You're giving up?"

Was she truly accusing me? "I'm not the one that let go, Abby," I said hurt by her claim.

"Abigail…" Charles started.

"Do you want me to believe that because there was a goodbye this time that it was supposed to happen this way? That's absurd!" she said stepping closer to where I sat. Charles stood watching Abby as she continued at me, "This time you get to live? Is that the difference? *You* are letting this happen. You are letting him walk away," she snapped. My hand had been fiercely tracing my collarbone as she spoke those last words. I don't know if it was my lack of sleep or sheer emotional collapse, but I had enough.

"I'm giving up?" I asked standing. "I'm giving up? You don't know what you are talking about," I finished severely.

"I know exactly what I am talking about. In case you've forgotten, I've watched this play out for the last century," she sneered.

"I'm guessing that's my fault too," I shot back.

"Ladies," Charles tried, looking between the two of us.

Disregarding her husband's attempt to diffuse the situation, Abby turned slightly so she could look out onto the grounds where Cole and Gracie were playing. The children's laughter brought with it a peace that put things back into perspective.

"Abigail," I said with a completely different tone, a calm, soft voice. "Your brother... Andrew and I..." My breathing was uneven as I tried to make her understand. "I very much feel like he did when I passed. He's just *gone*," I blinked, looking down at the decorative rug underneath my feet. "I'm confused," I shook my head. "I'm hurt. I'm tired. I'm scared."

When I looked back up, she had turned with tears in her eyes. "The last thing I need is for *you* to say that *this* is my fault. If I had my way..." I began to sob. Abby had covered her mouth and she nodded before stepping closer to me, embracing me in an all encompassing hug.

"I'm sorry for what I've said. I know what your feelings are for him," she swallowed as she leaned back and looked into my eyes. Charles stepped next to her, kissed the side of her head, trying to calm Abigail. He didn't want his pregnant wife to experience the stress she was under and I understood that. Without another word, Charles led her out of the room and came back a moment later.

"I'm sorry, Bethany… truly, I am," he said apologetically. The sun shone through the windows next to us and he gestured for us to sit on the sofas again. Sitting across from me, Charles' warm brown eyes stared back into mine, contemplating. "I know Andrew exceptionally well. I know that he has motives for everything he does. He's calculated and deliberate. He wouldn't end things if he didn't think it was for the best."

"Best for whom?" I challenged, pushing my tongue against the teeth on the left side of my mouth as the sobs settled into my chest.

"That memory you have from when the two of you were dancing at your brother's wedding reception – the glimpse you stole in the hand exchange where Andrew was sitting in the pew and I was sitting next to him," Charles led. The memory was clear in my mind. Charles had pleaded, '*Please Drew. Think about this. Please, I beg of you.*' I could still hear the desperation in Charles' voice and feel the anguished emotions that had resonated in Drew.

"Yes," I said revisiting the oddity, now giving it more attention than I had. Charles averted eye contact, something he never did. "You knew he was going to break up with me?" I asked wounded to which Charles nodded, sorrowfully. "What?" I asked standing up.

"Beths, I didn't know 'if' or 'when', just that it was a thought," Charles defended as he also stood and reached for me.

"No," I said putting my hands up. I took two breaths before my eyes found his. I felt betrayed and I was sure my expression showed it. "But..." I said shaking my head, recalling the conversation Charles and I had in the empty classroom where he promised me that everything was going to be okay.

"You have to trust me," Charles said rushing his words.

"What?" I asked with a growing anger. "YOU KNEW," I said flatly. When he had nothing to say, I turned and headed for the door.

"Beths!" Charles called after me. With a fleeting look back over my shoulder, I left the room, walked down the hall into the entranceway and slammed the front door behind me.

It was with angry tears and white knuckles that I steered the roaring Corvette down the cobblestone path.

When I got back to my grandparents' house I threw open the screen door, slammed the front door shut and slid down it onto the ground. My keys hit the hardwood floor as I tucked my knees to my chest and buried my face into my elbow. I felt someone's hand on mine.

From underneath my Lumberyard hat, I slowly looked up. "Hey," Gregg said sweetly pushing some of my hair over my shoulder. Sniffling, I wiped my eyes with my sleeves and nodded to him. I felt angry, betrayed, but mostly exhausted. Instead of helping me up, Gregg turned, leaned against the door and sat too. I tilted my head back, closed my eyes, and I took a long slow draw of air.

"You'll be alright, Bethany," Gregg said looking sideways at me.

I shook my head and looked down into my lap as more tears emptied out. Everything seemed to be unraveling. "I cry… all the time," I confessed.

"That means it meant something," Gregg advised.

"When will it stop?" I asked desperately.

"In time," he swallowed.

He stayed with me.

I heard a car pull up out front; the engine was unmistakable – it was 'the tank'. Knowing that Ryan wasn't due back from his honeymoon until tomorrow, it had to be Chris. I stood up, as did Gregg, and walked over to the center table, putting my keys in the bowl. After hanging up my sweater on the banister, I went into the kitchen to get a glass of water. When I came back through the kitchen door, both Gregg and Chris were sitting on the couch and turned. "Want to watch the game with us, Beths?" Chris invited, looking nervously at me. I knew that they had heard about the breakup and judging by the timing, I was sure that either my grandmother, who had a Ladies Guild meeting, or my grandfather, who had a football practice, had arranged that I would not be home alone. Gregg smirked and nodded towards the spot in between the two of them and I plopped down. Even though I was numb to the world, it was not numb to me.

—

I knew Sunday had come because it was time for Church. I had so much anger in me that it wouldn't have surprised me if the Holy Water burnt my skin when I dipped my finger into the fount.

Charles… Charles had known something was up. 'Ouch' doesn't even begin to cover it. Abby, although she apologized, had said things that still stung. Then there was Andrew who had left me with the memory of him walking away.

I prayed, if you could call it that. I yelled and I wasn't nice. I yelled in my mind as the preacher spoke to the congregation. 'I'm broken. Are you happy?' I looked ahead at the wooden pew in front of me. 'I can't do this.' My eyes fell. 'Why is this happening?' I begged for an answer with an exterior that would not let on to the chaos inside of me. I was shaken… that was certain. The pain continued to withdraw me, pulling me further and further into myself.

After Mass I laid on the couch, dress clothes and all. Physically unable to keep my eyes open any longer, I dosed off with my rage matched only by that of the ache. When I stirred a few hours later I could hear familiar voices in the kitchen even over the broadcaster on the television. I heard Ryan; he was home. Putting one foot on the floor, I paused overhearing the conversation in the next room.

"Ryan, I am telling you," my grandmother's voice said with great concern from the kitchen. I swallowed hard.

"Grams, she can't be that bad," Ryan said unaware of the extent of the state I was in.

"Ryan, she hasn't eaten a real meal in over a week," she continued and then I heard another voice.

"She's a mess, man. He did a number on her heart," Gregg added.

"Seriously, dude, she didn't say a word. She's half-zombie or something," Chris said.

Grams continued pleading, "Ryan, she's breaking down more and more every day." I placed my foot back under the blanket and continued to eavesdrop.

That's when I heard my grandfather's voice, "Olivia spends as much time with her as she can. She's stayed over almost every night. She doesn't know what to do for her. She's worried and, frankly, I am too." There was a pause before he continued, "Ryan, Bethany's very fragile right now."

"Guys," Ryan said trying to calm them down.

"I'm afraid," Grams cut in with a serious tone. There was silence in the kitchen. I rolled over on the couch, hiding my face in shame. I had been so consumed in my self-pity that I hadn't realized the affect it was taking on the people who loved me.

I heard the swinging door open and I pretended to still be sleeping. I heard *SportsCenter* click off but I continued to lay motionless.

A few seconds later I felt Ryan poke at my legs. "Hey Beths," he said trying to sound like he hadn't been warned that I wasn't doing well. "Beths," he said again moving my leg. Slowly turning my head, I acted like he woke me up. "What's up, kid?" he asked with his boyish grin.

"Hey, how was the honeymoon?" I asked, pushing myself up and looking at him. Ignoring my question, Ryan took in mine face and he stood alarmed.

"You look like hell, Bethany," he said grabbing my hands and pulling me off the couch, examining my puffy, swollen eyes and frail stance. I consciously looked away from him knowing that my eyes were purple, their newest color. I sat down and focused on the floor. "Stop that," Ryan said knocking my hand away from my collarbone; there was a bruised path from where I had traced many times over the past week. "What happened?" Ryan asked outraged.

"Ryan," I began defeated, my shoulders hunched.

"What did he do? Did he hurt you?" Ryan asked kneeling down in front of me.

"No. He," I said before looking back at him. "He did nothing," I finished choked. "Please," I begged my brother not to push any further as I put my tired head on his shoulder. Ryan hugged me and took me into his arms as I collapsed against him, crying. Scooping me up in his arms, my weak arms found his neck and held on to it. Ryan carried me to the stairs, headed for the attic but stopped at the first step. Grams was standing by the kitchen door with the dishtowel over her shoulder. Chris, Gregg and Gramps were in the doorway also having witnessed the pathetic scene as it unfolded but said nothing as Ryan continued up the stairs.

Chapter Eight
Waking Up

I was coherent enough today to look at a clock. As I placed my cell phone back on my nightstand, I laid awake trying to recall what it felt like to wake up and not feel this way. With my feet finding the cold, attic floor, I closed my eyes one last time, focusing on a picture perfect memory before pushing myself out of bed. "You alright?" I heard Ryan ask and I jumped seeing him sitting at the far end of the attic, watching me carefully. I nodded before making my way down the steps to the bathroom to get ready for school.

Ryan was waiting for me in the driveway in 'the tank' when I came out the front door. He didn't live with my grandparents anymore, having moved out right before the wedding to the house that I had designed and he had built for him and Kate. I didn't know if he had spent the night in the attic while I slept, or if he just had come to see how I was. Sadly, it did not bother me enough to ask.

As I walked towards his truck, I knew that it was not worth fighting with him about driving myself to school. So, I opened the passenger door and got in without a word. I should have asked him about his honeymoon, the house, the Lumberyard, anything, but instead, I just watched out the window as he drove down Main Street.

The weather was getting colder and the trees looked bare, as the leaves swirled along the curb with the passing breeze. The bright blue skies could have been thunderous storm clouds for all I cared.

"Did you eat breakfast?" Ryan asked over the ruckus 'the tank' made, breaking the verbal silence between us. Not remembering at first, I shook my head back and forth. "Have you eaten anything lately?" he questioned and I shrugged not able to recall. Hitting the breaks abruptly, my seatbelt did its job retracting tightly as my brother pulled over to the side of the road. Having seen enough for himself, Ryan could not take it anymore. I didn't know what to say to him, or to anyone for that matter. Ryan looked over at me and said, "Beths, it's going to be okay."

Unwilling to hear these words, I snapped out of my coma and yelled at him, "NO, IT'S NOT! IT"S NOT GOING TO BE OKAY, RYAN! HE JUST WALKED AWAY. THERE WERE NO SIGNS. HE JUST, HE JUST..." I buried my head in my shaking hands. My brother sat in the driver's seat, letting me scream, waiting to see if I would continue, but it was just tears.

"Come here," he said pulling me into his chest. He rubbed my back as I sobbed into his perfectly good shirt.

"Why did he do this? Why can't I see passed this?" I asked the questions aloud.

"I don't know. He's an idiot." Ryan said coldly.

"I don't know what to do," I croaked in between hysterics, desperate now.

Holding me tighter, Ryan looked out the windshield and said, "You get up every morning, you breathe and you get through the day. And after a while, the world starts to spin again."

"Ryan, what are you doing here?" Gramps asked as he opened the office door.

"Special delivery," Ryan announced, nodding back in my direction.

"Bethany," my grandfather said surprised that I looked responsive today. I tried to smile but I hadn't come that far yet.

"Well, some of us have to work, so..." Ryan grinned and jabbed my side. Leaning closer to me, he whispered, "If you feel like you're about to cry, you call me and I'll be here before the tear hits the ground. Got it?" he asked and waited for me to acknowledge that I had heard him. When I nodded, he added, "See ya later, kid," and kissed the top of my head. He playfully pushed me farther into our grandfather's office and closed the door behind him.

"Have a seat, Beths," Gramps said pointing towards the chair across from his desk.

My grandfather dropped the morning paper in front of me. On the front page was a picture of me from when I lived in New York and the headline read, 'Supermodel Supports Super Cause'. I recognized the majority of the article because it was the press release Abby had prepared and given to me, what felt like an eternity ago.

"Front page?" I asked as I looked up at Gramps.

"It's one of the beauties of living in a small town," he smiled, "Not to mention, you are, how do they say it? 'Kind of a big deal'," Gramps said; air quotations included.

"Where did you learn that phrase?" I questioned with what sounded like a laugh and felt like a smile.

"Chris," Gramps smirked as he leaned back in his chair, happy to see that I wasn't crying for once. "How are you feeling?"

"Okay," I shrugged knowing that I was not much farther than where I had been, even with the progress of this morning.

"Good," he said as the wind picked up outside the window. "So are you ready for the Gala on Friday?" I hadn't given any thought to the Gala so I shook my head. "Decided on a dress yet?" he asked. I hadn't, so I shook my head again. "Well, I am sure whatever you decide on will look beautiful," my grandfather complimented. "As for the time between now and then, I was thinking that maybe you should focus on something… productive, for the cause, of course."

"Yeah, I think I will," I nodded liking the idea of distracting myself. I knew it wouldn't be easy but it was worth a shot. My Bethany Reid 'training' would come in handy – all that smiling and pretending would *finally* be put to good use.

Like Ryan said, the world would start to spin again. I didn't know when that would happen but until it did, I had work to do, people to be thankful for and a life with chapters still left to be written.

I missed most of my classes, spending the majority of the school day in my grandfather's office studying up on the team that stood between the Sparrows and another state championship. They were good but Gramps knew what he was doing. I smiled at his comments and laughed at his sarcastic humor. I felt a little more like myself and I could tell my grandfather liked seeing me that way.

After the final bell, I walked to the parking lot, forgetting that I didn't drive my car to school. When I turned around to go back inside, I saw Charles walking Abby to their car before he headed to football practice. They saw me looking at them. It was an awkward moment, one that I did not want to be a part of.

Ryan pulled up in his truck, in between me and them, breaking the line of sight. My brother leaned over and opened the passenger door. "How was school?" he asked with a smile on his face, not aware that he had just saved me in more ways than one.

"Spent it with Gramps," I smirked and jumped into 'the tank'. I watched in the side mirror as Charles helped his wife into their car and closed her door, but stared after my brother's truck as we pulled out onto the street.

Olivia came over after her practice and, instead of finding me curled up in the corner, I was sitting on my bed with my cell phone in one hand and a pen in the other, writing a list of names on a piece of paper. Liv flopped herself happily on my bed, glanced at the upside down page and asked, "What's up?"

Scribbling down the last name, I spun the paper around and handed her the pen. "Here," I said as I scrolled through my phone. She looked over the list and her eyes widened at some of the famous names, causing her to look up at me, searching for an answer.

"This is an attempt to distract myself. Kind of like a constructive pastime," I tried, knowing how pathetic I sounded.

"Good," my best friend said, willing to do whatever it took to help me. "What do I do?" she questioned, fiddling with the pen.

"You just sit there and look pretty," I laughed as I made the first call.

"All these people…" she began.

"Are friends from New York," I explained. "And Liv," I said and she looked up. "You don't know how much it means to me that you are here… that you have been here for me. Thank you." She smiled but before I could say anything else I heard a voice on the other end of the phone.

"Well if it isn't Bethany Reid," the New York accent greeted me.

As I hung up my phone for what felt like the millionth time, Liv, who had moved to my makeshift desk asked, "How much?"

"Twenty."

"Do you realize that in the past three hours you've raised," she paused, adding up the numbers on the list in her head. Her jaw opened at the summation.

"Disgusting right?" I agreed as I plugged my phone into the charger as another battery line flickered out.

"Ridiculous is all," she said putting the pen down. "Aren't you supposed to just be a PR boost for the Gala?"

"Yes, but even though they tell me I'm helping it doesn't feel like I am. All I'll do is stand around, smile…"

"AND hand them a huge check," Liv added with a grin.

"Hopefully for a prenatal unit," I daydreamed momentarily of Charles and Abby holding their newborn baby. I could be upset with them but I knew their story; I knew that this baby was their miracle. Nevertheless, the thought quickly derailed me as Andrew crept back into my mind, igniting the heartache. Needing another distraction, I picked up my phone and scrolled through my contacts for a name I had skipped over. I looked up at Liv and as I put the phone to my ear, I asked, "You liked that gown I wore on the cover of the last magazine, right?"

"Yeah…" she said suspiciously. A grin washed over my face giving me away. Liv's smile grew too, and she clapped her hands in excitement at my fairy godmother-like connections.

"Well, well, well. Where the hell have you been?" I heard the voice on the other end say.

"Hi Michael," I smiled at the sound of his voice.

"What can I do for you, honey?" he said cutting to the chase like he always did.

"I need a favor."

"Uh huh," he said listening.

"The Hannah Nelson gown…" I started.

"The navy blue one," he knew immediately.

"Yes! Can you send it to me? And the ivory one we were working on with Natalie?"

"Yes… I thought you'd never ask," Michael said and I could picture the sly grin on his face. The level of noise in the background told me that he was busy.

"Thanks, you're the best. I'll send you the address in a few."

"You got it. Oh, and Bethany, if you decide to grace New York with your presence, I better be the first stop."

"Without a doubt," I grinned and hung up the phone, scrolling through my contacts again.

"Who are you calling now?" Liv asked, sitting next to me crossed-legged.

"You're going to need shoes too, right?" I smiled at her. She giggled as I continued my phone marathon.

"So, he knew," Liv repeated surprised when I updated her about Charles.

"Yeah," I moaned as our spoons crossed paths in the carton of ice cream we were sharing.

"Wow."

"I saw him today when I was leaving school. I know he's going to want to talk the next time he can get me alone."

"What are you going to say?"

"I'm going to let him talk."

"Good idea," Olivia said as she selectively scooped her next bite, maximizing her chocolate consumption.

"How did everything get so bad so fast?" I blinked at the thought of the whirlwind that had become my life.

"Honest opinion?" Liv said readjusting on the bed so we were eye-to-eye. She was the only one who knew the truth about Andrew, the Landon's and me, and had a third party perspective. Not to mention, as my best friend, she had my best interest in mind. I waited as she took a deep breath and spoke with honesty. "Mrs. Landon doesn't know who to be angry at. All she wants is for everything to be fixed. You can't blame her for that. Dr. Landon, poor guy, is trying to keep his loyalty to his brother-in-law AND to you. He's stuck between a rock and a hard place." Liv dropped her spoon into the carton and put both her hands up, exaggerating her next point, "As for Andrew... I don't get it." I nodded in agreement as she continued, "But, what I DO know is that he's not the only one that gets to move on," she said glaring back at me with one of those best friend looks. She was right. "Beths," Liv said, reaching over and touching my knee, "Stop rewinding and hit 'Play'."

"Yeah," I exhaled at her perfect advice.

—

Liv fell asleep shortly after midnight. Even with the baby steps that I had taken today, when the stillness of the night came, the pain felt like it grew stronger, but it hadn't. It was just that I was tired and my walls were down, leaving me susceptible to my insecurities and over thinking.

Wanting sleep, I closed my eyes knowing that there was a pretty good chance that I would be met with images of Drew. Sure enough they did, but for the first time since 'goodbye', I welcomed the memory of our last conversation.

He was standing in front of me, telling me that he couldn't do this anymore. That he thought he'd given us a fair try but that he couldn't pretend any longer. It was over.

I rolled over in bed and wiped away the tears. The clock read, '3:00 AM'. I would close my eyes again and again until his memory left me alone or until I fell asleep.

My eyelashes met several times and he was always with me. The pain did not diminish nor was I building a tolerance or becoming immune to it. As I let the memories unfold, I was left to think of what I would say to him. It was ironic to me that they were words that would burn a bridge that I so desperately wanted to cross.

Letting go of the anger that tempted me into a false comfort, I started to pray. I needed strength to 'climb this hill'. I needed the grace to overcome the weakness. In a small way, my prayers were answered as I slipped into a deep, long awaited, forgiving sleep.

When I woke a few hours later, I wasn't afraid. I wasn't angry. I was calm. I had clarity of mind as the ticking of the clock aligned with my heart. 'My heart,' I thought and sat straight up in bed.

Opening my nightstand drawer, I pulled out the prescription bottle which contained medicine that I hadn't taken for more than a week. Running had also fallen to the wayside when everything… changed.

Chapter Nine
Evermore

"I haven't been taking these," I said, handing the bottle to Charles after making sure he was alone in the teacher's lounge before homeroom. He stood up and the look of surprise on his face that I was in the teacher's lounge was matched by the surprise that I was not angry with him. In more ways than one, our heated argument was a thing of the past. "And I haven't been running either," I admitted. He took the medication and looked down at it. "Charles," I said waiting for a response.

"How long?" Charles asked with fear in his eyes.

"Since Andrew and I…" I began. The bell rang out in the hallway and he handed the prescription bottle back to me.

"We did do a heart scan on Saturday and there was no change," he said in doctor mode. "Meet me at the hospital after school and we'll do another and move forward from there."

"Okay," I said sliding the canister back into my bag. Charles looked especially reminiscent today of the years in which I met him. He wore a white shirt and brown suspenders underneath his knit cardigan with beige slacks and leather shoes, and his hair was brushed to the side. Charles saw the grin on my face from the echo of time I saw in him.

"What?" he smiled back at me.

"Nothing," I shrugged as we both turned for the door.

"Beths, I want to apologize to you… for knowing Drew's intentions and not telling you of them. I was put in an unforgiving situation and I need you to know that by not telling you, I was not taking his side."

"Charles," I said short of the door. "You and Drew were best friends when I first met you and the bond you share is like brothers. I've always understood that," I said respectfully.

"I appreciate that, Beths. But it doesn't make me feel any better," he sighed. Almost unloading, my old friend continued, "I didn't know that he would act so soon. I thought he'd..." Charles stopped himself, abandoning his sentence and stream of consciousness, jumped to another. "I've been preoccupied with the hospital, school, the team, the kids, Abby and the baby... Drew knew that and took advantage." Another teacher walked into the lounge. Charles and I could no longer talk as friends; I resumed my role as a student and he, as a teacher. We walked out into the crowded hallway together.

I saw Drew at his locker as Charles and I parted ways. I took a double take thinking that he might have been looking at me, that I wasn't invisible for once. I saw his head turn back to the locker, his jaw tight, clenched, but it quickly loosened when a letterman jacket wearing teammate punched his shoulder as he passed. Andrew turned at the gesture and smiled at Zach and Tyler who were on their way to homeroom. I shook my head, catching my reflection in some girl's locker mirror. My Bethany Reid facade was fully intact. I had done my hair and makeup, was wearing a cute dress and wore no mark of the breakup on the outside. I had retired the Lumberyard hat and sweatshirts that I had worn all of last week. In my peripheral vision I saw that Drew was still talking to his buddies. In order for me to get to my homeroom, I had to walk passed him. I took a deep breath and remembered who I was. I walked close enough that he'd smell my perfume and didn't dare to make eye contact. Walking by, I screamed internally, 'YOU MIGHT HAVE CHANGED YOUR MIND BUT I DIDN'T CHANGE MINE.'

A few feet away from him, I heard, "Beths," and I looked over my shoulder to see Jackson trying to catch up to me. I also noticed that Drew had looked over when he heard my name.

"Hey," I grinned as Jackson joined me, and tried not to overact to Andrew's behavior.

"You," my friend tilted his head. "You look great!"

"Thanks," I nodded knowing what he meant. "Baby steps…"

"Hey, I'm just glad you're walking," Jackson grinned and held the door for me.

I had made it to physics before I had my next lapse. Midway through the class, I couldn't stand the fact that Drew and I were sitting only a feet away from one another. I excused myself to the ladies' room and closed the stall door. The seven stages of grief were all mishmash into one giant wrecking ball that was hitting me over and over. I held my hand out, touching the opposite wall for support, and let out the angry tears which trekked down my face.

They weren't a sign of weakness. I had to break to stand a chance of being healed.

After class, Abby and I stayed behind. Alone in the classroom, we spoke at the same time. Half-smiling I yielded so she could speak first. "Charles and Andrew can be… difficult at times. They are both highly intelligent men who have a tendency to over think matters. Usually one of the two will balance out the other depending on the subject," she paused. "But in this case… with Andrew… I'm sorry, Beths. I'm sorry as a friend. I'm sorry as Andrew's sister. And I'm sorry as a bystander."

"You know what, Abby," I said sliding my books off my desk. "He's *not* the only love story in my life. You, my father, my brother, my grandparents, Charles, Olivia, Jackson… they are love stories and those relationships are the things that are saving me right now." A grin grew on Abigail's lips at my words.

"I've never thought of it that way."

"You tell Andrew that somehow. Slip it in to a conversation," I grinned at her. She understood what I was asking her to do – to make sure he knew that I would be okay. I wanted Drew to know that, partly vindictive but mostly for my own closure.

"I admire how strong you are," she said and then looked away as she continued, "I've tried to put myself in your shoes… with us swooping into your life and then him just ending things – *again*." I felt a twinge of pain and was glad she kept talking. "If you need anything..." she said placing her hand over mine. No memory was exchanged but I still expected one too.

"Thanks. Same with you and that baby," I smiled at her stomach before walking towards the door. "See you later, Abby," I swallowed as I headed to the parking lot.

Click. 'Pain is physical.' *Click.* 'Love is emotional.' *Click.* 'Faith is spiritual.' *Click. Click. Click.* I thought as the machine worked around me. These three things 'caused and affected' every aspect of my life. As much as I would like to separate them, deal with them individually, they were very much entwined.

As I put my jewelry back on, I watched as Charles selected and zoomed in on the new scan. "No change," he said relieved that I hadn't unintentionally caused any damage by my week hiatus from not taking the medicine or sticking to the cardio regimen. "Please, I beg of you, take these," he said handing me a new prescription bottle with a slightly higher dose.

"I will," I answered. He looked at me tensely. "I promise," I assured him.

"So are you ready for the Gala?" Charles asked as we walked towards the elevators. "Remember, the photo shoot is tomorrow at four in the lobby," he said as he pushed the elevator call button. I was glad he reminded me because I had completely forgotten.

"Okay," I said making the mental note.

"Beths," he said looking down at me.

"Yes Charles," I said knowing that what he was about to say would have nothing to do with the Gala or my heart condition.

"Perhaps I am crossing the line, if there is a line," he muttered.

"What is it, Charles?" I grinned at my old friend.

"It's in regards to Andrew," he warned and his shoulders turned inward when his hands found his pockets; his frame, still bigger than mine.

"Alright," I nodded and braced myself.

"He… Has he spoken to you since he ended things?"

"No," I shook my head. "Haven't you talked to him?" I asked assuming that over the past week the details would have been shared between the two of them.

"No," Charles replied with concern in his wise eyes. I was shocked by this revelation. The elevator doors opened and closed without me. "Bethany, don't be bothered by this."

"I am bothered by it," I half-laughed. "You two tell each other everything!"

"Not *everything*. Most things, yes," Charles smirked.

"Charles," I continued apprehensively.

"Don't worry," he said pushing the button again and changed the subject, "Take that medicine, do the cardio and please, try and get some rest."

"Me? Get rest?" I said touching my chest, then gestured to him, inferring that he was the one that looked tired.

"I'll tell you what," Charles replied as the doors opened. "If you get some rest, then so shall I," he smiled. When I stepped into the elevator he added, "You would worry about me and not yourself."

"Of course," I said matter-of-factly. "You sort of have a special place in my heart."

Charles smiled. "My affections for you are quite similar. I will see you tomorrow, Beths," he nodded amused. I stopped the door from closing, giving him an unexpected hug before I stepped back into the elevator.

"See you tomorrow Charles," I said. Acknowledging our own personal demons, Charles and I exchanged a caring gaze. As the doors closed and started down to the lobby, leaving me alone in the elevator and him on the floors above.

Kate called my name out as I walked through the lobby. "Hey," she said coming up alongside me, glad to see me.

"Hi," I said to my sister-in-law. It was the first time I had seen her since she had gotten back from the honeymoon.

"Do you mind running some errands with me? I get off in a few minutes."

"Um, sure," I shrugged.

"Great," her smile widened.

It didn't occur to me until I was sitting in my car waiting for Kate as to why she had spontaneously asked to hang out together. Normally, she would have included Olivia in the girl adventure. This invitation was in response to hearing about my breakup from Ryan and Liv, and I was grateful for Kate and the distraction.

She and I ran errands around town and talked about everything but Andrew. It was nice to escape even if it was only for a little while.

I was home for dinner and had some of my appetite back. There was a knock on the screen door shortly after my last bite. "Turner," my grandfather said stepping aside and welcoming him in. "Oh, I forgot," Gramps said turning to me at the table. "Jackson mentioned at practice that you two had homework to do. I forgot to relay the message that he was coming over," he said pointing for Jackson to have a seat at the dining room table.

"Hi Jackson," I said standing up with my empty plate. It was good that he wanted to get together. We had talked about possibly meeting tonight or tomorrow before school to go over the loads of homework.

Coming out of the kitchen I said, "Let me just get my books," as I headed up the stairs.

When I came back down, Grams had set out cookies and milk. "Thank you, Mrs. Taylor," Jackson said with his textbooks piled in front of him. "Ready?" he asked as I sat down next to him.

"Yes sir," I said opening up the laundry list of assignments.

—

A few hours later, I walked Jackson out to his car which was parked on the street. "Thanks for coming over, Jackson. I really needed to catch up."

"Same here," he yawned. Between practices and school, Jackson was burning the candle at both ends. "After Friday, I'll be human again," he laughed.

"Yeah, yeah," I said as he put his books through the opened passenger window and onto the seat.

"How are you doing?" he asked tilting his head. The porch light was too far behind me to give him a clear view of my diverting eyes.

I shrugged as I put my hands in my sweater pockets. "Better than the last time you asked me," I tried to smile as the seasonal chilly air whipped between us. The scent of the wind was clean and cold, sharply invigorating the senses.

"You're doing better than you think you are," he observed. "Baby steps, right?" he smiled as he walked around his car to the driver's door.

"Right."

"Night, Beths."

"Night, Jackson," I smiled and watched as he pulled away.

Maybe Jackson was right. Maybe I was doing better than I thought. But when it came time to crawl into bed, any progress I had made during the day felt far from where I found myself. Lying on my side, tears drenched my pillow. Instead of memories keeping me up tonight, my attention was on the present. I thought about where Andrew was right now. Was he sleeping, tired from practice? Or was he doing homework? Was he going over the financial papers for the hospital? Did I cross his mind? My mind tried to write a story that would appease my wrecked heart.

I did fall asleep, only reawakening the memories from today that continued to remind me that I was human.

Chapter Ten
Inklings

"Beths?" my brother asked rubbing his eyes as he stood in his doorway wearing nothing but his boxers. "Is everything okay?"

"Want to go for a run?" I asked standing on his front porch dressed in my running clothes. I had already jogged the two blocks to his new house which I had to admit, looked exactly like I had intended when I originally sketched it.

"It's freezing," he said shivering as a breeze blew passed him and into the house.

"Bethany?" Kate asked coming down the stairs in her robe.

"Hi Kate, sorry if I woke you up," I apologized.

"It's fine, my shift at the hospital starts soon anyway. Are you okay?" she asked.

"Yeah, I guess," I lied; neither Kate nor Ryan were convinced.

"I'll be right back," Ryan said heading upstairs to throw weather appropriate clothes on. I looked over my shoulder as another gust rushed by me. I noticed all the leaves on the sidewalk, brown and withered. It was both amusing and sad to me that I hadn't noticed the changing of the seasons. While my own personal season changed, drastic and turbulent, the town and I adjusted with every day.

"You're doing that press thing for the Gala today, right?" Kate asked, welcoming me into the alcove and closing the door behind me.

"Yes. Will you be at the hospital later?" I asked about the timing of her shift.

"Yup. If you want we can hang out for a bit."

"I would love that," I smirked, thankful that she would be around.

"Ready!" Ryan declared, coming back down the stairs, pulling a sweatshirt over his head.

"You haven't gotten a tour of the house yet have you?" Kate asked me excitedly.

"Ugh..." I said looking at Ryan.

"Babe," Ryan said taking the last few steps slower and scratching his head, looking at me for help. I let out a laugh at his expression and the sound caught me off guard, not having heard it so freely in so long. Ryan stood next to me, leaned his arm on my shoulder, and also smiled at my laughter before he broke the news to his wife. "Bethany designed the house."

"What?" Kate asked baffled.

"You know, like, drew it – so I could build it..." Ryan said awkwardly. I turned my head and he and I both laughed at his gracelessness.

"But how?" Kate questioned and stared at me.

"I just hope you like it," I said putting my hands up in the air, not wanting to step on anyone's toes, especially my sister-in-law's.

"Are you kidding? I LOVE THIS HOUSE!" she said giving me an unexpected hug. "But how?" Kate asked again, pulling back confused.

"I'll explain later," Ryan said as he kissed her on the cheek then proceeded to push me out the front door and we started our run.

"Bethany, over here," a photographer said as he pointed his lens in my direction. I stood with a group of the Directors as Bethany Reid – the model. I had prepared myself for the occasion. After my run with Ryan, I took a long shower and spent time doing my hair and makeup. I felt better in my own skin but the external transformation was just that, external.

I was making it through the day without a single tear – a new record. I didn't know if it was due to the fact that I was truly making some progress, or if I had just run out of them. Now the only flashes I saw were those from the cameras. Articles about the Gala were going to run in all the newspapers and media outlets in the surrounding counties thanks to Charles' connections.

"Great," another photographer said after taking another frame. "Can I get one with everyone?" he announced trying to get the attention of all the Board members mingling amongst one another. Almost as if on cue, out of the corner of my eye I saw Andrew walk in. He was wearing black dress pants, a crisp, white button up shirt, black tie, black suit jacket, polished shoes, belt and all… looking dashing as ever. Greeted by some of the hospital's biggest contributors, Drew shook hands and joined the group for a photo. Andrew was on the opposite side of where I stood. The other reporters also jumped in on the photo opportunity. More flashes meant more fake smiles.

"Miss Reid," a woman photographer said directing her assistant to lead me over for an individual shot. "It is such an honor to meet you," she said somewhat flabbergasted at whatever rank she thought I held as a model.

"It's nice to meet you too," I smiled at her even though I was dying inside.

"Do you mind if I ask you some questions for the article?"

"Sure," I said stealing a glance of Drew as he shook more hands and answered questions about the highly anticipated upcoming championship game.

I hated it, but he was perfect. The way he laughed, the way he readjusted his tie, the way he listened to people as they spoke… Once you've had perfection, how can anyone else compare? How would I heal when the cure was also the poison?

The Board enjoyed the public relations aspect of the pre-Gala festivities. I gratefully enjoyed the continuous and distracting interviews which allowed me to play the role of a perfectly happy Bethany Reid. However, the event was wrapping up and the reporters were collecting their equipment as I finished one of the last interviews, this one alongside Charles. The reporter was satisfied with the material he had collected and thanked us before stepping away. We then found ourselves standing with a small group of department heads who Andrew was making conversation with. My heart was in my throat but I kept my Bethany Reid poise, half-listening to the discussion as my mind tried to stay calm. An attractive college-aged reporter hung back from the rest of the parting journalists and came up behind me. "Miss Reid," he said and I turned.

"If you don't mind," he asked as he pulled out a pad of paper and a pen. "May I ask you a few questions for my University's paper?"

"Of course," I said taking a step aside but was still close enough for Andrew and the rest of the group to overhear in the limited space. "Sorry, I didn't catch your name," I said politely. I liked knowing who I was talking to before the questioning started. It made me feel less awkward, especially when the interviewer and I were close in age. It leveled the playing field and made the 'spotlight' a little less blinding.

"My name is Warren," he smiled and I nodded. "So," he began somewhat nervous, "what made you decide to help with the hospital's Gala?"

Recalling a precious memory from a time when Andrew and I still believed in each other, I almost directly quoted the response Drew had told me about why he did what he did. "I think it's important that people have a place to go. No one should lose the person they love because they didn't have the means to save them." Out of the corner of my eye I saw Andrew's head turn at my response. He was listening and didn't notice that I caught his reaction. My heart fluttered knowing that I had struck a cord with *my* Andrew and that I wasn't invisible after all.

"What would you say you have enjoyed most about your experience working with the Board so far?" Warren asked looking up at me, enjoying the interview.

"Everyone has been very kind and brings something different to the table. I'm honored to be a part of such an important cause." I knew that although Andrew's head had returned to the other conversation, he was listening intently now.

"I should probably ask you something like, 'What designer do you plan on wearing to the Gala?'" Warren said letting out a laugh, "but I don't really know much about fashion so... If you could have dinner with one person who would it be?"

"My father," I answered without hesitation. It was the first and only name that came to my mind. "He passed away when I was younger."

"I'm sorry," Warren said writing down my response, and wanting to move forward, continued with a less serious question. "Do you miss modeling?"

"No," I smiled and he enjoyed the answer as well.

"And last but not least," he said, making full eye contact with me, "Would it be inappropriate if I asked for your number?" Andrew's jaw tightened and his shoulders broadened. I stared at the reporter trying to fathom both the reaction I was covertly witnessing as well as trying to process what my response would be. "Off the record, of course," Warren added flirtatiously.

"Thank you for coming," Charles said, having overheard and casually stepping in, graciously walking the young reporter to the door. I stood frozen in the same spot as so many emotions flooded though me without my permission. Against my better judgment, hope was sparked in the aftermath of Andrew's behavior. I wouldn't dare look at him, giving away that I had been paying closer attention to him than anything else. I was now giving the memory I had of seeing Drew in the hallway when I though I caught him looking at me more clout. I kept up my Bethany Reid facade but I needed to get out of here. Charles had walked back over to me and I inconspicuously skimmed the back of my hand with his so that he would know what I had seen and what I was feeling.

Being the gentleman and friend that he was, Charles put out his arm, escorting me from of the space without it appearing that I was coming undone at the seams. I blindly, but gracefully 'stiletto-ed' my way down the hallway alongside Charles until we reached the nurses' station.

"Meeting's over?" Kate asked in her pink scrubs as she filled out a chart. When I didn't answer she looked up and saw that I was trying to process something. "What?" she said standing up and I just blinked uncontrollably and shook my head not knowing what to say. "Terri, I'm going to take my break now," Kate said to the woman next to her without looking away from me.

—

"Life would be a lot easier without emotions," I said to my sister-in-law over iced coffee in the hospital cafeteria.

"Yeah, but would it be worth it?" Kate asked as she brought her coffee cup to her lips.

"No, I suppose not."

"So what's got you so flustered?" she asked.

"Andrew Wicks," I said flatly. She leaned forward and listened intently.

"So," Kate said after I finished recapping what had happened. "He was eavesdropping on your interview and looked up at the answer you gave to the reporter because it was the same one he had given you when you were still together," she said rephrasing everything for her own comprehension. It hurt hearing her say 'when you were still together' but it was the reality. "And he heard the guy ask for your number… and he didn't like it?"

"Yes," I said taking a sip of my iced coffee.

"Sounds to me like he's not over you," Kate said closing the lid of her cup. "Not that I ever thought he was…"

"What?" I asked alerted.

"Beths," Kate said tilting her head. "The boy was *in love* with you, you never did anything to cause him to break up with you… you didn't cheat on him, lie to him… So tell me why he broke up with you without any sign?" she posed.

"I don't know," I said frustrated by the question I hadn't an answer for. "He changed his mind?"

"No," Kate said shaking her head. "Let's go back to right before he broke up with you – the wedding. I know two things. One, someone who is planning on breaking up with you the next day, does not defend you like he did to your mother. And two, when I saw him towards the end of the reception inside the Church, I distinctively remember him looking like he was at a funeral and not a wedding," she finished.

"Liv, at the wedding reception when you and I ran into Andrew on our way to the bathroom…" Kate said into my phone once we were in my car.

"Yeah, what about it?" Liv asked.

"Andrew… did he seem weird to you?" she said looking over at me while we waited for her sister's response.

"Well," Liv began, "Maybe…"

I then proceeded to explain to Liv the scene that had unfolded thanks to Warren, the college journalist.

Olivia was already on the front porch steps when Kate and I pulled into my grandparents' driveway.

"Did he really look up?" Liv asked, sitting across from me on my bed.

"Yes," I nodded wide-eyed.

"It is weird," Olivia said not wanting to speculate because it would open a can of worms that was just starting to close. But even she knew things didn't add up.

"BETHANY, TWO BIG PACKAGES FROM NEW YORK JUST CAME FOR YOU," Kate yelled up the stairs.

"That's the dresses," I said looking at Liv whose face lit up.

"Can we put this conversation on hold?" she asked super excited to try on her couture gown.

"Absolutely."

"What are you doing?" I heard a voice say from a Silverado as it rolled down Main Street next to me. The street was lit up with sparkling white lights, adding to the small town charm.

"Walking," I shrugged at Jackson who was leaning over the passenger seat, attempting to talk to me and drive at the same time.

"It's freezing out. You're crazy."

I stopped and turned saying, "Without a doubt... care to join?" Laughing, he pulled over, parked, then jumped out and threw me his letterman as he came around the back of the truck.

"Pneumonia your new goal?" he joked and I smiled, shaking my head and slid my arms into the preheated letterman.

"I just needed to think," I said recalling my reasoning for going for a walk after dinner.

"You can think indoors too you know," Jackson offered sarcastically.

Smiling I asked, "How was practice?" acknowledging his grass-stained uniform.

"It was good. I think we're ready," he said leaning into a cold breeze with a pained expression at the bite it had. "Coach gave us off tomorrow so we can rest up before the big game."

"That's nice," I nodded and enjoyed the cloud of white smoke caused by simply talking in the dropping temperature.

"I'm kind of freezing. Mind if we sit in my truck?" Jackson asked.

"Wimp," I joked as I jumped into the passenger seat. When he slammed his door, he started the truck and the heat was already on full blast.

"So how's Olivia?" he inquired.

"How's Andrew?" I asked back and we smirked at each other.

"Looks like we're in the same boat," Jackson said with his hands resting on the bottom of the steering wheel as he looked out the windshield.

"With no paddles and up the creek," I added, my sarcasm restored.

"Welcome back," Jackson acknowledged. I let out a short breath knowing that I was nowhere near normal.

"Don't worry, it gets better. Hell, I've been up the creek since the third grade," he said in a rather adorable way.

"Third grade?" I asked, happy for the distraction and friendly banter.

"Yup, Mrs. Burke's class," Jackson smiled more to himself and then turned a slight shade of pink. "But anyway," he said trying to change the topic of discussion.

"What? Did you two split a cubby or something?" I joked and heard laughter, real laughter, coming out of me.

"Funny Beths... real funny," he smirked. "I feel more like a pansy than some macho football player," Jackson said shaking his head.

"Oh come on, it's cute," I said giggling.

"Cute isn't exactly what guys like to shoot for," Jackson said with a funny expression on his face.

"Sorry," I smiled and was quiet for a few seconds before I opened my mouth, "I think you should know that Liv would really like you. If that's any consolation..."

"Thanks, I think," he grinned and hesitated, "If it's any consolation to you, I don't agree with what Andrew has done to you." I looked over at Jackson and knew he meant what he said in a kind way.

"Yeah," I said slightly nodding my head and looking at the dashboard.

"I know you were only dating for a few months but I know how much you liked him and how much he liked you," Jackson added as I leaned my head on the headrest. I let Jackson's words hit me because the fact that I had meant something to Drew at some point, whether it was a century ago or within the past few months, meant something.

"So what do we do now?" I rolled my head to the left and looked at Jackson.

"No idea," he said resting his left arm on the side of the door and looking out at the bright moon.

"Will you ever tell Liv?" I asked curiously.

"I don't know," he replied seriously as he leaned back in his seat. "I definitely won't while she has a boyfriend."

"She wasn't dating anyone before Bobby asked her out. Why didn't you ask her then?" I speculated. Jackson shrugged. It was one thing if my situation had no solution but Jackson's might. "Dude," I said turning in my seat so I was facing him and my casualness got his attention. I suppose I had been hanging out with Chris and Gregg too much. "You are the captain of the football team, you're smart, funny, and good-looking… why didn't you make a move?"

"I don't know," Jackson laughed. "I'm shy?"

"Not when it comes to your 'boys' or anything football," I said as I assumed the role of his conscience; his Jiminy Cricket.

"That's different," Jackson said trying to defend himself but I didn't say a word which made him feel like he needed to elaborate. "Football has always been my thing, and the guys are my friends. Girls, especially Olivia, are totally out of my comfort zone."

"You're talking to me!" I said pointing to myself, "I'm a girl."

"You're," he stuttered, "you're 'different'."

"You're right," I started sarcastically. "I AM different. I was the city girl with the modeling career who everyone in this town stared and pointed at but no one talked to for weeks!" I ranted with a smile on my face. "Geez Jackson!" I exclaimed, "I was the freaking town unicorn – everyone wanted to 'spot' the mythical creature but no one wanted to get too close! And you, you walked right up and introduced yourself with no problem! Like I was one of the guys..." I then tallied on my fingers as I continued, "You're the only person who didn't succumb to the Bethany Reid Syndrome, you're the ONLY guy in school who talks to me, you just happen to be the captain of the football team AND you're telling me that you can't even say, 'hello' to Olivia?"

"Bethany Reid Syndrome?" he asked with a contorted face. "Unicorn?" he then laughed.

"Not important," I said shaking my hands in front of my face. "The point is you are shy under very specific circumstances."

"Yeah, it begins with and 'O' and ends with 'livia'," he laughed.

"EXACTLY," I nodded slowly. "I respect you for not making a move while she has a boyfriend. It speaks volumes of your character, but seriously, if you like her like you say you do, then you shouldn't wait."

"Are you challenging me?" he asked playfully.

"What if I am?" I dared back.

"Fair," he grinncd, intrigued. "But that means I get to challenge you."

"Fair," I replied, sitting back in the passenger seat, waiting for him to tell me the stipulation.

"Would you marry me?"

"What? I'm not Olivia," I laughed.

"And I'm not Andrew," he shrugged, "But we'll make a deal, a pact."

"Okay," I said skeptically.

"Let's say I never get the courage to ask Liv out, and Wicks never realizes what a mistake he is making… that would mean we would grow old… alone."

"This is depressing," I said throwing my head against the headrest dramatically.

"Hear me out," Jackson said turning in his seat, laughing almost uncontrollably. "If we are both not married by the time we are forty, we'll marry each other," he suggested purely for entertainment purposes.

"Oh thanks," I started to laugh.

"You are very welcome," Jackson said holding onto the steering wheel.

"So does that make me your safety?" I questioned, looking at him sideways.

"Yeah," he shrugged laughing. "And I'm yours."

"Can we make it thirty-five instead of forty?" I requested.

"Okay, thirty-five," he chuckled.

"Eh, thirty?" I asked.

"Okay, thirty," he laughed harder.

"Deal," I said putting my hands out in front of the heat vents. "This 'boat' might not have paddles but I'm glad it has heat," I added. Jackson laughed so hard he got a stitch in his side.

"Thanks," I said as I jumped out of Jackson's truck about an hour later. We had lost track of time, talking about our upcoming midterms and other school stuff.

"That Turner?" Gramps asked as I climbed the front porch steps.

"Yup," I nodded.

"Practice ended almost two hours ago..." my grandfather said looking at his watch.

"He gave Bethany a ride home Jon, leave the poor boy alone," my grandmother smiled at her husband, noticing that I had a smile on my face from my time with Jackson. Grams was wrapped in the blanket she was still knitting, using it for warmth at the same time. Before I continued inside, I took a long look at my grandparents. They were iconic for love stories; all these years and still in love.

Maybe it did exist.

"Hey Beths," Chris said sitting at the dining room table next to Gregg who smiled, glad to see that I wasn't in hysterics like the last two times he visited. Surprised to see them here since Ryan had moved out, I stopped and took a closer look. Chris was setting up a game of Scrabble.

"Hi," I said placing my keys in the bowl on the center table. I took off Jackson's letterman which I forgot to give back to him. 'Oh well, I would see him tomorrow,' I thought to myself.

"Whose jacket is that?" Chris asked.

"Jackson's," I said and after seeing Chris' face, I clarified, "It was just to keep warm."

"Just checking," Chris said comically with his hands in front of him.

Ryan came through the kitchen door into the dining room as it swung shut behind him.

"Hey," Ryan said with a drink in his hand as he sat down opposite Gregg.

"You guys are playing Scrabble?" I asked skeptically watching Gregg hand Chris the bag of tiles.

"Yup," Chris said as though this was normal for them.

"You *want* to play?" I asked more directly.

"Who ever really *wants* to play Scrabble," Chris said before Ryan kicked him under the table. "Ow!" Chris grimaced as he rubbed his shin.

"The guys thought you might want to play," Ryan lied.

"Yeah we want to play. Want to join us?" Gregg asked unconvincingly.

"Do you even know how to play?" I asked Chris as I took my seat opposite him.

"You... make... words?" he asked plainly. I looked at Ryan who had obviously orchestrated whatever this was.

"Fine, fine," Ryan started. "The guys asked how you were doing and thought you could use some entertainment."

"What?" I asked looking from Gregg who averted eye contact to Chris who was trying to make a word out of the tiles he picked. "That's... really nice of you guys."

"Yeah, yeah," Ryan said wanting to avoid the mushy moment entirely. "Anyway, genius over here thinks he's going to win," he said pointing to Chris.

"Genius, G-E-N-I-U-S. Genius," Chris said matter-of-factly.

"You're an idiot, you know that?" Ryan said taking a handful of tiles and handing Gregg the bag.

On cue, Chris continued, "Idiot, I-D-I-O..."

BAM! Ryan wailed Chris with the Scrabble board.

"T!" Chris finished now having to pick up his tile pieces which had scattered onto the floor.

"Can we just play?" Gregg asked reaching for the directions as Ryan put the board back onto the table.

"We don't need those," Ryan said looking across at Gregg.

"You know what?" Gregg said placing the rules in between him and me, "I think I'll hold onto them. I have a feeling this could turn ugly really fast."

"I have no idea what you're talking about," Ryan said catching Chris trying to sneak a peek at Ryan's tiles. My brother reflectively covered his letters with his hand, taking it very seriously. Gregg handed me the bag of tiles and we both smiled at what was about to ensue.

I showered and changed into old sweats and a t-shirt and slipped into bed after the game of Scrabble with the boys. For the first time, reliving my day in the middle of the night wasn't painful.

The day's events were filled with promise, friendship, and more laughter than I had had in a while. The hope that was sparked by Andrew's reaction at the hospital meeting wasn't my only ray of light. Time with Jackson, my grandparents, Kate, Ryan, Chris and Gregg, along with the ever constant Olivia, Charles and Abby were all reminders of hope. There were so many lights on my horizon that Andrew, for the first time, wasn't the only one I needed in order to see. I found comfort in this and even in the darkness, my newest past, today, was a good memory.

"You awake?" I heard Ryan whisper up the stairs.

"Yup," I called down to him. He climbed the stairs and I turned on the lamp on my nightstand.

"How ya doing?" he asked, once at the top.

"Today was better than yesterday," I said as optimistically as I could.

"Good. That's good," my brother said sitting on my bed looking down between his construction boots. "You know Beths, you're the one who reminded me to pray for strength instead of an easier path," he said looking sideways at me. "I wanted to remind you of that." I swallowed and my eyes trailed over the pattern of the quilt that was keeping me warm. "Anyway," he said, leaning over and kissing the top of my head. "Night, kid," was all I heard before he turned off my lamp and headed back downstairs.

I cried but it wasn't over Andrew. I cried in effect of the love my brother had for me. I knew my brother loved me but in my time of need, in this trying season of my life, his love didn't fail. It was unconditional – it was a blessing.

"Thank you," I whispered. That was my prayer tonight.

Chapter Eleven
Unaccounted

I had my earphones in and volume up as I walked into school this morning. It was my way of saying goodbye to the world with the touch of a button. I saw Jackson at his locker through the crowded hallway and moved towards him, taking out one of the earphones. "Hey," I said but he was focused on something else. "Ugh Jackson," I said stepping closer. His eyes shot to me and then he nodded nonchalantly to the other side of him. Liv and Bobby were only a few feet away and they were having an argument. I realized Jackson was eavesdropping. Pretending as though I too was looking in his locker, I tugged at my other earphone, pulling it out so that I could double my chances of hearing.

"I don't understand what the big deal is," Bobby said.

"So you think it's okay to put your arm around another girl, that isn't me?" Olivia asked in a raised voice.

"It's not like I was doing anything," Bobby closed his locker harder than necessary.

"That's not the point," Liv said uncompromisingly.

"I have to go to class. We'll talk about this later."

"You bet we will," Liv snapped before he walked away. Not having noticed Jackson or myself, Liv walked down the hallway with the rest of the student body.

"Wow," I said when the scene had dissolved. Jackson pushed books into his locker. "You okay?" I asked looking up at the gentle giant.

"He's such a jerk. He's been flirting with Courtney since the St. Anthony's game," he said irately.

"What?"

"He has his hands on every girl he can. He thinks he's untouchable. He's always been like that," Jackson said and with the last book, he used so much force that I jumped. "Sorry," he apologized and then looked down at me.

"No, it's fine," I smirked and he smiled. I had become the poster girl for letting out my emotions in front of him. "Anyway," I changed the subject. 'Thanks for letting me borrow this," I said handing him his letterman jacket.

"Next time, try not to freeze to death, okay?" Jackson laughed as he threw on the jacket and we walked to our first class together.

Andrew wasn't in physics or biochemistry and I hadn't seen him in the hallways in between classes. He was, however, very present in the haunted recollections which played over and over in my mind like a broken record.

The bell rang, ending biochemistry and as I made my way to the door, Charles gestured for me to stay behind. When the class was empty, the look on his face scared me.

"Would you know where…" he began. "Do you know where Drew is?"

My eyes widened. "No, should I?" I answered. Charles leaned against his desk as his mind raced. "Do you know where he is?"

"No. I saw him this morning before homeroom but Abby said he wasn't in physics and he wasn't here either," Charles said motioning to the row Andrew sat in. "I'm sorry that I asked. I thought perhaps, by some off chance you might know…" Charles began to explain.

"You might want to ask Jackson," I suggested.

"That's not a bad idea," Charles said, open to suggestions.

The hands on the clock were working hard as the night crawled by. I had given in before. I knew there was a fight. I was human and tonight was another reminder.

I found my mind escaping to memories of days when I knew who Andrew was.

Time, a paradox, an overlooked phenomena, had kept such great order, allowing me to relive the untouchable flashes in both this lifetime and another. I denied sleep, not wanting to be its next casualty, and wondered where he was. Did he ever think about me or had he written off our past as a learning experience while I held on to it? No longer able to keep my eyes open, I took a deep breath and submerged into the torture that lay behind my closed eyes. There were seldom signs that it would ever end, but luckily, when sleep came, the pain temporarily subsided.

Chapter Twelve
The Gala

Feet on the ground, air passing through my lungs, I pushed myself out of bed as the morning light shone through the windows. It was pathetic, really, that I was already thinking about him. I had somehow become one of *those girls* that I used to make fun of. However, Andrew and I were different; at least that's what I told myself. Every day that passed felt like sand running through my fingers leaving me with nothing to hold on to.

The hallways were packed. As I made my way through the pandemonium, I could feel the excitement growing for the championship game tonight. Getting my books for my morning classes, I automatically looked over my shoulder in the direction of Andrew's locker but he wasn't there or anywhere in the hallways. My grandfather hadn't mentioned if Andrew was at practice last night. He hadn't spoken about football at all during dinner. Becoming worried I closed my locker and impatiently waited until physics for any sign of him.

His seat was empty. After class I stayed behind until everyone left so I could talk with Abby. "He didn't come home last night," she said as soon as the door closed.

"What?" I asked shocked.

Unable to hide her nervousness, she continued, "Charles asked Jackson and he had no idea where he might be. Charles checked his office at the hospital but there was no sign that he had been there. We thought that Drew would show up for homeroom today considering that the game is tonight, but nothing so far," she said closing her eyes, letting a tear slip. "He's never done this."

"Abby," I said wrapping my arms around her, trying to console her. "You need to relax. It's not good for you or for the baby…"

"What is he thinking?" she barked with angry tears. "First with you, then all the arguments Charles and him have been having, then this," she said shaking her head searching for an answer.

"Hey, hey," I said trying to find her eyes. When she looked up at me I shrugged, "It will be alright. You just need to relax."

"You sound just like Charles," she sniffled reaching for her lace handkerchief, an outdated prop.

"Here," I said handing her a clean tissue from my pocket. "I keep a supply these days," I grinned.

"Yes, well," Abby smirked back at me.

Relief came four classes later in biochemistry. Halfway through the class, Andrew walked in through the door and found his seat. Charles didn't miss a beat in his lecture but I could tell he was relieved but fevered by his arrival.

I stayed behind after class in the empty room. I wanted to make sure Andrew had cleared from the hallways so I wouldn't have to walk passed him at his locker. When the final dismissal bell rang, I figured it was a safe bet but I stopped myself when I heard Charles calling out Andrew's name in the vacated hallway. I opened the door slightly and saw Charles walking out to catch up with Andrew by his locker. He asked critically, "Where the hell have you been?" I stood frozen at his tone. Out of plain sight, a piece of me wanted to hear Andrew's voice, a big piece of me.

"That's none of your concern," I heard Drew say as he took out his car keys from his locker.

"None of my concern?" Charles repeated making sure he heard Andrew's short remark correctly.

"Charles, leave it alone."

"I can't leave it alone. You're actions are causing your pregnant sister, my wife and child, stress that they do not need. She was up pacing all night; all night Drew. There was no note, no phone call, nothing." When Andrew continued to stare into his locker Charles pushed further. "I asked Jackson and even Bethany…"

"Why would you do that?" Andrew interrupted at the sound of my name.

"Because I thought that by some chance she might…"

"What did she say?" Instead of answering, Charles simply acted like he hadn't heard the question. "Charles," Andrew requested.

"Where were you?" Charles asked again. "As your friend, I would have hoped you would have forewarned me." The two were at a standoff, neither conceding. "Fine," Charles said after a few seconds and started to walk away but stopped in his tracks and turned. "Muster the decency to see Abigail before practice to let her know that you are alright." Andrew nodded.

"How's Bethany?" Drew spoke before Charles turned.

"You lost the right to ask that question," Charles said with an annoyance in his tone.

"Charles," Andrew said with unguarded anger.

"You were successful in blindsiding her."

"CHARLES," Andrew's voice resonated.

"You've completely devastated her… again. Congratulations!"

"Stop it Charles," Andrew said warningly as he stared pleadingly into the eyes of his lifelong long friend.

"So you do have a conscience?" Charles pushed further.

"CHARLES STOP," Andrew ordered.

Stepping closer to Andrew, Charles stared intently at him and with an authoritative voice wryly said, "*Your* Bethany… is not your Bethany anymore. Understand that firstly." Drew looked down at the floor in between them. Charles continued to close the space unafraid. I could tell that all of this had taken a toll on him and his patience. "The best thing you have ever done for that girl is affording another man the opportunity to love her the way she deserves." A breath of air escaped Andrew, one that left him looking back at Charles shocked and hurt; it was the lowest blow possible. Charles, however aware of the pain he had inflicted on his best friend, leaned back composed and walked down the hallway passed the classroom where I hid and out the doors.

I felt for the wall and slid down to the floor and clasped my hand over my mouth so that the sounds of my crying would be muffled. I heard Andrew hit the lockers and then the other set of doors were pushed opened at the other end of the hallway.

"I'll get the door," I said as Liv waddled up the front porch steps with foam flips flops and our hands up in the air.

"I know I'm going to smudge a nail. It's only a matter of time," she joked as we walked into the house.

"Hey, Grams," I yelled, closing the front door.

"Let me see!" she said excitingly coming through the kitchen door at our arrival. I held out my hands with my newly polished French tip and matching pedicure. "Very pretty," she smiled. "What about you Olivia?" Liv put out her freshly coated nails which had a design on them to match her gown. "Perfect," Grams smiled.

"Thanks," Liv said admiring her nails again.

"Well don't let me get in the way of your pampering schedule," Grams said taking the kitchen towel from her shoulder. "Ryan said he will be by with Kate around eight."

"Okay," I said as Liv and I began to climb the stairs.

"Oh, and Beths…" she started.

"Yeah Grams," I said turning on the platform.

"How are you doing," she asked.

"Fine Grams," I lied, smiling for her and followed behind Liv up to the attic.

—

Over the blasting music, my best friend and I talked as we did each other's hair. Liv's fellow cheerleaders envied her invitation to the event; it was something that the town and surrounding towns saw as being exclusive and rightly so. However, Liv did feel a twinge of guilt that she would miss cheering at the championship game but all was forgotten the closer it got to the Gala.

As the sky outside the window darkened, it was time to slip out of our sweatpants and t-shirts and into our gowns that hung on the armoire. Liv went first. Finally accepting that her nails were completely dry, she held her dress to her as I zipped it up. "Do you think I need to tape it? I don't want any surprises," she laughed.

"No, I think you'll be fine," I said as I secured the clasp and fixed the silky train of the dress so it laid right. Liv stepped over to the antique mirror and her eyes lit up as she took in her appearance. I walked over to her side and grinned. "You look stunning," I said as she turned from side-to-side, ecstatic.

"Your turn," she said turning towards me in her excitement. I stepped into the heavy, ivory gown and with help from Liv, adjusted the bodice, tying up the front corset while she fastened the long row of buttons down the back. As I finished with the strings, Liv fluffed the layers of linen that now cascaded to the floor. I ran my hands over my waist, flattening the dress to my sides as Liv took two steps back. "WOW," I heard my best friend say. I looked up at my reflection and saw an elegant woman staring back at me. She was beautiful – and for the first time, I let myself believe it.

With my hair in long, curly locks and my makeup accentuating my features, I couldn't believe my eyes. I had been made up for the runway before, but nothing compared to this. The sweetheart neckline, feminine in every way, was fitted at my waist, controlled by the corset. The material, soft and airy was layered; the skirt floated to the floor. The cap sleeves were sheer and showcased my graceful frame. There was no need for beading; I sparkled in this dress. It was the essence of the time I was from, perfected in the light of where my story continued. It was months ago that I was working with Natalie, a designer in New York, to create this gown. However, now I realized that it was over a hundred years ago since I saw it through my own eyes. It was remarkable how much this dress resembled the one from my welcoming party. Had it not been a century apart, the dresses could have been mistaken as sisters.

Looking down, I saw a flash in front of my eyes; one that brought me back momentarily. When they readjusted, I became very aware that the minutes were closing in on when I would be at the Estate. The strength of this realization was equitable to how weak I now felt. Andrew would be there. There was no avoiding that.

"It's almost identical," I began to explain to Olivia.

"It's beautiful."

"Thanks," I smiled as my right hand found my collarbone. My father had picked out the gown the first time around.

"Are you okay?" she asked. I shook my head, honestly, as the tears began to build. "We won't go," she said simply.

"No, I promised Gramps, Charles…" I started.

"Beths."

"Liv, I have to do this."

"This won't get easier. He's going to be there," she said anticipating a breakdown. She did know me better than I would like to admit.

"I know."

"Okay," she nodded. "But if at any time you want to leave, you let me know and we are out of there." In a protective, best friend kind of way she continued, "Like… out of there… lightening fast."

"Got it," I answered with a small grin.

"BETHS! LIV!" Ryan yelled up from the first floor.

"WE'LL BE DOWN IN A MINUTE!" Liv shouted down to him. Looking back at me, she said, "I'm serious. You don't have to do this."

"Thanks," I said sliding into my heels one-by-one. "I'll be fine," I lied as I reached for my clutch and prayed for strength I knew I did not have.

Olivia walked down the stairs first and I followed a few steps behind. Kate was standing in the living room in a gorgeous green gown that was roused to the side. Ryan came out of the bathroom and was halfway into the living room when he turned to see his sister-in-law coming down the steps. "You look beautiful," Kate said to her younger sister.

"Thanks," Liv smiled.

"Nice dress," Ryan said to Liv punching her on the arm.

"Aw thanks Ryan. That might be one of the nicest things you have ever said to me," she said sincerely.

"Is that why it hurt to say it?" he asked, holding his side jokingly.

As I came into view, I saw my brother dressed sharply. "Nice tux, Ry," I complimented. The room got quiet as all eyes turned to me.

"What?" I asked subconsciously when Ryan found himself stuck between a father and a brother moment.

"That's right," Liv grinned, proud of her work.

"You look amazing," Kate said wide-eyed.

"Absolutely gorgeous," Grams beamed, touching her hand to her chest.

"You okay there, Taylor?" Liv elbowed my brother.

"Yeah," he said snapping out of it. "You look..." Ryan started seriously, "You look great, Beths. Stunning actually."

"Thank you," I blushed in response to the unprompted accolades.

"Are we ready to go?" he asked, checking his watch.

"Yes sir," Liv said heading for the door. "Shot gun!" she said claiming the passenger seat on the ride over to the Estate.

"You alright Beths?" Ryan whispered as Kate and Liv walked down the front porch steps, arm-in-arm toward the 'the tank'. I looked up at my brother and smiled with comforting eyes, trying to convince him that I was okay. I had taken notice of how he had hovered over the past week. He watched but hadn't asked or tried to start a conversation since the ride to school. I think he was waiting to see if my world had started to spin again.

"My stomach feels a little woozy," I admitted.

"You don't have to go…" Ryan said stopping short. I watched as Grams joined Kate and Liv at the truck where they were patiently waiting.

"Yeah, I do," I said. He looked at me and I looked at him. Communicating without words, we smiled at one another.

"Alright," he didn't argue. Putting out his arm, the two of us walked to 'the tank'.

As we pulled off the main road and onto the long, cobblestone drive, the Estate glowed in the distance. The grounds were black but the driveway was lit by lanterns. The illuminated house at the end was perfectly lit by small lights hitting the front and sides of the exterior, showing off its grandness. Couples were already arriving and walking up the front steps. It was easy to get lost in that first glimpse, but then again, it was the normal atmosphere and charm of the Estate.

There was a valet for the guests who parked the expensive cars one-by-one off to the side, making Ryan's truck stick out in a comedic way. "I don't care what you guys say, I love this thing," he mumbled as we piled out of 'the tank' and adjusted our dresses.

Grams and Liv were animatedly admiring the luxurious home, followed by Ryan and Kate who were closely behind them. I hesitated at the foot of the front stairs and looked up. Unlike other guests, I already knew how wonderful the Estate was, having seen it many times before. I also knew that nothing on the other side of that door would heal me.

I could feel myself coming undone with every step but I took them anyway. That strength came in response to the prayers I had offered up because I knew that I was not strong enough on my own. It was all I needed to get into the entranceway where I could not turn back. I was in.

The chandelier over the table was lit and the space was decorated much like my first night here; with hundreds of white roses and thick ribbon framing the archways and tables. The Beaux style was predominately evident.

I turned to close the front door behind me. My hand rested on the knob for a split second as my dream flashed in front of my eyes.

My father and I stood exactly where I was and we were both saying goodnight to guests as they left. He was happy, smiling and alive. His spirits were so high; he was excited for the chapters that lay ahead of us now that I had joined him in Ellsworth.

I could barely breathe; the moment was a thief. More images of that particular night flooded in front of my eyes, triggered by the smallest of things.

I swear I saw James Hughes standing at the top of the staircase right where he was when first introductions were made.

Blinking furiously, I realized the images were just my memories intruding on the evening. The once cherished recollections were becoming bitter; like ashes scattered after a magnificent fire. I should be farther along by now. However, the more I let myself think about how close I had gotten to that famous happy ending, the more it hurt to walk through the present.

My ears were bombarded with the chatter from numerous guests, none of whose faces were familiar. Separated from Ryan, Kate, Grams and Liv, I walked across the entranceway to the top of the staircase that led to the ballroom. I knew that Andrew, like my grandfather and Bobby, were not here yet; the football game would be ending shortly, but I still found myself searching for Drew among the crowd anyway.

I ran my hand along the classically decorated banister wrapped in dozens of roses and yards of ribbon which competed with one another down into the brilliant ballroom. The soft lighting illuminated the hundreds of exquisitely dressed guests talking and laughing amongst one another. A violin played softly somewhere in the distance; the notes were mesmerizing, sounding almost like two separate strands that were intertwining. It was so familiar that I expected to look beside me and see my father.

As my foot touched the last step, it was Charles who came up beside me. He looked at me knowing that I was reliving the moment. He too was reliving the memory. It was so different – the circumstances, the time… yet still, it was so reminiscent. "You are breathtaking," my dear friend said in all sincerity.

"Thank you," I spoke in what was almost a whisper, running my hands over the gown. He also looked the part in his tuxedo with a hidden eighteenth century twist. We smiled at the quirk of fate, what could be defined as an inside joke. Charles put his arm out for me to take; I accepted. I carefully picked up the back of my gown with my free hand and suddenly noticed the whispers and flashes of light that went off. Pausing, I looked up at the media presence, and with the mood around me changing, it jolted me into 'Bethany Reid' mode. We had walked a few feet before a photographer called out, "A few pictures, Miss Reid?" Charles nodded and stepped away from me as they captured the images they wanted. Meanwhile, I spotted Liv and my family finding their place at a table across the ballroom.

A new song began to play and I heard the violin's opening cords. My eyes shifted up to the sound and the anxiety returned as I waver back to Bethany Taylor. Charles recognized the melody as well and came to my side, excusing me from the public eye for now. Accidentally, my hand grazed his as I took his arm once more. I knew what he would see and feel.

He would first know that even though my appearance had improved since last week, I was no further along in my grief. He would see me hiding in the empty biochemistry classroom unbeknownst to him and Andrew that I overheard their confrontation in the hallway earlier. What I was most upset about was that he now knew the anxiety and fear I had of the Estate, a place I had once called my home. That mixed with the internal battle of seeing Andrew at some point this evening was my innermost secret and Charles now knew them all.

He blinked at me, refocusing as he came out of it, but without missing a stride, he led me to the head table in the front of the room. I turned my attention to the people sitting there; a few Directors from the Board and their spouses. I cordially greeted all of them and took the seat Charles had pulled out for me next to Abigail. Sitting down on the other side of me, Charles said apologetically, "I am sorry, Bethany."

A cold sweat washed over me. "For what Charles?" I swallowed and tried to look away. I was admittedly embarrassed. Abby had been conversing with one of the Directors who I recognized as being the hospital's Chief of Surgery. When she became aware that her husband and I were next to her, she excused herself from the discussion for a moment and turned towards us. She recognized my dress instantly. "You… that gown, you look…" she smiled but it disappeared when a reporter came up behind me and asked for a quick interview. I agreed and left the table – Bethany Reid ready. Not far from my two old friends, I answered the questions for that particular news outlet. On my return to the table Abby watched me carefully wearing her maroon gown with a swoop neckline. The gown had a high waist and billowed to the ground like an eighteenth century dress should. To anyone who knew our situation, the three of us looked almost comedic in our inability to shed the time-honored fashion. However, to those who did not know, we seamlessly fit in with the guests around us.

"Bethany," Abby started. By the sound in her voice I knew that Charles had made her aware of my true emotional state.

"Please," I said to her feeling the pent up tears in my eyes.

"Okay," Abby said, patting my knee as I took my seat. Knowing not to push farther right now, she helped to include me in senseless party conversation.

I had successfully completed dozens of interviews as Bethany Reid – a perfectly happy young woman who showed no signs of heartache. Unfortunately, the act only lasted a little while – it was a temporary distraction. Charles who was never more than an arm's length away the entire time, acted as the ice breaker and foot soldier. He introduced me to the generous guests around the vast room, stopping briefly at each table in between interviews. Charles had mastered conversation over the years; the foundation of his gift was rooted back to a time when speaking was considered an art form. I took notice of how he talked to different types of people – how he approached them rather strategically, customizing the topic of discussion, the airiness in his tone, his selection of verbal and nonverbal cues, the softness in his listening eyes… The culmination of all these things produced a harmonious, yet intriguing rhythm which left every acquaintance enchanted in his wake.

Whenever the spotlight was not on Charles, he watched me, seeing right through my façade, having bore witness to the true pain in our exchange. I lost track of how many pictures I had taken as a 'celebrity' with guests and for publicity use. Finally, Charles steered me over to a table with familiar faces, my family. Confident that I was safe in their company, he headed back to the head table to his wife's side and continued to attend to his hosting responsibilities. I stood next to Ryan's chair and he looked up. "How's it going?" he asked as he wiped his mouth with his cloth napkin and returned it to his knee.

"It's going well," I said playing with the bodice of the gown.

"Have you tried the pasta?" he asked pointing to his now empty plate.

"No, I'm not hungry," I answered looking around the beautiful room. It was unfortunately like a dagger to the heart; the unrelenting pain escaped from its temporary cage again.

"I can't believe I missed the game," Ryan said fiddling with his phone, messaging Chris who had gone to the town's Super Bowl. Ryan was still getting all the details.

"Me neither," I laughed knowing that he was here to support me and not for the pasta. "How'd we do?"

"We won by thirteen," Ryan smiled and held up his hand for a high five which Kate would not return in a setting such as this. Ryan rolled his eyes when Liv started to laugh.

"Beths," Liv said becoming rigid in her seat, motioning behind me towards the grand staircase. I turned slowly and saw my grandfather and Bobby dressed in their tuxes walking down the stairs. I knew that meant that Andrew would not be far behind. Ryan, also understanding, looked back at Liv and took a sip of water, not saying anything. Feeling another cold sweat breaking over me I said, "I'm going to go find my seat," and attempted to make a beeline to the head table. However, I hit some interference – a group of reporters. I sarcastically thought to myself that they seemed to be growing in numbers before putting on a smile that my mother would be proud of. Again, I was geared up as Bethany Reid.

Just when I thought I was content with my surroundings, I caught sight of Gracie in her pink dress darting up the stairs. I knew she only ran towards one person that way – Uncle Drew. I only had a few more seconds until he would come into my view. As I finished answering a question, I saw him walking down the stairs having already spotted me with the crowd of reporters. Gracie met him and hugged his leg. He stopped and looked down at the blonde haired, pink dressed little angel and kissed the top of her head as she rambled on about the party. Within seconds she was off running down the staircase towards Cole who was eating pasta at a children's table. Andrew's gaze fell on me again. I foolishly looked back at him and felt the blow I had anticipated. He was enthralling, beautiful and perfect in his black tuxedo. Like Charles, Andrew's outfit had a hint of an older time, a reflection of class that never went out of style. His white shirt contrasted with the black pants and suspenders which shown underneath his jacket before he buttoned it. His hands found his pants pockets as his foot touched the bottom step. A guest came up next to me, an older gentlemen and his niece asking for a picture. Looking away, the air was quickly disappearing from my lungs but I smiled as the image was captured.

"Hi," I heard Ryan's voice say as another reporter tried to interview me. I looked over at him skeptically. "I'm sorry but Miss Taylor is done interviewing for now."

"I thought it was Miss Reid?" the confused reporter questioned.

"It's TAYLOR," Ryan insisted through gritted teeth, shaking his head as he led me away to the middle of the ballroom where there was a designated dance area. A string orchestra played in the background and couples danced to the music. Ryan and I started to dance when I noticed Charles spot Andrew and then looked for me in the crowded room. Relieved that I was with my brother and not alone, he continued his conversation with some of the prominent donors. I then caught sight of Abby in her maroon dress off to the side. She had approached Andrew and now looked berate as he walked away from her to a group of men which included my grandfather, who were discussing the game. I turned my head and met Ryan's eyes, which were looking over my face. I knew that he saw how destroyed and deeply hurt I still was. Ryan didn't need a memory exchange to know that my life was driving me insane. In that moment, Ryan took the reins.

His eyes squinted in thought and I knew now was the time he would choose to speak. Ending the silence he said, "Beths, sometimes two hearts can't dance to the same beat." I stared at him after hearing his rather poetic advice. A grin broke out over his face and he added, "Now, do you want my real opinion?"

With a small smile breaking over my lips, I questioned, "Then what was what you just said?"

"That's what an older, smarter brother should say," he nodded. "You'll have to get over it. I'm learning as I go, okay?" he smirked.

"Okay, what's your opinion?" I asked amused.

"You're miserable and it kills me. You're broken and I know I can't fix you. There is nothing that can change it. So, I came here tonight with every intention of beating the ever-loving sh..." Ryan paused refraining from cursing as he looked in Andrew's direction. "Shit. I was going to beat the shit out of Wicks," my brother cursed freely, holding nothing back. "But, it looks to me like he's been beating himself up worse than I ever could." Meeting my taken aback expression, Ryan grinned. I hadn't gotten a long enough glance of Andrew to get a good look at him. "Seeing as how he isn't handling it well, any physical pain I would have inflicted would be nothing in comparison to the mental torture he is probably going through over letting the most amazing girl go." I let out a smirk, looking up at my brother. "Don't tell Grams I cursed," he requested with a grin. "She'll get the swear jar out again."

"Thanks Ry," I said giving him a hug as the song came to an end.

"Of course, Miss Taylor," he said hugging me tighter and then led us back to the table were our family was sitting. Gramps had just sat down next to my grandmother and was telling her and Kate about the victory. Liv was giggling as Bobby put his arm around her chair. "How was it?" Ryan asked, causing Gramps and Bobby's heads to turn. A detailed synopsis followed.

Abby came up next to me and motioned towards the head table. I followed her, finding our seats as Charles tapped a crystal glass with the back of his knife to get everyone's attention. Surprisingly, the small noise in the vast room avalanched as the guests gave him their undivided attention. Picking up his glass of champagne, he said, "Ladies and gentlemen, it is with a humbled heart that I speak to you this evening. If you would please raise your glasses…" Charles paused as hundreds of glasses were raised before he continued, "Let us toast to the worthy cause that has brought us together, and, if you will allow me, on behalf of Ellsworth Hospital and its Board of Directors, I would like to extend our deepest gratitude for your generous financial support and thank you for sharing your evening here with us tonight. Cheers." A round of applause filled the room at the short welcoming and waiters now came through the far doors, serving the main course on elegant China.

"Good evening," I heard Andrew's voice say politely just a few feet to my right. I dared not look up. I steadied my focus on an unimportant discussion another Board member and his wife were having with Abby about the lawn furniture they recently purchased. A few seconds later, Andrew was making his way down the table closer to me, greeting the guests in passing. "Good evening Ralph, Sophia," Drew said to the lawn décor specialists. "Abigail… Bethany," Drew said nodding towards me. I swallowed hard at my name coming from his lips but took notice of his appearance as Ryan had pointed out. My brother was right; Andrew did look like hell, especially for an archangel. It was obvious he hadn't slept and his face was drawn. His eyes seemed gray instead of their usual striking blue. Even so, his hair was brushed to the side, he was clean shaven… but I noticed that his shoulders were not as broad as I knew them to be. "Charles," Andrew addressed. Charles stood and put out his hand for Drew to shake. Andrew could not deny his brother-in-law's gesture or the inevitable exchange the connection would allow. It was not noticeable to the guests around us, but Drew's dislike for what Charles had just done was undeniable. They shook hands and Andrew proceeded down the other half of the table as Charles sat back down. Abby asked softly, "Charles…" wanting to know what her husband had seen. Whatever images and emotions that were transferred must have been significant because it took Charles longer than usual to adjust back to his senses.

"Coverly? He was in Coverly?" I asked as my voice cracked. Andrew had been in the neighboring town when he hadn't come home. It was a town Drew despised; it was the place of my father's accident. Charles nodded, deep in thought at the revelation. Abby's eyes looked back and forth as she tried to think of a reason why her brother had gone there, trying to justify his behavior.

"If you'll excuse me," I said to Ralph and Sophia who didn't notice anything odd, fully distracted by the delicious dinner set before them.

"Where are you going?" Abigail whispered touching my hand. Charles' head turned as well. Abby, unable to receive emotions or memories from the hand connection was safe from the anxiety I was experiencing.

"To find reporters," I said hoping that my escape to 'Bethany Reid Land' would outlast my temperamental mood.

Sure enough, an hour's time flew by. I would occasionally scan the room looking for him but I did so sparingly, not wanting to blow my cover.

"So, how does it feel?" Kate asked when I sat down next to her.

"Looks like Bethany Reid is back in the saddle," I said taking a sip of water from Liv's glass.

"I don't know how you do it with all of those photographers and questions…" Kate shook her head.

"You should have seen her when I was in my prime," I tried to joke.

"That dress is just gorgeous, Bethany." Grams said. I looked down at the beautiful gown… I ran my fingers over the overlay.

"If I didn't know any better," Gramps started and I looked up at him. He smiled at me grateful for my efforts this evening and the small help I provided to the charitable cause. "I'd think you've done this more than once or twice. You're doing wonderfully, my dear."

"Thanks old man." I grinned back.

"Can I get anyone anything?" a waitress with dark hair which was pulled back in a low ponytail asked the table. Liv pulled at my arm and I turned to see why. She whispered in my ear, "Just so you know, Andrew's been watching you the entire time. He's up on the landing talking to a group of men. He's distracted though…

he keeps following you," she stopped. "Oh, and he's drinking something… and it's not water," she said implying it was an alcoholic beverage. I was grateful that Olivia had been watching Andrew.

"Thanks Liv," I said indebted to her for spying.

"You would think since his cover is a high school student, he wouldn't be drinking…"

"I think I'm going to get some fresh air," I interrupted her. I needed to get away. She understood.

"Okay," she said before I walked swiftly over to the head table to get my clutch before heading out the archway onto the terrace.

Finally outside, I took in a deep breath and was caught by the sight of the lanterns sporadically lit throughout the extensive grounds. It looked perfect. How could it be so perfect and everything else be so wrong?

"Bethany," I heard a voice say from behind me.

"Charles," I answered knowing who it belonged too. He must have noticed my dash from the head table; my friend had been watching me as closely as he watched Gracie throughout the evening. We had made eye contact routinely, wordlessly checking in with one another. However, unlike Gracie who was asleep on a chair next to Abby, I was spiraling, getting closer and closer to having an emotional breakdown.

Charles came up beside where I stood and leaned his hands on the balcony railing in front of us, looking out over the grounds. Even in the colder months, the garden below the veranda gave off a floral aroma which was stirred by a breeze. Not neglecting the simple pleasure, Charles drew in a deep breath as his eyes searched into the darkness; the wavering lanterns casted shadows over the manicured grounds. "Beautiful night," Charles acknowledged.

"Yes," I nodded. Charles let out an unwarranted laugh and I looked back at him wondering what was so funny.

"Your gown," he explained, "It has been quite some time but Abby and I are in agreement that if we didn't know better, we'd say that you are wearing the very same dress you wore the night we were introduced."

"I thought the same thing," I grinned. "I guess my style hasn't changed."

"No, I suppose not," he smiled, shaking his head and standing up straight.

"Charles," I said abruptly. He waited for me to continue. "Why was he in Coverly?"

"Beths, I can only speculate…"

"Charles," I tilted my head. I knew he knew Andrew better than anyone and he was working with more information than I had. Charles put out his hand for me to take. Trusting him, I reached out to take his hand but he pulled back. Warning me, he said, "The memories are Andrew's; I'm merely passing what I saw from the connection. The emotions, the images... they're all his." Then his fingers locked with mine.

They came in hurried flashes; glimpses. First was of the scoreboard from tonight's game, then the strong sound of his voice calling out a play. The roar of the crowd was encouraged by the cheerleaders, of which Drew noticed Olivia's absence. Andrew's eyes shot up to the stands at the fifty yard line where I normally sat with my brother and sister-in-law but instead there were unfamiliar faces tonight.

More flashes brought the thunderous noise of crushing shoulder pads hitting one another as the offensive line met the opponent's defense. A row behind the battle, Drew scanned the field for one of his receivers. The cold was bitter and I could see the smoke from Drew's breath push out of his mouth as his eyes blinked before launching the football into the stadium light, only to be caught by his teammate forty yards away. Andrew then saw one of the defensive linemen break through and he felt the impact of the tackle. Then he heard the loudness of the crowd in response to the touchdown that was just made.

Zach helped Drew up and patted him on his shoulder pads. Drew nodded and ran off the field, switching with the special team for the extra point conversion. Adrenaline was something Drew was familiar with. It was the only thing he was running on.

I heard my grandfather's voice as the memory was fast forward. "Wicks!" I heard Gramps yell over the crowd which caused Andrew to snap out of thinking about how I would be arriving at the Estate right about now. "Come on, son, focus," my grandfather said looking him straight in the eyes. Drew took a drink out of a paper cup one of the water boys gave him and forced his attention back on the playbook my grandfather was holding... but Drew's concentration was fleeting.

They were in the locker room next, the whole team. They were up by fifteen points and the energy in the room was electric. They were two quarters away from the championship title. Jackson was talking over strategies for the second half, adjusting his line so that they would capitalize on the opponent's weakness. Andrew and Jackson's eyes crossed one another's and the two nodded. I could feel Andrew's confidence in his friend and I could see Jackson's trust in his quarterback.

Blurs, noise and a measurable anticipation swarmed Drew's senses as time ticked off the game clock. A victory was in the foreseeable future but Andrew's mind seemed to lose more and more ground with every second that passed. Before the last snap of the game, Andrew licked two fingers on his throwing hand and began to call out the play in a strong, authoritative voice. However, images of a sign that read 'Coverly' flew in front of his eyes. He had driven to the town the day before and he was remembering it. Drew had spent the night sitting by the embankment of a stone bridge were the accident had taken place. He was broken – devastated. He felt so much, he was carrying more than he could hold – I knew this feeling but it wasn't mine for once.

The truth of where he had been came out as the images played on. Andrew had waited to go back to the Estate when he was sure that Charles and Abigail left for school early the next morning with Cole and Gracie. He parked his Camaro, went into the house, showered, collected his things and had all intentions of making it to school for the homeroom bell. However my old quarters, distracted him enough that he, for the first time in over a century, entered it. It was here that emotions of indescribable loss billowed through him. He walked slowly until his hand touched one of the four posts. He sat down at the foot of the bed, his head dropped and he ran his hands through his hair – he had lost me… again. 'No,' he thought, wanting to wake up from this nightmarish reality. 'No,' resounded in his mind.

There were no images, as his eyes closed but the swirls of thoughts were clear. It was the 'can't-get-you-out-of-my-head', 'I-wish-there-was-another-way', 'hears-me-saying-his-name' kind of crazy. Drew opened his eyes to only close them again but this time his memory brought back me smiling at him. He shook his head and whispered, "Damn it," to himself. The image stung worse than any tackle he had ever taken.

As that memory left him, he took one last look at the formation before the football was hiked. Drew took three steps backwards, scouted his options and then handed the ball off to Duke who ran it for ten yards before being knocked out of bounds.

The flashes slowed as Andrew pulled up to the strategically lit Estate where dozens of cars were parked in an orderly fashion. Andrew parked his Camaro in the garage and could hear the guests from the Gala as he shut his driver's side door. He went straight upstairs, showered, dressed and took a moment in his room to tie his tie. He was tense, troubled, drained... With the sounds of laughter and celebration coming from below, Drew took a deep breath, knowing he needed to compose himself.

As he descended the first staircase into the entranceway, he took notice of Abigail's selection of decorations. The Estate was hauntingly familiar with the dim candlelight-like ambiance with the roses and ribbons cascading down the grand staircase. Drew tried to convince himself that he could make it through the night.

Andrew shook hands with guests as he passed them in the entranceway, asking if they were enjoying their evening and smiled back at them. It was when he saw me smiling for pictures and enjoying the conversation I was partaking in, when he stopped in his tracks. It was like a bullet to the heart. The setting, the time, the place... my dress... everything, it was as though the moment had rippled through time and it depleted any strength he had.

With one look I had crashed any hope, any excuse and any chance he had for tonight. An offer of whiskey was given to him by a passing waiter which he accepted, not taking into consideration the age he was portraying. A conversation was started by a gentleman to his left; one that he could not ignore without being impolite. So, courteously, Andrew entered the discussion but his eyes continued to follow me in the crowded ballroom.

He placed his empty glass on another waiter's passing tray and took the opportunity to bow out of the conversation when it no longer called for him and started down the staircase. His eyes locked eyes with mine when he was halfway down the stairs. He knew that the smile that was on my lips was a result of something a reporter had said to me. It had been two weeks since the last time he had seen me smile. In those few seconds before Gracie pulled at his arm, calling for his attention, I felt the burdened ache in his chest grow deeper. He was still taken by me.

Tonight he felt more like a ghost than a man, and he was certain that death would be kinder than this torment.

Drew was three drinks in before he attempted to make his way over to the head table where Charles, Abigail and I were sitting. He nodded and said hello to the members of the Board, aware that he was getting closer and closer to where I was. His heart pounded in his chest with every step. Andrew never thought he'd be my ex-boyfriend and didn't know how to act or what to do… all he knew was that I looked like I was getting along fine without him. That killed him even more. Charles' words from their exchange in the hallway earlier in the day resounded in his mind. 'The best thing you have ever done for that girl is affording another man the opportunity to love her the way she deserves.'

The thought of another man courting me disgusted him and he nearly lost his mind overhearing Warren talking to me at the press release for the hospital a few days ago...

Drew's mind stalled when the next group of 'hello's' belonged to his brother-in-law, sister and me. When Charles put out his hand for Andrew to shake, he knew that with the guests around them it was an inescapable gesture. Drew knew Charles would see all of it. Reluctantly, he made the exchange.

My eyes tried to focus as my sight became mine again but everything was still blurry from tears that had yet to fall. "Breathe Beths," Charles said holding my wrist so that my hand would stop anxiously rubbing my collarbone.

"I'm okay," I exhaled, ridding my eyes of the tears with the tips of my fingers so that they wouldn't mess up my makeup. I stared blankly out over the acres of land. Charles and I were both quiet.

Releasing the death grip I had on my clutch, I remembered what it held. Opening it, I pulled out the envelope with a check written for the hospital and handed it to him.

"What's this?"

"A donation," I said hearing the leaves in the trees warn of a breeze that was on its way. Charles grinned as he pulled out the check. "I called a few people," I added, not wanting to take credit for the large sum.

"You never cease to amaze me, Miss Taylor," he smiled at me.

"If you could do me a favor though and make sure the contribution is anonymous."

"Of course," my friend said putting the envelope in his inside jacket pocket.

"Designated to a state-of-the-art prenatal unit... There's a Landon on the way..."

He looked back at me and for the first time, I witnessed a glow about Charles, one that only fathers who were awaiting the birth of their child have. "Thank you Bethany," he said with a deep gratitude. I smiled and looked down but when I looked back up, Charles' attention was on someone behind me. I turned slowly to find the archangel standing a few feet away – tall, handsome and holding a glass of whisky. "Drew," Charles said and then looked at me silently excusing himself, walking passed the frozen figure and back into the ballroom. Even with what little light there was, I noticed how Andrew's suit fit his body in all the right places, giving his frame the justice other clothes could not provide.

It was clear that I was not invisible to him even though the silence was deafening. A cold gust blew in my favor, helping me stay aware that this was not a false reality. He and I were both here, together and alone. Hell was playing an evil trick or it was heaven's providence.

Drew rotated his drink in a circular motion in his hand so that the ice clinked against the glass. He walked up beside me, placed it on the stone railing and absorbed me with his eyes. "You look… absolutely beautiful, Beths," he adoringly remarked.

"Thank you," I said in a whisper. Drew put his hands in his pockets as I looked down at my gown. Feeling angry and a little bit stronger, I hit him verbally. "How was Coverly?" He didn't answer at first, partly taken aback that Charles had shared with me what he didn't want to share with Charles in the first place. He fumbled his confidence and the whisky was kicking in.

For the first time, I enjoyed his uneasiness. I enjoyed hurting him in some sick way. I knew that I would soon regret my words but when your heart is breaking, the future and its retribution seem so far away. I wanted answers and I needed to bypass the meaningless chatter that stood between not knowing and the truth. While my lips separated ties with my mind, I turned towards him with glassy eyes.

"Andrew," I said and he looked down at me hearing the heartbreak in my voice. "Why?" I questioned as a tear fell and with it, his composure. Taking a step closer, Drew dried my tears with his thumbs and then ran his hands into my hair, cradling my head behind my ears. This was the Andrew I knew; the one I loved.

"It is not enough to say that I am sorry," he said unguardedly. "But I am sorry," he exhaled, "truly sorry."

I would not so easily let myself forget the pain he had caused me. "After all this time," I said as my anger and confusion met. 'He had put us in this situation. He had done this,' I reminded myself. "Why put me through this again?" I reworded as a steady flow of tears silently slid down my cheeks. He tried to dry them again but I pushed him away and dried them myself. "YOU ended things… there were no signs." In shock of my rejection to his once welcomed touch, Drew stepped back devastated. "Why? Just tell me that," I pushed and when he had no explanation for me, I snapped. "You can be the strong and silent type, Drew, but look at the good it's done." This caused him to look back at me. "I have never asked anything from you. Not when we met, not while we were seeing one another… but now, I am asking you for one thing." When he still didn't answer the question, I glared at him before I turned for the ballroom.

"Bethany," he called out and caught my arm, turning me around. His face finally released the pent up expression of desperation which I knew he was feeling but had masked so well. Drew caught himself mesmerized by my lips but pulled away quickly, adding space and ran his hand through his hair looking up at the night sky.

"You," I said placing my hands on his chest. My fingertips touched his white crisp shirt and the suspenders under his tux jacket. "You broke my heart," I said exhausted. "All I want to know is if got what you wanted?"

Air escaped his lungs and he placed his hands on my wrists, "No. No I didn't," he said defeated. "Beths, I would do all of this again if it meant it led me back to you." I shook my head and looked down at the stones beneath the hem of my dress. "I would go back to the beginning... back through *all* of it. I would be grateful for the tortured nights, the pain – even if it meant it brought me to this moment." I felt my eyes narrow as he spoke. "You're worth it. You always have been and you always will be worth it," Andrew said and his jaw tightened when my eyes slowly looked up from the ground to his chest and then met his sight. I leaned into him and he wrapped his arms around me and kissed the top of my head. "I need you to remember this moment," he whispered into my ear. "I need you to remember what I'm telling you. I want this to be the memory that I leave you with. Not of me walking away."

My breath caught at his words. It was like he was saying goodbye; something he never got the chance to say last time.

"I don't want this to be it," I let out and he held me tighter still.

"I know."

"Do you know where Bethany is?" I heard Abigail ask from the other side of the archway inside the ballroom.

"You better get inside," Drew said releasing his hold on me and placing his hands back in his pockets. Looking up at him, I read over his profile even though it was ingrained in my mind. Picking up the side of my gown with my leading hand, I turned and unwillingly started to walk back towards the party but stopped and looked over my shoulder at him. Andrew was watching me walk away. "I love you," he said with tear filled eyes and swallowed hard.

I nodded and with quivering lips, I added, "In every age," quoting a familiar fairytale. My words touched him and we were perfect in that moment, broken or not.

Abby had stepped out onto the veranda and took in the scene. Without saying anything, she led me back into the crowded ballroom.

Abby knew I wasn't okay. Worried, she began to ask, "Bethany..." but my grandfather had come up alongside of us.

"Abigail, if you don't mind, I'd like to steal my granddaughter for a dance," he said very much taking notice of my faltering demeanor.

"Of course Jonathan," Abby nodded and walked back to her husband. I was sure she would share her alarm with him.

"Shall we?" Gramps asked motioning towards the designated dance area where a group of people were already dancing; Liv and Bobby included. "It's a wonderful event," my grandfather said as we swayed. I had zoned out, my thoughts were elsewhere as time gave pain the freedom to reformulate itself. "Beths," he said getting my attention and I looked up at him.

"Sorry Gramps," I apologized.

"Don't be. It's hard to think with a broken heart," he said causing me to surrender any front I thought I needed to put up for his comfort. "Bethany, it is none of my business," he continued paternally, "and it's definitely not my area of expertise per se, but I believe the saying goes, 'It is better to love and lose than to never have loved at all,' or something to that effect." My eyes filled as I looked around the room. "Personally, I think it's a load of horse manure," my grandfather continued, "Obviously, the person who said that didn't know what real love is because when you experience it, you don't lose no matter the outcome."

"Yeah," I said emotionally exhausted.

"Oh, Beths…" my grandfather sighed. "In my book, no one will ever be worthy enough for you. However, your grandmother reminds me that I can't keep you frozen in my mind as a little girl. Now, I'm no fool and I know that you fell hard for Wicks, which is what you're supposed to do when you like someone – you go all in, give it all you have. If it doesn't work out, then it doesn't work out. You move on, you make it through; we're all here for you."

"Thanks Gramps," I said hearing the confidence in his voice and I found my own again.

"Of course," he smiled. "But, I will tell you, I know that Wicks still being head over heels for you is not making this easier." I looked up at my grandfather who never spoke about things like this to me. "But, it's also very clear that you are still very much head over heels for him as well."

"What do I do?"

"My dear, real love is worth fighting for," Gramps smiled with his eyes.

"May I?" Abby asked suddenly coming up next to my grandfather and me. I looked over to see that she was dancing with Andrew who, like me, was not expecting her request to cut in.

"It would be a pleasure," Gramps said letting go of my hand.

Andrew and I found ourselves surrounded by dancing couples. He very slowly, but naturally, placed his hand on my waist and put out the other for me to take, but I hesitated. I didn't want memories from the past exchanged at the touch of our hands. I wanted to see Andrew, make a new memory, and not relive an old one.

I picked up the train of my dress and made sure it covered my hand before placing it in his. The material acted as a buffer and prevented a connection from being made. Picking up the train of my gown was also one of the few unchallenged and socially acceptable gestures that had descended though the decades. Realizing what I had done, Andrew appreciatively nodded as he gracefully led us over the marble floor in the elegantly lit room.

What I wasn't expecting was the trance that Drew and I fell under as we stepped in rhythm with one another. He was even more attractive and poised in his protective nature. As he guided us with an ever-changing closeness, Andrew would pull me near then separate the space but with a swift move, we were back together. It was more passionate than a kiss or an embrace. He didn't look away and I couldn't. When he released me into a quick turn, I didn't second guess that he would be there for the next step.

Our eyes again locked on one another as the music came to an end. I let go of his hand and dropped the material to the floor. My eyes found his polished black shoes and my hand instinctively began to trace my collarbone. "Beths," he broke the silence between us.

"Drew," I smiled looking up at him with watering eyes and forced a smile. Before he could say another word, I stepped around him and walked towards the staircase that led up to the entranceway. I needed to escape. I needed an empty room... my father's office or the dining room, somewhere I could release everything I was desperately trying to hold in.

Passing people with a painted expression, I climbed the steps giving no sign of my true state to the guests or the photographers. When I reached the top of the staircase, my fingertips grazed the top of the old, wooden, round table underneath the chandelier as I looked to the left and then the right deciding which way to go. There were a few people talking in the doorway to the left, blocking the way to my father's office. I decided to go head towards the dining room – that would be my haven.

Opening the double doors, I found the silent room in perfect order. I walked over to the windows and could see a few of the valets standing together talking out front, trying to stay warm. Taking a deep, controlled breath, I turned and leaned against the table under the window, another handcrafted antique. My eyes welled and the tears crested over onto my cheeks then trailed down my face.

The doors to the room opened, and with it came a burst of noise from the party. My brother closed the doors behind him before walking over to me. "Hey," he said taking me and my crumbling façade into his open arms. I knew he would have watched Andrew and I dance together; my brother probably saw my escape up the stairs and followed behind me. Ryan's hug held me while I broke out into sobs as pieces of my heart shattered.

Chapter Thirteen
Change

'Hospital Fundraiser Success' and 'State Champs' jumped from the front page of the *Ellsworth Edition*. Gramps was reading the paper at the dining room table, occasionally taking a sip of his morning coffee. I was dragging my scrambled eggs from one corner of my plate to the other. After last night's breakdown, Ryan had made it his priority to insure that I didn't spend the day in bed. In fact, he woke me up at eight, we went for our run, and he told me to be back downstairs for breakfast after I showered. There was a note from him waiting for me on my dresser after I got back from the bathroom with specific instructions.

Beths,

Don't bother looking for your 'I'm hiding from the world/depression' Lumberyard hat – I took it. Do your hair and makeup. No sweatpants or sweatshirts allowed.

You have thirty minutes before I come and get you for breakfast.

No, I'm not kidding.

-Ryan

I was now looking across the dining room table at my brother who was eating his second helping of breakfast while reading a section of the newspaper my grandfather had shared with him. I smiled to myself remembering how Ryan had carried me over his shoulder and down the attic stairs when I exceeded the thirty minutes I was allotted.

"Claire, is there anything you need from the store?" my grandfather asked as he stood with his empty plate, making his way to the kitchen.

"Just the usual," Grams answered with a smile as she cut her sausage delicately with her knife.

"Beths and I can get it," Ryan volunteered us, looking up from the paper momentarily. "I have to stop by the Lumberyard… we'll get the groceries on the way back."

"That's sweet of you, dear," Grams grinned. As happy as she was that Ryan had moved out to start his life with his bride, I could tell that she missed having him around. My grandfather paused with his back against the kitchen door and gestured for me to follow him.

Once inside the kitchen, Gramps placed his plate in the sink and turned when the door closed behind me. Speaking softly he said, "Beths, last night before we left Charles asked that I bring you to the hospital this afternoon for a heart scan."

"Okay," I agreed.

"The problem is that Ryan isn't going to let you out of his sight any time soon," my grandfather said folding his arms. He was right. Noticing Gramps' unchanging glare I knew where he was going with this.

"I can't tell him," I shook my head. "He'd freak out if he knew about my heart condition."

"You're going to have to tell him at some point, Beths."

"But…" I started.

"Wouldn't you rather he heard the truth from you?"

"Yes," I said defeated.

Holding the door open for me, he added, "After you." Reluctantly, I walked back into the dining room.

"Um, Ry?" I said trying to get his attention as I sat back down across from him.

"Uh huh," he replied, flipping the newspaper over and scanning the small business section. I looked up at my grandfather who stood next to my grandmother's chair and nodded for me to continue.

"Before we go to the Lumberyard, you think we could stop by the hospital?"

"Yeah, sure," my brother said not fazed by my request. I paused, unsure how to continue.

"Dr. Landon is expecting you at one," my grandfather chimed in.

Ryan looked up at this. "For what?" he questioned.

"I have an appointment with Dr. Landon at the hospital… for a heart scan," I elaborated. Ryan tried to compute what he had just heard and blinked quickly while it sank in.

"A heart scan?" my grandmother asked surprised, looking up at her husband who comfortingly touched her shoulder.

"I'm perfectly healthy," I stated, looking directly into my brother's eyes.

"Perfectly healthy people don't have appointments for heart scans," he said in true Ryan fashion.

"Okay, maybe I'm not *perfectly* healthy but I'm fine. Dr. Landon has been monitoring my condition…"

"Now you have a *condition*?" Ryan panicked and shot a glance at my grandfather.

"Ryan," Gramps said evenly.

"You knew about this!" Ryan stood up. His seat made a noise as it slid back against the hardwood floor. Gramps nodded but looked down at my grandmother who had her hand over her chest and concern in her eyes.

"Bethany," Grams started, wanting to know more. Ryan too listened intently and sat back down.

"It's okay. *I'm* okay. In New York I was diagnosed with a heart defect that went undetected since birth. I've been on medication for the past two years and do the recommended cardio like I'm supposed to… our morning jogs," I explained to Ryan. "Dr. Landon has been looking after me since I moved to Ellsworth. He's the one that told Gramps about everything."

"Charles wants to see her today," Gramps said lightly not adding any unnecessary drama.

"At one?" Ryan swallowed.

"Yes," I confirmed.

"Okay," my brother said still staring at me from across the table.

"You could have told me sooner," he said when the two of us were alone in 'the tank'.

"Ryan," I said rolling my eyes.

"DO NOT roll your eyes at me young lady," he said paternally as the veins in his neck pulsated. "Does mom know about this?" he asked but I didn't need to answer. I just gave him the 'are you kidding me' face. "I figured," he said more to himself than to me, hitting the steering wheel with the palm of his hand.

"Before you blow a gasket…"

"BLOW A GASKET? BLOW A GASKET! Beths, you have a heart condition. I didn't go to med school but I'm thinking this is pretty serious." I shrugged and watched the trees pass by the passenger window. "What's wrong with you… I mean with *it*… I mean…" he took a deep breath and composed his thoughts. "What exactly is the heart condition?"

I smiled at his lack of grace but answered in all seriousness, "I have Ventricular Septal Defect."

"English Beths!" he demanded.

"Everyone's heart has chambers. I have a hole in…" I began and instantly regretted my selection of words the moment they came off my lips. Ryan's grip on the steering wheel tightened drastically. I amended my last comment immediately by adding, "A *small* hole."

"I swear to…" he began to say under his breath. "You know that you're making me gray before I'm thirty, right? I hope you know that," my brother said looking sideways at me to which I laughed.

"Where are you going?" I asked when he made a left at the stop sign.

"The hospital," Ryan answered like I was crazy for asking him.

"Ry, Gramps said one o'clock."

"I know, so we'll be early," he shrugged.

"Dude, it's not even noon. What happened to stopping at the Lumberyard?"

"We're going to the hospital," he said leaving no room for discussion.

First Gramps knew, then Ryan and Grams, and now Kate. Ryan told her the second we got to the nurses' station. "Beths," Kate looked at me with concern when she heard the news.

"I'm fine," I assured her.

"What tests have you had? Have they done a cardiac catheterization?" she said in nurse mode. Ryan, out of his element, listened to the questions Kate asked.

"Can we talk about this over coffee?" I asked and Kate grinned.

"Sure. Debbie, I'm going to take my break," Kate said to one of the nurses sitting behind the desk. As Ryan, Kate and I walked into the cafeteria I saw Charles standing at the coffee vendor, waiting for his order.

"Char…" I started but recovered, "Dr. Landon."

"Beths," he smiled. Seeing the look of concern on my brother and Kate's faces and taking into consideration that I was scheduled for a heart scan today, it was clear to Charles that I had shared the news with them. Sensitive to the issue, Charles shook Ryan's hand and smiled at Kate, instantly easing the situation.

"I know I'm early," I began then looked over at Ryan, inferring that he wasn't taking the news too well.

"I don't know the first thing about medicine," Ryan said nervously.

"Well, I wouldn't know how to run a Lumberyard," Charles nodded. Ryan appreciated the mutual respect the two had for their fields.

"I have a lot of questions," Ryan said frankly as he discretely dried his sweaty palms on his pant legs. Kate tenderly placed her hand on Ryan's back and gave me a look of reassurance.

"I would imagine so," Charles nodded as the server placed two tall cups of coffee in front of him. 'Two cups,' I thought to myself – Andrew was here. A cold sweat broke over me. "Why don't you come upstairs after you order your drinks? We can do your scan now, Beths, and then I'd be happy to answer any questions you have."

"Thank you," my brother nodded gratefully.

"Of course," Charles said slowly, bowing out of the conversation.

"Kate, can you get me an iced coffee?" I asked. "Decaf." She looked confused, but recovered when I made to follow Charles.

"Sure."

"What floor?" Ryan called out.

"Fifth," I answered, in pursuit of an unaware Charles who was a few strides in front of me.

"Hi," I said pressing the elevator call button for him so he didn't risk spilling any coffee.

"Hello," he smiled back at me as the doors opened. Luckily, no one else got on before the doors shut. "I'm glad you told your brother," he said with a look of relief.

"Yeah," I exhaled.

"How are you doing?" he asked. I looked up at him. I didn't know how much he knew about last night. After talking with him on the veranda and handing over the check for the prenatal unit, I hadn't seen Charles for the rest of the evening. I knew how my evening had unfolded, but I didn't know about his – or what he saw between Andrew and I. "You know," Charles smirked and looked down at the floor when I said nothing. "I will say that if you didn't already have my utmost respect for the way you handle yourself, Beths, last night was a testament to the trophy of grace that you are."

"Thank you," I smiled up at my old friend as the doors opened at the fifth floor.

My heart stopped when I saw the door at the end of the hallway. Through the frosted glass I could tell that the desk lamp was on, and I knew that Andrew was only yards away. "We're looking over the numbers from last night," Charles explained. "He doesn't know that you are my one o'clock appointment. I'll tell him that it was moved up," Charles offered.

"Oh," I nodded but in that moment something inside of me changed. It was a moment of clarity. No, I wasn't going to be the girl that rearranged her life when my path crossed with Drew's. We had tried that already – last night was a prime example – and it hadn't worked. "That's okay. Saying hello won't do any harm." Charles looked surprised but said nothing, and led the way.

When I opened the office door for Charles, Andrew looked up from what he was working on at the desk. "Hey," I said, watching as he stood, taking the coffee Charles was offering him and looked from his brother-in-law back to me. Charles' eyebrow rose in amusement as the moment delivered itself. He was proud of me, proud of my confidence, with or without Andrew.

"Bethany," Andrew greeted in surprise.

"Sorry to interrupt, but my brother is here with me and I was hoping Charles could answer a few questions he has about my heart."

"No, that's no problem," Drew replied, comforted to hear that I had told Ryan. Charles, excusing himself, walked back to the door and into the hallway.

"I never thanked you for the dance last night..." I said to Andrew. "It was..." I hesitated, not knowing which adjective would do justice in trying to explain that moment. What I did know was that it was an instant where he and I got to be as timeless as we truly were.

"Yes," he said agreeing that there were no words to describe it. We smiled at one another, both reminiscing about the dance. However, when I let myself think about the relationship that could have been, I started to anxiously trace my collarbone. Drew noticed my nervous habit and I stepped backwards, retreating to the door. In one quick motion, Drew had placed down his coffee and walked around the desk. "Beths," he called out and I turned around in the doorway.

"I, uh..." he hesitated before his eyes locked on mine. Off in the distance I heard the chime of the elevator and then Ryan and Kate talking a mile a minute. Andrew looked passed me and I turned to see the two of them walking down the hall. My brother's shoulders grew when he saw me standing next to Andrew. It was a tense moment, but it was quickly deflated by Kate, who showed Ryan the door to the room where Charles was turning on the monitors.

"I should go," I said, starting towards the hallway but in the small space, our hands grazed one another's unintentionally. The connection was made.

I heard the music being played by the stringed orchestra come to an end before the images settled in front of my eyes. Through Drew's sight, I watched as I let go of the material of my dress after gliding over the dance floor with him. He was enamored just as I had been and it was when I stepped around him and headed for the staircase that Drew's trance on me was broken. He followed behind me, he was going after me. His emotions were very high, his senses failing because to him there seemed to be no one else in the ballroom, but us. Blurs around him would not stop his trek after me. He had made it to the bottom of the staircase which I was halfway up, when Ryan's outstretched hand pushed against Drew's chest. "No. You don't get to follow her," my brother warned angrily. It was clear he had been watching what had transpired. "You blew it. And if you know what's good for you, you'll leave her alone." Charles joined the two men and had overheard what Ryan had said. With no need to diffuse the situation, Ryan gave one look back at Andrew before he turned and made his way up the stairs after me. Thankfully, the guests around them hadn't taken notice to what had just transpired.

"Drew," Charles said.

"I can't," Andrew began and looked sideways at his brother-in-law. Charles nodded. Drew and Charles walked up the

stairs. I could hear the swishing of laughter and conversation from the guests around them but Drew felt like he was in slow motion. He was depleted of all hope, broken, tired... The two men continued up to the second floor and didn't say a word until they reached the study.

Andrew gripped the mantle of the fireplace while his other hand loosened the tie around his neck. He looked down at the floor but couldn't see it clearly because tears of anger and grief were at their peak. "Drew," Charles said closing the door behind him and the noise from the Gala lessened. Andrew looked over at his friend and shook his head. "I can't. I'm not strong enough," Drew breathed out. A shallow sob came from his chest and didn't stop. He clenched both hands on the mantle and watched as two tears exploded when they hit the hardwood floor. More fell as the fire's light shone off his polished shoes.

I turned my eyes to Drew's as they refocused. Andrew looked away, clearly not wanting to have shared what he had with me. It had been an accident. Charles was calling my name from the hallway, unaware of the split second exchange. "Coming," I called back to Charles. Slowly, I walked away from Andrew not having time to process any of this.

Click. Click. Click. The sounds grew louder and faster together while my thoughts swirled with the noise. 'What was going on? How... What?' I thought to myself.

The machine slowed to a stop and the door popped open. I could see Charles pointing to the screen explaining the latest scan to my brother and Kate. "So, she's okay," I heard Ryan ask when I entered the room. I saw the same red numbers blink cautiously when Charles zoomed in on the image. There was no change.

I knew that Charles requested the heart scan today because he was concerned that last night's excitement and the emotional strain it caused might have affected me. Fortunately, the results were no different than usual. Charles was kind enough to answer each question and address every concern.

About twenty minutes later, Charles looked over at me and instructed, "Just keep taking the medication and continue the cardio. In a month or so if there is still no change, I would like for Bethany to be seen by an old friend of mine who is a specialist in the field. I would be curious to know what his opinion is as we move forward."

"Move forward? As in surgery?" Kate asked.

"Yes," Charles said. "But there's no need to be alarmed. We won't worry about that bridge until we know that it's a bridge we need to cross."

"This specialist…" Ryan began to question.

"Let's just say that if Abigail were in Bethany's shoes, I would want her to be seen by him," Charles said, confidently recommending the other physician. Ryan looked over at me and nodded. He was worried, but he was happy that Charles was in my corner.

We stopped at the Lumberyard and the grocery store. Ryan had calmed down by the time we got back to my grandparents. He was tired from the long week, and the events from last night and today. I, on the other hand, was completely wired. As I unloaded the groceries my mind went from daydreaming of the exchange Andrew had unintentionally shared with me, to fending off unfounded speculations.

Drew had come after me… he was fighting himself. Why? Learning something new about the past changed the way I looked at the present.

I had made a decision and had to act on it. I grabbed my keys off of the table and headed out the door when I bumped into Ryan who was on the porch talking to Gramps. "Where are you going," he asked as I bounced off of him.

"Picking up Liv from work," I lied. "We might catch a movie or something. Girl stuff."

"Alright, have fun."

"Thanks," I said running down the stairs and turning back. "Thanks for coming with me to the hospital, Ry," I added, unlocking my car door.

"Yeah, yeah," he nodded. "Just be ready for our run tomorrow morning."

"Of course," I smiled and got in the car.

—

I knew Liv had plans with Bobby after she got off of work but I was hoping to catch her before her shift ended. "You knew that Drew tried to follow me!" I blurted out as soon as I got to the counter. Looking up from a book she was reading, her eyes grew bigger. "LIV!" I said forcefully putting my keys down and placing my hands on my hips.

"Maybe," she defended as she shut the book and looked up at the clock.

"Bobby does not have a record for being on time so I have about five minutes before you're saved by the bell," I said referring to the tiny ding that occurred every time the door opened.

"Fine," she said taking off her nametag and slamming it on the counter. We didn't need a hand connection to share a memory – Liv and I just understood one another. "I *might* have seen you two dancing... I *might* have been sitting next to Ryan when it was happening... I *might* have enjoyed watching him stop Andrew at the stairs and maybe – JUST MAYBE, I didn't tell you because it wasn't going to help you."

"Help me?"

"Beths, you have a history with this guy. LIKE A REAL HISTORY. It goes back way farther than any ex's should. AND the last time you two went through something like this, YOU ended up dead!" she let it all out and then took a breath. "I didn't tell you because..."

"You were trying to protect me," I finished.

"Yes," she tilted her head.

"Well... thanks..." I shrugged sheepishly.

"You're welcome. Are we done fighting now?" she asked distressed and I nodded. She came around the counter and we hugged. "Did Kate tell you that Ryan stopped Andrew?" she inquired but I didn't answer. Leaning out of the hug, her eyes narrowed, "Who told you?" I looked down at the floor afraid to tell her the truth. "ANDREW? WHAT! Are you kidding me? When?" Liv's voice got higher and higher with every question but the bell over the front door rang and Bobby walked in. Ironically enough, I was saved by the bell.

"Ryan and Kate know about my heart. I went for a heart scan. I ran into Andrew," I summarized quickly before Bobby could hear.

"But," Olivia said flustered, as Bobby got closer.

"Cover for me? Ryan thinks you and I are hanging out." Liv looked at Bobby, then at me. "Please!" I begged.

"Okay," she forfeited.

"Thanks," I smiled and walked by Bobby who was on his way to Liv. "Hey Bobby," I said in passing.

"Hi Bethany," he said.

"Where are you going?" Liv called out as Bobby reached the counter.

"I don't know. Somewhere quiet," I said as I looked back before closing the door behind me.

—

My car roared to life and I broke the speed limit on a road or two. I had slowed at the entrance to the Estate but I couldn't bring myself to turn in. Instead, I continued down the road and drove up the climbing, winding hill towards another place with less strings; a place where I could think better – alone.

The old barn where Andrew and I had our second first date sat up on the hill, unnoticed to everyone, overlooking the town of Ellsworth. It was like God's window and I found refuge here.

Closing the driver's door, I put my keys in my sweater pocket and walked to the front of my car. The blue sky above me was fighting with the yellows which in time fought with the oranges at the horizon. It was an untouchable sunset and after it was gone, the shades of dark blues and shades of black could not rival with the brightness of the stars as they took their place.

I was lying on the hood of my car, looking up at the night sky not caring that it was getting colder. My eyes blinked slowly as I thought about the accidental exchange Andrew had shared with me – the emotions were tied so closely to it, yet, I could not fully understand them.

With unfailing accuracy I could recall his eyes and how they pierced into mine. My eyes opened and closed, growing heavier with each passing minute. They touched one last time before I drifted away.

I heard gravel being kicked up and the roar of an engine. Then a car door opened and the archangel called out my name in fear, "Bethany!" The car door closed and I heard my name again. I opened my eyes and turned to see the headlights that belonged to

Drew's Camaro blaring at me. He had thrown his car into 'Park' behind mine and was jogging towards me. Seeing that I was okay, relief washed over his face as he slowed a few feet away. I slid off the hood and onto my feet.

Our eyes locked on one another but we didn't speak. It was as though we could not afford ourselves to use the energy we desperately needed in order to keep up our facades. Being the gentleman that he was, he conceded. "Olivia is looking for you. She hasn't heard from you, and she's worried."

Realizing I had fallen asleep and that time had escaped me, I looked down at my phone and saw that I was dangling close to missing curfew. I also saw the calls and messages from Liv that I had missed while I slept. I hadn't told anyone were I was going… only Liv knew I wanted to escape to somewhere quiet… that I had gone rogue. Yet, here Andrew stood in front of me. "Did she call you?"

"No, she called the Estate and spoke with Charles. I was standing next to him when he answered."

"You came looking for me?" I asked.

"I tried the football field first," he admitted. "I didn't think you'd come *here*," Drew said looking over at our shadows casted on the barn doors from his headlights. Drew clenched his jaw before he looked back at me. "I'm glad you're okay."

"Thanks," I said trying to decode his behavior.

"I'll follow you back to your grandparents," he said trying to detach himself from the conversation.

"You don't have to," I replied, as he turned to leave. Silence filled the space and instead of another piece of my heart breaking, something inside me clicked. For the calculated man I knew Drew was, nothing was adding up.

Andrew had dropped everything to come back to Ellsworth – *for me*. He left his life in Colorado and had to face going back to the town he thought he'd never have to return to – *for me*. Drew rearranged his life and faced personal demons to be near me, to be with me. He had waited a century – *for me*. And here I stood as he walked away from me.

I knew I was missing a vital piece of information because none of this was making any sense. This was a chance to fill in the blanks. I yelled after him, "I know you're not telling me something. And I know that you love me – you said it last night and you're saying it right now by being here."

Andrew stopped midstride and let out a breath of forced air before turning back towards me. He averted his eyes away from mine because they were filled with tears that he did not want me to see. I did see one or two hit the dirt and darken where they hit the ground. When he looked back up at me, he ran his forefinger under his nose, nodded slightly and unable to have this conversation, he turned back towards his car again.

"Andrew," I called after him but he kept walking away even though I knew he had heard me. "Drew!" I yelled, causing him to stop, hearing the pathetic longing in my voice.

I didn't want him to go. I wanted him to stay. I wanted to know why he came looking for me and what the emotions he felt in the exchange meant. Andrew stood with his back to me but slowly turned around.

His handsome face was torn with anger. "I DON'T WANT YOU!" he hollered as he charged towards me. Startled, I stepped back a few paces. His words echoed through my body. "I HATE loving you," Drew swallowed, still closing the space between us.

In between the barn and my car we stood inches from one another and the tears that fell from my eyes were a type of tear that I had never cried before. The look of complete frustration on his face burdened me. I didn't want him to hurt. I especially didn't want to be the cause of it. "Waiting all this time wasn't good enough for you?" he asked consumed. I tried for words but found none; his distilled anguish paralyzed me.

"I'm sorry…" I fumbled. My eyes dropped from his. Suddenly, he bent over in pain. "Andrew," I said worried. Then, he was hit with another stab causing him to lean forward with his hands on his thighs. His body faltered where he stood. Something was terribly wrong and he was fighting against it. A stronger onset of pain took Andrew's knees from him causing them to hit the earth. Drew's muscles contracted and his hands curled into the ground below him as agony overpowered him. "Drew!" I yelled kneeling next to the falling archangel while the bonds of time began to loosen their grip.

"Take it," Drew exhaled.

—

"CHARLES!" I cried, getting out of Drew's Camaro after throwing it into 'Park' outside of the Estate. "CHARLES!" I screamed again as the front door opened.

Charles, taking in the scene, hurried down the steps to the ailing Andrew fighting against an invisible torturer in the passenger seat. He pulled his brother-in-law out of the car, put his arm around Drew and leveraged him with the other, helping him into the house.

"What?" Abby gasped as she walked into the entranceway having heard the commotion.

"Beths, my bag – it's in the office." Charles ordered. I ran passed Abigail and found Charles' medical bag on the chair near my father's old desk.

Charles and Drew were three quarters of the way up the stairs to the second floor when I rejoined them. Andrew was sweating profusely, his breathing was forced and his hand clutched around the banister.

Abby went ahead, opening the door to Drew's room and pulling down the sheets on his bed. Charles helped Andrew get his legs over the side then checked his vitals.

Terrified, Abby stood feet away watching as her husband worked. Andrew grimaced and pushed through whatever was attacking him. I winced as Drew seemed to be slip further and further away – his stream of consciousness flickering.

Charles wrapped his stethoscope around his neck, stepped back and ran his hands anxiously through his hair. He was frustrated; he was unable to determine what and where the source of the pain was coming from.

"Charles…" I started to say, wanting to help in any way I could.

"What happened? In the moments before his symptoms started, what happened?" Charles asked desperately. "Was it sudden? Did he give any inclination?" Charles questioned. I put out my hand offering him the ability to see the scene that preceded Drew's collapse, hoping that it held an explanation.

Charles saw how Andrew had found me at the barn. He watched as Drew went from concerned to relieved, then to distant and cold, before becoming enraged. With Andrew's composure faltering, and his body following behind, Drew fell to his knees. The haunting words, 'Take it,' lingered as I broke the connection.

Charles slid into a chair close by and his eyes narrowed as he stared at Andrew, deep in thought. "Charles, what's wrong with him? Do something!" Abby begged.

Charles looked up and said unarguably, "There is nothing I can do, Abigail. This… *isn't* medical." Abby knelt down at her brother's bedside and placed her hand on his forearm as tears filled her eyes. Charles comforted his distressed wife, moving her to the chair he had been sitting in. Drew looked sick – weak. His coloring was gone, his eyes were closed, his muscles were tense, and his breathing was irregular. I had never seen him this way. Sweat ran down his forehead and his teeth were clenched tightly as another wave of agony washed over him.

"Charles, please, do something…" I said covering my mouth.

"Come with me," Charles ordered. Hesitant to follow, Charles took me by the arm. "Trust me Beths," he said guiding me with his other hand on my back, leading me to the hallway. He opened the door diagonal to Drew's, the door at the end of the North Corridor, my old chambers. Charles turned the light on and it was like walking into a memory. He waited as I rediscovered it in real time.

Andrew called out in pain and it echoed in the hall, making me cringe where I stood. I swallowed and felt my cold hands, overcome by nerves, trace my collarbone. This room, these walls, Drew and I… I was overwhelmed and began to panic. However, Charles saw this and locked eyes with me. Even in the midst of a storm, he was in complete control of himself and I took comfort in that. He uncrossed his arms and walked over to where I was. Placing his hands on my shoulders, he spoke, "Drew will be fine, Beths."

"How do you know," I challenged the certainty in which he spoke.

"He's not dying," Charles affirmed solemnly, knowing where my concerns lied. Then he turned back around and walked to the door, closing it. Charles leaned his shoulder against the armoire and slid his hands into his pockets. "At least not tonight," he said looking down at the old, hardwood floor with a look of astonishment on his face. The room was silent but my thoughts were loud, 'At least not tonight,' I repeated. 'What?' Unhurried, my old friend's eyes came back to me. "Beths, Drew is... *changing.*"

"Changing?" I challenged quickly.

"Like Abigail, age has found him. Time has found him." Charles pushed off the steady armoire and stood straight again. "This pain that Drew is experiencing, I believe is his confirmation, his catalyst. Very much like how Abigail's inability to exchange memories was confirmation of the change's end. I believe it's safe to say that Andrew will no longer have the ability as well." I swallowed hard and blinked slowly, stepping backwards and found the vanity stool with my fingertips. I sat down, still facing Charles, who gave me a moment to take this in. Charles then came around the bed and sat on the edge of it, across from me. "Are you okay?" he asked placing his hand on my knee. I looked up and shook my head. "It's alright Beths. It's all over," he whispered.

"What?" I asked confused by what he said. There were footsteps outside the door and then it opened.

"His breathing is getting worse," Abigail informed Charles who got up to attend to Drew.

This left Abigail and I in the room alone. I saw the fear in her eyes, so I stood up, walked over to her and gave her a hug. She hugged me back with a matched intensity. "What did you show Charles before in the exchange? What happened right before

Drew…" she began to question as we both sat on the bench at the foot of the bed.

"I was at the barn where Drew and I had our second first date. He pulled up behind my car. I must have fallen asleep and…"

"He found you," Abigail finished.

"Yes. He looked really worried before he saw that I was fine. When it was obvious that I was okay, he just started acting distant again. I yelled at him and he yelled at me." Looking at the floor, I tried to think of a way to explain to her in words the emotions that had been ignited between him and I. "It was like the day on the grounds," I said drawing the parallel, "The anger, the hurt, and then the fall out." Abigail nodded and looked down at her hands in her lap. "Charles thinks that he's changing, Abby," I told her but she wasn't surprised.

"I think he's right," she grinned.

"What?" I asked perplexed.

"I think he's right," she repeated, staring straight at me. Time had given her patience, a quality that she had not had when we first met.

I was not emotionally or mentally stable to have this conversation. Bidding for time, I looked at the unlit fireplace, stood up, walked over to it, knelt down, ran a match along the stone before touching it to the waiting, cold logs. When I returned to the cushioned bench, I felt Abby watching me but I didn't look over at her.

"Beths…" Abigail began, reaching out her hand for me to take. She could see the disorder in my eyes. As our hands touched there was no memory exchange; it was purely a gesture of comfort. "When Charles first took the job with your father… about a century ago," she smirked, "we were finally in a place financially where we could start a family, and we were very excited." Abigail's tone changed as she continued, "Unfortunately, Charles and I couldn't seem to get pregnant. We tried for months and started to believe that it was never going to happen for us. That was right before you came to Ellsworth. Watching Jonathan with you, the relationship you two had… I wanted that so badly for Charles. You and your father gave Charles and I hope again."

Abigail slowly let go of my hand and instinctively retreated hers to her lap, where her other hand was. Whether Abby realized it or not, her back straightened, her chin rose and her feet crossed beneath her, resting to the side. She sat poised like the polished woman she had been raised to be. Time had no affect on her good manners, nor did they go out of style. I smiled at her proper reflexes but was reminded of the weight of the conversation when she carried on.

"Even with that renewed hope, Charles and I still couldn't conceive and I felt broken; like a failure. I had this wonderful, wonderful husband who I knew would make a great father and I couldn't *give* him a child. It absolutely devastated me," she confessed as tears began to well up in her eyes. I touched her forearm as she smiled through the tears. Then she took a deep breath and said, "After your father passed away and then you... when we realized that we were 'frozen', any chance that Charles and I thought we might have with having our own child was gone. Pregnancy is all about change and our bodies wouldn't allow it. So, barren or not prior to the agelessness, now we most definitely weren't going to be able to have a baby."

Abby was quiet for a moment, reliving the years of uncertainty. I saw the raw sadness in her eyes. I never knew this about them and it killed me to hear their struggle. These were two people who I knew would make fantastic parents and they couldn't for so long.

"Charles is a wonderful man and I am blessed to be his wife," she said as tears slid down her face. "I know that when we exchanged our vows neither of us expected to celebrate the number of anniversaries we have," she laughed and blotted her cheeks with the back of her hand. "We both wanted a big family... but in good and bad times he has led me. He's been my stronghold and has loved me through it all." Abby looked across at the fire as it crackled. "And now, somehow, here we are... and I'm pregnant," she shook her head, beaming as she touched her stomach. Abigail took a deep breath and added, "Every child that Charles and I have taken in over the years – whether it was for a month or a few short years... we treated each of them like they were our own." She looked sideways at me and added bewildered, "The funny thing is... because we couldn't have children of our own, we actually ended up having more children than we could've ever dreamed of."

With this, she smiled and all traces of her sadness were gone. I was taken by what she had said, the profoundness of her journey – how it had come full circle. I couldn't imagine how many young souls they had guarded in their time. Their curse had become a blessing for so many others.

"Have you thought of any names?" I asked wanting to lead her out of the past.

"We haven't talked about it yet, but if it's a boy, I would think Charles would want to name him after his father, William, or Will. If it's a girl, I would love to name her Charlotte after Charles."

"Beautiful," I smiled.

"Not as charming as Luke or Haverly," she said without thinking. I felt the stab of a memory I had long forgotten come to the forefront of my mind.

Years ago, Drew and I were walking from the foot of the cobblestone path back to the Estate. We were under the oak alley as the morning light casted shadows of thousands of leaves dancing in the wind. Being young and in love, he and I stayed up into the early morning hours, exploring each other's hearts... He would sit in the doorway of his chambers and I would sit in the space of mine, and when we weren't talking about the present, we would fall prey to daydreaming of our future. Our conversation continued after breakfast today, before he had to depart. "I want twelve children," he joked wearing his riding attire, boots included. His shirt was pushed up over his forearms, his hair was still damp and his eyes were as blue as ever. He was missing his overcoat because it was over my shoulders. It was a chilly morning and he, of course offered, not accepting a refusal.

"Twelve?" I laughed.

"No," he grinned. "Four or five… or six," he said kicking a small stone under his foot. He then turned his head and flashed me his most charming smile. "How many do you want to have?"

"Four," I answered matter-of-factly… too, matter-of-factly. I had given it thought and it was now evident.

"And do you have names in mind?" he inquired, pleasantly surprised and very much curious.

"Do you?" I said throwing the question back at him.

"Perhaps," Drew smirked. Clearly, he had thought about it too. Not only did this make me feel better, but it also took my breath away.

"Will you tell me then?" I blushed.

Andrew ran his tongue over his lower lip before divulging, "Luke, if there is a boy."

"Luke," I repeated as I felt a smile melt across my face at hearing him speak the name. "Luke…?"

"Luke Fenton," he said choosing his deceased mother's maiden name for his future son's middle name. "Do you like it?" he asked somewhat timidly.

"Yes," I replied, looking down at my skirt which I held above the ground so it wouldn't get dirty so early into the day. It

was a burnt rose color and complimented the near permanent blush on my cheeks. "And if there is a girl?"

"I believe it is your turn to answer," he countered, transfixed by the topic.

I knew the name I would say because I pictured her in my mind having his eyes... "Haverly Elizabeth," I said softly. Drew stopped walking, so I stopped as well. "Do you not like it?" I nervously asked but the smile on his lips assured me that he did.

"Haverly Elizabeth," Drew repeated and stared back at me. "I adore it," he nodded. "As long as she takes after you more than me," he added with a grin and put his hands on either side of the opened overcoat that hung over my shoulders, stepping closer. "I have never," Andrew said with a flicker in his eyes, "in my life, felt this way before."

"Neither have I," I agreed. With his thumb, he tilted my chin up and then his hand touched my neck, bringing me into his kiss. It was soft, slow... when he pulled away, the wind would kiss our lips but then ours were back together again. I felt more complete than I thought possible in that moment. It was the sound of horses galloping that made us break away. Drew protectively pulled me closer to his side, standing in between me and the approaching guests.

"Good day," a few of the gentlemen said, tipping their hats as they passed, heading toward the house. Amidst the dust that was kicked up, I saw the front door of the Estate open about twenty yards away. My father stepped out also dressed in his riding gear, *alongside a few servants who were laughing with him before welcoming the men. Charles was behind them and Abigail handed her husband his gloves. I watched as the guests dismounted their horses and first shook my father's hand, then Charles'. As Andrew and I joined them, they greeted Drew as well.*

"Miss Taylor," they said bowing slightly, and I curtseyed once for all of them.

"We'll return later on this afternoon," my father said, coming over to me and kissing my cheek. "Hold down the fort?"

"Yes sir," I smiled back at him and our green eyes reflected perfectly in one another's before my father slipped his foot into the harness and mounted his horse.

Looking back over his shoulder, my father waited for Andrew to get on his horse. Drew and I shared a smile before I walked over to Abby who was standing by the formidable front door. Realizing I was still wearing Drew's overcoat, I slipped it off and handed it to one of the servants to give back to Andrew. When Drew put it on, I smiled to myself. I had slipped a letter I had written to him in the inside pocket of the overcoat and could not wait for his correspondence. It had become something we did regularly, but however frequent, they were always captivating.

I didn't know it then, but he would hold onto that letter for more than a hundred years...

As I let go of the memory I felt a tear slide down my face. "I'm sorry," Abby apologized, realizing how she had rekindled the past. Trying to recover but only making matters worse, she added, "Luke and Haverly are beautiful names."

Hearing them aloud again only brought more anguish and tears to my eyes. I held off so many memories that came flooding back in response to this one. In my mind, it was like coming across a drawer that had been locked but was now wide opened. Instead of letting myself get lost in the past, I let myself get lost in the present.

"Beths," Abigail tried consoling me, but I stood up and turned away. As I brushed the tears from my eyes, I saw that I was standing across from the vanity mirror. Seeing my reflection, I walked closer to it, placed my hands down and reexamined the old piece of furniture. My hairbrush, heavy in its metal setting, sat untouched next to unspooled ribbon and other trinkets that brought back more memories. Seeing my old things I felt, for the first time, like the ghost I was in this place.

Abigail stood and her reflection was over my shoulder. "Beths, what I was trying to tell you... before I got sidetracked," she said as I slowly circled back to her. "I found out only a few hours ago, so please don't think I've been keeping this from you," she prefaced.

"What is it?" I asked.

"Bethany, there is nothing that could separate you and Drew – not even him."

"Abby, what are you talking about?" I asked exhausted in every way.

"I can't tell you how many arguments him and I have had since I heard he broke things off with you. But as you know, Drew shut down any inquiry, refusing to discuss it. Charles told me that even if I couldn't understand why my brother did what he did, that I should trust him because he was a grown man who knew what he was doing. Well, that didn't sit well with me and to make matters more frustrating, I couldn't exchange memories with either of them because I had changed. To think of all the years I had the ability and now when I needed it, it was gone…" she said annoyed, but refocused her attention in order to stay on point.

"Charles honestly didn't know the scope of Drew's plans at first, but I think he started to figure things out the night they won the division playoff game… the day before you dropped off Drew's letterman jacket." Abby motioned for me to join her again on the bench and I did as she suggested. "I was in bed when they got home from the game. It was late. I heard Charles and Drew exchanging words with one another downstairs. They were still going at it when they reached the study where Drew's been sleeping since the breakup. I think it's because he couldn't stomach walking passed your room but, regardless, I saw both of their feet pass in the light from under the door. Then I heard the study door close and their words escalated. It was muffled so I got out of bed and by the time I reached the hallway, I could hear glass breaking and banging noises. When I opened the door, the two of them were throwing punches at one another and the room was in complete disarray. To see them… fighting!" Abby said outraged.

"They stopped when they saw me; they tried to compose themselves, tucking in their shirts, taking inventory of their recklessness... They both tried to formulate some sort of apology. Cole and Gracie had woken up from the noise and had come out of their bedrooms. I handed Gracie to Andrew and Cole to Charles, leaving them responsible to see that the children were put back to bed while I attempted to put the room back in order. Drew ended up sleeping in Gracie's room and Charles in Cole's to avoid my wrath. In the midst of sweeping up glass and moving furniture back to where it belonged, I tried to figure out what would have caused this. Charles must have discovered the true motive behind Drew's behavior and when he challenged him, they took their frustrations out on each other."

"The next morning I went downstairs to make breakfast only to find that Charles and Drew – who were still not talking to one another – had already prepared it. They were sitting at the dining room table, reading their respective sections of the newspaper when I overheard Gracie ask them why they had been fighting. Cole was quick to ask how long they were going to be punished for." Both Abby and I laughed. "Charles and Drew looked at one another but said nothing. They were still at odds. When I walked into the room, they both stood up and could tell that I knew something was up. However, in my own tactics, I didn't ask like they thought I would. Time would tell and tensions need to die down."

"In the next few days, they eventually began to speak to one another. It was either about football or the hospital; both business related and necessary to discuss. Then at the Gala, when Charles and Andrew shook hands, Charles was able to see that Drew had gone to Coverly the night he was missing." Abigail stopped herself knowing that she was now jumping around, making it difficult for me to follow. She started again, "Andrew came looking for you earlier because Olivia called. She said she was worried because she hadn't heard from you and was the only one who knew you were by yourself. Since it was getting late and your brother and grandparents would be expecting you home soon, she thought perhaps, you had come to the Estate."

"Charles had answered the phone and Andrew was in the office with him. Before Charles had even hung up the phone, Drew was out the door. Charles was not too far behind him but when I saw Drew fly out of here, I stopped Charles. I had enough of being in the dark and I told him that he needed to tell me what was going on. He told me everything."

"Told you what?" I asked confused.

Abby took a deep breath, "Over the years, the three of us have had our theories as to why we stopped aging. We knew for certain that the change didn't happen instantly, and that it happened in some sort of order. We've had plenty of time to question the past. There have been seasons in our lives when we became frustrated with our situation. There have been seasons when we feel forgotten and depressed. No one is meant to be here for as long as we have." There was an unnerving ache in her voice which brought me to a new level of awareness in regards to the challenges they had faced.

"Our theories were just theories – we've had nothing to hold them against. It wasn't until a few weeks ago, when I found out that I was pregnant, that we were finally given some validation."

"Charles, Andrew and I have all agreed that the moment on the grounds when you passed was the starting point." Methodically, Abby explained, "I was the last of us to see, but the first person to believe that you were *gone*. I knew the second I saw you in Drew's arms that you had passed. That was my trigger. And the moment I saw you in my physics class, I reacted the same way – I believed it was you immediately, even before interrogating you. The moment I saw you was my trigger, and the start of the undoing. Finding out I was pregnant, that my body had changed, was further proof. The loss of the hand exchange was affirmation that I was no longer 'connected' to Charles or Andrew."

"I had thought for the longest time that Andrew had been the one that changed first. It made sense because he lost you. But while my trigger was *my* sight, Drew's was devastation and heartbreak, and that isn't an instant kind of pain. It worsens with time; memories form and if given the power, they haunt you."

"Andrew, being the exceptionally bright and rational man that he is, put these things together. He knew that sight and believing was my trigger, and that heartbreak was his." Abigail paused and looked me straight in the eyes, "Drew also believed that in order for Charles to get a chance at changing… a try at growing old with his growing family, Drew needed to change – it was part of the order of things. Andrew believed that Charles' trigger was linked to the helplessness he felt in not being able to save you and, in turn, not being able to prevent the anguish Drew and myself endured after we lost you."

"With the added pressure of the newest Landon entering the world in a few months, it put a time crunch on the state of things. Not only was there a sense of urgency but, at the end of the day, Drew was still faced with the reality that his trigger was losing you. There was no way around that. He had finally gotten you back, and now his only chance at a future with you couldn't truly start if he couldn't age. It was a double-edged sword." Abby stood up and walked to the fireplace where the fire raged inside. My eyes followed her across the room.

"Charles said that Ryan's wedding was the tipping point for Drew. At the time, Charles didn't understand why. However, when Drew watched you walk down the aisle, then saw Ryan and Kate exchange their vows… he wanted that for the two of you. It only escalated when he looked over and saw Charles and I in the pew next to him; his brother-in-law was ageless as my stomach grew bigger – that's when Andrew knew he couldn't prolong what he feared he'd have to do. Toward the end of the wedding reception…" she began but I interrupted her.

"He acted strange," I said recalling how I had stolen a hand connection while we danced. Andrew had cut the exchange short but it was long enough for me to see Charles ask Drew to 'think about it'. I could feel the strong emotion that had resonated through Andrew but now, I knew their true meaning and could identify the drive behind them. After he realized what I had done, Andrew had excused himself and went into the Church. The next day, Drew broke things off with me. The timeline, for the first time, made sense. "But why not tell me? Why didn't he…" I began to ask and answered my own question. He couldn't tell me. He couldn't warn me because if his trigger was true heartbreak, I couldn't know. If I did it wouldn't be real.

"He loves you." Abby said plainly. "And his love for you is not just the affectionate type. It has no limits. He did this for you… for the both of you. For Charles, for me, and the baby," Abby explained. I closed my eyes and felt my fingertips reach my collarbone.

"This theory," I began to question, "does it mean Drew started to change when he broke things off at school?"

"I think Drew thought that it would be enough. But that's where he was wrong. Charles kept it to himself that he didn't believe that heartbreak was Drew's trigger. And in the days and weeks that followed, things only got worse for Drew. Of course, he was frustrated that he hadn't changed, but the reality that he just let go of the love of his life, that he had caused you pain – that's what wore on him. He couldn't come to you with the truth because there was a real possibility that he would never change if he did. Charles also couldn't say anything because he didn't want to risk that chance either."

"When Drew asked you for his letterman jacket back, that was out of desperation. He was hoping that it would trigger whatever it was to break but when it didn't work, he became more disgusted with himself."

"Charles was with Drew the first time he suffered the loss of you. When Drew showed the same signs of torment after the breakup, Charles tried to help. The night they fought, Drew's guard had been down. After a few inescapable questions, Charles quickly discovered that Andrew was far worse than he could have ever anticipated. Drew nearly lost his mind last time and Charles saw echoes of it in Drew's silence."

"They're both struggling," Abby said speaking on her own behalf. "They're wrestling an invisible, shapeless enemy – time. The complexity of everything – Andrew's tie to you, the reasons behind his actions, his relationship with Charles, his connection to me, this house... and then there's Charles, putting it all together, trying to be there for his best friend, to be strong for me who had no clue what was going on while also being there for you, but not being able to tell you. AND, on top of all of that, he was relying on Andrew to change but didn't want to add pressure that he knew Drew was already placed on himself." Abby took in a much need breath.

"Drew thought everything through, or at least he thought he did. He pushed you away, secretly hoping that you wouldn't give up on him, or move on. When he changed, he could explain himself to you and beg for forgiveness. After all, this *is* the second time he has broken your heart," she said keeping count.

"Abby!" I said surprised

"Two times," she reminded me by holding up two of her fingers. "You do realize that he even went as far as to tell people that *you* broke up with *him*."

I shrugged my shoulders. Out of everything she had just told me, that seemed to be the least strange thing to think about. Abigail rolled her eyes and explained, "If it were 1888 and a man broke things off with a woman, it would ruin her reputation. To avoid dishonor, he would say that she broke things off." Abby stated this to remind me of the ways we had once lived. My eyes widened thinking of how the locker room rumors that I had broken up with Drew had spread like wildfire. My eyes blinked quickly as the dots connected. Drew had thought of everything for this to work in my favor, regardless of his outcome. I was overwhelmed.

"Beths," she said taking my hands in hers and looked down. In her best friend way, she continued, "Last night after you left the Gala, I went looking for the two of them. I found Charles and Drew in the study. I didn't want to interrupt, so I stayed in the hallway. I heard Andrew tell Charles that he didn't know how much longer he could do this. You could hear how the burden of his sacrifice was wearing on his soul. It was heart wrenching." Abby swallowed.

Before I could ask her why she was telling me this, she looked up at me with a grin that I wasn't expecting. "Drew said that he wouldn't stop fighting because the love of his life was worth every try."

My heart skipped, the butterflies were back and I smiled before I cried into my hands. Andrew had been strategically and willingly acting for our benefit. He had never stopped loving me; rather, he had been fueled by it in every choice that he made whether it was easy or not. As my crying turned into sobbing, Abby hugged me and I hid my face in her shoulder. "It's okay," she whispered, rocking us slightly back and forth.

There was a soft knock on the door and we looked up to see Charles holding a sleepy-eyed Gracie. Charles, seeing me this way, was immediately concerned and handed Gracie to his wife. Abby excused herself, walking down the hall to put the little one back in bed. Charles brought me into his chest and hugged me tightly as my hysterics began. My old friend held me patiently, waiting until the sobs subsided.

"It's going to be okay, Beths," Charles promised.

"Can I see him?" I asked, drying my face with the handkerchief he offered me. My room felt like the waiting room at a hospital. I just wanted to see Andrew.

"Yes, of course," Charles said stepping aside and letting me lead the way. I walked to his bedside in the poorly lit room. Andrew was experiencing sporadic dives of pain. The torment had not lessened – he was adapting; locked in, waiting it out... fighting.

"I'm going to check on Abby," Charles said stepping out. I heard the doorknob click close and the sound of Charles' footsteps softened until they were gone.

Looking down at Drew, I traced over his face with my eyes wondering how this man could continue to amaze me after all this time. He had risked it all for the people he loved. Knowing everything that I now knew, it was difficult for me to keep it together. In the stillness of the room, I watched as his hand which rested on his chest, rose and fell with every labored breath he took. Believing that he was not frozen any longer, I wanted to hold his hand and for the first time since 1888, I could without a memory exchange. The simplicity of just holding his hand was a miracle in its own right. The gesture, taken for granted, was profound; one soul choosing to hold onto another.

I knelt down and reached my left hand out, sliding my fingers into his. Nothing happened; I relaxed. Why it had happened so quickly for him compared to Abby was a question I would save for a later time. Then, without warning, his fingers closed over mine. I covered my mouth with my other hand and tears filled my eyes. Drew knew I was here with him and even though there was no exchange, I was still flooded with emotions – my emotions. I wanted to tell him that I knew. I wanted to tell him that I loved him. I wanted him to tell me everything. However, a part of me wanted to yell at him. Yet, another part of me wanted him to look me in the eyes, grab either side of my face, kiss me and never stop. I didn't want him to be in pain anymore. I wanted… I wanted...

I stopped myself. Seeing him lying in bed, weak and struggling, I wanted to hold him as much as I wanted him to hold me. I slid in bed next to him and curled into his side, our hands still intertwined. I was there with him, *for him*, for now.

I lingered between sleep and being awake when Andrew finally stirred. He took a deep breath and then I felt his head turn and his lips kissed my forehead. His fingers pushed further into mine and with what little strength he had, he pulled me closer next to him. By the time I looked up to see his face, he was sleeping again, exhausted from what the night had brought. But the episodes of pain were over.

Relieved, I looked up at the ceiling and noticed rays of light peaking through the window drapes. Getting out of bed, I kissed Drew on the cheek then quietly left his room. Tiptoeing down the hallway and the stairs, I met Charles in the entranceway. He had walked out of the dining room and was holding a cup of coffee to his lips. We stared at one another for a moment and with one long look had a full conversation without a single word. I could tell he knew Abby had shared some of what she had learned yesterday with me, but I could also gauge that there was more that I did not know. Perhaps, even more than what Abby knew. Charles picked up the keys to Andrew's Camaro and handed them to me. We both smirked at one another. There was time and place for everything, we all had learned that. Right now was not the time to sort things out. Now was the time to accept the things we could and find the courage for the things we couldn't.

I turned and opened the front door to see that Drew's car was parked where I had left it. My Corvette was still up at the barn but that was at the bottom of my list of concerns. Charles stepped out on the landing and taking a sip of his coffee, watched as I got into the Camaro and started the engine. I pulled away from the Estate underneath the oak alley in the early morning light.

As the Estate got smaller and smaller in the rearview, I heard myself whispering an unscripted prayer for the people behind me. Through blurry eyes, I pulled off the cobblestone path and onto the main road, losing sight of the Estate entirely. The morning glow came through the windshield and hit me with its silent force. I pushed the accelerator and felt the power behind it carry me down the open road.

Chapter Fourteen
Aftermath

I pulled into my grandparents' driveway and could see a sleepy Ryan getting up from the couch through the front window. He and my grandfather walked onto the porch ready to yell at me for 'disappearing' and completely disregarding curfew as I got out of the Camaro. Ryan stopped himself though when I ran to him and began to cry into his shirt. I was vulnerable and he had always protected me. My brother forgot his anger momentarily and hugged as he looked over at my grandfather not knowing what to say.

"Bethany," I heard my grandmother call as she came out onto the porch. I looked passed my grandfather who had also lost his anger for the time being to see Grams reaching for me. Ryan let go and she shooed him and Gramps back into the house so that she and I were alone.

"Are you alright?" she asked as we sat down on the steps, her arm around my shoulder. I nodded. Physically, yes, I was fine, tired but fine. "Were you with Andrew?" she asked and I nodded again. "It's very unlike you... very unlike him, to do something like this. Missing curfew, not calling..." Grams said scattered, yet collected. I could tell that she, like Ryan and Gramps, had been very worried about me.

"I'm sorry," I apologized, appreciative of the concern my family had for me.

"Beths," my grandmother started. I swallowed nervously, realizing that she would ask me questions about where I had been and what had kept me from making a single phone call to let them know that I was okay. I couldn't answer any of her questions truthfully. I couldn't explain the real cause and, to make matters worse, I was so exhausted that I couldn't even think of a decent lie. "I'm sure you're tired, I think we all are," she grinned. "Let's say that you go up to your room and sleep for a little. After you've rested, you and I will sit down and talk about what happened." I was shocked. I thought for sure I would get the third degree; if not from Grams, then from Ryan and if not from Ryan, then certainly from my grandfather. I deserved it.

"Are you sure?" I questioned, still in shock.

My grandmother laughed and said, "Yes." She leaned in and said softly with a smile on her face, "Let me tell you, when Ryan first moved in with us, your grandfather vetoed some of his curfew misdemeanors, so I think I can pull some strings. Although, I will say, Ryan did manage to get home *before* the sun came up," she smirked and patted my knee before getting to her feet. "Just leave the boys to me," she added gesturing for me to go into the house and straight up to bed. "We will talk later," she reiterated and I kissed her on the cheek before going inside.

Gramps and Ryan were sitting at the dining room table and watched as I headed for the stairs. "Ep," Grams chirped when he thought I was trying to sneak by. Both he and Ryan were surprised when Grams intercepted their request, but they listened nonetheless.

I wearily trekked up to the attic. My brain was overloaded. All I knew for certain is that everything – everything had changed again.

Epilogue

I heard my brother's truck pull into the driveway. Then another car drove over the gravel. I heard my grandfather's voice say hello out front and then a car door closed. It was Gracie's laughter that made me open my eyes and sit up in bed. I listened as my grandmother opened the front door and greeted Abby. Getting out of bed and creeping down the attic stairs over a few squeaky boards, I was able to eavesdrop unnoticed.

"Where were you?" Gracie's little voice asked playfully as my brother and grandfather came in behind them.

"Ryan and I were at Church," my grandfather answered her sweetly.

"I'm sorry to just stop in like this," Abby said politely. "This is for you," she added.

"Apple pie," my grandfather said extinguishing my curiosity.

"Homemade," Gracie chimed in proudly. I was sure she had helped in some capacity. "Because it's Ryan's favorite."

"It is," I heard Ryan laugh at the fact that Gracie remembered.

"It's the least we can do for keeping Bethany out last night." My family left a silence for Abby to fill. "Charles and I want to thank not only her, but you as well. If it weren't for Bethany happened to be with him when he got sick and brought him back to the Estate so Charles could see too him. Drew would

-667-

probably still be out in the cold…" she stopped, preventing herself from rambling. "I realize that Charles or I should have called but we were just so distracted with the condition my brother was in that it escaped us. Again, I am truly sorry. I can't imagine how worried you all must have been about Bethany."

Gramps, forgetting his anger entirely, asked, "Is Wicks okay?"

"Not as of right now but Charles believes he will be fine," Abby exhaled, relieved. "Gracie and I just wanted to stop by and say thank you. We are truly grateful to Bethany. And again, Charles and I apologize."

"It's fine Abigail, really," my grandmother interjected. "We're glad Andrew will be okay."

"Thank you," Abby responded and I could hear the smile on her face. "Please tell Bethany that Charles will be by later today with her car."

"I will," Gramps assured her.

"Alright Gracie, it's time for us to go," my old friend said picking up the little one.

"Bye Mrs. Taylor! Bye Coach!" the Gracie said. "Bye Ryan," she giggled.

"Bye Gracie," I heard Ryan chuckle. Then I heard the front door open and close before I snuck back upstairs in time to see the Bentley pull away.

I knew Grams wanted to talk about what happened last night. I knew my brother wanted answers too. I could only imagine the amount of pacing he had done not knowing where I was. Even if he had driven passed the Estate, my car wouldn't have been there to tip him off. And my grandfather, well, this was new to him – having a daughter/granddaughter to worry about; it was different dynamic. I hadn't expected Abby to do what she did but it was truly perfect. She had set the stage for me, telling my family as much of the truth as she could. Now my grandparents and brother would all be on the same page and confident that my staying out wasn't done out of rebellion. 'Thanks Abby,' I thought to myself before grabbing my towel and heading downstairs to shower.

I turned the hot water on and stepped into the steam. As I put my face in the stream of water, I smiled to myself. I didn't know what the future held but it felt more like a beginning than an end.

Made in the USA
Lexington, KY
15 June 2014